RUNAWAY Cecilia

Catherine Duffy

First published in Far North Queensland, 2025 by Bowerbird Publishing

ISBN 978 1 7640739 1 2 (print)
ISBN 978 1 7640739 2 9 (ebook)

Runaway Cecilia
By Catherine Duffy

Cover & Interior Design: Bowerbird Publishing
Editing: Crystal Leonardi & Georgie Montague

Distributed by Bowerbird Publishing
Available in National Library of Australia

Bowerbird Publishing
Julatten, Queensland, Australia
www.crystalleonardi.com

Dear little me, we did it!

In loving memory of Faith Briggs, who listened.

Contents

The Legend of Princess Lilia

It was many and many a year ago
In a kingdom by the sea,
A princess lived in a castle there
Her beauty sweet as a lily

This was a child, adored by all,
In this kingdom by the sea
Loved with a love that was more than love,
Marred by a woman's envy

This was the reason that long ago,
In a kingdom by the sea
When darkness fell and clouds grew cold
The king's crowning glory

Was stolen by a matron there
From the bosom of the queen
And smuggled on a pirate ship
To a kingdom o'er the sea.

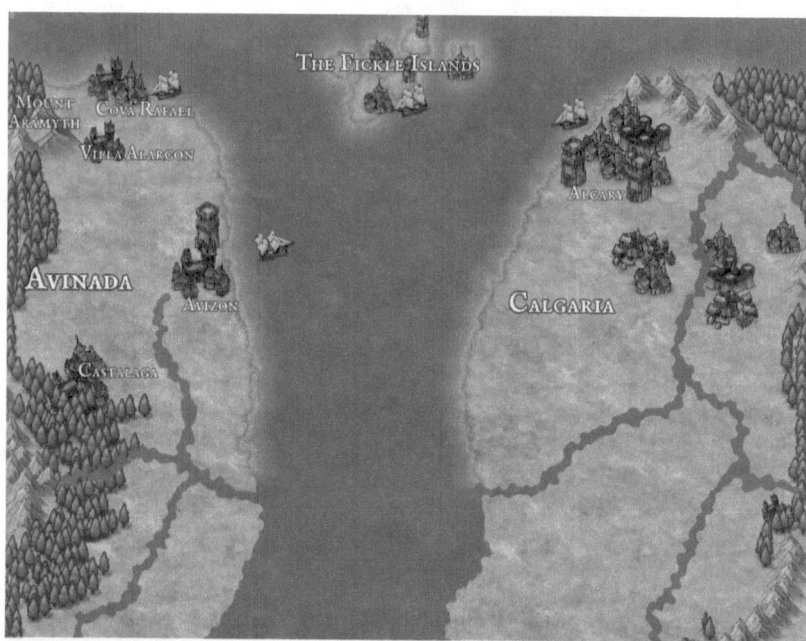

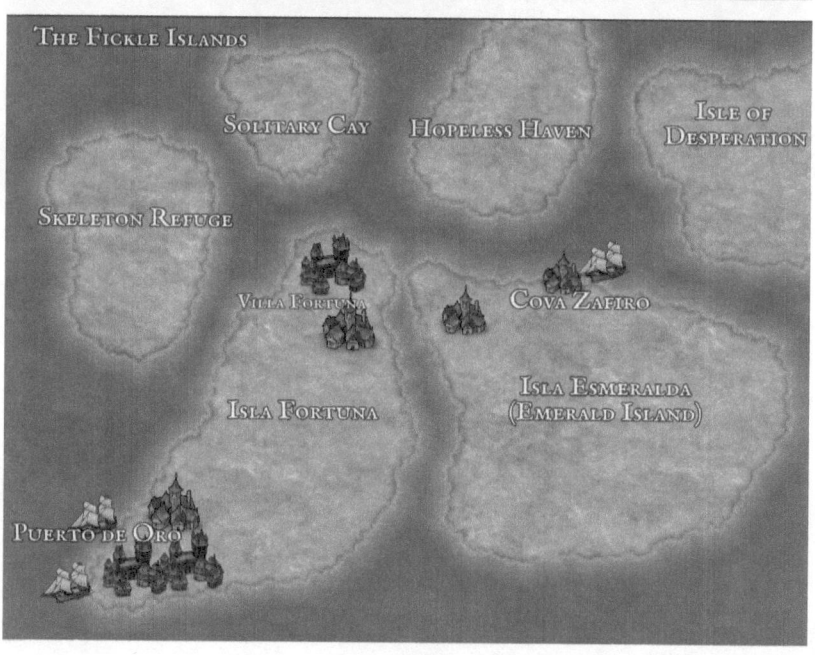

PRELUDE

16 Years Earlier

Fridolina Calderon was dead.

In her place stood Duchess Frida Alarcon, wife of Duke Leonidas Alarcon, ambassador to the king.

But the duke was dead and there was nothing left to stand in the way of her revenge. Starting with The Royal House of Calgaria.

***

The diamond chandelier mocked Frida as it twinkled in the centre of the grandiose ballroom.

Go home intruder, it seemed to say, *you don't belong here.*

Draped in crimson silk, her neck and ears dripping with rubies, she feigned indifference to the prying eyes of the gathered crowd, peering out beneath their golden locks.

With her smooth honey gold complexion, and dark hair piled fashionably on her head, she stood out among them; the only splash of red in a sea of blue, green and gold.

Yet, the objects of her attention were completely oblivious to her.

Absorbed in their own conversation, draped against matching golden thrones on a dais on the edge of the of the marble ballroom, King Lars and Queen Minerva paid her no attention.

Frida bristled as she watched them from the edge of the crowd, dancers twirling past her, oblivious to her rage. She barely registered the drink offered to her by a pale servant, a crystal goblet filled to the brim with sparkling wine.

"I did not expect to see you here, Your Grace. I had thought the royal couple would have misplaced your invitation," a familiar voice greeted from her shoulder. Startled, she cleared her throat, turning to meet the owner of the voice.

Clad in a red brocade suit, medals pinned to his chest stood King Vicente of Avinada. His brown eyes glinted with mischief under the light of the chandelier. With unruly dark curls and a prominent dimple, he was the picture of a roguish boy rather than a ruler.

"I am the wife of a duke, I am entitled to be here." She sipped on her wine, the bitter aftertaste settling on her tongue.

"You are a widow. And you parted ways with my sister on less than amiable terms," he gestured to the queen on the raised dais.

"I'm surprised you decided to show up at all."

"What can I say? I'm full of surprises."

"Indeed you are," his lips tipped into a teasing grin.

She rolled her eyes, "Where is your wife? I would not have thought Queen Isabel would miss such a soiree."

The king shifted, "She is not fit to travel in her condition. The fifth in line to the Avinadan throne will make his appearance any day now."

Frida fought the urge to roll her eyes. For all Vicente's talk about not being in love with his wife, she had managed to bear him five sons.

Ignoring his presence as best she could, she turned her attention back to the Calgarian royal couple, still oblivious to the world around them.

They did not deserve to celebrate anything after the pain they had caused her. Their frosty blue robes matched the ice in their hearts.

Crowns of thin silver adorned their heads, the colour muted against the king's blonde hair, yet stark against the queen's dark locks.

Her fellow Avinadan should have looked as out of place as Frida felt, but Queen Minerva emanated a quiet grace and dignity the duchess had always envied.

Time had been kind to the couple. Neither the king nor queen had aged a day since Frida last saw them, when they were wed. When they betrayed her.

Her future had been ruined by their selfishness. Her chance to rule, stolen.

She wanted nothing more than to see them falling to their knees, their royal airs and graces shattered on the altar of their grief as they threw themselves at her feet and wept.

The sound of shattered glass echoed on the marble tiles, tearing her thoughts back to the present. A few patrons glared at her – ladies of nobility, dressed, ruffled and stuffed within an inch of their lives in feathers and fine silks, contempt seeping from their sharp, blue eyes.

"Let's get you away from the drinks," King Vicente suggested, guiding her from the crowded ballroom as the band picked up a quick tune.

Servants scurried to where they had been standing moments before, clearing the area of smashed crystal. It took Frida a moment to register the goblet had slipped from her hand.

They made their way to a shadowed corner of an outdoor balcony. The cold, marble terrace was mostly empty of revellers, save a handful of couples seeking a sliver of privacy.

She warmed under Vicente's touch as he took her hand to examine it. Now they were away from the action, she let herself relax a little.

"Let me examine this," he frowned as he took her hand, his fingers light against her skin.

"You're not a medic," she protested.

"I've seen enough wounds to patch someone up," his frown eased. "You seem preoccupied tonight."

She held her breath unconsciously. It had been so long since they had a moment alone together.

"It's the first time I've been overseas without Alistar," she shrugged, hoping he would believe the excuse.

He frowned, as he traced her hand with his thumb.

Since their son was born, they had found it increasingly difficult to find time to meet. The moments they shared were short and hard to come by.

"I think you'll live." She sucked in a breath as Vicente's fingers caressed hers, his lips trailing her knuckles, her wrist. Her thoughts drifted to the last time he had handled her so tenderly.

"My lady," A young man's voice startled them from the shadows, "you have received a summons."

Vicente jumped back, dropping her hand like a hot coal. The memory of his touch lingered on her skin for a moment.

Frida faced the intruder, a short young man with dark blonde hair and beady eyes.

She cleared her throat, glancing at Vicente.

"My apologies, Your Majesty," she stepped away from him, "my attentions are required elsewhere. Goodnight."

He caught her wrist as she turned to leave. She gritted her teeth, resisting the urge to wrap herself in his arms. He turned her shoulders to face him.

"When can I see you again?"

Her eyes narrowed, her lips pursing into a hard line as her heart tore itself apart.

"You can't."

After tonight, nothing could be the same. He could know nothing of her plans.

Gathering her skirts and her resolve, she followed the servant through the brightly lit ballroom, into marble hallways and hidden corners of the palace.

***

Cutting through the servant's quarters, Frida paused to take off her red suede heels, the clip clop of her shoes echoing down the marble halls. Her companion led her through winding corridors and shadowed walkways, stopping now and again to wait for servants to pass, their grey uniforms blending into the walls around them.

Eventually, he led her around a quiet corner in a new wing of the palace, the mosaic walls covered in various pieces of shining gold, green and blue tiles. Checking to make sure they hadn't been followed, the servant gently pushed open a panel in a white marble wall, hidden under a painting of wildflowers, the only one in the magnificent hallway. If she listened hard enough, Frida could almost hear the distant trill of the fiddle or sweet melody of the grand piano in the ballroom.

The panel opened to reveal a small room, no larger than a storeroom where Frida could change clothes.

Her companion leaned past her to fumble with an oil lamp. Her bare feet slapped on the tile as she tapped it impatiently, crossing her arms in a huff.

"We don't have all night, Mars," she snapped.

With an apologetic glance, the young man finally set the lamp alight, the warm glow illuminating the small room. It was stone and largely empty save for a few dresser cabinets and various items of small furniture. A pile of neatly folded servant's clothes lay atop one of the dressers.

Frida slipped inside, tugging Mars in with her. His eyes widened as she closed the door behind her.

"Turn around if you're sensitive," she huffed.

He obeyed.

"You found the girl?" she asked as her deft fingers worked the lines of her corset. She heard Mars shift uncomfortably, but a quick glance over her shoulder revealed him looking stoically at the ceiling.

"Yes, Your Grace. She is in the west nursery. I have distracted the guards, so they should not pose a problem."

"You're sure?"

He nodded, eyes still fixed on the roof above them.

"There are no other children in the nursery tonight?"

He shook his head, "Only the princess and her cousin."

Frida turned around, her ebony locks tied into a tight bun. In the grey servant's uniform, she looked pale and non-descript, save the dramatic make-up around her dark eyes and scarlet lips. Mars turned tentatively around to face her.

"Lead the way," she ordered, slinging a satchel over her shoulder. They could leave no evidence behind.

Mars nodded, his thick eyebrows furrowing as they looped back through long marble halls, their slippers barely making a sound on the cool tile.

While the entrance to the grand hall had been swarmed by guards, the rest of the palace seemed deserted, save for a few burly servants. Frida had given Mars enough coin to bribe some servants away from certain halls for the evening. Servants who could not be bribed were moved to different sections of the palace, leaving the nursery largely unattended save for the royal nannies. Even they had been allowed time away to enjoy the celebrations. Still, the pair stuck to the shadows.

If Mars' information was correct, there would only be one nanny in the wing at this time, preoccupied with a distraction he had set up earlier.

It was not hard to find the wing in which the royal children slumbered. Mosaic animals decorated the nursery, the smallest area of the palace. Mars had mentioned the royal cousins were loath to be apart, and despite their tender ages, continued to share a bedroom.

Checking the hallway for any sign of movement, Mars and Frida slipped quietly into each room until they found them.

Each child was asleep in their own bed pushed against opposing walls. The room was surprisingly tidy on the girl's side, however the boy left much to be desired. Figures of horses, knights, dragons and dull swords littered his side of the room, whereas only the princess' teddy had fallen to the ground beside her bed.

Frida stood watching the children for a moment. The princess lay on her side, her dark hair splayed against her pillow as she faced her cousin. The young boy slept like a starfish on his back, snoring softly. She fought the urge to throw a pillow over his face.

"Your Grace?" Mars whispered, his voice loud in the stillness of the room.

Frida nodded at him, his outline visible from the warm glow of light emanating from the gap in the door.

He revealed a white handkerchief from his pocket and a vial of chloroform from the other. He measured small drops before covering the girls open mouth, cradling her small body against his own. The girl did not struggle, much to Frida's relief.

From the other side of the room, the boy groaned.

Mars met Frida's gaze, in the dim light. Wordlessly, they turned back the way they came.

Light streamed into the room as a young woman in a royal blue uniform entered. The nanny.

"Who are you?" she asked as Frida stepped in front of Mars, attempting to block her view.

"That is none of your concern," Frida snapped, crossing her arms.

Her heart lurched as the woman peered around her to see the little princess thrown over Mars' shoulders. The woman's scream rang across the quiet hall, the sound bouncing off the tiled walls. Jumping into action, Frida slapped the intruder, her heavy rings leaving an ugly gash on the woman's cheek. She stumbled backwards, clutching the side of her face. Frida took a step forward, one hand searching for a dagger that wasn't there.

Still, it was enough to frighten the girl. She screamed again, the sound filling the room. How long would it be until someone answered? Frida didn't want to wait to find out. She shoved the woman against the nearest wall. A sickening crack filled the room as she fell to the ground. Frida didn't dare look down.

"Lilia?" the young boy asked, sleep clouding his voice, "are you there?"

"Go back to sleep!" Frida shushed him as Mars stepped past her.

"Who are you?" he asked, his drowsy eyes settling on her.

"I'm no one. Go back to sleep."

At this juncture, Mars stepped into the light, revealing the young princess asleep over his shoulder. The boy screamed.

"Run!" Frida yelled, bursting into action. Mars followed close behind.

The clean marble hallways blurred together, swirling into one long runway as Mars shot in front of her. They hurried through a maze of doors and unfamiliar walkways. Frida's head swam, lungs burning as they burst into the cool night air.

A dark carriage waited for them in the shadows of the west wing. How they got there, Frida could not remember, but there was little time to think. They pressed on towards their driver.

The lanky older man leapt into action, stamping his cigarette under a heavy boot, his dark cloak flowing behind him as he opened the door of the carriage. The black woodwork shone with recent rain.

Frida's legs pumped under her, her toes pinching as she fought to keep her feet in her shoes. She barrelled into the carriage, swinging herself onto the plush seats, before turning to Mars and helping him load the child inside. The carriage rocked as he threw himself in behind them.

The door slammed shut against the frame seconds before the carriage lurched forward. Frida examined the girl as best she could under the lights of the palace as they hurried through the royal square and into the bright city of Alcary. Fireworks lit the sky in celebration, each boom reverberating like a harbinger of doom in her ears.

Her heart sped in time with the horses' galloping hooves. Had anyone followed them out of the nursery? Would Vicente suspect her involvement and blow her cover?

Though they surged through the city, would they reach the docks before someone found the princess missing?

She watched the girl's chest rise and fall at a steady rhythm.

"What will you do with her?" Mars nodded at the small figure resting against Frida. The duchess positioned the girl so her head was resting in her lap, the rest of her small body lying against the plush seat. The girl had curled into a ball, as if not wanting to take up space, even in sleep.

"I will raise her as my own. Then, I will return her to her parents and claim her inheritance as mine."

Mars' thick brows furrowed, creating an angry V on his forehead.

"You will return her? Why?"

"Because her throne is rightfully mine. She may a princess, but through her, I will be queen."

Catherine Duffy

1

The Mission

The clang of metal on metal rang out across the room. Marcus kept his eyes trained firmly on his opponent. Matched in strength and size, they circled each other on the stone floor of the outdoor courtyard. He surveyed his partner, a dark-haired young man in training gear, his blue eyes fixed on Marcus' weapon.

A sword flashed in the corner of his eye, but he would not take the bait. His opponent set his lips into a thin line, a dead giveaway.

Taking advantage of his partner's impatience, Marcus waited for the young man to strike. Just when he thought he had given up, the opponent lunged, but Marcus was quick to parry the attack.

"Are you ever caught off guard?" his opponent grunted.

"Never, Your Highness." Marcus smirked, as he lunged forward, the tip of his sword grazing his opponents padded shoulder.

After years of training together, Marcus knew the prince's fighting style almost as well as his own, anticipating the prince's next move with uncanny accuracy. The prince shook his head, his dark curls bouncing like coils around sharp blue eyes as he let out a tired laugh.

"This is why you should become Chief Sentinel. You're always prepared for anything," said the prince resuming his position on the training mat.

"Bodyguard and best friend are two very different roles," Marcus replied, settling into position and lifting his sword into the air.

"I'll need you to keep me out of trouble when I'm Crown Prince."

"Good luck with that," Marcus shot back, raising an eyebrow. "You'll just drag me into your schemes."

The prince opened his mouth to protest.

"Cervantes." Their commanding officer's voice boomed across the room.

"Duty calls," Marcus excused himself with a wry grin and exaggerated bow.

Prince Derek rolled his eyes, a smile spreading across his face as he watched his friend cross the yard.

The clang of blades continued around Marcus as he made his way across the vast courtyard. Soldiers in grey padded uniforms continued fighting, their rapiers sizzling as parries were blocked and spurned. Casting his eyes quickly about the room, Marcus noted there were more men in training this afternoon than usual.

With the prince's investiture quickly approaching, the king had made sure to double the security around the event. The kingdom had remained in peace for well over a decade, but tensions were rising with the western kingdom of Avinada. No doubt the king would want to speak with Marcus about the security concerns.

Prince Derek had recommended Marcus for the position of His Highness' Chief Sentinel, head of the prince's personal security guard. Marcus hadn't accepted the position yet. He preferred to earn his rank, not be seen as merely the prince's friend.

He nodded in greeting as he approached his commanding officer. Major Nilson was the picture of authority. His uniform was ironed within an inch of its life, not a single black thread out of place. His neatly trimmed moustache rimmed a hard mouth, centring his angular face. A pair of steely blue eyes peered out from under thick black eyebrows as cold and hard as a winter glacier.

Marcus stood at attention in front of him.

"Sir." He raised his hand in salute.

"The king wants to see you in his study. Immediately." The major's voice rose above the clatter of metal on metal.

"Yes, sir."

After a sharp salute, Marcus turned on his heel. A cool breeze and a touch of destiny hung in the air.

***

A light sweat had broken out across the back of his neck by the time he reached the heavy oak doors of the king's study. A cool breeze filtered through the open-air hallways as he crossed from one side of the palace to the other, cooling him slightly.

Marcus navigated the familiar halls and courtyards of the grand estate with ease, taking well-worn shortcuts and quiet servants' passageways.

Within minutes, he found himself standing in front of the king's study. Lions' heads emblazoned each door, their golden mouths open in a soundless roar.

Taking a deep breath to steady his nerves and straighten his uniform, his fingers grasped the lion's golden mane, the knock sending a shudder through his knuckles.

"Enter," called a muffled voice from the other side of the door.

The study was a sanctuary amid the palace's chaos, the distant clang of swords muted, replaced by the soft rustle of parchment.

Papers littered the floor beside King Lars' mahogany war-table in the centre of the room. The rest of the study remained neat and orderly, except the king himself.

His cerulean robe hung loose from his broad shoulders, his white shirt rumpled. He'd pushed his usually tidy blonde hair haphazardly from his face. He lifted his head as Marcus approached; hazel eyes rimmed with dark circles. Lack of sleep aged him, crow's feet appearing at the edge of his eyes. He smiled wanly at Marcus.

"I trust Prince Derek has already entreated you to become Chief Sentinel?" he asked, briefly turning his attention away from a small wooden chest in front of him.

"Yes, Your Majesty." Marcus nodded, eyeing the box.

"And you've accepted?"

"Not yet, Sir."

The king's brow quirked up in a question. Marcus wet his lips nervously, a knot twisted in his stomach. The weight of the crown's expectations pressed against his shoulders, heavier than any armour.

"Is there something stopping you?" The king asked, leaning his hip against the table, arms crossed.

Marcus hesitated.

"While I am honoured to be considered, I believe there are others who deserve the role more. If I am to be offered a promotion, I would like to have earned it through merit, not preferential treatment."

The king stroked his chin.

"Wise words from a young man," he said finally.

Marcus exhaled slowly, careful not to let the king see his relief.

The king returned his attention to the chest in front of him, popping the lid open to reveal red velvet lining and a small stack of papers. Marcus inclined his head, his curiosity piqued.

"What do you know of the recent rumours surrounding the whereabouts of my daughter?" he asked, changing the subject.

Marcus thought for a moment.

"There was talk the Avinadan ambassador had been enquiring into a number of noble families who had adopted daughters around the time Princess Lilia went missing. I have not heard if any of the rumours are true."

The king turned back to the chest, gesturing for Marcus to stand beside him. As he did, King Lars handed him a thin slip of paper.

"What is this?" Marcus asked.

"Read it."

He opened the creased letter, tracing smudged fingerprints.

Hvalgard Dynasty, 121
His Royal Highness, King Lars of Calgaria
The Marble Palace

Your Majesty,

I write with haste to inform you of a line of inquiry I am undertaking with Queen Isabel of Avinada as it pertains to the disappearance of your daughter, Princess Lilia.

It is our belief that after the young princess was kidnapped, she was adopted into a noble Avinadan family.

The Queen believes the princess resides in the north of the country, as the ward of Señorita Frida Alarcon, widow of the late Duke Leonidas Alarcon. I believe you once knew her as Doña Fridolina Calderon.

However, there is another young woman who may be of interest. Lady Estella Logarzo, adopted daughter of Don Federico Logarzo. It is understood both of these young girls were taken from Calgaria around the time the princess was kidnapped.

According to my sources, the former was plucked from an unknown orphanage, while the latter was allegedly orphaned from a noble Calgarian family.

The queen and I are soon to obtain evidence from one of King Vicente's trusted advisors, who has been working with us on these matters. We believe we can collect enough evidence to determine which of these young ladies is your daughter and convict those involved in her disappearance.

I will write soon when more details have been confirmed.

Your Majesty, I would not mention this if I did not think it important. Duchess Alarcon's ward, from the little I have seen of her, bears an extraordinary resemblance to Queen Minerva.

I have attached three small portraits of the Señorita Cecilia for your perusal.

Sincerely,

Hugo Montoya,

Duke of Castalaga

Avinadan ambassador to Calgaria

The king's hazel eyes shone.

"The pictures?" Marcus gestured to the chest on the table.

The king pushed the box towards him. Inside, were three small portraits. Marcus shuffled through them quickly.

There was no mistaking the young girl in the pictures. Her different coloured eyes, one hazel and one brown, could be missed by the untrained eye, but there was no mistaking the resemblance between this girl and the portrait hanging over the king's shoulder. Lilia's final picture.

In each card, the girl appeared older.

In the first picture, she looked no older than eight, dark braids tumbling over her back as she stood at the shoulder of a stately young woman noted as Duchess Alarcon on the back of the card. A young boy also appeared in the painting, not much older than the girl himself.

The second image featured the princess, no older than twelve, pictured again with the young boy who had grown taller, his blonde locks determinedly in the way of his eyes. The final image seemed to have been painted recently, a stray splotch of paint on the edge of the border, while no longer fresh, was still smooth.

This one confused Marcus. Why would the box include a picture of young Queen Minerva? He glanced at the king, his brows furrowed.

"Look closer," The king instructed.

Marcus obeyed, examining the portrait a second time.

Checking the eyes, he realised, he was looking at a picture of Princess Lilia.

The shape of her face was the same oval as Queen Minerva's, and her nose was similar to the king's. The tip of her lips seemed poised in a small smile, yet sadness wrapped around her like a cloak.

A name was scrawled in pencil on the bottom edge of the paper. Cecilia Alaracon, 20.

Marcus reunited the images with the letter in the box, placing them gently in a pile in the middle.

He glanced at the king whose eyes followed the paintings.

"I have prayed so long for my daughter to return," said the king, his voice low. "For sixteen years, hope seemed lost. I am afraid to let it bloom again."

He sighed and ran a hand through his golden locks. In the faded yellow light, it was hard to see the grey peppering his hair.

"As much as I love my nephew, I care for him like my own son, nothing has dampened the longing to be reunited with my daughter. When you become a parent one day, you will understand."

Marcus nodded. Finding Lilia wasn't just about fulfilling a royal wish; it was about restoring hope to a family and a kingdom—one he'd sworn to protect.

"As king, it is my job to ensure the nation has a hope and a future, someone they can look forward to leading them when I am gone. Derek has proven himself to be a capable leader, and parliament has no issue with me naming him as my official heir."

It had been a battle for Derek to be recognised as a prince, given the unsavoury condition of his birth, especially once Lilia's birth cemented her as Crown Princess.

"You have proven yourself a loyal and trustworthy man, Captain Cervantes, and a good soldier. I want you to bring my daughter home."

"It shall be done," Marcus vowed.

The king placed a hand on his shoulder, the weight of his words hung heavily between them.

"As a reward, I will restore to you, your fathers land, wealth and titles, upon your return."

"Sir-"

The king held up a hand.

"I should have stood up for your father when your grandfather disinherited him for marrying an Avinadan woman. Perhaps if I had, things would be different for you."

Marcus shook his head, grasping for something to say.

"I know you think Derek recommended you because of your longstanding friendship, but I have spoken with your superiors and they speak highly of you. Do not discount yourself, Marcus."

The soldier nodded.

"I will let Prince Derek know not to expect you around palace grounds for a few weeks. You are to board the *Real Sorrento* immediately after supper. You will be sailing with Captain Catalina. I will let you sort out the rest of the mission with her."

"Yes, sir." Marcus nodded.

"My only request is that you bring my daughter home as soon as possible. My wife and I are excited to see her again."

"You have my word."

"Good." The king's grin widened, the gesture lighting up his whole face.

For a moment, Marcus glimpsed what the king must have looked like in his younger years, his strong features softened at the edges, his hazel eyes shining with delight.

"Captain Cervantes," the king returned to formalities, "I hope you understand the necessity of secrecy in this operation. No one can know what you are doing, not even the prince."

"Yes, sir."

The king nodded as he tucked the chest in one of the drawers in his mahogany table. A knock at the door signalled it was time to leave.

Marcus bowed low as the king dismissed him, before turning and walking out of the room and into the path set before him.

The grandeur of the palace was lost on him as he began to formulate a plan, half-conscious to stay out of the prince's way. He turned down a hall leading to the Rose Garden, a shortcut past the training hall where he could pass unnoticed. He wasn't ready to face his friend just yet.

"Copper for your thoughts?"

Marcus flinched as Prince Derek settled into step beside him. He exhaled a smile, mustering the energy to greet his friend.

"I thought you were still in training."

"Finished early to grab a snack," the prince took a bite from an apple, offering another to Marcus, who shook his head.

"What did my uncle want?" the prince asked, his mouth full.

"To go over some safety concerns before your investiture." Marcus shrugged.

"Just you?"

"And some others."

"Who?"

Marcus pursed his lips. He could lie well enough to fool most people, but Derek knew all of his tells. There wasn't much you didn't know about someone you spent your whole life training with.

Derek chewed thoughtfully.

"Does this mean you'll be Chief Sentinel then?"

Marcus hesitated, "I'm thinking about it."

"Still?" Derek's eyebrows shot into his forehead. "You've had weeks to think about it. This is the opportunity of a lifetime for you."

Marcus shot him a teasing grin.

"Yes, because being the royal babysitter is the highest honour in the kingdom."

Derek flinched, hurt flashing in his eyes, "Don't joke about that."

"Sorry," Marcus pulled away.

Although the prince had seen combat, the memory of his nanny dying the night Lilia disappeared still troubled him.

Marcus kicked a stone into Derek's path. The prince returned the favour. It was a game they had come up with as children. A silent peace offering.

"There was nothing else my uncle wanted from you?" Derek pressed, passing the stone back.

Marcus shook his head, thankful they were approaching the soldier's barracks, eager to put distance between them. The prince frowned but said nothing until they reached the wooden gate at the front of the complex.

"You know, I'm surprised Uncle Lars hasn't said anything about Lilia in a while," Derek broke the silence between them. "It's hard to celebrate when Aunt Minerva wears that forced smile all the time. It's as though she wants to be doing this for Lilia, not me."

"You can't be too hard on her," Marcus offered, "she lost her child. But you are like a son to them."

"That's what they say," Derek shrugged, tossing his apple core into the carefully manicured garden. "Anyway, I must get going. Duke Oleksander has invited me for dinner this evening. I suspect this has more to with finding me a match with one of his daughters than it does about his politics."

"And this is a surprise to you?" Marcus smirked.

Noble families had always thrown their daughters at Prince Derek. He pretended to object to the attention, but secretly Marcus thought, he thrived on it.

"Course not, but as pretty as his daughters are, they're not exactly riveting conversationalists."

"Well, let me know how it goes," Marcus clapped him on the shoulder.

"Always. Have a good night."

"Goodnight, Your Highness," Marcus threw him a mock salute. Derek rolled his eyes, flashing a wry smile over his shoulder as they walked in opposite directions.

Marcus hurried into to the barracks. Supper would be served soon. He had to pack quickly.

***

Prince Derek watched his friend scurry into the soldier's quarters through a nearby set of bushes close to the barracks. It wasn't like Marcus to keep things from him. He hadn't meant to listen at the door during Marcus' conversation with the king, but the temptation had been too great.

Now, his friend was betraying him – finding a foreign woman to put on the throne of Calgaria. It didn't matter that Lilia's disappearance had haunted his family; she was nothing but a distant memory to him.

The prince watched the barracks a little longer when an idea struck him. He untangled himself from the vines, walking quickly to his chambers. If he wanted to retain his claim to the throne, he had to act before it was too late.

2

A Secret Uncovered

"Happy Birthday Cecilia!" Frida burst into the room.

Cecilia groaned, squeezing her eyes shut against the blinding sunshine streaming through her curtains. Covering her head under the thin blanket, she turned her back to the window.

"Five more minutes?" she moaned.

The night before had brought her a fitful sleep full of strange dreams of ships in the night, a dark, empty palace and the lingering lingering thunder of horses hooves.

Sleep had eluded her until the early hours of the morning, the sun now mocking her through the bay window.

"It's time to get up. You've slept the day away and we have many things to do." Frida stripped the covers back, revealing Cecilia's petite frame. She was curled in the foetal position, her linen pyjamas as dishevelled as her dark hair, splayed across her pillow.

"It's my birthday, please can I have just five more minutes?" Cecilia yawned.

"No," Frida threw a dress at her, her dark features settled into a sour demeanour.

"If you wanted to sleep longer, you shouldn't have spent the night reading. Now get up. The servants have drawn a hot bath for you. It'll likely be cold by now," She snapped as she swept out of the room, her scarlet skirts trailing behind her.

With a final groan, Cecilia forced herself out of bed, making her way to the small, tiled bathroom attached to her suite. Her godmother was right, a bath had been drawn for her. Wilted lilies lined the tepid water. She undressed quickly and lowered herself in, hoping the water would wash her thoughts away.

Though it was her twenty-first birthday, a day she had been looking forward to for years, it felt the same as any other. Frida was her usual brusque self and despite the revelries planned for the evening, Cecilia was not looking forward to entertaining a bunch of strangers, most of whom would come to gawk at the nation's most secluded bachelorette.

Holding her breath, she submerged her head underwater, as if to hide herself from prying eyes before she entered the party. Frida had spent weeks – months - training her to be the perfect hostess.

"Now, if you begin to feel uncomfortable, what do you do?" Frida had asked, tapping Cecilia's shoulders to straighten them.

"Smile and move on," Cecilia sighed.

"What don't you do?"

"Hide away in the library until the party's over."

Frida managed a tight smile.

"Very good."

With burning lungs, Cecilia emerged from the water to find two servant girls waiting at the foot of the tub. Dressed in the same brown uniform, it was difficult to tell them apart, with their dark braids and steely blue eyes. Still, Daphne's proud chin and freckled cheeks were hard to miss.

"Her ladyship sent us to help you get ready," she mumbled, stepping forward.

Cecilia sighed resting her head on the edge of the bronze tub. If Frida had sent servants to help her, it was to keep an eye on her and prevent her from sneaking into the library.

"Go ahead," Cecilia conceded, water splashing the tile as she pushed herself out of the tub.

She dried herself quickly, changing into a blue day dress before the girls sprang into action. Once she was changed, one set upon brushing her hair while the other painted her nails.

The sisters chatted lightly about the upcoming celebrations.

"The flowers are divine. They smell almost as sweet as the sticky puddings coming from the kitchen." Delilah said, holding out pink lilies for her sister to weave in.

"I can't wait to see all the young men in their finery," Daphne sighed dreamily through a mouthful of hairclips.

"I heard King Vicente is bringing all of his sons to the ball. Apparently, he wants to use it as a way to find suitable wives for them."

"I heard the duchess arranged someone to marry Alistar and she's announcing it tonight."

"If anyone were to marry Alistar it would be- ow!" Delilah glared at Daphne who poked her in the ribs.

Cecilia caught the girl's sheepish expression.

"If Alistar were to marry anyone it would be me. That's what you were going to say, isn't it?" Cecilia raised a brow in question.

Delilah nodded.

"I suppose that is what everyone expects. I half expect it myself," Cecilia admitted with a sigh.

Regret tugged at her chest as the girls shared a furtive look. It had been so long since Cecilia spoke freely with anyone, was she so desperate to admit such a thing to gossiping servants?

"Your hair is ready, señorita." Daphne set the final pin in place.

"Thank you." Cecilia leaned back into her chair, dismissing them with a wave.

Her mind whirled at their conversation as she settled into the plush cushions at her bay window, thumbing the pages of a nearby book. Morning sunlight spilled into a lazy afternoon. Only when Daphne and Delilah returned to touch up her makeup and help her change into her gown did Cecilia register the day had passed her by. She shuddered smoothing her skirts in front of her floor-length mirror. Would Frida really announce an engagement at her birthday ball? Was it so hard for her godmother to let someone else have the attention for one day?

A bump at the door startled her from her thoughts.

A shadow flickered at the gap as the door bumped against the frame. Had she not seen it, she would not have known what had happened. Her heart raced in her chest. Who had been watching her and for how long?

Swallowing the lump of fear in her throat, she waited a few seconds before cracking the door open and peering down the hall. A tall silhouette hurried down a corner. Not stopping to think, she followed.

***

Sticking to the shadows, Cecilia was careful not to stumble over her slippers as she followed the stranger down the familiar sandstone hallways to the main hall. She recognised the black and white servants livery, but could not place the face.

Frida had hired extra servants for the evening, but there was something about the boldness of this one that piqued her curiosity. At the very least, someone needed to tell him not to snoop where he wasn't supposed to.

The distant thrum of activity faded as she turned the corner, watching the young man turn into the library. Before she could follow him further, Frida's shrill laughter echoed through the hall. Cecilia froze. Tentatively, she backed away from the door, following the sound to the grand hall. She slipped through the heavy velvet curtain separating the hall from the ballroom.

Frida had not yet changed into her evening gown, although her ebony curls were piled fashionably on top of her head, revealing ruby teardrop earrings hanging almost to her neck. She stood with her advisor, Count Mario Sanchez, their backs turned to Cecilia.

She crouched beside the sandstone banister, careful not to peak over the edge.

"I know Isabel doesn't like me but I doubt she would be clever enough to go to such lengths to get rid of me," the duchess chuckled.

"After you made Vicente appoint Alistar as ambassador to Calgaria, Isabel is desperate to get rid of you. Even if it means digging up old rumours." Mario replied.

"She would say anything to curry favour with the king. Not that's she's had favour with him since their wedding."

"She's given him five sons."

"And? Just because they have children, doesn't mean he loves her. The only reason he hasn't left her is because the people love her. Saints know why."

"All the same, be careful with how you conduct yourself with him tonight." Mario cleared his throat, "Speaking of matrimonial matters, when will you tell Cecilia that we are to wed?"

Cecilia covered a gasp with her hand.

"At the ball tonight. Hopefully that will keep Isabel from looking too deeply into my affairs. After all, why would I troth a princess to a count?"

"You are certain the girl remembers nothing of her past?" he asked.

"Of course. I will tell her in due time, obviously, but she need not know for now."

"And what of Isabel snooping for evidence? We eliminated Ambassador Montoya, but the queen's suspicion grows."

Cecilia chanced a glance over the banister to catch Frida shaking her head, dark curls springing around her ears.

"I trust that evidence linking us to Calgaria at the time of Lilia's disappearance has been well hidden at your discretion."

Mario nodded. "I've hidden it in the library where no one would think to look."

Trumpets blared, cutting off Frida's next words. Cecilia flinched, ducking her head beneath the banister.

"Is it not early for guests to arrive?" Mario asked.

"Yes. I still have to change! Then I must check on Cecilia. Goodness knows if she's ready yet."

The clip clop of Frida's heels had long since faded when Cecilia peeked over the banister again. It was empty. Snatching her skirts, she hurried up the stairs and back to her room, collapsing against the door.

What on earth had she just heard?

What did Frida mean she wouldn't troth a princess to a count? Was Cecilia not an orphan, as she had been told all these years? And why would Mario want to marry her anyway?

Cecilia pushed herself off the floor long enough to flop onto her bed, her mind a mess. She couldn't stay in Villa Alarcon. Not anymore. Her twenty-first birthday had meant she would be free of Frida's expectations. She had dreamed of travelling the world, or at the very least traversing Avinada. The last thing she wanted was to marry.

And if Mario spoke the truth, if she wasn't an orphan, she would have to find her family.

Sourcing an old leather satchel, she packed it with what she assumed would be necessary for travelling. A change of clothes and her meagre savings. She would swipe some food and water skins from the kitchen on her way out, and if she had any time, look for the evidence Mario mentioned.

"Cecilia," Frida knocked on the door, "the first guests have arrived."

Cecilia dropped the satchel by her feet, kicking it under the bed.

"Thank you!"

Frida pushed the door open, frowning as she cast a critical eye over her. Cecilia was sure her godmother would find fault with the bustling navy skirts or black rosettes lining her shoulders and collarbone.

"I will send one of the servants to fetch you when it's time to make your entrance," she said instead.

"I will be here," Cecilia gestured at the room.

"Yes," the duchess raised a brow, "Make sure that you are."

An awkward silence stretched between them before Frida gathered her crimson skirts and swept out the door.

Not for the first time that day, Cecilia was left alone.

3

The Imposter

It was easier to infiltrate Villa Alarcon than Marcus had thought. Posing as a manservant, he was able to move from one section of the villa to another. It suited him, getting to know the ins and outs of the grounds without raising suspicion.

For a week, he had spent the days moving furniture, decorating hallways and ballrooms, making sure everything was spick and span for Señorita Cecilia's birthday ball. But when his supervisors weren't looking, he was searching for the evidence Ambassador Montoya wrote of in his letter to the king.

In his servant's uniform, Marcus slipped into rooms unnoticed, including the otherwise abandoned library. The only person who frequented the room was Señorita Cecilia, although he was careful to stay out of her way, preferring to observe her from afar.

Ambassador Montoya was right, she bore a striking resemblance to Queen Minerva. That alone could be proof enough she was the lost princess, but he knew Parliament would need something more concrete.

Nothing had appeared yet. The only evidence something was amiss with Duchess Alarcon were snippets of gossip from long-standing servants. One thing that remained consistent was the duchess' disdain for Calgaria.

"The duchess used to be good friends with the Calgarian royals," Cook had shared with him as he helped her knead bread the night before.

"Then what happened?" he asked, rolling the dough into a ball.

"The rumour was the duchess was engaged to King Lars, but they couldn't announce it 'til after his father's funeral," she lowered her voice.

"Then?" Marcus leaned in.

"Then after his brother was crowned king, the new King Oslo announced Prince Lars' engagement to Princess Minerva as part of a peace treaty between our nations. He had been staying in Avinada and apparently, the couple got quite close. Frida was furious. Her father died shortly after and she blamed it on them."

"Why?"

"Dunno," Cook shrugged, "But she married Duke Alarcon to save face. He was summoned to Calgaria but died on the voyage over. Frida blamed his death on them too, Saints know why. He was twenty-years her senior and not in the best health."

Marcus tried to prod her for more information, but once the dough was rolled and ready to set, Cook's lips were sealed.

Nothing about it made sense, and time was running out to find evidence before Duchess Alarcon dismissed the new servants. He could not afford to weasel his way into the villa a second time.

He had attempted to search Señorita Cecilia's rooms until he realised, she was still in them. The blare of trumpets startled him as he doubled back to the kitchen.

"Ah, there you are Julian. We are almost ready to begin the final preparations for the guests." Juan Carlos grunted as Marcus swept into line. The other servants stood in two neat rows peering at him from under uniform caps.

"Sorry, I seem to have gotten lost again," he straightened his livery, joining the rest of the team.

"Yes, you seem to be quite good at that." The butler crossed his arms. Marcus bristled under the weight of the older man's gaze. Juan Carlos, had been an amiable fellow, but as Marcus soon realised, was quick to run out of patience. If he suspected Marcus was up to something, the entire mission could be compromised.

Marcus began formulating a plan while Juan Carlos droned on about the final preparations. With all the servants busy cooking, cleaning or serving, it would be easy for him to slip out and join the festivities.

Once he was satisfied there were no faults in his plan, he returned his attention to the butler.

"Alvaro, Severo, Julian— you'll be serving the guests on the floor."

"What?" Marcus blurted.

Juan Carlos' face turned stony. The other servants murmured in anticipation around him. Marcus kicked himself inwardly. A soldier did not talk back to his superiors, much less a servant.

"Were you not listening? Santo mio! Why must I be cursed with such ignorant rabble?" Juan Carlos rubbed his face with his hand.

"If you are not out serving in the hall in fifteen minutes, consider yourself on notice."

With that, the older man stomped up the stairs, leaving a string of curses in his wake.

Deflated, Marcus slipped in with the rest of his crew, mirroring how they arranged glass flutes on silver trays. Tonight was his only chance to get close to the two noble ladies and find out which of them was the princess. Between now and then, he had to figure out a way to slip in and out of the ball unnoticed.

Ignoring the glares of his fellow servants, Marcus hurried out of the kitchen and into the servants' hall. It wasn't far from the library, which in turn was not far from the ballroom. He'd already packed his disguise, he just had to hope Juan Carlos didn't intercept him on the way.

4

A Beautiful Distraction

Marcus managed to slip out from the ballroom under the guise of getting more wine. Instead, he'd detoured to the library to change before re-entering as a guest.

Guests bustled around the ballroom, their masks and skirts glistening under the twinkling chandeliers. He slipped in easily with the crowd, searching for his first target.

Lady Estella Logarzo stood a head taller than most of the women and half the men in the room.

Her long, blonde hair tumbled in polished waves down her shoulders. She was dressed in a simple, pastel blue gown that accentuated her slender figure.

Her blue-grey eyes fixed on him over the rim of her crystal wine flute as he approached her. She lowered her drink and flashed him a dazzling smile, which lit up her whole face. He returned the gesture, picking two flutes from Severo carrying a full tray, careful to hide his masked face.

"Can I offer you a drink?" he held a glass out to her.

"You may," she said, downing the last of her drink, to accept his offer.

"I don't believe we've been introduced," he accepted her white gloved hand, "I am Duke Aurelius Reddan. And you are?"

"I am Señorita Logarzo. But you can call me Estella, all my friends do."

"It's a pleasure to make your acquaintance Señorita," he brushed a gentle kiss against her satin knuckles, earning him a pearly grin.

"Reddan?" she tested the word on her tongue. "That is in Calgaria is it not? What brings you to a ball so far from home?" she asked.

"I am in the country for business. I am at this ball because I heard Avinadan's throw the best parties," he winked.

A rush of pink stained her pale cheeks. Perhaps it would be easier to get her to talk than he thought.

"And what do you do for business?"

"Trade."

"Which one?"

Marcus ran his tongue over his teeth to buy him some time. She was astute and a little bold. He'd have to be careful she wouldn't catch him out.

"Wool."

"Alpaca or sheep?"

"Both," he sipped from his wine flute.

"Ah, I'd better not introduce you to my father then. He has been thinking of investing in the wool trade for a while. If I brought you to him, you'd never get away."

"A fair call. Besides," he cast his eyes over her, "I'd like to enjoy myself without talking of business tonight."

Her smile widened, "I think I can help with that."

Marcus chuckled. She was a handsome young woman and every inch the Calgarian lady – tall, high cheekbones and eyes as blue as the winter glaciers. He paused, no – one eye was blue. How could he have missed it?

"You have two different coloured eyes," he blurted.

Her bright laughter filled the air as he flashed her a sheepish smile, raking a hand through his dark locks.

"Forgive me, I hadn't meant to say that out loud."

"I know," her eyes danced, "I get that a lot."

"You know in Calgaria," he said, leaning in towards her, "they say having different coloured eyes is a sign of royalty. You wouldn't happen to be the lost princess would you?"

She flashed him a coy smile.

"And how many women have you tried to charm with that line?"

"Just one."

"Oh?" her cheeks reddened a second time.

"Forgive me for asking, and you may tell me to leave you alone if this question offends, but there are rumours you, yourself are from Calgaria. Is that true?"

Any hint of annoyance did not cross Estella's soft features.

"Can I tell you a secret?" she asked, her eyes sparkling as she drew closer to him, so they were a hairsbreadth apart.

He nodded.

"Lord and Lady Logarzo are not my real parents. They adopted me from Calgaria when I was five years old."

Marcus' eyebrows shot into his forehead. This was not news to him, but he was surprised she had shared it so openly.

"Oh?"

She shrugged casually.

"My parents died when I was young. They were high nobility within the late-King Oslo's social circle. One day they went to a ball and never returned. The next thing I knew, Duke Logarzo, my father's cousin, came to take me to Avinada."

"And you have not been back since?"

She shook her head.

"My father does not like to talk about the past. I'm afraid I don't know much about them."

Marcus placed a reassuring hand on her elbow. She smiled softly at him, her eyes shining.

"I always liked to fancy myself as Calgaria's lost princess as a child. My hair was naturally a few shades darker than this," she said toying with the blonde locks tumbling down her shoulders.

"My adopted mother began dyeing it when I was young so I would look more exotic. Besides, my eyes are the wrong colour. Everybody knows Princess Lilia's colouring was dark."

"Well, your eyes are beautiful anyway," he offered.

Trumpets blared as a herald announced Señorita Cecilia's arrival. With a smile and a bow, he disentangled himself from Señorita Logarzo's attention and made his way toward the centre of the room. He turned with the rest of the guests to watch Señorita Cecilia descend the steps.

His breath caught at the sight of her.

Her dark brown locks were pulled into a fashionable updo, with two styled strands of hair framing her face. Her brown and hazel eyes roamed the crowd, flashing a smile brighter than the lamps blazing around the room.

She exuded a quiet grace and beauty as she descended the steps with the air of a princess.

Her golden skin glowed under the light of the chandelier. A simple pendant hung in the hollow of her neck, at her exposed collarbone.

There was no mistaking it.

This was Princess Lilia. She was his duty.

He stepped forward, a sea of people parting for him, holding its collective breath as she drew near. He was vaguely aware of the duchess suggesting an opening dance. This might be his only chance to engage with Cecilia Alarcon. He would not waste it.

5

Handsome Stranger

Cecilia's heart hammered in time to the music filtering from the heavy velvet curtain, hiding her from view of her guests. Her feet were rooted to the floor as Frida's conversation echoed in her mind.

Why would I troth a princess to an earl?... Evidence connecting us... Knows nothing about her past.

Something about it tugged at a distant memory she couldn't quite place. What did she have to do with a Calgarian princess?

Trumpets blared from the top of the stairs, the sound ringing in her ears long after they had stopped. She wiped her sweaty palms on her silk dress, regretting it immediately.

"Announcing Señorita Cecilia, ward of Duchess Frida Alarcon, of Avinada," The herald boomed, his voice cutting through the hubbub of the ballroom.

Gathering her skirts, Cecilia took a deep breath. Masked faces peered out at her from every corner of the room as she descended the sandstone staircase, clutching the banister for support. The room was bursting at the seams, with women in colourful dresses and men in a dazzling array of suits.

She counted the steps under her breath, her lips frozen in a smile as the weight of hundreds of eyes pressed down on her shoulders. Frida did not have many friends. Everyone had come to see *her*.

She recognised King Vicente and his gaggle of sons, their faces hidden beneath matching burgundy masks. Mario Sanchez in his ridiculous pinstripe suit stood out like a sore thumb.

A soft murmur broke through the hush. Snippets of conversation drifted up as she moved closer to the crowd.

'Queen... Spitting image…"

Frida met her at the bottom of the stairs. Despite the dazzling array of colour in the room, the duchess was the only woman dressed in red.

Frida met her gaze, her dark eyes flashing with something sinister. It was gone in a moment, replaced by a mask of joviality. Still, Cecilia's stomach twisted. Her godmother held a manicured hand out to her. Not missing a beat, Cecilia took it, her face never betraying her discomfort.

They were so well-practiced in keeping up the façade, it almost steadied Cecilia's nerves. She knew what to do, what to say and how to act from this moment on.

If Frida had taught her anything, it was how to pretend nothing was wrong.

"Your Royal Highnesses, lords, ladies and gentlemen," Frida addressed the crowd, "Thank you for being here tonight to attend the birthday of a most beloved goddaughter."

The room erupted into applause. Frida grinned. Her dark eyes shone through her crimson mask as she turned her attention to Cecilia.

"It has been an honour and a privilege to care for you over the past sixteen years. You have always been like a daughter to me and now it is time for you to create your own path." Her manicured nail scraped the side of Cecilia's unmasked cheek.

Cecilia gritted her teeth, her stomach flipping at the announcement she knew was about to come.

"As you all know," Frida continued, turning back to the crowd, "It is customary for celebrations to begin with a dance. Tonight, we are not only celebrating Cecilia's birthday, but also her engagement."

The crowd thrummed with anticipation.

The young Duke Alarcon made his way to the front. Cecilia barely recognised him in his dark green suit and mask. She tried in vain to ignore Mario who crept up beside Frida. He looked ridiculous with his greasy black hair pulled back, his goatee plucked within an inch of its life.

"I would also like to take a moment to congratulate my son, Duke Alistar Alarcon, on his recent appointment as Ambassador to Calgaria," Frida announced turning the attention onto her son.

A murmur ran through the crowd at the juncture.

Whispers scurried across the room. The weight of her godmother's expectations threatened to suffocate Cecilia. She blinked back tears of frustration. If only she could lock herself away in the library and never face civilisation again.

Frida's fingers dug into her arm. It took a moment for Cecilia to realise she had just been asked a question. She glanced at her godmother.

"It seems Cecilia is still shy when it comes to choosing a partner to open the dancing," Frida announced, garnering a chuckle from the audience. "Perhaps she can start with her new fiancé?"

The crowd applauded. Mario stepped forward, manoeuvring himself in front of Frida and Cecilia. Before the duchess could open her mouth, a young man slipped through the throng, his face covered by an intricate black and gold mask. He looked like something out of a fairy tale; tall, dark and handsome. And he was walking straight at Cecilia.

"Before your fiancé whisks you away for the evening, may I have this dance?"

6

Dances & Chances

Something about the way the stranger looked at her flipped Cecilia's stomach in a way that was unfamiliar but not wholly unpleasant.

Frida shifted beside her, face creasing into a frown. The slip in her godmother's façade was enough to push Cecilia into action. She had never defied her godmother before.

Steeling her courage, Cecilia took the stranger's hand.

"I would be delighted," she said in a voice that was not her own.

The stranger grinned, eliciting butterflies in her stomach, as he led her to the centre of the floor. The crowd pressed together, giving them ample space as the band picked up a lilting tune.

The stranger pulled her close, keeping one hand in his and placing the other gently between her shoulders.

"Do you trust me?" he asked softly.

Letting out a shaky breath, she nodded.

"Yes."

He pulled her close and she caught the scent of dust and lemon, reminding her vaguely of servants. He guided her expertly through the dance, the crowd fading as she focused on her strange new partner. They said nothing, only the sound of strings and flute filling their ears. He anticipated her every move with ease. Where she would usually trip over her partner's feet, he held her steady. When she was unsure about a twirl, he would maintain their pace or follow through, even twirling himself and garnering a laugh from the crowd.

She grinned. She'd never had fun dancing before, especially not in front of a crowd. Trying not to blush under his warm gaze, she glanced over his shoulder, registering nothing but the cream wallpaper and blazing lanterns adorning each pillar of the room. When she finally looked back at him, it was as though she were floating on air. Her feet flitted on their own accord, following as he swept her along.

The song came to an end before she was ready. With a final twirl, he spun her out to the crowd before drawing her back into him. Cecilia stood breathless; their gazes locked as the crowd erupted into applause.

The stranger took a step back to release her, lifting her hand before bowing. After a moment, she found her footing and curtsied. They repeated the gesture to the crowd.

"Thank you for a wonderful last dance my lady," the stranger brushed a kiss on her bare knuckles. Before he could speak again, Frida stepped onto the dance floor and looped her arm through Cecilia's.

"Thank you for that display, sir," Frida said. "I'm afraid I did not catch your name before the dance."

He gave her a dazzling smile.

"Duke Aurelius Reddan, my lady," he winked.

A murmur went through the crowd.

"Well, thank you for your dazzling display," Frida said at last. "It is not often my goddaughter looks so graceful on a dance floor. I must commend your efforts."

"It is not often I have the pleasure of such a beautiful, well-practiced partner." He winked at Cecilia who blushed in earnest.

Frida cleared her throat, "Well, that's one way of putting it. On that note, it is time for the announcement we have all been waiting for." Frida ignored Aurelius as he settled back into the crowd.

Cecilia tried to ignore the weight of his gaze as Frida took her hand, leading her back to the centre of the dance floor. This time, she could not escape her fate.

Her legs grew heavy. Sweat prickled her skin. Her stomach twisted itself in knots, nausea bubbling into her throat as Frida's voice echoed through the hall.

"It is my honour to announce Señorita Cecilia will be joined in marriage to Count Mario Sanchez."

Mario stepped forward, his lips pushed back into a smile as he took Cecilia's hand from Frida. A polite applause filled the air as Mario bowed to the audience. Cecilia stood frozen, barely able to breathe.

"Bow with him," Frida's breath was hot on Cecilia's neck. "And smile for goodness' sake! This isn't your funeral."

Cecilia forced her features into a practiced smile as Mario squeezed her hand. She let him pull her back to the dancefloor, her limbs numb with dread.

She tried not to flinch when he took her sweaty palms in his, resting his other hand uncomfortably low on her waist. The band may as well have picked a funeral march, the music was so slow and mournful. Another waltz.

Mario's beady eyes were hooded with desire beneath his crimson mask. Disgusted, she turned away from him, determined not to look into his pinched face.

She found Duke Reddan who was watching them closely. Señorita Estella had sidled up beside him, briefly capturing him in conversation. Cecilia knew she had no right to be jealous, but something ugly stirred in her as she watched Estella bat her pale eyelashes at him.

When the duke returned his attention to Cecilia over the rim of his wine flute, her knees weakened and she stumbled. Unprepared, Mario stepped back, letting her fall to the floor.

In a moment, the duke was by her side.

"Are you alright?" he knelt beside her. "Do you need to get some fresh air?"

Frida was beside her in an instant.

"What's the matter with you? Get up!" She demanded, tugging Cecilia to her feet.

Cecilia shook her head, resisting her godmother.

"Water," she rasped.

"Someone fetch her some water." The duke ordered holding a hand out to steady her. With a quick glance at Estella, Cecilia took it. Aurelius put her arm over his shoulder, helping her to her feet. The crowd parted as he guided her to a stool in a quiet corner of the room.

Frida clapped her hands and all eyes returned to her.

"While the bride-to-be recovers from the excitement, let us continue to celebrate the happy news. Please, eat, drink and toast the young couple," she said raising her glass. The band began to play a happy tune.

From this distance, Cecilia could see Frida was close to breaking point, though she put on a pleasant façade. She dreaded to think what would happen when Frida cornered her for a moment alone.

She was glad of the duke's company as he knelt in front of her, his conversation light.

"Are you alright?" Estella asked removing herself from the crowd to kneel beside him.

Cecilia fought the urge to roll her eyes. Estella had never concerned herself with her before.

"I'm fine." Cecilia flashed her a wan smile, hoping it would be enough to wave her off.

Estella stood and placed a hand on Aurelius' shoulder.

"Let me know if you need anything," she said, barely sparing a glance at Cecilia.

His polite nod was quite satisfying as Estella slipped to the edge of the crowd, glancing back at the duke. He didn't turn back.

A servant appeared at her side with a tumbler of water. Aurelius turned his face away as she plucked it from him.

She gulped it down, water spilling from her lips and cheeks onto the front of her dress. She wiped the water from her mouth with the back of her hand. She froze, glancing at Aurelius, embarrassed to be caught in such an unladylike gesture.

"Do you need some fresh air?" he asked.

She nodded, taking his proffered arm as he led her out onto the adjoining balcony.

A handful of couples loitered under the spilled moonlight. Only a few revellers strayed at the edges of the open doorways, the final bite of winter keeping gossipers at bay.

Goosebumps ran up Cecilia's arms as an evening breeze picked up. She rubbed her arms with her hands.

"Would you like a jacket?" Aurelius asked, shrugging off his jacket to reveal a crisp, white buttoned shirt, the cuffs embroidered with strange flora.

Cecilia shook her head, but the duke draped it over her shoulders anyway. She savoured the warmth of it.

"I'm from Calgaria. This is not cold for me." He said, leaning against the stone banister.

"Thank you," she leant her forearms on the railing. "What brings you so far from home?"

"I'm here on a mission," he admitted.

"Oh?"

"To seek adventure," he winked.

She laughed, the sound echoing on the sandstone walls.

"What's so funny?"

"Nothing. Just – it must be nice to have the freedom to live in such a way." She shrugged, a tinge of jealousy clouding her voice.

"You wish to explore the world?"

"I-"

"Cecilia, there you are," Alistar interrupted them. They turned to face the duchess' son, his usually tidy blonde hair, falling into his vivid green mask.

Aurelius inclined his head at the duke who barely glanced at him.

"I'm feeling slightly better now that I've had a chance to take in the fresh air," Cecilia admitted, glancing at her companion.

Alistar ignored him.

"I didn't know mother was going to promise you to Mario," he continued. "I would have stopped it if I had known."

Cecilia shook her head.

"They had planned this for quite some time. I only found out today."

"No." Alistar balled his fists by his side. "No, I should've seen this coming. I should've said something. Why didn't you tell me?"

"I only found out an hour ago. There was no time to tell anyone. Besides," she shrugged, her voice low, "there's nothing you could've done. Once her mind is made up, there's nothing you can say to sway her."

"No." Alistar shook his head. "You can still get out of this. I will talk to my father. You mustn't marry Mario. You were always meant to be mine."

Aurelius cleared his throat.

Alistar finally looked at him, his face red.

"If I may cut in," Aurelius said carefully, "perhaps now would be a good time to take Señorita Cecilia somewhere private - away from prying eyes and ears."

"A wise suggestion. Thank you," Alistar agreed taking her wrist. "Come Cecilia."

She hesitated. She didn't need Aurelius' approval, but somehow, she wanted it.

She met his steady gaze, his expression hard beneath the dark mask.

Alistar tugged her wrist again. She let him lead her back into the ballroom, sticking to the edge of the crowd as they made their way into the villa's sandstone halls. She turned back as they reached the door leading to the main hallway. Would Aurelius follow them? Did she want him to?

With a final glance at the crowd, she stepped into the hall and hoped she was not making a mistake.

7

Snippets of Gossip

Marcus slipped into the ballroom after them, careful to avoid Lady Estella who waved to him from the edge of a crowd of young ladies.

He hesitated, flashing her a quick smile before turning back to the din. He could just make out the top of Alistar's blonde head above the swelling crowd, Cecilia close behind him.

The mood had shifted considerably in the few minutes he had spent on the balcony. An unspoken tension hung in the air as murmurs ran through the crowd. Dancers moved jaggedly across the cleared floor, restless and ungraceful.

"Why would Duchess Alarcon troth her goddaughter to a count of all people?"

"She looks like a young Princess Minerva doesn't she?"

"Who?"

"The king's sister, don't you remember her? She married a foreign king."

"Blue and black do not suit the señorita at all! Who is responsible for that terrible gown?"

"Don't be ridiculous Gregorio. And stop drinking – wine goes straight to your head."

Marcus listened to snippets of gossip as he trailed Alistar and Cecilia to the other side of the room. He watched them duck through the door, careful to keep a safe enough distance between them when another conversation pricked his ears.

"Do you remember the rumours from when the duchess first adopted Cecilia?" a noblewoman dripping in pearls asked her companions. Her eager listeners, two young ladies and an older woman, shook their heads.

Marcus stopped close to the edge of the group, keeping his back to them as he pretended to admire a large portrait of dancers hanging on the wall in front of him. He glanced over his shoulder as the ladies shook their heads.

The older woman leaned in. Marcus took a careful step back, straining his ears.

"People said the duchess held a grudge against Queen Minerva for stealing her fiancé years ago. The duchess was supposedly engaged to King Lars when he was still only second in line to the throne. Then his father died and his older brother became king and he was betrothed to Queen Minerva.

"It was a political match. Our kingdoms were at war with each other, but even blind Bartimaeus could see those two only had eyes for each other from the day they met. Still, the duchess thought there was something between her and the prince and accused Minerva of stealing him. As far as I know, they have never reconciled."

"And what does this have to do with Cecilia?" asked one of the young ladies.

"Hush. Listen to the story." The older girl admonished.

The older woman continued.

"Not long after Princess Lilia disappeared from Calgaria, Doña Alarcon adopted a little girl from an orphanage. Before this, she had been what you would call a socialite. Queen Isabel had tried to bar her from societal functions for years, after she found out Alistar was King Vicente's child. It never quite worked out."

The older woman lowered her voice, "After she adopted Cecilia, rumours began to swirl in foreign circles that she had somehow taken in the lost princess. As the rumours grew, she began to shut herself and her children away."

"Is that why Cecilia hardly goes to parties? I thought she was just socially inept."

"Lucia! What is wrong with you?" The girl's mother scolded.

Marcus sipped his wine.

"Some say Cecilia looks like Queen Minerva, but I've met the queen a handful of times and I can't see the resemblance," the woman concluded.

Marcus raised his eyebrows at the painting.

As the conversation turned to music and dancing, Marcus turned his attention to the mission at hand. Leaving his goblet on the gold-painted buffet beneath the painting, he continued weaving through the crowd. He ducked his head as he passed Juan Carlos who had taken a young servant aside.

"Have you seen Julian? I sent him to get wine more than an hour ago and he hasn't returned."

The servant shook his head.

A hand gripped Marcus' forearm like a vice.

He turned to see Duchess Alarcon, grinning at him like a predator sizing up its prey.

"Ah, Duke Aurelius. I had hoped you were with my goddaughter," she greeted.

Marcus inclined his head politely.

"Alas, I am not, however I thoroughly enjoyed her company. Now, if you will excuse me Doña Alarcon, I'm afraid I must retire. I have an early start ahead of me." He tried to pull his arm from her grip.

"But the night is only beginning!"

He flashed her a wan smile, "I am afraid I cannot stay, though it has been a very lovely evening."

Her smile turned sickly sweet as she loosened the grip on his arm, her fingers lingering for a moment. An uncomfortable shiver ran down his spine as her eyes roamed over him.

"It is a shame we could not keep you here longer. I would have liked to get to know you more."

"Likewise." He stepped away, eager to put as much distance between them as possible. "Now, if you will excuse me."

"Don't hesitate to come again Duke Aurelius. I look forward to your next visit."

Another man may have fallen for her charming smile, but all Marcus saw was a viper in a crimson gown.

8

Plan of Escape

A wall of people pressed in against Cecilia despite Alistar leading her through the edge of the crowd. An upbeat tune grated in her ears as dancers flocked to the open floor. Her stomach rumbled at the sight of decorative pastries held aloft by servants, the smell of rich food teasing her empty stomach. When was the last time she had eaten?

Before they reached the door, a swarm of ladies surrounded her, wishing her well with her engagement. Her sweaty hands slipped easily in and out of their grasps as she smiled and nodded her way through the uncomfortable pleasantries.

"What a fine bride you will be," said a woman drenched in pearls.

"It's an unusual match, but I'm sure you'll be happy together,' said another.

Smiling, she waved them off as quickly as possible, snatching snippets of gossip along the way.

"Well, I've lost five crowns. I thought for sure the duchess would troth her to young Alistar-"

"She's marrying beneath her station."

"Did you see the way the duke looked at her as they opened the dancing?"

The murmur of gossip turned to silence as they made their way down the sandstone hallway, away from the ballroom.

"Where are we going?" She struggled to keep up with Alistar's long strides. He said nothing until they reached the library, shoving her inside.

The tension in her shoulders eased a little as she walked through the familiar room. The smell of dust and paper would have calmed her save for the ball of anxiety knotting itself in her chest.

Alistar stood by the bay window, the room lit softly by the glow of lights on the balcony. Due to the curve of the building, they would be able to see out, but no one could see in. During the day, she had a spectacular view of the manicured garden overlooking the woods. Tonight, it was covered by stars and shadow.

"We should go back to the party," she began, "Your mother-"

"Forget about my mother," He snapped, pushing off from the window.

Her stomach twisted under his hard gaze, shadows dancing across his sharp features. A storm was brewing behind his brown eyes.

"Cecilia, you know I have always loved you," he reached for her hand. "Ever since we were children I knew if I was to marry anyone, it would be you."

She stumbled backward into a bookshelf. "Alistar-"

He held up a hand, "Let me finish. Please."

She swallowed her nerves, hot tears stinging her eyes.

"I know accepting my position as ambassador put me in a difficult position with you. Queen Isabel would not allow me to have such a high position and the nation's most elusive bachelorette. If you would give me some time to get settled in Calgaria, I will come back to marry you."

Cecilia shook her head.

"Your own mother wouldn't allow it. She wants me to marry Mario as soon as possible."

"And what do you want?"

She stepped back, struck by the question. If she told him what she wanted, would he believe her? Would he help her?

She looked out the window, the outline of Mount Aramyth flickered in the near distance. What she wouldn't give to be standing on the mountain than standing here with Alistar.

She sighed. He would not let her go without an answer.

"I want... to have the freedom to make my own choices," she said finally. "I want to find out who I am in the world. Who my family is."

He nodded eagerly.

"I can give you that. If you marry me, you can have all the freedom and family you want."

Cecilia shook her head. He didn't understand. If she married him, she would be trading one cage for another. And she would never escape her godmother.

"Alistar, I can't marry you. I'm sorry," she slipped her hands from his grip.

"No," he pleaded, "No. No, I don't think you understand Cecilia. You were always meant to be mine."

His grip tightened around her wrist like a vice.

"Alistar, let me go!" she pulled away from him. "I cannot change your mother's mind."

"Why not?" He whined, oblivious to her struggle, "Just tell her that you love me. You do love me, don't you?"

She took a shaky breath not quite meeting his eyes.

"I care about you."

His shoulders relaxed as he leaned forward. She put a hand out to stop him.

"But not the way you want me to."

His face crumpled.

She slipped her wrist from his grip as he raked his hands through his hair. He paced the floor, uncomprehending.

Cecilia flinched when someone cleared their throat behind them. Duke Aurelius emerged from the shadows, knocking on a wooden bookcase. Alistar swung around to face the intruder, hand ready at the decorated scabbard on his hip.

"Sorry to interrupt," Aurelius greeted.

"What are you doing here?" Alistar growled.

"I have been sent to fetch you both," the duke explained. "I understand His Highness would like to make a speech congratulating you both on your recent good fortunes."

Cecilia felt his dark eyes on her, despite the shadowed room and black mask he continued to wear. Alistar's own mask lay discarded on the floor. He took a deep breath, running a hand over his face.

"Alright. I shall escort Señorita Cecilia back to the ballroom. Thank you, Your Grace." He offered his elbow to her.

She hesitated. The last thing she wanted was to go back into the ballroom and face the snake pit waiting to criticise her. Not to mention the tongue lashing she would receive from Frida later. Briefly, she remembered the satchel she'd hidden earlier.

"If I may," Aurelius stepped in, "can I suggest you enter separately? It would look awfully suspicious if you were both to enter at the same time."

"What would be suspicious about that?" Alistar frowned.

"While Señorita Cecilia's appearance remains intact, you appear dishevelled, Your Grace."

Alistar swore, then excused himself.

"Fine. I'll go in first. But you owe me a dance at least," he pointed a bony finger at Cecilia.

"Of course," she nodded.

"What about you? What will you do?" Alistar turned to the duke.

"I will escort Señorita Cecilia back to the ballroom and then I will say my goodbyes."

Alistar narrowed his eyes at the duke. Cecilia could see the cogs turning in his mind as he decided what to make of him.

"Fine," he smoothed his golden hair. With a pained look at Cecilia, Alistar turned and strode out the door.

"Thank you, Your Grace," she let out a shaky breath. "I suppose we should begin making our way back to the ballroom?"

"Not if you don't want to," he shook his head. "It's your party, you can decide when, or if, you want to make a reappearance."

"You don't know my godmother." She shook her head. "She will drag me out of here as soon as she realises I'm not with Alistar."

"So, leave," he shrugged, "Run away."

A laugh escaped her.

"You can't be serious?"

"Haven't you ever thought about it?"

"Well, yes," she admitted, surprised by her own candour, "But it's not feasible, is it?"

"It can be."

"How…?" she hesitated the weight of her question pressing down on her, "Do you think about running away?"

"All the time."

"What do you have to run away from?"

He flashed her a teasing grin, "Responsibilities."

"But would you really do it?" She couldn't mask the desperation in her voice, "Would you run away if you could?"

"From a situation like this, yes. In fact, I'd go right now."

"You're not serious?" she scoffed.

"Why wouldn't I be?"

"Because," she tried to think of an excuse, "I'll get in trouble."

"Then come with me."

"Why should I? You're a stranger. Why should I trust you?"

"You trusted me on the dancefloor."

"That was different," she blushed, glad for the darkness shrouding the room.

"You're right. I am a stranger," he glanced at the door. "But I can see you're unhappy here. From what I've observed, your godmother treats you like a commodity rather than someone of inherent worth and value. I want to help you."

She narrowed her eyes at him.

"Why?"

"Because everyone deserves a chance to be free."

She paused, catching her hands in front of her as she picked at her nails.

"What if Frida finds out you helped me?" she asked.

"I'm not worried about that."

"Maybe you should be."

"Is that a threat?" he raised an eyebrow.

Cecilia tilted her chin, suspicions. Why would a wealthy man, a duke at that, help her run away? What was his motivation?

"Why do you want to help me, specifically? Why not Señorita Estella or one of the other ladies in the ballroom?" She jerked her head at the door.

He took a tentative step towards her. Her shoulder brushed the wooden edge of the bookshelf behind her.

"Those ladies are nice enough, but they don't need to run away. Besides, I assume you don't have a lot of experience in the matter."

"And you do?"

He nodded.

"What's in it for you? If I'm so ill experienced, wouldn't I just slow you down?"

He crossed his arms in front of him, even under the dim light his eyes seemed to dance with amusement. She wasn't sure if she should be comforted or offended.

"I'd feel more at ease knowing I didn't leave you stranded in the woods, than if we went together."

"So, you would bring me along to ease your conscience?"

"Correct."

She surveyed him again, crossing her arms over her chest.

She could see nothing objectively wrong with him. He was handsome and his tailored clothes hinted at a slender athletic build. He was obviously fit, and wouldn't look out of place with a sword in his hand. Dark, mysterious, and vaguely foreign - the more he spoke, the more she heard a lilt to his voice that was almost musical.

He glanced at the floor to ceiling windows over his shoulder. The warm glow of the party shone brightly against the cool sandstone, down to the lush green lawn. Beyond it lay a grove of trees that stretched to the base of Mount Aramyth.

"If we're going to leave, we should go now while your godmother and guests are preoccupied with the party," he suggested.

He was right. The longer she took to make up her mind, the greater the chance they would be caught before they had a chance to leave. Frida would never let her out of her sight then.

"Alright," she agreed, "but if you start acting dishonourably, I'll turn you straight in to the authorities."

"Deal," he stuck out his hand.

She took it, the warmth of his touch lingering on her skin.

"Now, the first rule of running away is to wear suitable attire." He clapped his hands together. "Ballgowns are... not the easiest clothes to move around in. Shall we stop by your room to change?" he asked.

"Actually, I prepared something earlier," she admitted disappearing briefly behind two bookshelves and returning with a small leather satchel.

"So much for being undecided," he said, impressed. "It's a good thing I happen to have something I prepared earlier as well."

From another shelf, he produced his own satchel.

"How-?"

"Later. Right now, we need to change and get going. Your absence won't go unnoticed much longer."

They each took different sides of the room to change, returning in plain travelling clothes. Cecilia held her gown over her arm.

"What do we do with this?" she asked.

"We'll have to cause a scandal," he warned, tossing the various pieces of his suit and her dress haphazardly about the floor.

"That's not the kind of girl I am!" She gasped at the implication.

"We can clear your name later, but right now we need the guests to think otherwise. This is the only way that will buy us some time and give you a motive to run away. Now, do you trust me?"

"Do I have a choice?"

He paused, "Of course you do. You always have a choice."

Something about the earnestness in his voice calmed her.

"Alright," she said slowly, "I'll trust you."

He held out a hand, "Then it looks like it's time to run away."

9

Runaway Cecilia

Shadows flickered at the corner of her eye, her heart skipping a beat as they hurried through the empty halls. The muted sound of music and merriment grew distant with each step as they detoured through the villa's gardens. A cool spring breeze tugged at her hair as they neared the stables, the smell of fresh hay and dust lingering in the air.

"How do you know this place so well?" Cecilia whispered as they crept through the back door. Their boots crunched on dry straw as they paused by an empty stall.

"I don't," he peered around the corner, "I just have excellent navigational instincts."

He motioned for her to duck as a stable hand came into view. Heart beating in her throat, she waited until the crunch of boots faded into the distance. She flinched as a horse nickered nearby.

Aurelius peered over the edge of the stall. Satisfied no one was around, he hurried to the tack room, Cecilia following close behind.

"How quickly can you saddle a horse?" he thrust a saddle into her arms. She grunted under the unexpected weight.

"As quickly as you need."

They hurried to the nearest stalls, saddling their dark steads quickly.

"Before I forget," Aurelius led a thoroughbred from the stall, "I didn't introduce myself properly."

Cecilia flashed him a puzzled look as she walked beside him, leading her mare to the stable's back entrance.

"If we're to run away together, you should probably call me by my name."

"Isn't your name Aurelius?"

He shook his head, mounting his horse.

"My name is Marcus."

"I'm Cecilia," she swung onto her horse, "but you already knew that."

"Halt! Who goes there?" a third voice called out.

They turned to face a young man, his arms full of buckets and brushes.

"Run!" Marcus yelled urging his steed into a gallop, Cecilia following close behind.

"Wait! Guards!" The stable hand called from behind them.

The rush of wind in her ears drowned out the chaos of the stable. Moonlight spilled over sweeping, wide fields spreading out before them like a great green ocean. Marcus' voice was lost on the wind, as he veered into the lush woodland. She followed, clearing a path to the base of Mount Aramyth. Dry branches crunched underfoot as they raced through the narrow walking track leading into the mountain. Stones flicked at her legs, their sharp edges pelting against her trousers as they rounded a corner.

A distant whistle sliced the air, followed by dogs barking.

Snatches of light from Villa Alarcon shone between the trees, quickly devoured by the dense thicket of trunks and vines. A smattering of warm rain filtered through the foliage, clinging to her skin and hair. Dirt turned to mud as Marcus guided them through a sharp turn. The rush of water did nothing to drown the sound of dogs howling in the distance.

She swallowed her fear. It was too late to turn back now. Urging her steed faster, she tightened her grip on the reins as they cleared a fallen log.

"Sharp left," Marcus called from beside her.

"But that's the creek!"

"I know," he threw her a wink before charging into the water.

Throwing a quick prayer to whatever saint was listening, she followed. She shuddered as the icy water engulfed her legs, splashing her sides and arms. Glaring at Marcus, who spared her only a cursory glance over his shoulder, she followed him across to the other side. She shuddered as the wind tore at her wet clothes, biting her skin.

The rush of horses' hooves drowned out any chance of conversation as they raced through the scrub, dry branches and tangled vines scratching at her clothes, dragging her backwards. *Stay,* they clawed at her.

Cecilia shook her head. She had to go. She had to find answers.

Marcus swung right, Cecilia rushing to follow as they began their descent down the mountain. The thud of hooves on dirt matched the beat of her heart until there was nothing in her ears but a pounding *badum, badum, badum.*

Marcus pulled at her sleeve for attention, motioning her to slow down. She blinked. Trees gave way to grey boulders. The moon shone brightly above them. She strained her ears; the hounds had stopped howling.

In the near distance, a warm orange glow emanated from a cluster of houses. Beyond, a distant white speck scanned the black horizon, beckoning them onwards.

"There's a cottage not far from here where we can spend the night," Marcus stretched his arms in front of him.

"And how far is not far?" She readjusted herself in the saddle.

"As long as we keep a steady pace, maybe another hour."

"An hour?"

"We'll be undercover for most of the way. I promise you can have a hot cocoa when we get in," he clicked his tongue to urge the horse into a canter.

She rubbed her eyes. The reality of running away was quickly beginning to lose the romance of her daydreams.

"Lead the way, I suppose," she sighed, picking up her reins. The familiar sound of hooves on dirt filled the silence between them.

Crickets picked up their nightly tune, a bird cooed high above them; the only hint of its presence as lazy raindrops fell haphazardly onto her skin.

Perhaps, on another night, she would've appreciated the trail. Marcus slowed the pace as they rounded another corner. Trees and vines pressed in on them from all sides until they reached a wide trail. He sidled up beside her, the horses clip-clopped over the muddy path.

"Marcus," she tested the name slowly.

"Yes señorita?"

"You're not really a duke, are you?"

He flashed her a charming smile, "What gave it away?"

"I didn't think dukes were the type to run away so easily."

"You'd be surprised," he swung out to avoid a tree.

"What would nobility run from? Aside from criminal activities, perhaps?"

His dark eyes twinkled under the moonlight, "Are you calling me a criminal?"

"No," she shook her head, "although I'd prefer to know if I'm running away with one."

"No," he chuckled, "I'm not a criminal."

"Then what are you running from?"

He patted his horse's neck thoughtfully, "I'd like to think I'm running to something, rather than from anything."

"What are you running to, then?"

"Adventure," he winked, a mischievous gleam in his eye.

His horse leapt forward, racing down the narrow track. Cecilia charged after him, his laughter echoing through the cathedral of trees. He was still laughing when she caught up with him, his smile infectious.

A distant howl rose from the shadows behind them. Merriment died on Marcus' lips as he peered into the trees behind her.

"Let's keep moving. We're not far from the base of the mountain."

Cecilia nodded, her skin crawling under the shadows. She strained her ears for any sign of pursuit, but all she could hear where her horse's hooves thudding in time to her heart.

10
Safehouse

Branches scraped Marcus' arms as they raced through the thicket of trees down the side of the mountain. The landscape rushed past, its beauty lost to him as the horses thundered down the track, rocks and pebbles spraying his legs.

The smell of damp grass filled the air as they burst into the open, moonlight spilling onto the world below. Grassy fields spread out before them, a sea of silver-green beneath the moon. Beside him, Cecilia clung to her horse for dear life, her face as white as the knuckles holding the reins.

A shadowed cottage rose from the side of a grassy hill as they drew near. A single lantern lit the southern gable, a red scarf flowing gently in the breeze.

He threw a glance over his shoulder at Cecilia, gripping his reins in one hand.

"Over there," he pointed.

Cecilia nodded as she followed him to the right.

They slowed as they drew close to the cottage. Marcus let out a low whistle as they reached the gate. A wooden door swung out at the side of the house to reveal a woman, wrapped in a faded brown shawl hurrying towards them. She stopped at the gate, resting a calloused hand on the wooden pole.

"The red duke trades in winter. What does he offer?" the woman's voice was young and clear.

"Wool of alpaca and sheep," Marcus replied.

"Always a pleasure to see you Marcus," the woman smiled, the gesture lighting her face.

"Likewise," he slipped off his steed. Cecilia followed suit.

"Allow me to introduce my companion," he held his hand out for Cecilia to join him. "Jeleni, may I present Señorita Cecilia. Cecilia, this is my friend Jeleni."

"It's nice to meet you," Cecilia smiled politely.

"And you," the young woman held out her hand.

Cecilia hesitated a moment before shaking it.

"I'll take the horses," Jeleni released her, reaching for the reins. "Liz's got some hot cocoa on the stove for you."

"Thank you," Marcus handed over the horse gratefully. He stretched his legs as he walked, not wanting to be caught by any pursuers in the open. Cecilia followed, mute.

"Don't worry," he murmured as they reached the front door, "We'll be safe here 'til the morning."

Cecilia nodded. For the first time he noticed the weariness in her shoulders, and red eyes.

A second young woman appeared at the door to hurry them in.

"Don't just stand there! Come in," she greeted, dragging them both inside. "Have a drink and a bit to eat," she ushered them into the cottage. She doled out mugs of steaming cocoa and offered a plate of cold meats, fruit and crackers once they were seated on a plush sofa in the *sala*.

"Thanks Liz," Marcus sighed, leaning his head against the low headrest, "but I think a bed and change of clothes are in order."

"Of course," Liz agreed, glancing at Cecilia who failed to stifle a yawn. "We can get better acquainted in the morning."

With very little coaxing, Cecilia followed Liz through the small house to a spare bedroom.

Marcus unlaced his boots and stretched out on the couch. Jeleni spared him a brief glance as she re-entered the house.

"Comfortable there?

"Mm-hmm."

Jeleni rolled her eyes affectionately. "My sister-?"

"Here." Liz entered the *sala*. She turned to Marcus, voice low, "This Cecilia, she's not Calgaria's lost princess, is she?"

Marcus took a sip of cocoa. "I believe so."

Liz and Jeleni shared a look.

"Well then," Jeleni shrugged, "she's a long way from home."

***

Frida traced the well-worn path on her tapestried rug. Cecilia's ball had been cut short soon after she disappeared. Rumours of her whereabouts swirled around the ballroom at an alarming rate.

"I saw her run off with Duke Alarcon after the dance," a pearl-drenched guest had told her companions.

"Have you seen Duke Reddan? I've been looking for him everywhere," Señorita Logarzo asked her.

Alistar had not long returned to the ballroom, eager to seek out his father, when Frida noticed something amiss. Extracting herself and Alistar from the festivities had been a tedious task. Guests came up to congratulate them as they made their way out the door.

"I told you mother, they will be coming in any moment now," Alistar assured her as they hurried down the empty hallways.

"What have I told you about trusting the word of a stranger? Did you not see the way he looked at her while they were dancing? Tell me I did not raise a fool."

Alistar stared at the ground, a sullen expression on his face.

Frida sighed, rubbing her temples with one hand. By the time they reached the library, a nervous sweat had broken out on the back of her neck.

The library was empty, a few rows of disturbed shelves the only evidence anyone had been inside.

"This is Cecilia's," Alistar picked up a discarded navy slipper beside a worn plush sofa.

Outside the door, an urgent buzz filled the air as servants rushed around the hall, murmuring to each other in low voices.

She narrowed her eyes at the unseeing servants.

Something was wrong.

Outside the window, frenzied voices rang out. Despite the thick glass, she caught the word 'escape'.

"Is something wrong here?" Mario demanded from the doorway. Frida turned to face him, forcing herself to smile.

"Everything's fine," she assured him at the same time Alistar said, "Cecilia's missing."

Frida groaned. Mario swore.

"You don't think she ran away, do you?" Alistar toyed with the shoe.

"You promised me she knew nothing about the plan!" Mario pointed a finger at Frida.

"I didn't tell her. She must have found out some other way," she glanced at Alistar.

"Don't look at me," he held up his hands, "I don't know what you're talking about!"

"It doesn't matter now," Frida sighed, "we have to find her and bring her back."

"And what of the guests?" Mario crossed his arms over his pudgy frame.

Frida rubbed her temples again, "I'll tell them Cecilia has taken ill."

He shot her a long look.

"What else do you expect me to do, Mario?" she snapped.

"I expected you not to lose her in the first place!"

"If you want her back, by all means – my resources are at your disposal."

He tilted his head, narrowing his beady eyes, "Including Brutus?"

"Yes. Now go," she waved him off.

Mario didn't wait to be told twice. Alistar on the other hand, continued to stick around.

"What should I do, mother?" he asked.

"Leave me to think for a moment," she waved him off. "Go back to the ball, and if anyone asks for Cecilia, tell them she's taken ill."

"And if they ask for Aurelius?" he nodded at the pile of clothes on the floor, an obvious distraction.

Frida shrugged, "He was leaving anyway. First ship back to Calgaria I think. Actually," a thought occurred to her, "Ask your father to close the ports, tonight if possible."

Alistar nodded, his face grim. She didn't watch him leave.

News of Cecilia's illness had spread through the room almost as fast as the rumours of her disappearance.

Frida's smile remained plastered to her face as she watched the king and her guests clamber into their carriages, the moon mocking her in its brightness. Surely someone would have seen Cecilia and apprehended her?

Silence pressed in on her from the four walls of her suite as she waited for news from her tracker. The guests had long since disappeared, their chatter fading into the night as she watched the last dregs leave.

A cup of chamomile tea lay abandoned on the small wooden table beside her settee. She picked it up, the drink cold and bitter on her tongue. She poured the remnants into a small potted plant beside the chair. It was an unladylike gesture, one that had amused her late husband.

She was almost sorry to have killed him.

Still, he never would have believed the child she carried was his, nor would he have helped her take Cecilia. Absolute power, he told her once, corrupted even the best people.

So, he had to go.

A knock on her door startled her from her thoughts.

"Come in." she ordered settling back into the plush seat.

A stocky man with close shaven grey hair inclined his head at her before stepping into the room. She frowned as his heavy boots tracked mud onto her pristine rugs. She would get the servants to air them out later.

"Brutus," She greeted, setting down her cup, "did you find her?"

"Yes, Your Grace."

"Where?"

"She and the rogue are spending the night at a small cottage on the edge of Cova Rafael. If we amass a regiment to get there at dawn, we can catch them and bring the young lady back."

"Let it be done," she commanded. "But I want to come with you. I wish to personally make an example of the rogue and anyone who helped her escape."

"As you wish, my lady," Brutus placed a fist over his chest.

Frida dismissed him with a wave of her hand. He gave her a cursory bow before turning on his heel and stalking out the door.

With a long sigh, Frida dropped into her sofa, pulling her red silk dressing gown around her shoulders.

"You will not humiliate me and get away with it," she spoke to the sky outside her window. "Mark my words, Cecilia. You will rue the day you crossed me."

11

A Narrow Escape

Cecilia tossed and turned as the grey edge of dawn seeped in through the thin curtains. She flinched as a rowdy cockerel burst into song by her window. A woman's voice cooed softly from the other room as voices filtered through the thin walls.

Yawning, Cecilia stretched her aching limbs, pushing off the stiff yellow bedcovers. She rubbed her palms, her hands sore from where the reins had dug into her skin.

"Señorita, are you awake?" Liz knocked on the door.

"Yes," Cecilia padded across the small room to open it. The woman grinned, holding out a pile of clothes.

"We didn't have much chance to get acquainted last night," she greeted. "My name is Elianza, but you can call me Liz. These are for you."

"Thank you." Cecilia took the clothes, laying them on a neat pile on the tangled sheets.

"They might be a little big, but you'll feel better wearing fresh clothes on your journey." Liz nodded at the pile of clothes Cecilia had hastily draped over a chair the night before. It was all she could do to change from her damp clothes into the nightclothes Liz had provided her before collapsing into bed.

"Thank you," Cecilia repeated.

"I'll let you get changed," Liz's smile never wavered as she withdrew to the hall, clicking the door shut behind her.

Cecilia wandered over to the porcelain washbasin on a small vanity near the window, the floral print faded from years of use. A matching, chipped water jug lay beside it, which she used to wash her face and hands, the water greying as she rubbed at her skin. It was not as luxurious as yesterday's bath, but it would do.

Changing into the travelling skirt and blouse Liz had lent her, she fixed her hair with a heavy white hairbrush, untangling grass and leaves along the way. Checking herself in the small mirror beside the door, she tucked in her blouse and entered the hall.

Marcus' voice filtered from the small hallway as she entered the *sala*. Liz sat opposite him on a plush wooden stool, a steaming cup of cocoa in her hands.

"She awakens," Jeleni announced as she entered from the kitchen, offering Cecilia a steaming mug. Cecilia took a tentative sip.

"Have something to eat," Liz implored, offering her a plate of fried bananas from the low wooden table in front of her. Unable to ignore her rumbling stomach, Cecilia stabbed a piece with a fork.

"How'd you sleep?" Marcus asked as she settled on the small plush sofa beside him.

"Fine," she said avoiding his gaze.

He'd changed into travelling clothes, the faded beige shirt showing off a lean figure. His brown clad legs stretched out in front of him, worn leather boots peeking out below the table.

"That's good," he said swallowing a mouthful of banana. "We have to leave soon. There's a ship waiting for us in Cova Rafael that we can't afford to miss."

"We?" Cecilia's brows furrowed.

"You didn't think I'd leave you here, did you?" he flashed her a smile.

She shook her head, "Where are we going?"

"Calgaria," his brown eyes twinkled, "Home."

"I'll get the horses ready for you," Jeleni excused herself, taking an empty plate to the kitchen. "It sounds like you're in for a long journey."

Silver light filtered through the soft curtains. Cecilia shifted on the couch, taking in the quaint room as Liz and Marcus chatted about travel routes and weather. Books of various sizes lined a small wooden bookcase to one side of the room, trinkets and ribbons scattered haphazardly on the shelves. A tall stool stood opposite them, draped in a threadbare, yellow doily, adorned by a vase of fresh flowers.

"Have you been to Calgaria?" Liz asked. It took a moment for Cecilia to register the question had been directed at her.

"Uh, no," she shook her head, "but I would like to go. Frida said something about my parents being from there."

Marcus and Liz shared a glance.

"Is that a terrible idea?" Cecilia worried at her lip.

"No," Marcus leaned forward, "not at all. What do you know about them?"

"Nothing, really," she shrugged, self-conscious under the weight of their collective gaze. "Frida said something about taking me there one day, that's all."

Jeleni yelled a warning as a carriage squealed to a halt outside.

Cecilia froze, "That sounds like Frida's carriage."

"Damn. She must have found us," Marcus stood, picking up his satchel.

"This way. Hurry." Liz ushered them down the hall, their conversation forgotten. They followed her into the small room across from Cecilia's, shutting the door behind them.

Cecilia gasped as Marcus pushed a vanity away from the bedroom wall. Liz pulled the rug underneath to reveal a trap door. Together, they tugged it open to reveal a narrow, dark staircase. Cecilia's heart hammered in her chest as Marcus plunged into the darkness.

"Hurry," he held out a hand to her. Swallowing her fear, she took it.

"There's a false wall at the end of the tunnel and a small peephole you can check to make sure the coast is clear. Jeleni would've saddled your horses by now. Go. Stay safe."

"You too," Marcus replied.

Cecilia fought down a wave of panic as Liz shut the door, the vanity scraping into place above them. She stumbled after Marcus, still gripping his hand as they pushed through the narrow tunnel, rough stone grazing her arms.

"How did she know we were here?" she mumbled as they came to a stop in front of a wooden wall.

"We must've been followed," he let go of her hand.

"But I thought we lost the trackers?"

"I suppose they were better than I bargained for." His hands searched for purchase on the wall in front of him. He pulled on a small square to reveal a peephole. Cecilia held her breath as he peered through it.

"All clear," he grabbed her wrist, "come on."

He pushed against the wall, giving way to the soft dawn glow as geese and chickens clucked around them. Frida's shrill voice rang out from somewhere nearby. Despite her trepidation, an idea began to form in Cecilia's mind as she followed Marcus to the horses. Doubling back, she hurried to a stall, which had been converted to house geese and chickens.

"What are you doing?" Marcus hissed, one foot already in the stirrups as she unlatched the stall, herding the unruly foul toward the barn door with a rake.

"Get out of here! Shoo!" She shooed the birds, steering them out into the open. It was enough, the birds squawked and scattered, scurrying into the garden.

Cecilia raced back to the stall, swinging herself onto the dark mare. A grin crept across her face as Frida shrieked.

"Get that thing away from me!" the duchess cried.

"What on earth?" Marcus turned to her bewildered.

"Let's go catch the fun," she threw him a clumsy wink.

Marcus chuckled, charging after her as she raced into the rising sun.

Together, they swung around the cottage, clearing the low wooden fence. A handful of guards scrambled after the geese, their red coats flailing as they attempted to apprehend the unruly flock, while the rest reached for their horses. Frida wailed as she hurried to the carriage, pushing past her confused guards.

"Catch them! Kill them!" she shrieked.

Cecilia's knees trembled as she steadied herself in the saddle. She couldn't be sure if Frida was referring to them or the geese and she wasn't going to wait to find out.

12

Cova Rafael

Verdant green fields swept past as the sun bathed the earth in a warm golden glow. A strong breeze did nothing to cool the sweat beading her skin as they raced past a second village outcrop. A slice of blue appeared beyond the horizon as they rested briefly at the top of a small hill. Marcus kept a look out as they urged their horses into a walk.

If she hadn't already been panting from exertion, the view might have taken her breath away. Mount Aramyth stood like a sentinel behind them, her presence large and imposing. Beyond them, green fields stretched out, dotted by the occasional patch of burned fields, and just beyond the horizon, lay the edge of the Cerulean Sea.

The smell of salt water and freshly burnt sugar cane carried in the wind.

"Beautiful, isn't it?" Marcus glanced at her as they continued down a grassy path, toward the entrance of Cova Rafael.

"Yes," Cecilia agreed, unable to tear her gaze from the landscape.

A worn dirt road came into view as they entered the outskirts of the portside town.

Cova Rafael looked like a small fishing village from their vantage point on the hill, but as they drew closer, the town sprawled out in all directions. They slowed to a walk, blending in with a smattering of other travellers. Cecilia slid off her horse, standing close to Marcus as a bored guard glanced at them, his face as bright as the faded red uniform he wore.

"Welcome to Cova Rafael," he grumbled, waving them along.

"After you," Marcus gestured Cecilia to enter first. The horses trailed along behind them, Marcus pulling on her wrist every now and then to keep her out of harm's way as people pressed around them, keeping his head down.

Cecilia, on the other hand, watched the bustling village openly. Voices overlapped as stall holders enticed passers-by with an array of fresh produce. She scrunched her nose at the smell of frying fish, the cook arguing with a neighbouring stallholder. As she hurried past, she caught sight of rising brick buildings supporting crumbling wooden structures.

Cova Rafael had been a sleepy fishing village throughout most of Avinadan history, its only claim to fame a tragic love story between an Avinadan prince and Calgarian princess. Now, with tensions rising in the east, the king had decided to fortify the village.

Marcus pulled her into an alley, putting a finger to his mouth. She quirked a brow at him as the horses shuffled nearby. Heavy boots thudded behind them, the familiar red flash of a guard's uniform hurrying past.

"Does Frida know we're here?" she whispered, chancing a glance into the busy street.

"I don't think so," he shook his head, "but I can't imagine it would be too hard for her to figure out where we are. We have to hope she hasn't tried to close the port yet."

Marcus glanced into the street again, checking the coast was clear before leading her and the horses through the streets again. Carts rolled by, children jostled past, running after each other. Men and women in straw hats called out prices for produce to see who could garner the most customers.

Cecilia held onto Marcus' shirtsleeve, so as not to get lost. They stopped near a quiet stall, tying their horses to a lean-to. An older woman shuffled behind a charcoal stove. Two children no older than ten peered at them from where they were assembling pastries at a small table nearby.

"Hungry?" he asked, nodding at the stall.

"Don't we have a deadline to keep?" she raised an eyebrow at him.

He opened his mouth to reply, when a loud voice boomed above the busy street.

"Attention citizens!" A young man with a pinched face and crimson military jacket called out from a balcony across the street. The gold ensign on his armoured breastplate glinted under the bright sunlight.

"Port Rafael is henceforth closed to ships and sailors. Anyone looking to leave the city by foot or by boat must first be searched by military personnel. Anyone attempting to leave without permission will be held in custody," the guard announced.

Shouts of dissent mingled with disappointed gasps as the crowd took in the news.

"I guess we'll have to eat some other time," Marcus sighed, untying the horses.

"What are you doing?" Cecilia stared at him, "Didn't you hear what he just said? We can't leave!"

"With all due respect señorita," he gave her a level stare, "they're looking for you. For us. They'll search every house, every ship and every business until they find you. Then what do you think will happen?"

"They'll return me to Villa Alarcon," she mumbled.

"Exactly. You don't want to go back now, do you?"

She shook her head.

"Stick with me," he handed her horse back to her. "If anything happens, head straight for the docks. Look for the *Real Sorrento*. She's a triple masted ship, flying the Calgarian colours."

"Which are?" she pulled her horse closer.

"Blue and white." They ducked into another alleyway, waiting for soldiers to pass, their horses blocking them from view. Instead, a group of red coats strayed close to the edge the alley mouth.

Marcus dropped the reins, pulling Cecilia against the brick wall behind her.

"What are you doing?" she gasped as he placed a hand by her ear, leaning in.

"Do you trust me?" he was close enough now she could catch the scent of sweat and leather on his skin. His eyes glowed amber under the pale morning light.

A harsh laugh broke out beside them, but Marcus' steady gaze never wavered from her own. Nerves bubbled up in her throat, threatening to spill over. Her heart hammered in her chest.

What was he doing? This was not the place to try an illicit a romance! She broke his gaze, willing herself not to blush, her focus instead settling on a crumbling stone statue at the end of the alley – a woman on her knees, her face raised in a cry. Her uplifted hands were missing some fingers, and half an ear had been chipped away, but Cecilia knew the figure instantly.

Princess Aramyth, the Calgarian princess and doomed lover of Prince Rafael. Their tragic history was often cited as the start of Avinada's feud with the eastern kingdom, though it was so long ago no one could tell if it was fact or fiction.

"Let's keep moving," Marcus pulled away, tearing her attention from the statue. She followed him out of the alley, the red coats moving ahead of them. She spared a final glance at the stone woman. What must she have been like to bring kingdoms to war?

The already crowded streets pulsated with people pressing together from all sides. Cecilia and the horses slipped in behind Marcus. She tethered herself to his shirtsleeve as they bustled their way through the crowd. Most people continued in the direction of the markets – if they were to be turned out of their houses, they might as well catch the gossip.

"I heard they're looking for a couple on the run," a man told his wife.

"Haven't you heard? Apparently, Señorita Alarcon ran away with some foreign duke!" A woman draped in fine silks grinned at her equally finely dressed companion.

"Bloody Calgarians," a second man burst. "They have no decency! They think they can come to our shores, steal our women and not face consequences! I'll show them!"

Cecilia wiped sweat from her damp brow as they finally reached the edge of the crowd. The bay opened below them, two paths diverging from the marketplace to the docks. To the right, houses were built into the rock, square homes rising outwards, blending together as locals navigated smooth sandstone pathways. A short distance below, wooden planks paved the way for sailors and stevedores unloading the ships.

"Halt. Who goes there?" a voice boomed behind them. Cecilia glanced at Marcus, who flashed her a reassuring smile.

"Good morning, sir," Marcus greeted jovially, extending a friendly hand toward the guard. "Fine day for sightseeing, isn't it?"

"You're travellers?" the young man rested a hand on his sword hilt.

"Yes," Marcus pulled his hand away, "From the south."

The soldier brushed his short beard thoughtfully.

"Your accent," he narrowed his dark eyes at Marcus, "it sounds almost Calgarian."

"My father's sin," Marcus chuckled, attempting to lighten the mood. "My mother is Avinadan."

"And what about you?" The soldier turned his attention to Cecilia, "Where are you from, señorita?"

"Here," she squeaked. Embarrassed, she cleared her throat.

"What business have you in Cova Rafael?" The soldier stepped closer, his eyes roaming over her petite form. She took a tentative step back into Marcus, who laid a hand on her shoulder.

"We're on our honeymoon," Marcus flashed her a warm smile. Her stomach tightened as she returned her attention to the soldier.

"From where?" he pressed.

"Avizon."

"And you chose to visit this godforsaken backwater?" the soldier scoffed, shaking his head. "Well, with a wife like yours, I doubt you'll be leaving your lodgings much anyway."

Cecilia's cheeks heated as Marcus' mouth hardened into a thin line. The soldier's lips peeled back into a predatory smile, his eyes lingered on Cecilia.

"Your eyes. They're two different colours," he noted.

Cecilia's heart sank to her stomach.

"You must be Señorita Alarcon… We've been looking for you." he grinned.

"Run!" Marcus yelled.

"Guards! Seize them!" the soldier shouted lurching toward her. Marcus stepped in front of her, pushing her backward.

"Go!" he ordered. Her fingers slipped from the horse's reins as she raced in the direction of the cliffside village. Her legs pumped beneath her, feet pounding the pavement as she burst through the crowd. A whistle pierced the air. She turned back. Marcus. She couldn't leave without him.

Before she could move, a pair of meaty hands grabbed her arm. She screamed. A sickening crack crunched the air in front of her, a plump guard in a red coat crumpled to the ground.

"Keep moving," Marcus' voice tore her back to reality. Turning on her heel, they raced through the narrow streets. Whistles blared behind them. Cecilia blinked back tears as they tore through side streets and back alleys. Heavy boots kept pace behind them.

"We need to split up," Marcus panted beside her.

"What?" she stumbled. Marcus' steady hands caught her before she could fall, pulling her along as they ducked into another alley, pausing to catch their breath.

"It's the only way."

"You're crazy!"

"Do you trust me?" A thin trail of blood smeared his chin, but he didn't seem to notice. His amber eyes sparkled with mischief under the early morning sun. They had a deadline to keep.

"I'm beginning to think I shouldn't."

His lips tipped into a grin.

"I promise I'll make this worth it," he squeezed her hand. "I'll distract the guards while you take the path to the docks. Do not stop for anyone."

She nodded. After a moment's pause, he checked the alleyway.

"I'll see you soon," he promised. The soft pressure of his hand lingered even after he'd ducked out calling the guards after him. She waited until the thunder of boots died down before peering around the corner. Satisfied no guards were about, she cast off.

Her legs protested as she broke into a run. Keeping the docks to her left, she focused on putting one foot in front of the other. Beside her, the sun cast a soft golden light over the cerulean waves. The beauty was lost to her as struggled onward, lungs burning in her chest. A trio of red coats flashed in front of her. She ducked beside a food stall, her back to the street as she waited for them to pass. Her legs trembled beneath her as she sucked in a breath.

It would be so easy to stop running, to wait for someone to find her and turn her into the authorities. Then, at least she could rest. No, she shook her head, she couldn't go back. There was nothing left for her at Villa Alarcon.

Besides, she had to get to the *Real Sorrento*. Maybe they could help her rescue Marcus.

With renewed energy, she picked up the pace. Her foot caught on a wooden stall, bringing the structure down. Fresh produce rolled into the path as the stall holder cursed her out.

"Sorry!" she brushed herself off, "I'm sorry!"

"Stop that woman!" a guard yelled behind her.

Guilt settled in her chest as she pressed into the crowd, squeezing past fruit sellers, fishmongers and rowdy children, some of whom joined in the pursuit. The further she ran, the less dense the streets became. Until she ran out of road.

A stone building towered over her, its shadow blocking the sun. Below her, houses littered the edge of the bay, a narrow path snaking into the village and a little further out, the port.

"It's a dead end, señorita," the young soldier's voice rang out behind her. One eye was already sporting a smart black bruise, while blood ran down his cheek and chin as his face cracked into a menacing smile. He took a deliberate step toward her.

"I've caught your little companion," he sneered. "He looks a lot worse for wear now. I'd be surprised if he could open that pretty mouth of his."

Cecilia's heart lurched in her chest. What had they done to Marcus?

"Cecilia," her name carried in the wind. For a moment she could swear she heard Marcus' voice. She chanced a glance at the village below. A swarm of guards appeared behind the young soldier, their grins' mirroring his own.

"Come with me," he swiped at her, "I'll go easy on you."

A chill ran up her spine at his menacing smile, something sinister illuminated his black eyes. She took a step toward the ledge, the breeze tugging at her skirts.

"Actually," she flashed him a wan smile, "I'd rather take my chances with the fishes."

Heart pounding in her chest, she stepped backward from the ledge and fell.

13

Real Sorrento

A jolt shot through Cecilia's legs as she fought for balance. If she hadn't spied the mattress on the roof, she wouldn't have jumped. Steadying her trembling legs, she looked at the soldiers peering down at her from the ledge.

They wouldn't wait.

Pushing herself off the mattress, she rolled onto the rooftop, stumbling to a faded brown door.

She had barely touched the handle when it swung open, missing her nose by an inch. A girl, not much younger than herself, stared at her, a basket of clothes perched on her hip.

"Excuse me," Cecilia squeezed past the girl.

Her feet pounded down the narrow staircase, voices filling the house. She burst into a crowded *sala*, the little room packed with fishing gear. The occupants fell silent as she entered.

"Who are you?" A dishevelled man asked from the sofa, a glass of ale poised half-way to his lips.

Upstairs, the girl screamed. Cecilia bolted for the door, swinging it out to reveal a young boy, about twelve, with a stack of fish slung over his shoulder.

"Who are you?" he asked.

"How do I get to the docks?" Cecilia ignored his question. He jerked a thumb behind him.

"Thank you," she called as she raced down the stone stairs.

The stench of fish and salt permeated the air, assaulting her nose. She fought the urge to gag, an unpleasant heaviness on her tongue. The further she ran, the stronger the stench became. Her eyes watered, lungs burning as she stumbled past fishmongers, sailors and stevedores.

"What's a pretty thing like you doing in a place like this?" someone called after her.

"Hey señorita, what's your going price?"

She bristled, forcing herself forward.

"Cecilia!" A familiar voice called out.

She slowed, turning to see where the voice had come from. Hooves thundered along the wooden path. Facing forward, she found Marcus, astride a dark horse, his hand out-stretched. Reaching for the last dregs of energy, she pushed forward, reaching for him.

"Not so fast!" strong fingers grasped at her clothes. Fingernails dug into her back. She screamed as Marcus pulled her onto the horse.

"Are you alright?" He yelled over the din.

"Fine," she swung her leg over the horse, clinging to Marcus as she steadied herself behind him. A soldier yelled after them, his curses lost to the wind.

Hoofbeats thundered in her ears. A guttural cry. A flash of blue beneath them. A heavy jolt as the horse landed on something solid. Her head throbbed from crashing into Marcus' shoulder. The ground surged beneath them, the roar of waves filling her ears. Blood bloomed in her mouth; she'd bitten her tongue on the landing.

A cheer erupted from the crowd behind them as guards shouted at one another, pushing and pointing at their ship. Vessels, large and small sailed past as they pulled away from land.

"That was quite an entrance," A woman's voice floated from somewhere in front of them.

Cecilia peered around Marcus' shoulder to see a young woman draped in a blue military jacket, her dark hair pressed smooth against her brown skin. Her long legs were clad in military style trousers and shining black boots. She tilted a proud chin at them, her dark eyes sparkling with amusement, yet her straight-backed posture exuded an air of authority.

"You know me." Cecilia could hear the smile in Marcus' voice as he slipped from the horse, "I don't mind a grand entrance now and then."

The woman shook her head affectionately, an easy smile on her lips.

"Who's your friend?" she jerked her chin at Cecilia.

"Captain Catalina, I present to you Señorita Alarcon." Marcus offered Cecilia a hand to help her dismount. She took it gratefully, leaning on his arm while she willed her legs to stop trembling.

"Cecilia Alarcon?" the captain narrowed her eyes.

"Yes," Cecilia gave her a polite smile.

"Hmm," Catalina turned to Marcus, "You bring me a noblewoman and a horse on the same day. Aren't you full of surprises?"

"Yes, well," he cleared his throat, "it couldn't be helped."

"A word. In my office," she jerked a thumb at the worn wooden door behind her.

"Of course," Marcus nodded. "Señorita?"

Catalina shook her head, "Just you, Cervantes. I'll speak with Señorita Alarcon soon enough."

Marcus shot her an apologetic smile.

"I'll find you," he promised.

"Sebastian," Catalina addressed a swarthy sailor, close by, "show Señorita Alarcon around the ship. See if you can find Bella or Jeremy, I'm sure she would be grateful for some youthful company."

"Aye captain," the sailor inclined his head. With a final glance over his shoulder, Cecilia watched Marcus follow the captain into her quarters.

"Come, I'll introduce you to the others," the sailor offered his burly arm.

Cecilia hesitated. After the chaos of the morning, she wasn't in the mood for meeting new people. All she wanted was a clean bed, a warm bath and the brief respite of sleep. Still, she couldn't be rude to her host, or whoever these people were.

"Thank you," she took his arm. With a final glance past the helmsman, she watched the Avinadan coastline slip into the distance. The boat surged beneath her feet. Regret tugged at her chest, tears sparking in her eyes. Would she ever see her home again?

"Señorita?" Sebastian's brows furrowed in concern.

Forcing a smile, she rested a light hand on his damp arm. Avinada was her past. But her future? It was as wide and unknown as the ocean.

***

"So, you managed to find the princess within a week of infiltrating Avinada," Catalina leaned back in her mahogany chair, a dull silver tumbler poised at her lips. "I have to admit, I'm impressed."

"Oh, ye of so little faith," Marcus grinned, sitting opposite her. Papers littered the desk between them, half-filled ships logs overlapped maps. A compass lay discarded at the edge of the table. Marcus pushed it forward to save it from falling as the ship dipped into the water, buoyed in an instant by the waves.

From the window behind Catalina's shoulder, Avinada flickered in the near distance, Mount Aramyth peaking over the horizon under the morning sun. He yawned, fighting the fatigue that pulled at him.

"So, what did you manage to find out about the girl?" Catalina set her glass in front of her, shuffling through a small stack of papers.

"You can see for yourself, she's the spitting image of Queen Minerva."

"Maybe so," she shrugged, "but Parliament is going to need more evidence than that."

"That's why," Marcus pulled a box from the satchel at his feet, "I brought this." He pulled out a long, black velvet box. He'd found it while hiding his satchel in the library in Villa Alarcon. Then he'd almost lost it, and the horse, during the fight in Cova Rafael.

Catalina set her papers down, leaning close to inspect the box. He handed it over.

"What am I looking at?" She surveyed the worn velvet, the silver edges rusted and chipped with age. She turned it over in her hands before opening it. Folded pages peaked out from beneath the velvet lining.

"Receipts from Doña Alarcon's journey from Avinada to Calgaria a few days before the king and queen's anniversary celebrations sixteen years ago," Marcus smiled triumphantly.

"Is that all?" She shuffled through the rest of the papers, the parchment yellow and creased from age-old folds.

Marcus shook his head. "The first receipts were from her solo journey to Calgaria. The other receipts show she booked passage for herself, a young man and a small child from Calgaria to Avinada."

"Doña Alarcon has a son, does she not? Perhaps he was the child."

"No," Marcus pressed, "One of those pages is a letter from her mother the week she went away. She left Alistar with his grandmother in Entander because he was sick. And if you see here," Marcus pointed to a faded scrap of paper, "there is a letter of payment to the orphanage at Cova Rafael."

"So, she adopted a child? Is that not common knowledge?" Catalina sipped her drink. Marcus sighed, the burden of knowledge weary on his shoulders.

"Why would Doña Alarcon pay for passage for a child across the ocean, one whom she did not arrive with? And why would she pay to adopt a child from an orphanage in a remote fishing town, three months later?"

"It makes no sense," Catalina agreed.

"What if she used the orphanage as a cover?" he argued, "Hiding Princess Lilia until such a time as she could adopt a child without raising suspicion?"

"You're leaning into speculation," Catalina warned.

"I know," Marcus nodded, "but if you had just kidnapped the crown princess of a rival kingdom, what would you do with the child? You wouldn't take her into your home right away."

Catalina twisted her mouth in thought, considering the theory.

"I suppose that's plausible," she agreed.

Marcus leaned back in his chair, "And another thing."

He pulled the satchel out again, retrieving a thin velvet pouch and pulling the top open. He poured the contents into his open palm, a small gold chain spilled onto his tan skin. A pendant, smaller than his thumb, glinted in the morning sunlight. A lion's head was emblazoned on the trinket, it's mouth open in a silent roar. The royal Calgarian ensign.

Catalina reached for the necklace, studying it closely. She turned the pendant in her hand, running her thumb against the warm metal

"The royal crest," her breath caught.

"Turn it over," Marcus instructed.

The captain's eyes widened in realisation. Stamped in small letters around the edge, was a name: Lilia Sigrid of Alcary.

"Lilia's chain," she gasped.

"How could a foreign noblewoman come to be in possession of such a fine item belonging to the crown princess?" Marcus asked, eyes gleaming with satisfaction.

"So, Cecilia...*is* Lilia?" Catalina's words were almost drowned by the constant lap of the ocean.

"So it seems," he leaned back in the chair.

"Does she know?" Catalina handed the necklace back.

Marcus shook his head as he returned it and the velvet box, into his satchel.

"As far as I know, Cecilia knows her parents are Calgarian, but nothing more. I think she may suspect she is the princess, but she hasn't said as much to me."

Catalina tapped her chin in thought.

"Stay with her anyway and see what else you can get out of her. She seems to trust you. Use that to your advantage," she instructed.

"Aye, captain" Marcus threw her a mock salute.

"You're dismissed," she waved him away.

Marcus stood, giving her a proper salute and turning on his heel.

"Just one thing," Catalina called once he reached the door, "try not to get too close. The last thing we need is for you to break the princess' heart."

Marcus threw her a charming smile, "Since when have you known me to do such a thing?"

"You're too much like your brother," her lips thinned into a sad smile, "You break hearts everywhere you go."

Ignoring the weight in his chest at the mention of his brother, Marcus flicked her a final nod as he stepped into the bright sunlight. He was determined not to follow in his brother's footsteps. He would complete his mission without letting his emotions get in the way.

Just make sure your heart doesn't turn to stone, a voice echoed in his head. He shook off the thought. He could charm the princess without falling for her. He would get what he needed, get her home and receive a handsome reward for his efforts. Nothing more, nothing less.

His mouth set in a grim line.

This is just a job. Do nothing but your duty. And don't get distracted.

14

New Friends

Crewmen hurried about the deck, barely glancing at Cecilia and Sebastian as he escorted her to the forecastle. She barely paid any attention to him, her stomach churning at the open ocean before them. Her eyes squeezed shut as the breeze tugged at her shirt, the taste of salt and sunshine settling on her tongue.

"We have set a course for Avizon," Sebastian said, apparently oblivious to her discomfort. She glanced sidelong at him, his dark eyes fixed on the horizon.

"Are we not due to head to Calgaria?" she asked.

He shook his head. "We must go to Avizon to resupply and then we will make our way there."

"How long will that take?"

"Ah, there you are," Marcus greeted from behind them.

Cecilia turned at his voice. He raked a hand through his dark locks in a vain attempt to keep it from tangling in the wind. He wore the same charming smile she had come to expect. Her stomach churned again, as the boat rocked beneath them.

"Marcus," Sebastian unlooped his arm from Cecilia's to clap his hand in greeting.

"Shouldn't you be keeping us on course at the helm?" Marcus grinned.

"I was just showing Señorita Alarcon around the ship," Sebastian nodded at her, "but now you're here, perhaps you can introduce her to the others. I must be getting back."

"Of course," Marcus agreed, glancing at her.

"Thank you," Cecilia called as he walked across the deck. Sebastian turned, nodding briefly as he continued.

"So, how much of the ship did Sebastian show you?" Marcus asked, leaning against the guardrail.

"Only the deck," Cecilia hung back from the edge. Marcus nodded, not looking at her.

"How do you like the view?"

She shrugged, "I'd like it better on solid ground."

From her vantage point at his shoulder, she could see the corner of his mouth tip up in a smile.

"You get used to it," he shrugged. "The worst thing the ocean can do is kill you."

"There are better ways to die than drowning."

He glanced at her then. Sadness flickered behind his eyes, his mouth setting into a hard line.

"Come, I'll introduce you to the others," he pushed off the edge, leaving her standing on the deck. Finding her feet, she hurried after him, catching up when he entered the cramped galley. The roar of the ocean was slightly dampened by the sound of sailors' laughter as boots and rope thudded above them. A gull cried somewhere in the distance.

In the cramped hallway, she squeezed close to Marcus, keeping out of the way of other sailors. Almost directly in front of them, stood a faded green side door which swung out before Marcus had a chance to knock.

A shock of blonde hair poked out from the door, attached to the tallest man Cecilia had ever seen. The young man stooped in the cramped space, his pale head barely an inch from the top of the doorframe.

"Hullo Marcus," his accent was strong, lilted, "long time no see."

"Jeremy," Marcus took the man's proffered hand, "good to see you. I'd like to introduce our latest arrival, Señorita Cecilia."

Jeremy's dark eyes alighted on her. She saw nothing sinister in his wide smile.

"Good morning," he offered his hand. "It's a pleasure to make your acquaintance."

Hesitating, she took it, offering him a polite smile.

"We've come to see if you or Bella were free to join us above deck for some fresh air," Marcus continued.

Cecilia slipped her hand from Jeremy's as he shook his head.

"She's helping her uncle prepare some decorations for the festival tonight and I'm taking stock of supplies before we dock in Avizon," he flashed them an apologetic smile, "otherwise I would."

"Ah," Marcus shrugged, "no matter. We will see you at the celebrations?"

Jeremy nodded, enthusiastically, "I wouldn't miss it."

Cecilia followed Marcus back through the narrow galley and onto the deck. Despite the ocean breeze, the morning heat pressed down on them like a cloak.

"Is it possible to get freshwater so far out at sea?" she asked as they passed bronzed sailors, sweat glistening on their brows, shirts rolled up to their elbows.

"We have barrels of drinking water to last us a while," he reassured her. "Why? Are you thirsty?"

Cecilia shook her head. In truth, she was parched, her lips were dry and cracked. Still, she didn't want to impose.

"I'll get you some water. Sit... here." Marcus led her to a small barrel near the forecastle. Satisfied she wouldn't move, he hurried across the deck, disappearing into the galley. Squeezing her eyes shut, she pressed the toes of her boots into the deck beneath her. Wind rushed in her ears, battering her cheeks.

One, two... Marcus will be back soon and you won't be alone. She thought.

It was two minutes before Marcus' boots stopped in front of her.

"Are you alright?" he asked, kneeling on the deck.

Cecilia nodded, taking the proffered cup of water.

"Not used to sailing," she mumbled.

He watched with concern as she downed the cup.

"Are you feeling nauseous? Headache-y?"

She shook her head. Her stomach growled. She pressed into it, hoping he wouldn't notice. He frowned as she glanced at him.

Her stomach twisted again, although this time she couldn't be sure it was from hunger pangs.

A sailor strolled past them, carrying a crate full of oranges on his shoulder. He stumbled as the ship dipped beneath them. Cecilia clung to the edge of the barrel, watching as two oranges rolled towards them. Marcus swiped them from the floor dusting them off against his shirt.

"Hungry?" he asked.

This time she couldn't stop the growl that escaped her stomach.

"Me too," he smiled. "Your godmother and the guards at Cova Rafael interrupted our breakfast plans."

"That was quite rude of them," Cecilia agreed as he retrieved a dagger from his boot. Her eyes widened in alarm as he cut into the fruit, "You had that on you this entire time?"

"Yes." Juice spilled between his fingers. "Would you prefer I wasn't armed?"

She hesitated for a moment, then shook her head. Hadn't she watched him fight off a slew of the king's guards at the docks? Did she really expect him to be unarmed while fighting?

"I suppose I hadn't really thought about it," she admitted, taking a proffered orange slice.

"I try not to use this one if I can help it. Emergencies only," he wiped the dagger on his trouser leg.

"And this constitutes an emergency?" she licked the sweet juice from her lips.

"Like I said, we haven't eaten today," he bit into an orange wedge. Gulls circled overhead, their impatient cries ringing across the clear blue skies. "So," Marcus chewed thoughtfully, "you haven't told me why you're running away."

Cecilia tried not to choke on orange juice, "It was your idea!"

"You didn't have to take me up on it," he laughed.

Cecilia frowned, "I didn't feel like I had much of a choice."

"The choice was always yours, Señorita. Though you seemed to have made up your mind before we met," he eased into a smile, wiping juice from his chin with a shirtsleeve. She averted her gaze.

"I never wanted the life Frida laid out for me. And when I overheard her say she would betroth me to Count Sanchez... I didn't want to wait."

Marcus paused, waiting for her to continue.

"He's been the duchess' advisor since I can remember and... well, it's not a nice feeling to find out a man who watched you grow up wants to marry you." She picked at the orange peel. "Before the ball, my godmother said something to him about hiding evidence linking them to Calgaria, and making sure I didn't remember my past. Whatever that means."

She cast her eyes over the rail to the blue-grey ocean beyond.

"Do you know what she meant by that?" He offered her another slice.

"No," she shook her head, shifting on the barrel as she accepted the wedge.

"And you don't know what the evidence was?"

"There were rumours around the orphanage. I'd been taken in not long after the Calgarian princess' disappearance," she crossed her arms. "but what does that matter now?"

"This is your past, Señorita. Your future. It matters a great deal."

Something about the earnestness in his voice struck her. She thought for a moment before answering.

"They said my eyes and accent were strange. I stopped speaking after my first month in the orphanage. When my godmother adopted me, someone mentioned my resemblance to Queen Minerva. She forbade me from repeating or questioning it. She forbade me from speaking about my life before she took me in." Cecilia paused, chewing another slice before speaking.

"I hoped...it's silly to say it out loud," she shook her head, "but as a child I thought I wanted to be Calgaria's lost princess. At least then I would have a family who wanted me."

Marcus' face fell into a frown. There was no malice in it – only sadness reflected in his deep brown eyes. Cecilia looked away. She didn't want his pity.

"Can you remember anything before she adopted you?" he asked.

She shook her head. He offered her a sad smile.

"We'll find out what happened to you. I promise."

She nodded, not quite believing him. Still, if he was confident he could help her find evidence of her parents, maybe she could try to believe it to.

He gave her the last orange slice.

15

Missing Pieces

Rage brewed and bubbled until finally it boiled over. The duchess' perfectly styled curls had been pulled apart in a haphazard crown, framing a stony face and blazing black eyes.

Mario Sanchez was the bane of her existence and she was determined to be the bane of his in turn.

A cacophony of books, scrolls and journals scattered the usually pristine library floor. A wooden horse figurine lay on its side, its front leg missing. Furious, Frida picked it up and pitched it across the room. The crack of wood on stone was not as satisfying as it should have been.

"You called?" Mario drawled, leaning against an empty bookshelf, its contents scattered on the tile. The heavy timber held him upright as he swayed on his feet.

His white shirt was crumpled, half tucked into faded black trousers. A dark moustache and heavy stubble framed cracked lips. If his bloodshot eyes weren't sign enough, he reeked of alcohol.

"What the hell have you been doing in my library Mars Erikson?" she snapped.

He jolted forward at the use of his true name, beady eyes bulging out of their sockets.

"I'm not the one who made this mess!" he argued, leaning an arm against an empty shelf to keep him steady. "You made this all on your own."

"I'm not the one who was in charge of keeping Cecilia's papers hidden. That was your responsibility and you've failed," she pointed a bony finger at him.

"One would think," he settled back to his usual indifference, "if it was your responsibility to care for the girl, evidence of her parentage would be yours to hide also."

"This was the only thing you needed to do for sixteen godforsaken years, Mario!" she yelled. "This was the only evidence we had to present her to Lars and Minerva after your wedding and it's all been for naught!"

She sank to her knees, knocking over a pile of leather journals. Her eyes stung, but she would not let him see her cry.

"You promised you would help me steal a kingdom. Now you've gone and lost the key," her voice cut through the silence of the room.

Mario crossed his arms, avoiding her gaze.

"What do you want me to do about it? She's halfway to Calgaria by now," he mumbled.

Frida tilted her chin at him, "How do you know that?"

He shrugged, "I asked Brutus to follow her."

Frida straightened, smoothing her hair.

"If they're sailing to Calgaria, they'll have to resupply on the Fickle Islands," she mused.

"Oh, that reminds me," Mario reached into his pocket, handing her a crumpled envelope.

"What's this?" Frida snatched it from his slimy hands.

"A letter from the king," Mario shrugged.

"Which one?" She broke the wax seal – a single ship pressed into the stamp.

Her eyes widened as she read the letter once and then again.

"Well?" Mario demanded as the silence grew loud.

Frida rolled her eyes at him, letting the air settle as she straightened her hair.

"It seems Pirate King Anders has requested my presence, post haste," she preened.

"Why?"

She fought the urge to slap him as he snorted.

"It seems, he'd like to offer us a deal," her lips pulled back in a grin. "Tell Brutus to meet us in Puerto de Oro. We leave for the Fickle Islands in the morning."

***

Cecilia rested her hand on the doorknob, the metal warm under the afternoon sun. After sharing the orange with Marcus, he had introduced her briefly to Bella, the ship's nurse with whom she would share a room.

The young woman couldn't have been much older than Cecilia and her soft brown eyes and friendly countenance quickly set her at ease.

"I'm sure we're going to be great friends," she embraced Cecilia in a warm hug, "but first, you need to rest. Jeremy tells me you've had a long journey."

Cecilia nodded, grateful. Adrenaline had kept her awake for most of the day, her nerves on edge the further they sailed from Avinada. Marcus had caught her yawning several times in quick succession and suggested she rest. She wasn't going to argue.

"If you need anything, don't hesitate to come and find me," Bella said once she'd shown Cecilia their room in the officer's quarters. "I will either be downstairs with my uncle, or in the medic's cabin helping Jeremy."

"Thank you," Cecilia smiled, fatigue threatening to take her where she stood.

Bella smiled, closing the door behind her, leaving Cecilia to her thoughts and the constant sway of the ship. At some point, the waves had carried her to sleep.

When she emerged from their quarters a few hours later, Cecilia found herself summoned to the captain's cabin. Wiping remnants of sleep from her eyes, she knocked on the cabin door.

"Come in," Catalina called from the other side.

Dust and parchment tickled her nose as she fought the urge to sneeze. Catalina sat hunched at her desk, turning a small velvet box over in her hands. She glanced up when Cecilia came in.

"Take a seat," she gestured at a wooden chair opposite her desk. Cecilia sat.

"Do you recognise this?" Catalina slid the box to her.

Cecilia shook her head. "Should I?"

Catalina shrugged, "Take a look inside."

Cecilia frowned, studying the box. Flakes of silver peeled at her touch; the velvet rough under her thumb. It reminded her of a box of mints she found in her library when she was a child. She'd suffered a sore stomach afterward. This box opened with a satisfying click.

Inside lay a small golden pendant.

"What is this?" she asked, not taking her eyes from the necklace. It seemed familiar somehow, she was sure she had never seen it before.

"I was hoping you could tell me," Catalina leaned back in her chair.

Cecilia shook her head. "I'm sorry. I don't know."

She pushed the box back to Catalina who pushed it back again.

"Are you sure? Have a closer look," the captain's mouth set into a thin smile. It wasn't a suggestion.

Gingerly, Cecilia picked up the pendant, admiring the lion's head, it's mouth open in a silent roar. She turned it over, her thumb pressing against faint lettering. A name.

Lilia Sigrid of Alcary. Royal House of Hvalgard.

The ghost of a memory tugged at her mind. 'My Lilia, min Elskling', a man's soft voice whispered in her ear. Tears sprang to her eyes. A tight hug, the smell of mint, a shock of blonde hair flashed in her mind before she could grasp them.

"Do you recognise it at all?" Catalina pressed, drawing Cecilia's attention back to the present.

She blinked, shaking her head.

Catalina's lips pursed. "What do you know about your parents?"

"Nothing," Cecilia took a breath to steady herself. "Like I told Marcus earlier, Frida never told me anything about my parents, and she forbade me from discussing them."

Catalina nodded, casting her eyes briefly out the window before turning back to her. Cecilia shifted under the captains scrutinising gaze.

"Have you heard the rumours of Calgaria's lost princess?" Catalina folded her arms over her chest.

"Of course," Cecilia nodded, "who hasn't?"

"Have you ever thought you might be the lost princess?"

Cecilia snorted. If the captain's eyes hadn't narrowed, she might have thought she was joking.

"You're serious?" she scoffed.

Catalina leant forward on the desk, leaflets scrunching under her elbows.

"We've gathered information on Princess Lilia. As you know, she was stolen from The Marble Palace sixteen years ago. Our sources tell us Lilia was smuggled into Avinada, potentially stashed in an orphanage, and adopted by a noblewoman."

"And what does that have to do with me?" Cecilia asked, a knot forming in her stomach.

"I think you know."

Cecilia picked at her nails, a nervous habit she couldn't seem to break.

"I can't be the princess," she mumbled more to herself than the captain.

"What makes you say that?"

She shrunk into the chair. It was true she didn't know her parents or her past. Sure, she had dreamed she might be the lost princess, but so had every girl in the orphanage. Something tugged at her chest at the sight of the necklace, but that didn't prove anything.

Besides, how could she be sure the captain was telling the truth? What evidence did they have aside from a pretty piece of jewellery?

"I just can't," she stammered, "I'm not anyone special. I'm just an orphan from Cova Rafael."

"Marcus seems to think otherwise," Catalina said matter-of-factly.

Cecilia fought the heat that rushed to her cheeks. Nervous, she tucked a strand of hair behind her ear.

The captain sighed, "What do you remember of your life before Duchess Alarcon? Before the orphanage?"

Cecilia twisted her mouth in thought, eyes casting over the ocean. She shook her head. Then, "I remember a boy screaming."

Catalina pushed her chair closer, leaning onto her elbows. Cecilia kept her eyes on the horizon, the golden sun danced along the edge of the world.

"A woman was there. She hit someone, I think... Then I was in a carriage. It was dark and bumpy. Thunder rolled around us. My eyes were closed but I remember bright lights flashing."

"And then..." Catalina urged.

Cecilia paused. She shook her head.

"I'm sorry."

Catalina flashed her a tired smile, "At least you remembered something."

Silence hung in the air between them. Catalina filled two cups of water, handing her one. Cecilia took it gratefully, sipping to avoid any more conversation. The gentle rock of water on wood filled the air as Catalina surveyed her maps.

"Out of all the other girls, why do you think I am Princess Lilia?" Cecilia asked, unable to bear the silence any longer.

"For one thing," Catalina leaned back into her chair, "you bear significant resemblance to Queen Minerva."

"That doesn't mean anything without proof," Cecilia countered.

Catalina's mouth curved in a smile.

"That's exactly what we're looking for."

"So, what do you need from me?"

"At this point, your memories, although there's not much we can do to force you to remember anything. Perhaps the festival tonight will refresh your memory. Eir Astra is one of the most important holidays in Calgaria."

"And what if I still can't remember anything after that?" Cecilia burst, her voice desperate. "Or if my memories don't align with the story of Princess Lilia?"

Catalina watched her unfazed, "If you are not the princess, that will help us narrow down the woman who is. And if you are her, well… we can count that mystery solved."

Cecilia nodded, unsure what else to do or say.

"Unless you can uncover five years' worth of memories right now, I suggest you go and enjoy the festival." Catalina gestured at the door.

"I… thank you," Cecilia stood, the chair scraping behind her.

"If you do remember anything, let us know."

"Us?"

Catalina opened her mouth to speak when a knock at the door interrupted them. Not waiting for an answer, Marcus poked his head in, leaning against the door frame.

"Celebrations are about to begin." He announced, flashing his usual charming grin. Cecilia fought the flutter in her stomach. Between Catalina's suspicions and Marcus' perpetual charm, the journey was getting too much for her nerves.

"We'll be out soon," Catalina waved him off. Not waiting to be dismissed again, Cecilia followed him out.

16

Eir Astra

The world was bathed in gold when Cecilia stepped out of the captain's cabin. Salty air bit her cheeks, whipping loose hair around her face.

What had, mere hours ago, been a traditional ships deck, had been transformed into a cosy outdoor setting. Long tables were arranged in two long rows, white tablecloths held steady by heavy trinkets and bowls of fruit. Decorative lanterns hung from the railings of the forecastle, the coloured paper glowing under the sun's golden rays.

Cecilia found Bella lighting tea candles by the forecastle, tucking them into lanterns, careful not to set them on fire.

"What is this?" Cecilia pointed at the pink lantern in Bella's hand. Now she was closer, she could see delicate floral prints had been painted on the sides.

"We're getting ready for the Festival of Eir Astra. Here, hold these," Bella handed her a handful of paper lanterns.

"What is it?" Cecilia fiddled with the edges

"It's a Calgarian festival celebrating the god Ilio and his guidance in leading Queen Astra's victory from foreign invaders," Bella explained, as Cecilia passed her a lantern. "In her honour, we light lanterns and say a prayer for peace.

"That's beautiful," Cecilia watched her light a candle.

"If you're into that sort of thing," Marcus greeted from behind them. Beads of water dripped from his dark hair which he pushed from his eyes. Droplets hung on his dark shirt, tucked into equally dark, thick trousers. Only his leather boots and belt remained unchanged. He winked at her, his lips tipping into a teasing grin.

"You don't believe?" Cecilia managed, realising she'd been staring.

Marcus shrugged, "No amount of lantern lighting has endeared Ilio to me."

"It's not the act of lighting the lantern, Marcus," Bella admonished, taking another lantern from Cecilia, "it's the heart behind the prayer."

"Maybe Ilio doesn't listen to Avinadans," he countered.

Bella crossed her arms, "Ilio is not bound by race. Besides, you're Calgarian."

"Half Calgarian."

"Ah there you all are," Jeremy burst into the fold, a perpetual smile on his lips, "the festival is about to start."

A hush fell over the deck as the crew gathered around in a semi-circle, Sebastian standing in the middle of the crowd.

"Hundreds of years ago, when Calgaria was barely a country," Sebastian began, his voice carrying in the gentle wind, "a peasant girl, Astra, was chosen out of a thousand women to marry King Eirik. When the Syracusians came from the north to invade Calgaria, they pillaged the kingdom and took the king hostage, believing the people would turn against the Queen and turn the land over to them."

Cecilia held her breath.

Sebastian continued, "she called on Lord Ilio, the Almighty Creator. It was said Queen Astra prayed ceaselessly day and night, refused to light a single lantern until her husband came home and their enemies retreated.

"Instead, she relied on Ilio who it was said made the stars shine brighter to guide her path and plans."

Sebastian picked a lantern from the railing holding it high in the air. Bella nudged Cecilia's elbow, urging her to bow her head. Cecilia followed suit. The gentle lap of waves against the hull filled the air as

Sebastian blew out the lantern. Little by little, darkness fell across the deck, the sun casting a deep purple net across the sky. Cecilia peaked out from the corner of her eye. Two officers trailed along the edges of the railing putting out the lanterns from one end to the other.

"After a time, Ilio not only delivered Calgaria from her enemies, He returned King Eirik unharmed also. The Festival of Eir Astra is not only a reminder of the queen's faithfulness to Ilio and her victory, but of His faithfulness to His people."

Marcus found a spot beside Cecilia, clasping his hands in front of him.

"Now we pray," he whispered, leaning in close. She caught his wink before shutting her eyes. She had never learned how to pray. Frida prayed to myriad saints but her prayers always sounded like demands.

Dear Ilio, or whoever is out there, please help me find out who I am, she thought.

Someone handed her a leaflet of paper. She opened her eyes to find Bella walking along the circle handing out bouquets of coloured paper. Cecilia toyed at the edges – pink lilies.

A soft tune floated from the edge of the crowd. Two young men, clad in pale officers' jackets, stood at the bowsprit. One held a delicate flute to his lips, the other plucking at the strings of a well-worn viola.

The crew picked up the tune. The words were foreign – Calgarian, she realised - yet somehow familiar.

A lullaby from years gone by.

'It was many and many a year ago, in a kingdom by the sea...'

17

Journey to the City

"Cecilia, are you ready?" Bella's voice floated from the other side of the room.

"Why must we get up so early?" Cecilia grumbled, pulling on her boots. "It's not even dawn yet."

"We need to get in and out of Avizon before the guards can catch us," Bella looked sheepishly at her own boots, "rather, before they can catch you."

Cecilia sighed. Though they were stopping in the city to resupply, she was still technically on the run. If she were to be caught, it would spell disaster for her and her companions.

She rubbed a tired hand over her face. She was dressed in the same white blouse and brown skirt Bella wore; her new wardrobe borrowed for the journey into the city. Cecilia yawned, tying her laces. What she wouldn't give for an extra hour's sleep.

They had sailed along the edge of a storm the night before, the ship tilting and pitching at odd angles. Bella had knitted furiously in their cabin, counting rows to help settle Cecilia's nerves. It helped, marginally. Cecilia had been so sure they would sink or be shipwrecked. Not even Marcus' jovial greetings after the storm could pull her from the anxiety that tugged in her chest like a cavernous well.

Only the promise of making landfall in the morning helped Cecilia sleep as the ship eventually evened out to a steady pace.

"Must I accompany you into the city if I'm such a liability?" she yawned.

Bella shrugged, giving her a sympathetic smile. "You heard Catalina. It's likely safer for you in the safehouse than on the ship. If Marcus' theory is correct, they'll be searching for you on every ship that docks in the capital."

Cecilia sighed. Bella was right – they all were. How could a royal naval ship explain a stowaway?

Stretching her arms, she replayed yesterday's conversation in her mind.

"Ah, good, you're here. Take a seat." Catalina greeted them from where she sat at her desk on the far side of the room. She had barely glanced at them as they filed in, Cecilia trailing behind Bella, Jeremy and Marcus. The girls squashed together on the small sofa, Jeremy and Marcus sitting at the small dining table opposite the captain's desk. Sebastian joined them also, preferring to stand at Catalina's shoulder as she shuffled papers into a neat pile.

"As most of you know, we are to dock in Avizon tomorrow morning," Catalina began. "The king has made preparations to inspect every ship docked in the harbour before the Ambassador's ceremony in two days' time. Obviously, we cannot be found with a stowaway on our ship." She threw a pointed look to Cecilia.

"She's not a stowaway. She's a runaway," Marcus winked at her, before turning back to the captain.

"If we're caught with a runaway," Catalina continued, "it could spell disaster for us and our mission. We'll need to hide Cecilia somewhere safe."

"We could go to the markets," Bella suggested, glancing at Jeremy. "We need to pick up supplies anyway, and the markets will be busy with people."

"And soldiers," Sebastian pointed out.

"The last thing we need is anyone recognising Cecilia and arresting us," Catalina conceded. "Marcus, have you been in touch with Antonio lately? Perhaps he could hide her for a few hours?"

"No." Jeremy interrupted, his mouth hardening into a thin line, "I would not leave a dog I liked with him, let alone these lovely ladies."

Bella's cheeks flushed as Jeremy's gaze lingered on her for a moment, before turning back to the conversation.

Cecilia caught Marcus watching her.

"What about the safehouse?" he suggested, turning back to Catalina and Sebastian.

Catalina frowned.

"It's out of the city and no one would think to look for her there," he continued.

"It's further from the docks than is feasible. If you miss the ship, you'll have to make your own way out of the harbour," Catalina leaned back in her chair. "Who knows how tricky that will be with guards swarming the perimeter."

Cecilia tried to follow along as her companions hashed out a feasible plan.

"Alright," Catalina clapped her hands together once an agreement had been reached. "The three of you will take Cecilia into town. Buy what you need and have them sent to the docks before making your way to the safehouse. When I send word for you, double back as quickly as you can. I'll stall as much as I can if I have to."

So it was, Bella and Cecilia rushed from their quarters as stars twinkled above them, the sun still slumbering past the horizon. Cool wind whipped at their cheeks, biting Cecilia's nose and ears. Not for the first time did she wish to be curled up in bed.

Had she known running away required this much action, she might have thought twice about it.

Marcus and Jeremy met them at the gunwale, a rickety rowboat perched just below the ships edge. Did they really expect her to climb into it?

"Morning," Marcus grinned, "fine day to be on the ocean, isn't it?"

"If you say so," she grumbled. It was too early in the morning to deal with his perpetual peppiness.

"I for one can't wait to get out of this wind," Jeremy greeted, rubbing his hands together.

"Let's just hope it doesn't rain," Bella agreed.

"Alright," Catalina appeared behind them, Sebastian a sentinel at her shoulder, "just a reminder – get into Avizon, buy the supplies and Ilio willing, come back to the ship this evening."

The company nodded their agreement.

"Should anything go wrong, meet at Rosalina's safehouse, then come here. Understood?"

"Aye, captain," Marcus saluted her.

Catalina dismissed him, "Off you go, then. See you in a few hours."

Cecilia shivered under the cool air, pulling her borrowed cloak tighter around her shoulders.

Marcus climbed in first, followed by Jeremy, then Bella and finally herself.

She stumbled on the seat, almost smacking her head on the edge of the small boat and toppling over the edge. Marcus caught her before she could fall, drawing her back to the relative safety of the boat.

"Careful," he flashed her a tight smile, "precious cargo."

Heart hammering in her chest, Cecilia settled in beside Bella, counting the seconds as the boys lowered the ship onto the water.

The sun peaked over the horizon, bathing Avizon in a grey haze. Palacio Esmeralda watched over the waking city, the constant flash of a lighthouse glinting off its solitary golden spire. The city sprawled below it, square buildings stacked on top of each other as it meandered down the hill, all the way to the docks. Lush, green mountains surrounded the city, cupping it against the grey ocean.

Cecilia yawned again, the constant thwap of the oars against the water slowly carrying her thoughts away.

It was going to be a long journey.

18

Avizon

"You don't need to keep staring at her you know," Jeremy mumbled under his breath as he kept pace with Marcus. The *Real Sorrento* had sailed ahead of them, revealing the city bathed in an early morning glow. Fishing boats sailed past, earning them curious glances as they passed by.

"I'm not staring," Marcus grumbled, switching to Calgarian.

"Can't say I blame you," Jeremy replied, pulling on the oars as he slipped into his native tongue. "If she's really the princess, you can't afford to take your eyes from her. Though I'm sure that's not the only reason."

Marcus ignored Jeremy's teasing grin, instead picking up the pace. Pink rays nudged at grey clouds as they made their way to the docks.

Gulls cried overhead, their hungry caws ringing across the early morning sky. Marcus glanced over his shoulder. The city was close enough now to see the buildings closest to shore, golden squares and shadows of humanity going about their business igniting the cityscape.

He turned his attention back to the view in front of him as he pushed the oar into the water.

The grey ocean lay unbroken ahead of them. Cecilia sat on the edge of her seat, half-listening to Bella as she fixed her eyes past Marcus' shoulder at the city behind him.

He had largely avoided Cecilia since the Festival of Eir Astra three nights ago. It hadn't been intentional at first. As the king's guard, there were certain duties he needed to attend to, lines of enquiry he worked on with Catalina in her cabin.

It was in one of these moments Catalina reminded him of his promise. To put his duty for his country above all else and to save his heart from pain. The more time he spent with Cecilia, the harder it was not to think about her. Yet... how could he protect her if he didn't spend time with her?

It was all too complicated. She seemed to be ignoring him too. Or trying to. She stayed out of his way as much as possible if they were on deck. They might have been able to avoid each other completely if it weren't for Bella and Jeremy. The pair of them always contrived plans for the foursome to be together, particularly at mealtimes.

It wasn't that he didn't like Cecilia. If all he had to do was keep an eye on her, he could handle that from a distance. But even putting distance between them couldn't keep his mind from her entirely.

"Are you alright?" Cecilia asked, snapping Marcus out of his thoughts.

"Hm?"

"You've stopped rowing," she pointed out.

Marcus looked around at his companions. Bella smiled knowingly as Cecilia returned her attention to the city. Jeremy rowed on silently, flashing Marcus a frustrated frown as he rowed harder against the current.

"Sorry," Marcus mumbled as he picked up the slack. He fixed his eyes on the horizon again. *Onetwothree, onetwothree,* he mumbled under his breath as he kept time with Jeremy. The little boat surged beneath them as he worked his aching muscles against the current.

Stop thinking. Keep rowing, he berated himself.

The sun had slipped above the horizon, bathing the world in a sea of gold as they navigated the small boat to a quiet berth.

Marcus leapt onto the gangway, working with Jeremy to moor the boat.

Heavy footsteps pounded nearby.

"Who goes here?" a gruff voice grunted behind Marcus.

He turned to face a sun-weathered guard in a faded red jacket, his grey whiskers brushing a crumpled off-white shirt.

"Hullo there," Jeremy called from the boat, "We are humble fisheries, sir. We ran into trouble with the boat and decided to return to shore."

The soldier narrowed his eyes at the men then cast his eyes over the boat.

"Where's ya gear then?" He asked, crossing his arms.

Jeremy stared at him blanky.

"Fishing gear," Marcus hissed through his teeth.

"What'd ya say young man?" The older man leered at him, cupping and ear with his weathered hand, "Speak up now."

Marcus cleared his throat.

"I said it's not here. We lost it."

"Fisheries don't lose their gear easily," the old man crossed his arms. "What business had you on the water this morning? Truth, now."

Marcus feigned a sheepish smile, glancing between the soldier and his companions.

"Alright, you caught us," Marcus admitted, "we're not really fishmongers. My friend and I thought we would impress these young ladies by going for a turn in our dinghy to catch the sunrise. We got into trouble and were saved by a passing ship who loaned us this boat."

"Then how come ya not disembarking with 'em?"

"My father is a stevedore and forbade me from taking his boat. He would not be pleased to hear if I lost it, especially with young ladies in tow."

The old man rubbed his chin in consideration, not quite convinced.

"What's ya name son?"

Marcus hesitated. "Cervantes. Claudio Cervantes."

The guard narrowed his eyes at Marcus, before scanning the rest of the group.

"Don't let me catch ya endangerin' these young ladies like this again, y'hear?"

"Yes, sir." Said Marcus and Jeremy in unison.

He turned to Bella and Cecilia.

"And don't ya let these fellas take ya out on the water again," he eyed them suspiciously, "they seem like trouble."

"We won't." They promised.

The guard watched as the group disembarked, following them to the end of the dock.

"That was close." Bella huffed once they had made their way to the edge of the dock.

"A little too close," Jeremy agreed. "Thank goodness for your silver tongue, Marcus."

He clapped him on the shoulder. Marcus said nothing, instead focussing on the path ahead as the crowd began to grow the further they moved into the city.

The smell of fried fish and bitter alcohol hit their noses as they meandered through the early morning crowd.

Marcus and Cecilia trailed Bella and Jeremy who walked arm in arm. He glanced at Cecilia who looked everywhere except him. He swung his leather satchel over a shoulder. It was light – only the barest necessities packed inside.

Beside him, Cecilia stiffened.

"What's wrong?" he stopped beside her, "Has something happened?"

"No," she shook her head, "I thought I saw something strange. That's all."

"What was it?"

"Nothing. Let's keep moving."

Goosebumps prickled his skin as he looked around, scanning

the crowd for any signs of danger. Apart from a set of guards in faded red coats a few stalls ahead of them, nothing seemed unusual. Still, he kept close to Cecilia, guiding her gently around a young family milling around a food stall.

Children kicked a ball around one end of the street, ragged men and women begged for scraps on the other. A young guard watched a group of young women pass by a market stall selling perfumes, too focused on the group to pay any mind to them.

Marcus offered Cecilia his elbow, standing taller as she accepted it.

"Anyone hungry?" Jeremy asked as they approached. He and Bella had walked ahead, oblivious to Marcus and Cecilia trailing along in the crowd.

"I could eat," Bella nodded, "What about you two?"

Marcus ignored the rumble in his stomach. He wanted to get to the safehouse as quickly as possible and they still needed to pick up supplies.

"I'm fine for now." He lied.

"Cecilia?" Bella asked, "what about you?"

Ahead of them a group of teenagers ambled along the narrow path, their laughter bubbling into the melting pot of noise around them. The further they walked, the more stalls cropped up around them selling everything from rugs and coats to dresses, fabric and food.

The familiar smell of fried dough and cinnamon permeated the air as they moved to one side of the street, keeping her out of the way of traffic.

"I could do with a snack," Cecilia said finally.

"That settles it then, we'll eat now." Jeremy grinned.

"You know Rosalina will have enough food to feed an army by the time we get to the safehouse," Marcus pointed out as the group swarmed around a stall selling fresh tortillas.

"Yes, and by the time we get there, we'll have worked up another appetite," Jeremy countered. "Besides, we've just spent the last hour rowing a lifeboat. I think we need some sustenance before trekking through the city."

The smell of fried corn filled the air as two sun-weathered women grinned at them from behind the stall, their hands occupied rolling dough or clapping it into perfect circles. Marcus sighed, but didn't argue. His stomach was rumbling too loudly to ignore.

Jeremy stepped up to the stall to place an order when a familiar figure caught Marcus' eye. The old guard from the docks stood to their left, flanked by two young men in crisp red coats. He knew it was time to leave when the old man pointed at him.

"We have to go. Now." Marcus ordered, grabbing Cecilia's arm.

"But I just ordered the food." Jeremy protested.

A shrill whistle rang through the crowd as the guards surged toward them. Marcus gripped Cecilia, pulling her through the startled crowd and into the busy market stalls beyond. He glanced over his shoulder to see Bella and Jeremy running hand in hand behind them. They would have to split up.

He flicked two fingers to his left before tearing off to the right. He trusted Jeremy would understand the signal.

Beside him, Cecilia panted as she struggled to keep up. He shifted his grip on her arm. This time, he was determined not to lose her. Avizon was much bigger than Cova Rafael. One wrong turn and she could slip away from him for good.

He guided them into a small alleyway, a rickety fruit stall providing a brief cover as a flash of red coats rushed past.

"Do you always invoke the wrath of city guards? Or is this a new habit of yours?" she panted, leaning heavily against a wall.

"A habit of mine? I thought this was your idea of fun," He countered, a teasing grin played at his lips.

He earned a small smile as she shook her head at him. Leaning against the wall, he checked the street for more red coats, gripping her arm as he pulled her down another alleyway. This time they turned into a residential street, leaving the safety of the market crowd behind.

Their feet pounded the cobbled pavement as they passed sandstone buildings with terracotta rooves. Golden light reflected from glass wind chimes swinging gently from windows above them. Another group of children chased a ball around the street, their bare feet kicking up dust, while old men sat smoking at wicker tables. The smell of rum and tobacco filled the air.

Marcus ignored the ache in his limbs and hunger pangs in his stomach as he slowed slightly to let Cecilia catch up. She gripped his arm again, digging her fingers into his shirtsleeve.

Music filled the air around them, a quick, jovial tune, at odds to the danger behind them. A whistle pierced the air, followed by whoops and hollers from bystanders leaning out windows as they ran past. Marcus glanced over his shoulder quickly. Red coats rushed forward, blocked briefly by the children's game.

Ducking into a side alley, Marcus weaved them carefully through the narrow paths between dilapidated buildings, sticking to the shadows, when they finally ran out of breath. His lungs screamed for air as he ran a dry tongue over cracked lips. He tasted the salt of sweat and ocean.

They were headed towards the outskirts of the city, away from the port, where poorer families lived a dozen to a house. Faded clothes hung on washing lines above their heads. Dirty children squealed, chasing each other in the narrow street ahead of them. He pulled them into another side street as another whistle blew, scattering the children into the shadows.

Somewhere along the line, their fingers had twined themselves together. It was a strange thing to notice as they hurried down the street. Marcus spared a glance over his shoulder, making sure to keep Cecilia to his right. A cool offshore breeze blew the hair out of his face as they reached the very edge of the city. Only a rusted, iron fence separated them from a drop into the cavernous ocean depths. The sun had risen, the blue sky mirroring the sea below.

Scanning the area, Marcus recognised the dense grove of trees around them. They were close to the safehouse.

"Come on," he pulled Cecilia into the thicket.

"But the guards-"

"They won't look for us here," he assured her.

"How do you know?"

"Because," he hesitated, "I know a good hiding spot. Come on."

Cecilia followed, catching her breath as they picked their way through the little jungle. He matched her pace, keeping an ear out for the familiar crunch of heavy boots. The trees grew so thick it was hard to make out anything beyond a few feet ahead of them.

He hardly dared speak until they reached a small clearing by the cliff's edge, the ocean roaring below them.

"Are you alright?" he asked once he was sure no one could hear them.

"I've had better days," she admitted.

He grinned, raking a hand through his hair.

"So have I."

"You're talking to me now?" she tilted her head at him.

Marcus frowned, "What do you mean?"

She huffed, dropping her hand from his.

"You've been ignoring me for the better part of a week and now I'm just supposed to trust you again? After running away from guards a third time?"

"We don't have a choice."

"Don't we? You told me I had a choice before. And now what? You save me a few times, pretend like I don't exist and then swoop in like Prince Rafael?"

He scoffed, "And what do you suggest I do? Let the guards take you away? Deliver you on a silver platter to your godmother and say, 'Here she is, the princess who gave up on running away.'"

Cecilia raised a suspicious eyebrow. He shook his head, stepping forward.

"Forget it. We need to get to the safehouse now before the

guards close in on us." He walked along the edge of the thicket in the direction they'd come from. Cecilia paused a moment before following.

"How do I know this isn't some elaborate scheme to deliver me to them anyway?" she argued. "You could take me to Frida right now and be handsomely compensated."

He huffed, raking his hand through his mussed hair again. Every second they spent arguing was time for the guards to catch up. Time, they needed to spend putting distance between them.

"We don't have time for this," he snapped. "If I wanted to hand you back to the duchess, I would've left you at Villa Alarcon, but... those weren't my orders."

"What orders?"

Damn. He'd said too much.

He ignored the question, using her hesitation to pull her with him and hurry them forward.

"We need to get to the safehouse now and we can't run if we're too busy arguing."

She stopped short, pulling him backward, "Do I have a choice in this?"

He recognised the challenge. He wanted to say no. To tell her there were no choices but to go with him and escape to Calgaria. He could order her as a soldier of the king. Or pick her up and carry her to the safehouse.

He sighed. He would rather bring her to the palace willingly than worry about her running away again. Besides, who was he to deny her freedom, even if she wanted it from him?

"You always have a choice," he mumbled.

Silence hung between them, broken only by the distant howl of the wind.

"Fine," she sighed, "I'll go with you. For now."

They were quiet, as they picked their way out of the thicket and onto a street lined with old, double-story houses. They were close.

A whistle blasted the air behind them.

Marcus' mouth curved into a smile as her hand slipped in his and they broke into a run.

19

Rosalina's Safehouse

The world passed in a blur as Marcus guided her through the street and into yet another alley. The city seemed to be littered with little alcoves and places to hide. It was a wonder the guards hadn't taken to hiding in them yet. Ahead of them, a squadron of red coats raced down the street.

A raggedy man stood under a broken lamp post smoking a cigar, his back turned to them. A pair of lovers ambled along the path arm in arm, unfazed by the chaos. The gentle rush of waves in the distance was replaced by the sound of their boots on cobblestones.

"This way," Marcus guided her, pulling her hand gently as they hurried down a quiet street. Despite the lack of guards, they stuck close to the walls, hurrying past houses with their heads down. Her hand, sticky with sweat, was still linked with Marcus' as they approached a solitary grey house near the very end of the street, teetering on the edge of a green hill. White sails were visible in the near distance, ships sitting in grey berths, waiting for repair.

Marcus rapped twice on the faded blue door, paused and rapped a second time.

Not waiting for an answer, he pushed the door open, the two of them stumbling inside before a strong breeze slammed the door shut behind them.

Cecilia wasn't sure what she had been expecting when Catalina mentioned a safehouse, but this wasn't it.

The smell of beef stew and fried corn welcomed them into a cosy little apartment, the cream-coloured walls adorned in a mixture of family portraits, landscapes and children's drawings.

A young girl with eyes too big for her small face squealed in delight as she threw herself at Marcus.

"Adelita! How is my favourite little mischief maker? Have you been good for your Abuela?" Marcus greeted swinging the girl in his arms.

Giggling, the girl nodded.

"That's my girl." Matching her grin, he swung her expertly onto his hip, turning to Cecilia.

"Adela, I'd like you to meet my friend Cecilia. Cecilia, this is my niece, Adela," he gestured between them.

"Hello." Cecilia gave the girl a polite smile.

Adela hid her face in Marcus' shoulder, only to peek out a few moments later and give her a little wave.

"She's not usually this shy," Marcus chuckled apologetically.

They had stepped into the *sala*, a small room with two sofas and an armchair arranged to create a cosy, intimate setting. A mess of coloured papers lay strewn across a low table in the centre of the room, an assortment of crayons spilled on top of them.

A weathered brown woman came out of the kitchen through a curved archway, her eyes widening in surprise as she wiped doughy hands on a faded grey apron.

"Mijo, is that you? Come, eat. Who is your friend?" She asked with a warm smile at Cecilia, who returned the gesture.

"Hola Mamá," he greeted, giving her a kiss on the cheek as she enveloped him in a hug, Adela still in his arms.

"I'd like to introduce you to my friend Cecilia. Cecilia, this is my mother, Rosalina."

"You are most welcome in my home," the older woman grinned, wrapping Cecilia in a tight hug.

"Thank you, Señora.".

"How long are you staying for, mijo?" Rosalina asked, turning back to the kitchen. Cecilia followed Marcus who followed his mother.

"We're staying for lunch. Possibly until dinner, possibly until breakfast. We're not sure at this stage," he set Adela onto the floor.

The older woman gestured for them to sit at the small dining room table at the end of the kitchen. Cecilia sat, Marcus beside her while Adela ran into the *sala*, reappearing a few seconds later with an armful of art supplies. Cecilia froze at another knock on the door.

Two short raps, a pause and two short raps.

"Bella and Jeremy haven't come in yet have they?" Marcus asked, straightening up.

Rosalina shook her head. "No, it's only been me and Adela at home this morning."

Marcus frowned as he walked into the *sala*, patting his hip for a weapon.

Cecilia watched from the small dining room, holding her breath as the door opened. Jeremy stooped through the small entryway; a jovial grin plastered on his face. Bella trailed behind him, her usually tidy curls frizzed in the salt air. A tear in Jeremy's sleeve gaped at them, exposing a shallow cut on his pale skin.

"You look like you've seen better days," Marcus greeted as he shut the door firmly behind them. The trio hurried to the dining room taking up the empty spaces at the table.

"Well, it's not every day you get chased by the king's guards," Jeremy clapped Marcus' shoulder, "What happened to you? We lost sight of you once you took off into the crowd."

"We tried to lose them through the *barrio* and eventually took refuge in the trees. We were followed by a squad of guards but we shook them off." Marcus explained as he settled in beside his niece.

Jeremy rubbed his face with his hands. "And how long have you been here?"

"Half a minute," Marcus shrugged, "You seem to have spent an awfully long time in the city."

Jeremy held up a beaten leather satchel.

"Once we lost the red coats, we stopped to get supplies, most of which we addressed to the *Sorrento*. Thanks for the satchel by the way. If you hadn't lost it in your hurry to get away from the guards, I would've been hard pressed to carry these."

Jeremy opened the bag to reveal a heshen sack, various fresh fruits spilling onto the table.

"I was wondering where that went," Marcus nodded at the satchel.

"Who's hungry?" Rosalina set a tray of bowls in the centre of the table. Cecilia's stomach rumbled at the smell of beef broth and coriander. Adela, who scampered from the table, reappeared with a plate of thick tortillas, the corn dough mingling deliciously with the stew.

"Come. Eat." Rosalina ordered, a proud glint in her eye.

They didn't need to be told twice. Cecilia sighed in delight as the beef and carrots melted in her mouth. A corn cob bounced in the bowl as she dipped a generous piece of the crispy tortilla in the broth.

Cecilia said little as she listened to the chatter around her. Rosalina joined them at the table, her soft brown eyes glinting in the warm kitchen glow.

It was clear to see Marcus favoured her colouring. He had her full lips and bright, brown eyes. Where Rosalina's hair was curly and peppered with grey, his dark locks fell in waves, framing his face. Cecilia supposed his chiselled jaw must favour his father.

"Will Mamá be coming home tonight?" Adela asked Marcus as the chatter died down. He shared a strained glance with his mother before turning back to Adela.

"She promised she would do her best to come-" he started.

"And here I am."

To Cecilia's surprise, Catalina stood in the doorway. It took a moment for her to recognise the captain without her sky-blue naval coat. Instead, she wore a long, blue travellers cloak, the hood pulled back to reveal her dark plaits.

"Mamá!" Adela squealed, leaping into Catalina's arms, burying her face in her neck.

Catalina squeezed her eyes shut, holding her daughter tightly.

"Welcome home, mija," Rosalina smiled widely, "Food is ready. Come, there is enough room for everyone."

Catalina squeezed into the empty space between Bella and Cecilia. Adela ignored her meal in favour of holding onto her mother.

"Adela, let your poor Mamá eat before you glue yourself to her side," Rosalina ordered her granddaughter gently. Adela frowned but did as she was told.

"So," Catalina said as she ladled a bowl of soup, "I saw a number of guards running around as I was walking through the city. That wouldn't have anything to do with you now, would it?" she looked pointedly at Marcus.

"Now, what gave you that idea?" he shot her a teasing grin.

Catalina rolled her eyes as she took her seat at the table. Even without her usual livery, she seemed every inch the leader despite the casual setting. Cecilia wondered if she ever switched off from being a captain.

"So, Cecilia," Rosalina turned the attention back to her, "how do you know my son?"

Cecilia shifted in her seat uncomfortably, pushing her spoon gently around the almost-empty bowl.

"It's a bit of a long story," Marcus said.

"We have time, don't we?"

Marcus looked at Catalina who gave a small nod. He recounted the journey with minimal detail, glossing over the brush with the guards in Cova Rafael and their landing in Avizon.

"So, you are sailing to Calgaria then?" Rosalina smiled at Cecilia, "That must be exciting for you?"

Cecilia nodded, "It feels like a blur."

"And what are your plans when you arrive?" the older woman pressed.

Cecilia avoided the question with a mouthful of soup.

"I don't know," she replied after a moment.

"We'll help you find something," Bella reassured her, flashing her a warm smile.

Cecilia nodded tersely.

Jeremy picked up the silence, filling it with anecdotes about the journey and what he had bought from the Avizon markets.

Adela begged her mother to go with them, but was refuted. When her tears threatened to spill over, Marcus entertained them with swashbuckling stories he had been reading on the voyage.

The day drew on, leading into the evening and eventually to night. Cecilia helped Rosalina light the candles.

They couldn't leave the house, not while guards remained on constant patrol in the city streets. Every now and then guards would yell at someone to move on.

Marcus and Catalina took turns peering out the dark curtains, watching the sun sink lower as the patrols became less frequent.

"We'll stay the night here," Catalina said once the sun dipped below the horizon.

Adela cheered in delight, throwing her arms around the captain. It was a strange sight, Cecilia thought; the stoic, stony captain made human by a little girl.

"What about the safety checks on the ship? Won't they ask questions if you're not on board?" Marcus asked.

Catalina frowned, "Sebastian has everything covered. If the guards get curious, I'll say I got lost in the city."

Marcus' mouth twisted to the side, but he dropped the subject.

Adela's bright laughter soon turned to yawns as she curled up next to her mother on the sofa. Catalina stroked the girl's dark hair out of her face absent-mindedly, her own eyes becoming heavy with sleep.

Rosalina found places for everyone to sleep – the boys on various sofas, Bella and Cecilia sharing a bed in another room and Adela and Catalina on the couch.

"It's not much, but it's the least I can do," Rosalina offered apologetically.

Cecilia shook her head, her limbs aching with exhaustion as she followed Bella and Rosalina down the short hallway to a separate room.

"I'm just thankful for a blanket and a pillow at this rate," Bella said, her voice thick with sleep. By the time Rosalina left the room, the girls had collapsed in a heap on the bed.

20

Fragments

Grey pre-dawn light streamed in through the kitchen window as Marcus poured himself a steaming mug of coffee. He had tossed and turned on the sofa, his limbs aching as much as they had when he fell asleep last night. He tried to avoid his reflection in the window. He didn't need to see the dark circles around his eyes to remind him of the nightmares that plagued him.

He had been dreaming about Claudio again – the day he died. He had been sheltering a group of young soldiers after their boat was laid under siege by pirates. He died covering their escape.

Sighing, he leaned against the kitchen counter as Catalina crept into the room.

"Care for a coffee?" Marcus asked, making sure to keep his voice low. Jeremy snored softly on the small sofa in the *sala*, one arm draped over his eyes to block out the glow of the streetlamp outside the window.

"Thanks," Catalina cradled the proffered cup.

"How'd you sleep?" he asked, taking another sip of his coffee.

"Awful. Doesn't look like you got much either. Nightmares again?"

He shook his head. It was easier to lie when he didn't open his mouth, but her questioning brow forced an answer.

"Tried thinking of a way to get out of the city this morning." He set the cup down.

"And? What did you come up with?"

He spread his empty hands out in a sweeping gesture.

"Ah. A classic plan," she murmured into the cup.

"Do you have any better ideas?"

She shrugged, taking a long sip. "You could wear a disguise. I'm sure Rosalina has some dresses that could fit you."

"Very funny," he picked up his cup again.

Catalina grinned, "I thought so."

Before Marcus could retort, Rosalina padded into the kitchen. He poured her a cup.

"Are you having breakfast before you leave?" Rosalina asked unstacking pots and pans from the counter and placing them back on the stove.

Catalina shook her head, "I have to go once I finish this."

"Can I come with you?" A small voice asked from behind her.

Adela rubbed her tired eyes, her face rumpled with sleep as she watched her mother set her cup down. Catalina's smile was apologetic as she crossed the kitchen to kneel in front of her daughter, taking her small hands in her own.

"Not this time cariña," Catalina rubbed Adela's arms gently, pushing stray strands of hair from her smooth cheek, "but I promise the next time I come home, we will go on a big long voyage together."

"You say that every time," the girl whined, stomping her foot.

"Adela..." Rosalina's voice rose in a warning.

Tears spilled down Adela's cheeks as her chest heaved with sobs. Marcus stepped toward her when Catalina enveloped her daughter in her arms.

"Don't leave me, Mamá..." she begged.

"I'm sorry cariña but I must go. They need me at the docks."

"But *I* need you! *I* want you to stay. Please Mamá! Please don't leave me!" Adela cried.

Jeremy appeared at the doorway, Bella and Cecilia at his shoulder. Marcus flashed them an apologetic smile.

"Is everything alright?" Bella asked no one in particular.

"We're fine," Catalina replied tightly.

Catalina picked up Adela and carried her out of the room, her sobs fading with each step.

"Coffee anyone?" Marcus offered.

He didn't wait for an answer as he began doling out coffee cups to the trio. He joined them at the table, getting up again to help Rosalina prepare breakfast.

When the smell of fried eggs and beans filled the kitchen, Catalina emerged with a red-faced Adela. The small girl sat beside Cecilia, determined to fight her trembling lip and silent tears.

"Eat something Adela. You'll feel better when you're not hungry," Catalina urged.

Adela shook her head, folding her arms stubbornly across her chest. Marcus glanced at her, his heart tugging at the sight. Adela was the spitting image of Claudio at that age and just as stubborn.

Beside her, Cecilia leaned toward them, her hands cradled around the still steaming cup.

"When I wouldn't eat my dinner, my godmother would forbid me from going to the library until I finished everything on my plate," she said.

"You lived in a town with a library that opened at night?" Adela asked, wide-eyed.

Cecilia shook her head, a small smile playing at her lips.

"My godmother never liked books, but Villa Alarcon, where I grew up, had an extensive library thanks to her late husband."

Adela's ears pricked up.

"You lived in a house with a library?" she asked, impressed.

Cecilia nodded.

"It's my favourite place in the whole world. I practically lived in the library. If Frida really wanted to punish me for something, she would lock the doors and hide the key."

Adela gasped, "Then what did you do?"

"First," Cecilia lowered her voice conspiratorially. Adela leaned in, uncrossing her arms, "I would scheme with my friend Alistar for a way to get the key. If that didn't work, we'd run away into the woods until it was time for dinner. But most of the time, I would collect books and hide them in my room so if Frida locked me out again, I would still have something to read."

"Wow." Adela looked at her as if she was a hero.

Catalina slipped out of the room as Cecilia regaled Adela with her favourite tales. Marcus caught her on the way out. They didn't speak until they were outside the little house. Grey clouds threatened to spill overhead. A solitary seagull glided in the air above them before swooping down to the shipyard.

"Be careful on your way back," Catalina ordered, "the last thing we need is more guards on our tail."

"I know," Marcus promised, "We'll be careful."

"Thank your mother for me. She does so much, looking after Adela."

"I will."

They walked side by side down the street as the first rays of dawn broke lazily over the grey horizon. Market-goers made their way languidly down the smooth stone paths cutting through the pale green cliffside. He glanced at Catalina, who was keeping pace with him despite a far-away look in her eyes.

They stopped at the end of the street, watching a young man sneak out the backdoor of a house, a young woman watching him from behind faded yellow curtains.

"Marcus, I wanted you to know, this might be my last voyage," she said, drawing his attention back to her.

He furrowed a brow, "What do you mean?"

"Adela needs me and I need to stop running from my responsibilities. She's growing up so fast and I'm worried I'm not going to know my own daughter one day. I promised Claudio I would take care of her-"

"And you have."

"No," she cut him off, "I have been providing for her. I have made sure she is safe and fed and clothed, but she is growing up before my eyes and before I know it, I could be a stranger to her. What kind of mother would I be then?"

"You have been good to her." Marcus wrapped an arm around her. She sighed against him. Catalina was the closest thing he had to a sister, and after Claudio's death, he had promised to look after her and Adela. It was a promise he did not take lightly.

"Claudio would want me here with her," she said, "not sailing the ocean and finding her a stranger each time. She is the only thing I have left of him. And," her voice trembled, "your mother won't be here forever."

Marcus rested his head on her chin.

"Whatever you need to do, we will always support you, Cata."

"Thank you."

They stood for a moment longer before Catalina stepped out his embrace, straightening herself.

"You better begin to say your farewells. We must leave soon."

Marcus nodded. He watched as she walked down the street, carving her way through the early morning market crowd until she was out of sight, before turning back to his mother's house.

Neither of them noticed the stranger standing on the street corner, watching them from a distance.

21

Chasing Shadows

The city buzzed with anticipation as the foursome made their way through the bustling city streets. Donning faded travellers' coats, Marcus and Cecilia disguised themselves as servants for Bella and Jeremy who ambled arm in arm ahead of them, his traitorous blonde hair hidden beneath a wide-brimmed hat. Marcus fought back a pang of nostalgia as an image of Claudio flashed in his mind. He'd donned the Avinadan cap at his wedding to Catalina almost a decade earlier. It was one of the few things his mother had kept.

Rosalina kitted Bella in one of the old dresses she had worn in the Calgarian court, a floor length, forest green number that trailed along behind her. It was fine enough to be considered rich, though it was several years out of fashion. Nevertheless, Bella looked every inch the lady and Jeremy was proud to have her on his arm.

Cecilia on the other hand, trailed beside Marcus, her face hidden under a dark cloak. Rosalina managed to find a pair of trousers from Marcus' adolescence, taking them in to fit the young maiden. He'd also equipped her with a weapons belt and a dagger, just in case.

"This is for emergencies only," he warned, placing the dagger in her trembling hands.

"I don't know how to use it," she shook her head.

"Here," he unsheathed a dagger from his own belt, "I'll show you."

They'd spent the next hour going through basic self-defence techniques until she felt confident enough to handle the blade without shaking.

"You won't have to use it in the marketplace," he'd reassured her before they left. "If danger presents itself, Jeremy and I can handle it. The dagger is merely a precaution."

She nodded, nerves bobbing in her slender throat. He looked away.

Around them, stallholders shouted their prices, an assortment of tunes flickered around them, street buskers stationed at various points throughout the city. Old buildings propped up against new structures. A tall clock towered above them, its ancient spire and iron numbers a leftover from the country's brief occupation by the Calgarians two centuries before.

A commotion picked up ahead of them, drawing Marcus back to the situation at hand. Men shouted in the street, threats soon turning to fisticuffs as red coats flashed past the group to break up the fight. Marcus pulled Cecilia forward, hurrying to catch up to their companions who took refuge by a small storefront. Despite the heat pressing down on them, the windows remained perpetually frosted over. A weathered sign hung in the small window of the green door, its paint faded and peeling.

"Is everyone alright?" Marcus asked as they gathered at the mouth of the small alley.

"I think we should take a respite," Jeremy suggested, Bella's fingers turning white around his bicep. Marcus nodded.

"Any objections to hiding out in this shop for a few minutes?" he asked. "At least until the red coats are gone."

At his companions' silence, he stepped up to the door, twisting the rusted handle. The door gave way with a thud. A tinkling bell heralded their arrival.

Marcus coughed, inhaling a mouthful of dust as he stepped inside. Cecilia stumbled into him.

"Sorry," she mumbled, "I- achoo"

"Prosit," Marcus held out a hand.

"Takk," she replied. Her brows furrowed in confusion.

"Where did you learn that?" He looked impressed.

She shook her head, "I... don't know."

"What's the hold up?" Jeremy called from the street behind them.

"Sorry," Marcus stepped out of the way. Cecilia followed.

"So, you know Calgarian?" he asked ducking into a narrow aisle.

"I don't think so," Cecilia trotted along behind him, "I was never taught."

The small shop was filled to the brim with bookshelves, stacks of leather and clothbound books lining each cabinet. Someone had arranged heavy leather tomes in piles across the floor. Old journals scattered across various tables, their pages faded yellow with age and disuse.

Marcus picked his way along the cramped aisle, careful not to knock anything over.

"Can I help you?" a crackled voice came from beside him. Marcus readied a hand on his dagger.

An old man as faded and crumpled as the tomes behind him appeared from around the corner. Rusted circular spectacles framed hazel eyes and a wizened face lined with wrinkles. He raised grey bushy eyebrows at Marcus.

"I said, can I help you?" this time the question came in Calgarian.

Marcus shook his head.

"No, thank you. We were just looking," he took a step back, bumping into Cecilia. A book thudded onto the floor between them. He reached down to pick it up at the same time she did, their fingers brushing on the leather cover.

She looked up, her hood falling to reveal her face. A single dark braid tumbled down her shoulders, a wisp of hair framing her cheek. He pulled his hand back, refraining from tucking it behind her ear. Behind them, the old man gasped.

"My queen," the old man fell heavily to one knee, "no- it can't be..."

Cecilia gasped as the weathered man took her hand in his, murmuring something under his breath. She glanced at Marcus who snatched his dagger.

"What's going on?"

"Cecilia?"

Bella and Jeremy appeared behind the man, exchanging confused glances with Marcus.

"I think there's been a mistake, sir," Marcus addressed the old man.

"No mistake," he said, pressing his forehead to Cecilia's knuckles. His eyes shone with tears as he lifted his face to her, "the princess has returned."

Cecilia snatched her hand from his grip, cradling it with her other hand, a wild look in her eyes.

"We should go," Marcus addressed the group, not taking his eyes off the old man.

"Please, take anything you want," the old man's gaze never shifted from Cecilia. Marcus stepped between them, weapon at the ready.

The hunched man didn't appear to be a threat, his grey robes hung loose around his thin frame. Thinning grey hair hung around his ears, his pale skin worn and wrinkled. A small breeze could easily knock him over.

Still, Marcus had fought less likely foes before. Despite the man's apparent affection for Cecilia, it didn't mean he wasn't still a threat. People acting from a place of love could still harm the objects of their affection.

Marcus glanced at Jeremy; Bella tucked safely behind him. His friend nodded.

Glancing behind him, Marcus nodded at the door, hoping Cecilia would take the hint. She did. Scurrying to the front of the shop, she met Bella and Jeremy. Marcus walked backwards, keeping his eyes trained on the shopkeeper who babbled in Calgarian, his words gargling together as he barely refrained from sobbing.

In any other situation, Marcus might have felt pity for an old man so far from home. But he had a duty to uphold and a crown to protect.

His eye caught on a silver cover. He paused, sliding the book from its place in the shelf.

"How much?" he asked the old man.

"Take it," the storekeeper replied.

Marcus frowned, pulling a gold coin from his pocket, laying it on the empty space on the shelf.

The man shook his head.

"To know the future queen has been in my shop is payment enough."

Marcus kept walking, keeping an eye out for any more threats.

Pain flashed through his shoulder as he banged into the doorframe. He didn't flinch.

Scanning the shop once more, he turned into the alley where his companions waited just outside the entrance, sticking close to the alley wall.

With a final glance at the greying man, Marcus shut the door firmly behind him.

"What was all that about?" Bella asked, still clutching Jeremy's arm.

"It doesn't matter now," he glanced at Cecilia her gaze fixed firmly on her boots. He ignored the quick pounding in his chest as he shouldered past Jeremy, his boots thundering down the stand stone steps, "We're late."

22

Salvador's Taverna

Cecilia's cheeks burned as the four of them joined the rush of the city. Marcus forged on ahead, Bella and Jeremy trailing after them. Had Bella not caught her wrist, Cecilia would have easily lost herself in the swelling crowd.

A flutist picked up a tune, its sweet melody lost to her as the old man's words repeated themselves in her mind. Why had he called her the future queen? And why was Marcus so standoff-ish?

"Liz! Jeleni!" Bella screamed, startling Cecilia from her thoughts. She followed her friend's gaze. Ahead of them, two tattered young women dragged their feet as guards led them through an arched, stone gate. One of the women glanced vaguely in their direction, dirty blonde locks falling into her eyes.

Cecilia's heart sank. Liz and Jeleni had been captured.

And it was all her fault.

Bella let go of her wrist as she flung herself into the crowd. Marcus blocked her before she could get far.

"Let me go!" she protested, attempting to sidestep him. But Marcus was quicker.

"Don't cause a scene," he hissed, snatching her arm, keeping her in front of him.

"That's not fair! They're my sisters!" she argued, angry tears rolling down her rosy cheeks.

"I know," his voice was gentle, but firm, "but we can't rescue them now."

"Why not?!" She struggled against him.

Marcus' mouth hardened as he shook his head.

"There's no time."

"Please, just let me see them!" Bella pleaded.

Cecilia glanced back at the gate. The sisters had disappeared, the iron doors clicking shut with a resounding thud.

"You don't think the guards will find it suspicious, four travellers wanting to visit two criminals?" his grip tightened.

"They're not criminals! And you're hurting me!"

"Unhand her Marcus!" Jeremy stepped forward, his hand resting on the hilt of his dagger.

Cecilia's heart thundered in her chest. Would Jeremy really hurt his friend? What was she supposed to do if something happened to Marcus? She reached for the dagger at her belt, the iron hilt sending a cold shock through her sweaty palm. She wasn't sure she could use it against her companions, but she had to do something.

With a final glance at the iron gate, Marcus released Bella, "I just don't want to do something that will put our mission in danger."

Bella's eyes shone with angry tears. Jeremy pulled her into a tight embrace. She sobbed into his shirt.

Guilt pressed down on Cecilia, as oppressive as the morning heat. The last time she had seen Liz and Jeleni was when they had helped her escape from the cottage near Mount Aramyth. Their imprisonment was likely Frida's doing.

"Surely, there must be something we can do?" Cecilia asked Marcus. He finally looked at her, his face unreadable.

"They helped us," she continued, "we have to do something to help them."

From the corner of her eye, she saw Bella peering at her from under Jeremy's protective arm. Still, she avoided her friend's tearstained face. The hope in her eyes only served to twist the knife of betrayal further.

Marcus raked a hand through his hair. He met Jeremy's stony gaze with a defeated one of his own.

"I might have an idea," he said slowly, "but you're not going to like it."

Jeremy shook his head, "If it helps Bella's sisters, I'll do anything."

Marcus let out a long sigh.

"Alright," he shrugged, "then I hope you remember the way to Salvador's Taverna.

***

Salvador's Taverna was a dilapidated building on the edge of the docks. A steady stream of working men and women flitted through the doors, despite the early hour. Shrill laughter and bawdy tunes filled the air.

The acrid smell of sour liquor and tobacco hit Cecilia's nose as they walked through the charcoal doorframe, faded smoke staining the wall around it. It looked as if someone had attempted to burn the place down, but couldn't finish the job.

She stepped around discarded glass bottles and cigar butts, expecting a similar reception inside.

Instead, they were greeted by colourful women with painted faces, their dresses too short to be decent. Cecilia's chest twisted strangely as a dark-haired woman flashed Marcus a flirtatious smile. He returned the gesture, accepting a crystal wine flute from her tray and whispered something in her ear.

The woman smiled revealing dull yellow teeth, and pulled Marcus behind her. The group followed, weaving past a bar of rowdy men, and dolled women. By the time they reached a secluded table at the far end of the tavern, Cecilia had contrived a number of ways to dispose of the waitress.

"Are you alright?" Bella asked beside her.

"I'm fine," Cecilia snapped. She glared at Marcus who, oblivious of her foul mood, spoke quickly with the waitress. He flashed the girl an easy smile, proffering her a sample of golden coins. The seductress tipped her head back in a mirthless laugh, brushing a hand on Marcus' bicep.

Cecilia glared at the woman as she walked away, glancing over her shoulder at Marcus. To Cecilia's relief, he didn't return the gesture.

"You're right, I don't like this idea, Marcus," Jeremy hovered behind a chair, "I think we should leave."

"But you only just arrived!" a jovial voice greeted from behind them. Cecilia flinched at the intrusion.

She turned to find a young man, not much older than themselves, standing with his arms open in greeting. His burgundy shirt revealed a lean physique, his dark pants adorned with various weapons hanging from his belt. His face was framed in a dark halo of hair and neatly trimmed beard, too dark for his pale skin. There was something familiar about the crinkle in his hazel eyes as he looked at her.

"Well, well, well, aren't you far from home?" he grinned.

Marcus cleared his throat, turning the man's attention to him.

"Antonio," he nodded, "we've come to ask a favour."

"Of course you have," Antonio's smile deflated, "but first you must sit. I haven't had the pleasure of Calgarian company in a while."

"In a place like this?" Jeremy snorted, "I find that hard to believe."

The stranger shot him a long look.

"I was going to say I haven't had the pleasure of civilised Calgarian company in a while, but you, *little brother*, are an exception."

Bella and Cecilia shared a confused look as Jeremy shook his head.

Antonio gestured for them to sit. A window hung above them, grey clouds rolling in over a rough, blue-grey ocean. Cecilia imagined she could feel the waves rocking beneath them.

"So," Antonio waved for a waitress, "care to tell me what this is all about? I assume you're not here to introduce me to your girlfriends."

Jeremy's hand curled into a fist on the table. His face darkened.

"We're here for a favour," Marcus interjected before Jeremy could open his mouth.

"Yes, you said that already," Antonio nodded.

"There are rumours you're the best person to break someone out of prison." Marcus lowered his voice as the waitress came past with a tray of ale. She flashed Marcus a winning smile. To Cecilia's satisfaction, he ignored her.

Antonio leaned forward on the table, "You of all people should know not to listen to rumours."

Marcus nodded, "Perhaps. But if a man like you can fake his death to an entire country, it may not be so far-fetched to believe he can infiltrate any prison in the city."

Antonio licked his lips, his gaze shifting between Marcus and Jeremy.

"How much did Lucian tell you?"

"All of it," Jeremy snapped, "Unlike you, I don't keep secrets from those close to me."

Antonio's features darkened for a moment.

Cecilia glanced between the three men, neither willing to budge from their positions.

"What do you need?" Antonio asked finally.

"There are two women who have been falsely imprisoned. We need to get them out," Marcus explained.

"Ah," Antonio's eyes glinted, "it's always women with you, isn't it? Although this one, despite the disguise, might be the prettiest yet." He winked at Cecilia.

She avoided his gaze, flicking her attention to Marcus instead. His mouth hardened into a thin line, his hand curling into a fist on the table.

"These women have helped me many times over the years," he addressed Antonio, "I cannot sit by and let them rot in prison."

"And how much would you be willing to pay?"

Jeremy scoffed, "You're only willing to do this for money? Not for honour, or respect or because it's the right thing to do?"

"You have much to learn about this life Lucian Jeremiah. Besides, what reason is there to do anything if you're not getting paid for it? Must I remind you that you are getting paid for your services aboard the *Real Sorrento*?"

Jeremy launched himself at Antonio, grabbing him by collar of his shirt.

"I am serving my country for more than just money," He growled.

Antonio cast his eyes over Bella.

"Oh, I can see that." He said, before flicking his attention back to Jeremy.

Marcus put a hand on his friend's shoulder. "He's not worth it."

Antonio nodded, not taking his eyes from his brother, "You should listen to your friend. You wouldn't want to start a brawl now, would you?"

Cecilia glanced around the room. What had moments before been a bustling tavern, had frozen in time. Burly men stood watching from their posts at the bar or nearby gambling tables, weapons at the ready. Waitresses scurried behind the bar or various patrons, ready to make an escape if necessary.

"Jeremy," Bella murmured, drawing his attention back to her. He followed her gaze to the crowd. He cleared his throat, letting go of Antonio's collar, dusting himself off as he returned to his seat.

"Now then. I think we can work this out like civilised people." Antonio clapped his hands together and the room returned to its revelry. "Let's go into the other room to discuss prices. The ladies can stay out here, unless you would like to negotiate one of them?"

Marcus glared at Antonio.

"You go ahead Marcus," Jeremy leaned back in his chair, "I'll stay here and make sure none of Antonio's men bother the ladies."

"Suit yourself," Antonio shrugged.

Marcus balled his hands into fists but said nothing as he followed his host through the main part of the tavern, disappearing up the stairs. Anxiety pulled at Cecilia's stomach as she watched him walk away. Something wasn't right.

23

Deal with the Devil

"I think I know, but I have to ask," Antonio gestured for Marcus to shut the door behind him, "who's the girl?"

"Which girl?" Marcus returned the question as he picked up a wooden trinket from the nearest cabinet.

To Marcus' surprise, Antonio's office was spacious and tidy, a far cry from the one he had left in Calgaria.

A plush green sofa sat beneath a window overlooking the grey morning. Antonio stood at a drink table beside his desk, the small space crowded with various coloured bottles.

"Don't play coy with me," Antonio offered him a glass, "the one you can't take your eyes off."

"Cecilia?" Marcus shook his head, feigning interest in the maps lining the walls, "She's no one."

"Cecilia." Antonio repeated, elongating her name. The chair creaked as he plonked himself into it, stirring a stack of papers on his otherwise orderly desk.

"She matches the description of Lady Alarcon's missing ward, especially with the two different coloured eyes. There are rumours she might be the lost princess of Calgaria. Although you already knew that."

"Like you said," Marcus shrugged, "they're just rumours."

Antonio swirled his drink, "Perhaps, but this one looks like the real deal."

Marcus crossed his arms. He didn't have time to waste playing Antonio's silly games.

"How much will it cost to get my friends out of prison?"

"That depends," Antonio sipped his drink, "How much are you willing to give?"

Marcus eyed him. A lifetime ago they'd been friends. Now, he was just another shady businessman.

"Just name your price."

"Alright," Antonio set his glass on the desk in front of him, "I want a cut of your share."

"What share?"

"The share of money you get when you return Cecilia to Calgaria."

"I never said there was a reward," Marcus tilted his head, "or if I was taking her to Calgaria."

"You didn't have to," Antonio shrugged, "I know how much King Lars would pay for her safe return. Besides, you're the Crown Prince's bodyguard – who would be better than you to bring her home? Not to mention she looks exactly like her mother. You know I know her mother, don't you?"

"I know you used to. Before your self-imposed exile."

Antonio put a hand to his heart in a mock wounding gesture.

"Ouch," Antonio put a hand to his heart in a mock wounded gesture, "that hurt."

Marcus rolled his eyes. "Am I supposed to sympathise with you after you abandoned your brother and your responsibilities so you could live like a criminal?"

"Much as I like you Marcus, if you're inclined to insult me, I'm less than inclined to help you." Antonio twisted his glass on the table.

Marcus sighed. This was a mistake. They didn't have time to negotiate.

"Doesn't matter now," Antonio took another swig of his drink, "you always get what you want somehow. Although, it's usually the prince who gets it for you."

"I can fend for myself," Marcus snapped, his fist curling at his sides. "I am not the prince's lackey."

Antonio narrowed his eyes, tilting his head at him, "Keep telling yourself that."

Marcus gritted his teeth. He would not let Antonio get under his skin.

"How is Catalina these days?" Antonio changed the subject, "Is she still crying over that brother of yours?"

"Take care with how you speak," Marcus' knuckles tightened, his nails biting into his skin. It would be so satisfying to knock him down a peg or two.

"I'm sorry. That was rude of me," Antonio apologised, "All I ask is a twenty per cent cut of whatever reward you get for presenting Cecilia to the king."

Marcus looked through the window over Antonio's dark head at the ocean. Grey clouds blocked the sun as angry waves clambered to the sky.

"And if I don't take the money?" Marcus levelled his gaze at Antonio.

"Don't take the money?" he scoffed. "Marcus, for all your pomp and façade at being an honourable man, we both know no one does something for nothing. This is a chance to reclaim your fortune, restore your family name. If nothing else, the king will make sure you are handsomely compensated."

"Or," fire burned in Marcus' dark eyes, "perhaps money is not my main motivator. Unlike you."

"Perhaps," Antonio's mouth quirked to the side, "but I know that's why you joined the Calgarian army when you could have stayed right here in Avinada. You wanted to become a spy, get close to the king's inner circle and do something that would restore daddy's reputation for marrying a foreign commoner. Look at you now. Bodyguard to the prince. Lackey to the king. And yet, we don't forget why we start things."

"You obviously did."

Antonio set his glass down carefully. "Do you want my help or not?"

Marcus paused for a moment, gritting his teeth.

"Yes."

"Then don't insult me."

"Fine," Marcus said eventually, "I'll give you five percent."

"Well, that's a start."

***

Cecilia was only half-listening to Bella and Jeremy's hushed conversation when she caught sight of Marcus. Relief washed over her for a moment, until she caught his stony gaze. His mouth was set in a hard line, one hand resting on the dagger on his belt.

Antonio trailed behind him, a jovial smile on his lips that didn't quite reach his eyes.

"We've come to an agreement," he announced, the pair of them standing over the table. "I will help you, for a price."

Something between a gasp and a sob emanated from Bella's direction as tears sprang to her eyes. Jeremy squeezed her hand.

"Thank you," she breathed.

"Don't thank him just yet," Jeremy warned, flashing Antonio an indignant stare, "he hasn't delivered anyone."

"For what it's worth Lucian, I will get those ladies out of the hell that is Avizon prison," Antonio addressed him, his voice softening.

"Your word doesn't mean much," Jeremy spat.

Hurt flashed across Antonio's pale features. He masked it quickly, turning to Marcus instead.

"It was a pleasure doing business with you," he said, offering his hand.

Marcus shook it, "I wish I could say the same."

Antonio let out a short laugh and slapped him on the back. Marcus met Cecilia's eyes and looked away.

"You should be on your way. You wouldn't want to be late returning to the *Sorrento*."

Cecilia trailed behind her companions, picking up the rear as they followed Antonio out of the establishment. The crowd had thinned since they first entered, the majority of people now flooding the streets. Cecilia's heart thumped as she noticed red coats, this time in pairs, weaving in and out of people.

"I'd wish you safe travels," Antonio leaned against the doorframe, "but where's the fun in that?"

"Thank you," Marcus nodded.

Antonio waved them off as they stepped into the morning sunlight. The sun was higher in the sky than expected. They were running dangerously behind.

24

Ambush

Cecilia fought to keep up with Marcus and the others. Bella clung to Jeremy's arm as they wove through the crowd. People pressed in around them, catching them up in the swell of traffic as it moved to the centre of the marketplace.

She stumbled on a piece of loose rock, her hands finding slippery purchase on a nearby wall. More people pushed past, pinning her against the wall as she scanned the crowd for her companions.

The smell of fried fish mingled with salty ocean air, churning her stomach. Townsfolk of every colour from the rich to the poor milled around a raised platform in the centre of the square. Guards in bright red coats surrounded the perimeter of a raised dais. Others stood scattered among the people, their weapons glistening under the silvery sunlight.

Cecilia gasped as a hand pulled her forward.

"I'm not losing you here," Marcus grumbled. His fingers dug into her skin as they weaved through the edge of the crowd. A trumpet blared across the hubbub; the city's general bustle reduced to a hush.

"Maldito!" Marcus cursed. "The ambassador's presentation."

It took a minute for his words to register. The king would present the new ambassador to the city before sailing to Calgaria.

Alistar.

"We have to go," Marcus pulled Cecilia along, "now."

She winced as his nails dug into her wrist before breaking into a run. The city blurred around her – flashes of yellow stone walls, a red scarf, the smell of salt and spice in the wind.

By the time they caught up to Bella and Jeremy at the mouth of yet another alley, Cecilia's lungs burned for air.

Her legs trembled as they slowed to a stop.

"Are you being followed?" Jeremy asked, gripping Bella's hand, ready to run.

Marcus shook his head.

"Ambassador's swearing in," he explained, "We have to keep moving."

Cecilia fought to keep up with Marcus as they hurried through the docks. They pushed past burly, sunburned stevedores grunting their frustration as the foursome slipped between boxes of cargo.

Cecilia's heart sank as they neared the *Real Sorrento*, two red coats guarding the gangway to the ship. She pulled her hood low over her face, hoping the guards would not ask questions.

Her fears were briefly allayed as Sebastian's familiar figure appeared on the gangway. He jogged down, towering over the two guards who did not move from their post. His dark eyes fixed on Marcus, his face creased into a frown.

"You're late," Sebastian greeted, his white shirt damp with sweat, "Catalina won't be happy."

"Occupational hazard," Marcus clapped Sebastian on the arm.

Nestled between Bella, Jeremy and Sebastian, the guards took no notice of her. Still, she fought to steady her breath as they hurried up the gangway, onto the ship's deck.

The *Sorrento's* crew stood at attention, each officer clad in the same blue military jacket as their captain. Their black boots shone even under the muted sun, weapons ready at their sides. Most paid her no attention as she congregated with her companions on the deck.

Catalina met them at the top of the ramp, hands on her hips. She looked as formidable as Cecilia had ever seen her. Her tanned face wore a frown as deep as the ocean. Her narrow eyes darkened, her fury aimed at Marcus.

"You better have a good explanation as to why you're late," she snapped. "I almost had to call the authorities on you."

"That would've been a bit awkward, given we're not exactly sympatico at the moment." Marcus gestured for the others to pass by him.

Though Catalina's frown was not aimed at her, Cecilia flinched anyway. Marcus' face remained neutral under the captain's stony glare.

"Had you arrived earlier, we could have hidden our runaway without anyone noticing," she hissed, throwing a pointed glance at Cecilia. She stepped closer to Marcus lowering her voice, "Unfortunately, this ship is crawling with soldiers until the duke is sworn in."

"Can we not hide in our cabin?" Bella suggested, sidling up beside Cecilia. Her stomach clenched. They had avoided the topic of Bella's sisters in the tavern, but there would be no escaping it once they were tucked away in their room.

Catalina opened her mouth to speak at the same time a trumpet blared. Cecilia flinched as the crowd cheered, picking up a tune as it meandered through the town square. Despite the heat, goosebumps crawled up her arms, it was too late to hide, or to abandon ship.

As if reading her thoughts, Marcus tugged at her wrist.

"Come with me," he said, not looking at her.

Ignoring her hammering heart, she followed him to the stern of the ship. Bored guards stood at intervals along the rail, their gazes cast across at the hive of activity on the docks.

Cecilia adjusted the hood over her face anyway.

Marcus leaned against the rail, scanning the open ocean. Grey waves clambered to the sky, crashing one over the other. The sun hung in muted splendour, a patch of blue peaked out from behind a cage of white clouds.

Steadying her breathing, she forced herself to watch the grey-blue waves in the distance, the constant push and pull rushing in her ears.

Another cheer erupted from the docks to their right, this one closer than the last. Cecilia gripped the edge of the railing.

"Are you ready for the next part of the voyage?" Marcus asked, breaking the silence between them.

"You're talking to me now?" she asked, a bitter edge to her voice.

"Was I not talking to you before?" he frowned.

She cast her gaze back to the ocean, her fear overtaken by annoyance.

"You've barely spoken to me all morning and now you expect to be chummy again? Who do you think you are?"

Marcus crossed his arms.

"Forgive me for trying to keep you safe," his brown eyes darkened. "I didn't realise I had to narrate everything while we were running for our lives."

"But we weren't running for our lives this time." She whirled on him. "You've barely said a word to me since we left Salvador's Taverna and you still haven't explained the incident at the bookshop."

Marcus shook his head, incredulous, "I'm happy to answer your questions, but when pray tell, did you think I'd have the time?"

She crossed her arms over her chest, scanning the ocean again. She hated to admit he had a point.

"I suppose we have a few minutes while we cast off," he sighed, leaning his arms on the rail. "What do you want to know?"

"Everything," she shrugged, "Why did you almost start a fight in the bookshop?"

Strands of dark hair brushed his stubbled cheek as he shook his head, the corner of his mouth tipped into a smile.

"That," he glanced at her, "was not my intention."

"Then why were you so..." she paused, looking for the right word, "brutish?"

He followed her gaze to the distant horizon, the constant crash of waves filling the silence between them.

"Sometimes, people get an idea into their heads, about a person or a position, which makes them unpredictable. They can say or do something foolish."

"Do you think he was a fool for calling me a queen?" she frowned.

"I didn't say that," he shook his head again, raking a hand through his wind-mussed hair, "but it is a dangerous assumption for him to make."

"Why?"

Marcus met her eyes then, his face unreadable.

"Because if people start to think you're lost royalty, well," he lifted a shoulder in a half-shrug, "we might have a fight on our hands to keep you safe."

Something about the twinkle in his eye when he smiled made her stomach tighten.

"Maybe if you stopped dragging me into danger, you wouldnt have to fight for me." She countered.

Something akin to hurt flickered across his face, nearly stopping her in her tracks. Pushing off from the rail, she stalked off, hoping to put as much distance between them as possible. Traitorous tears threatened to spill down her cheeks. How had Marcus gotten under her skin so easily?

She was beginning to lose count of the number of times he'd saved her, but did he have to be so smug about it?

Cheers turned to screams on the docks interrupting her thoughts. Gunshots rang in her ears as people on the shore ducked for cover. She watched, as though in slow motion, a regiment of guards rushing up the gangplank to the ship, a familiar blonde head peeping out from the middle of the group.

Fear constricted her throat. Her feet moved before she knew where she was going.

The boat dipped on a rough wave, sending her stumbling on the deck. She gasped, arms flinging out in front of her, hitting something solid.

"Oof," Marcus grunted helping her up.

"What's going on?" Cecilia couldn't hide the tremble in her voice.

"I don't know." Marcus looked around the deck. "But we need to get you to the galley."

"Weapons at the ready! Lower the sails!" Catalina shouted orders from somewhere above them.

The ship rocked beneath them as they cast off, gliding quickly through the busy harbour. Cecilia reached for Marcus, her fingers digging into his wrist. Surely, they weren't leaving now? Not with Alistar on board?

As if on cue, Alistar poked his head out from beneath his guards. He grinned as soon as he saw her, jogging across the deck to greet her.

"Cecilia! What are you doing here? Did you come to Avizon just to find me?" he embraced her in a tight hug, "How fortuitous!"

Marcus cleared his throat beside them.

Noticing his presence for the first time, Alistar frowned. Marcus glanced between them. Though she had done nothing wrong, a strange sense of guilt gnawed at her. She stepped away from Alistar, crossing her arms over her chest. Why should she care what Marcus thought of the duke's display? It wasn't like Alistar was a stranger to her. They'd grown up together.

She straightened her shirt, steadying herself as the ship dipped beneath them.

"Duke Aurelius," Alistar addressed Marcus after a moment, "what are you doing here?"

"I could ask you the same thing, Your Grace." Marcus crossed his arms over his chest. "I wasn't aware this was an ambassadorial vessel. What happened at the docks?"

Alistar shrugged, "Unruly crowd."

The two men surveyed each other. Finally, Alistar broke the silence.

"I thought you were in Avinada for business? Why the hurry to get back?"

Marcus frowned. "Forgive me Your Grace, but I don't think that's any of your concern."

Cecilia glanced between them, their stony gazes levelled like swords. Alistar bristled beside her. He hated being addressed as a duke, though it was his proper title. His status as a prince was never officially recognised, but he liked to style himself as one anyway.

"As a prince of this realm, and as Cecilia's..." he searched for an appropriate term, "friend, I think it is my right to know why you're attempting to flee the country with her."

A muscle worked in Marcus' jaw before he answered.

"No one is attempting anything, Your Grace, I am simply helping a lady on her travels," he glanced at Cecilia, "And, not that it's any of your business, but I must return for the investiture of Crown Prince Derek."

"Huh." Alistar clucked his tongue.

The deck thrummed with activity, boots thumping on timber, crew members calling to each other.

Alister glanced at the passing harbour, taking Cecilia's hand.

"Perhaps we should go below and let your friend attend to his duties," he addressed her though his eyes never wavered from Marcus, "I'm sure there is something he can take up on the deck to keep himself occupied."

"I am attending to my duties," Marcus stepped forward, his hand resting on the hilt of his sword, "You are the one getting in my way."

"And what duties are they?"

"I promised Señorita Cecilia I would look after her on this voyage," Marcus glanced at her, "And I never break my promises."

The sharp edge in his voice forced Cecilia to look at him.

Having shed his travelling cloak, Marcus looked like any other deck hand, his shirt bound in a brown sash at his waist, stopping at the edge of his dark trousers tucked into worn leather boots. Only the array of weapons hanging from his leather belt separated him from the sparsely armed crew. His white shirt billowed on the breeze, stretching out like angel wings. His dark eyes burned with something she couldn't quite put her finger on, and there was an edge to the polite smile he threw at Alistar.

"Yes, well," the duke cleared his throat, "I can take care of her from here."

Marcus took a threatening step towards him. Alistar, cowed, stumbled backward into a deckhand.

"I can look after myself." Cecilia piped up. Marcus glanced at her as a gentle thwip shot past her ear.

A sharp heat spread through her arm, static shooting through her fingers.

A scream pierced the air, followed by her name. Marcus was beside her in a moment, shielding her body with his, shouting for help.

Cecilia bumped against him as he drew her onto the deck floor, a sudden surge of pain following. She glanced at her arm and immediately wished she hadn't.

A long wooden arrow embedded itself into the flesh between her elbow and shoulder. Dark blood ran in rivulets down her arm, dripping onto the wooden deck.

Her lungs constricted at the sight. She forced herself to breathe. Marcus held her upright, cradling her against him.

"I'm here. You'll be fine," he reassured her. She wanted to shake her head, to tell him it wasn't fine, but her body froze, unable to follow a simple command.

Jeremy was beside her in a moment, examining the wound.

She was vaguely aware of someone hauling Alistar away, his terrified shouts mingling with the hurried orders Catalina snapped at the crew.

"Cecilia, how many fingers am I holding up?" he asked, holding up his hand.

Three, she answered in her mind. Instead, she blinked at him, her tongue lead in her mouth.

Jeremy's lips pursed into a thin line.

"Can you stand?" Jeremy asked instead.

Cecilia nodded, despite her trembling legs. She leaned on Marcus, her knees buckled beneath her. Bile rose in her throat as the ship pitched and swayed.

"Get her to the medic's cabin. Now!" Jeremy ordered.

Like a prince in a fairy tale, Marcus swung her into his arms. Above his concerned brow, the sky remained impossibly, blue, the clouds parting at last to reveal a flash of spring sunshine. It would be a fine day.

What a shame to waste it, she thought as Marcus hurried after Jeremy into the medic's cabin. Bella stood at the door, fingers moving quickly to tie an apron on top of her gown.

Tender hands laid Cecilia on the hard wooden table in the centre of the room. Without Marcus holding her, she shivered in the cool cabin air. Her vision blurred as she scanned the room, Jeremy hovering at her shoulder while Bella sorted through a variety of vials and instruments. Marcus stood beside her; a hand frozen in the air between them as if she might break if he touched her.

Jeremy set to work, procuring a set of bandages to staunch the flow of blood.

She gasped as Bella applied something cold to her skin.

"Marcus," Jeremy ordered, "hold her hand. This is going to hurt."

Cecilia hadn't noticed Marcus' face pale until he stepped closer. He hesitated a moment before taking her hand in his. Bracing herself for pain, she focused on the gentle stroke of Marcus' thumb against her skin. He glanced at Jeremy, fear flashing in his eyes. Cecilia's heart hammered against her ribs. If Marcus was afraid, what did that mean for her?

"You'll be alright," he flashed her a tight smile, though she suspected he was trying to reassure himself also.

It was too late. A guttural cry burst from her mouth as her arm burned with searing pain. For one horrible second, she focused on the acuteness of the metal inside her arm. Blood thundered in her ears. Desperate, she gasped for air, forcing herself to breathe as panic set in.

"Bella, give her another dose," Jeremy ordered, "this isn't looking pretty."

A tin cup was forced between Cecilia's lips. A bitter liquid burned her throat. Firm hands held her steady as she curled upward, gagging at the wretched taste. Gentle hands laid her back on the table.

"Easy does it," Marcus murmured, stroking hair back from her face.

Dark spots blurred her vision, fatigue creeping at the edges of her mind. Her eyelids drooped as she struggled to focus on Marcus, his brow etched in concern.

With the last of her energy, she squeezed his hand.

The image of his reassuring smile burned in her mind as darkness finally consumed her.

25

A Taste of Friendship

Cecilia startled awake. The sound of horses thundering through the city, the sky splitting into brilliant colours were replaced by the constant thrum of waves against the ship's hull. Her fingers gripped the sweat-soaked sheets, the remnants of her dream fading as her eyes adjusted to the dim cabin light.

Her arm throbbed, the pain banishing all thoughts of dusty carriages and faceless royals to the memory of metal embedding itself in her flesh.

Taking a breath to steady herself, she examined the wound. A brown splotch marred an otherwise crisp white bandage wrapped around her left arm, sans arrow. She flexed her hand. Apart from a tight twinge and some static in her sleepy fingers, the pain had reduced to a dull ache.

Someone had moved her to a cot in the far corner of the room. Flickering candles and an assortment of bandages lay on the centre table Marcus had laid her on earlier.

Wincing, she struggled into a sitting position, careful not to bump her arm against the wall.

Taking a moment to compose herself, she reached for the steel cup on a square table beside her. To her relief, it was filled almost to the brim.

She drank deeply, water spilling down her chin, onto her thin blanket.

A mournful tune filtered through the cabin walls, drawing her attention from the gentle rock of the ocean.

Taking a moment to let the world stop spinning, she swung her legs carefully over the cot. Her bare feet barely made a sound as she padded to the door, testing the handle. It swung open without a sound.

The deck was quiet, most officers appearing to have gone below for the night. Cecilia wondered what time it was. The medic's cabin bore no clock and the candles had been fresh.

Still, she kept to the shadows. She would drink the stars to her fill before making her way back to bed. The last thing she wanted was to have someone prodding her about her arm.

A shadow to her right caught her attention. It was hard to make him out in the dim light, until he raked a hand through a dark mess of hair.

Even under the deck's dim candlelight, Marcus looked more worn than he had a few hours ago. His shirt hung loose on his lean frame, untucked from his dark pants. He'd lost the brown sash somewhere and his belt was empty of weapons. He rested one hand on his hip, the other facing the sky. He lifted his face to the heavens, eyes closed as he paced back and forth against the rail, silent words streaming from his lips.

Cecilia startled as Sebastian and Jeremy appeared in front of her. She ducked behind a barrel, keeping low to the ground. Jeremy held a candle between them, half of his face bathed in the warm glow, the other cast into shadow.

Sebastian stood beside him, their backs to her.

"Is Marcus... praying" Jeremy paused, his voice low.

Sebastian shrugged. "Seems so."

"I haven't seen him pray since Claudio died. Why would he start again, now?"

Sebastian folded his arms across his broad chest, giving his companion a long-suffering look. "Perhaps it has something to do with the unconscious girl in your cabin."

"Oh?" Jeremy's brows furrowed as realisation dawned on him, "*Oh.*"

"It's been three days," Sebastian continued, "I trust your methods, but even I am beginning to worry. A poisoned arrow is hardly an easy cure."

Jeremy frowned.

"I've done all I can. The rest is up to Ilio," He looked up at the heavens. "King Lars will have my head if we bring back her body, but I hate to think what he'd do to Marcus."

"The arrow could have been meant for the duke. If so, Marcus could remain in his role as the prince's protector," Sebastian shrugged.

"I'm not so sure," Jeremy shook his head, "I doubt Marcus would forgive himself if Cecilia died on his watch."

"Nobody could've seen the arrow coming."

"That's what I don't understand about all this," Jeremy frowned. "Who would have cause to hurt her?"

Sebastian paused. For a moment Cecilia wasn't sure he would speak again.

"I can't imagine Prince Derek would be too thrilled to hear his cousin could be on her way home," Sebastian said eventually. "If Cecilia is the the princess, the Calgarian crown is her birthright."

Jeremy's lips pursed into a thin line.

"But to kill her? Surely that's a bit much, even for the prince?"

Cecilia shifted on her knees, eager to hear more when something metal clanged to the ground beside her. Flinching at the sound, she turned to move away.

Someone gasped behind her. Too late.

"By the stars!" Jeremy gasped, his pale face turning white under the moonlight, "you scared me."

"Sorry," Cecilia mumbled, standing to dust herself off. There was no point hiding now.

"What on earth are you doing out of bed?"

"I-uh," she glanced at Marcus who jogged towards them, joining Sebastian at Jeremy's shoulder, "I was looking for some water," she finished lamely.

"There was a jug on the table. I'll find a fresh pitcher for you." Jeremy turned to leave.

"No, I have some. I just-" she scrambled for an excuse, "I can't lift the jug."

Three pairs of eyes settled on her bandage.

"I'll help you," Marcus offered, stepping past Jeremy.

She took a step back.

"You don't need to."

He shook his head, "Please. I insist."

Heat rose to her cheeks as she recalled Jeremy and Sebastian's conversation. She refused to look at either of them, lest they realise she'd been eavesdropping. Instead, she nodded. "Thank you."

She hurried back to the cabin, acutely aware of every move she made until she was wrapped in the safety of the scratchy cot blanket.

Marcus shut the door behind them, pouring water from the pitcher without a word. She kept her eyes on the tin cup he offered, not daring to glance at him should he already be watching her.

He set himself up on a chair beside the cot. She swiped a sweaty palm on the blanket. Why did she care so much what he thought of her? He said himself he was ordered to bring her to Calgaria. Discomfort twinged in her chest at the thought.

"How are you feeling?" he asked when she emerged from the cup.

"Better," she nodded, cradling it in her hands. "How long was I out for?"

She already knew the answer, but for some reason, she wanted to hear him say it.

"Three days," he replied, his voice matter-of-fact, betraying none of the emotion he'd displayed a few minutes earlier.

"What did Jeremy give me?" she kept her voice light to ease the tension.

"That's anybody's guess," he settled into an easy smile, "but it worked."

His eyes lingered on her a touch longer than necessary. She turned her attention back to the empty cup, trying to find something to talk about in its shadowed depths. The last time they had spoken, she had snapped at him that she could take care of herself. Now she sat, wounded and defenceless and he had spent the last three days praying for her recovery.

"Does it...still hurt?" Marcus jerked his chin at her arm, breaking the silence between them. She nodded, adjusting herself on the cot.

"It aches," she admitted, not quite meeting his eyes. Her stomach growled, filling the empty room. Her cheeks flushed again.

"Here," Marcus fished an orange from his pocket, "I thought you might be hungry so I swiped some of these just in case."

In one smooth motion, he plucked a dagger from a small scabbard on his boot, giving it a cursory wipe on his shirtsleeve before slicing into the orange. At this point, she was too hungry to care where the dagger had been.

He peeled the fruit, the rough skin forming a circular shell as juice spilled down his sun kissed hand. She plucked the proffered fruit from him gratefully. Sweet citrus burst on her tongue. A satisfied sigh escaped her lips as sticky juice spilled down her chin. Marcus offered her a scrap piece of bandage.

Fighting a fresh wave of embarrassment, she took it from him, wiping her face and hands as she devoured the fruit.

"I wanted to thank you," she swallowed, wiping her hands on the sticky fabric, "for helping me. Even when I said I didn't need you... I was wrong."

To her surprise, Marcus didn't mock or derive her. Not like Frida would have done, demanding an apology. Instead, he offered her a smile, his brown eyes flickering with familiar warmth.

"It's what anyone would have done." He offered.

She shook her head. "I'm not sure I could've in your position."

"You never know," he leaned back in the chair. "You'd be surprised at what you can accomplish under pressure. Another?"

She nodded as he procured another orange slice.

"I suppose you have a cool head thanks to your military skills."

He shrugged, averting her gaze. She watched him cut a second orange into wedges. Still, her curiosity gnawed at her, refusing to let go.

"Is that why you were so..." she scrambled for the right words to convey her question, "why were you so standoffish with the bookshop owner?"

Marcus plucked a wedge from beside her.

"He made a dangerous assumption about you," he said finally.

"Is there any truth to it?"

His lips pursed into a thin line, dark eyes hardening. He looked away. Still, she pressed on.

"I don't remember much of my life before living at Villa Alarcon, and I do not wish to hope, but," she paused, stroking the cups' cool handle, "I cannot see why you would be taking me to Calgaria if there wasn't a possibility I am the lost princess."

Marcus exhaled, wiping his fingers on a bandage scrap.

"You're right," he nodded, finally meeting her eyes, "there is a chance you might be her."

A strange sense of relief washed over her at his admission, as though a heavy weight she didn't know she'd been carrying had vanished from her shoulders.

"That's what made the man's display of allegiance so dangerous," Marcus pressed on. "There may be peace between our countries now, but if word were to spread that Calgaria's lost princess had been raised in Avinada, or worse, stolen by an Avinadan, it could likely start another war."

"So, you're bringing me to Calgaria to eliminate the threat?" she reached for another orange slice.

Marcus' brows furrowed, "We're not going to kill you."

To his surprise, she laughed, "Well that's a relief."

"You'll likely be examined for questioning before a decision is made," he said, serious.

"A decision?"

"On whether you're the Crown Princess or not."

Cecilia balked, an orange slice poised at her lips.

"Crown Princess? But isn't Prince Derek next in line to the throne?"

Marcus nodded, chewing on an orange slice.

"He was assumed heir to the throne after Princess Lilia disappeared, but he won't be officially named as Crown Prince until the end of spring - if the princess is not found."

She tilted her head at him, confusion written across her features. He took a breath before explaining.

"Prince Derek was the byproduct of one of King Oslo's... indiscretions, and is the late king's only child. After King Lars took the throne and Lilia was born, he was never considered a legitimate heir. At least not until King Lars adopted him."

Cecilia picked at the polished orange skin, bits of bitter white flakes falling onto the scratchy blanket.

"So, if it turns out I am the lost princess, what will that mean for Prince Derek?"

Marcus sighed, a frown tugged at the corners of his mouth.

"I don't know," he said in a voice so soft she wasn't sure he meant for her to hear.

He pushed the silver tray toward her, offering her the last slice. Gingerly, she took it.

In silence, he scrounged around the cabin for another scrap piece of fabric to wipe their hands with. Cecilia toyed with the material, the sweet citrus embedding itself into the grooves of her palms.

"Oh, I almost forgot," Marcus reached behind the water jug, resuming his position on the chair beside her. He produced a thin silver rectangle, handing it her.

"What is this?" She asked, the book's soft material sending a thrill down her spine. The smell of dust and old pages lingered as she flicked through the pages.

"It's a collection of stories from Calgaria," he relaxed into an easy smile. "I thought we could use it to help you learn the language before we arrive."

"Oh," was all she could manage. Despite using the library in Villa Alarcon, no one had ever bought her a book before. If there was a story she wanted to read that the duke did not have, she would use the meagre savings her godmother gave her to purchase it.

To have someone buy her a book, even if it was a practical gift, meant the world to her.

"Thank you," she hugged it to her chest, eyes shining, "but I don't know Calgarian."

Marcus' smile widened.

"If you want, I can teach you."

She nodded, blinking back tears. Despite her joy, she was determined not to let him see her cry.

They set to work until the candle burned low and Cecilia's eyes began to droop. Marcus had tried making himself comfortable on the chair, but it was no use. Despite his eagerness to teach, she could see fatigue catching up with him by the subtle drop of his shoulders.

"Maybe it's time we stopped for the night," he suggested, stifling a yawn. Cecilia nodded, settling back into her pillows.

Without a word, he plucked the empty cup from her fingers, filling it with water, and setting it on the table beside her, making sure it was close enough for her to reach. She gathered the leftover orange skins, which he disposed of.

"Thank you, Marcus," she yawned, "for everything."

"You're welcome, señorita" he flashed her a wink.

The corners of her lips tipped up into a smile, which was soon covered by a grimace. Her arm throbbed as she hit the tender wound against the cabin wall.

Marcus was by her side in a moment, his hands hovered at her elbow.

"I'm fine," she shook her head.

He pursed his lips. "You're sure?"

She nodded, cradling her arm as she changed the subject.

"Is Calgaria truly as cold a place as the stories say?" she fought another yawn.

"Colder. Maybe sometime I'll tell you more about it," he covered his mouth, sleep catching up with him, "but I think we both need some rest."

She nodded, her eyes already drooping as she nestled into the soft pillow. Marcus found an extra cushion, propping her injured arm atop it.

"You don't have to do this," she whispered, as he drew his hand away. He was so close she could feel his breath on her hair. She fought to keep her own breathing steady.

He shook his head, dark waves brushing against his ears.

"I want to," he offered her a tired smile, pulling away from her as quickly as he'd tucked her in. "Sleep well."

She offered him a weak smile as sleep threatened to overtake her. The door clicked shut behind him and for the first time since arriving on the ship, she felt truly alone.

Yawning, she brought her uninjured hand up to her pillow, tracing wayward lines on the cool surface. The scent of citrus mingled with book dust on her skin. Despite herself, she smiled. Perhaps Marcus was a bit prickly, but he wasn't so bad after all.

The constant push and pull of the ship tugged her to sleep, but it was the memory of Marcus' strong arms cradling her as he hurried to the cabin that haunted her dreams.

26

Royal Treatment

Frida's boots crunched on gravel as she exited a dusty black carriage. The journey from the docks to the palace should not have taken longer than an hour, but the streets had turned to chaos after rumours Alistar's ship had been shot at.

Frida hurried up the grand marble steps of the palace. Palacio Esmeralda loomed above her, the emerald roof catching the early afternoon sun. She groaned. She should be on her way to the Fickle Islands by now, but instead she had received an urgent summons from the king.

Sweat clung to her neck and brow, heat pressing in on every side until she reached the imposing brass doors. Waving the summons with the king's royal seal at the stationary guards, she passed through without issue.

She scowled as a palace servant ran down the golden hall to meet her. She could imagine the delight in Queen Isabel's eyes when Frida entered the court, dripping in sweat.

"Your hat Doña Alarcon?" the servant asked, his hand poised to take the new black top-hat fascinator she bought when she arrived in the city the day before.

"Absolutely not," she snapped. Her usually tidy curls had no doubt turned into a menacing frizz atop her head, and she was certainly in no mood to let the queen see her ruffled.

Already she could feel the perspiration settle on her neck despite the standing lace frill on the back of her dress to keep the sun from burning her skin.

Regret was not an emotion she felt often, but she had to admit this perhaps was not the best day for wearing the king's favourite red satin dress with black gloves and trimming. The fabric would betray her dilemma in the heat.

With a huff, she fumbled for her fan as the servant dressed in red and gold livery escorted her from the golden entryway through the luxurious hall.

Portraits of long dead rulers lined the rich green walls. Frida's heels echoed on the gleaming marble floors, muffled only when she crossed extravagant tapestried rugs.

While she was used to a life of luxury, it was hard not to admire the array of marble statues lining the outdoor courtyard, as the servant led her into an alfresco hallway, half of which was ensconced by luscious flowers in spring bloom.

She feigned indifference, following the servant up the paved steps and through a set of tall brass double doors, the Avinadan sun blazing at eight points on each door.

The air changed when they stepped inside. Surrounded by marble and tile, she pulled her sleeves tighter as a cool spring breeze wafted from an open window somewhere.

King Vicente sat on an ornate golden throne centred on a marble dais, bathed in afternoon sunshine. Trees swayed gently in the wind behind him, the expansive royal gardens visible through the tall glass windows behind the dais.

Queen Isabel posed beside the king on her own matching throne, her golden hair catching in the sunlight.

Frida kept her scowl in check as she approached them, her black leather boots clip-clopping on the white tiles.

She glanced around the room expecting to see hundreds of noblemen in their robes as the king held court, the queen and her ladies sitting a polite distance away. Instead, the throne room was empty and the gallery had been moved away.

"I suppose you're wondering where your audience is," Queen Isabel said by way of greeting.

It took every ounce of strength for Frida not to launch herself at the queen. Her very voice grated on Frida's nerves. How the king had remained married to the viper, she knew not. Instead, she smiled, curtsying low to the king.

"I confess I was expecting a public audience, Your Majesty. I assumed anything which relates to the ambassador had to have a public hearing."

'And I have a right to share my side of the story before you make me a villain,' she thought.

The queen gave her a forced smile, "You have the right to speak, but you should not expect what you say to be heard or believed."

Before Frida could say anything, King Vicente cleared his throat.

"Duchess Alarcon," he addressed Frida. They were always formal in public, but the sound of him using her title always grated on her.

"Yes, Your Highness?" she asked sweetly.

From the corner of her eye, she could see Queen Isabel cross her arms.

"It is understood your goddaughter may be involved in an assassination attempt involving your son, Duke Alarcon, as he embarked on his journey to Calgaria. Such an attempt, especially by someone of your own household, must be dealt with swiftly."

Frida balked. Catching the satisfaction in Isabel's smile, she schooled her features into a neutral expression.

"Of course, Your Majesty," she folded her hands in front of her, "What do you wish me to do?"

The queen mumbled something under her breath.

"Isabel!" The king hissed, before addressing his mistress, "I apologise for my wife's behaviour-"

"He may, but I do not." The queen interrupted, fire in her emerald eyes.

"In any case," said the king, attempting to regain control of the conversation, "As the *Real Sorrento* has not yet been intercepted and neither Duke Alarcon or Señorita Cecilia have been brought back to Avinada, the palace will hold you for questioning."

"What? But I had nothing to do with this! I swear it!" Frida burst.

Queen Isabel grinned, "Oh you may not have anything to do with an attempt to murder your son, but you have plenty of reason to harm another person on that ship."

"And who, pray tell, might that be?" Frida snapped.

The queen paused a moment before answering, her smile dripping with satisfaction.

"Princess Lilia of Calgaria."

Frida's eyes widened, "Cecilia has nothing to do with the Calgarian royal family. She was an orphan when I found her."

"I did not say it was Cecilia, although you have solved that mystery for me. After all, she bears and extraordinary resemblance to Vicente's sister, Queen Minerva, don't you think? Not to mention your bastard son Alistar. Do they not know they are cousins? Is that why you tried to silence her before they could reach Calgaria?"

"I attempted to do no such thing!" Frida stepped forward. "Vicente, control your wife!"

The queen narrowed her eyes at Frida, all semblance of civility dissipated into thin air. The king glanced helplessly between them.

"Oh, so you think you can just waltz in here and claim authority over my husband in *my* court when you have been summoned for questioning?" Queen Isabel demanded. "I suppose you would like to spend an evening in the dungeons."

"Better an evening there than another second here with you." Frida spat.

"That's enough." King Vicente boomed.

Though his voice ricochetted, his request fell onto deaf ears. "You're acting like spoiled children."

The women glared at each other. Frida hated how regal Queen Isabel looked in her floor length gown, the pale pink fabric complimenting her pale skin. Pearl drops covered every inch of her torso, grey furs draped elegantly over her throne. The golden crown on her bright blonde hair twinkled contemptuously at Frida.

The queen's green eyes blazed with fury. For a moment Frida had to admit she looked like an avenging angel. But the duchess had no fear of gods or men.

It was the king who spoke next, though Frida realised too late, he was not addressing her.

"This is why I wanted to do this privately," The king grumbled at his wife.

"If I had left the two of you alone, who knows how long it would be before you found a bed and emerged from it?"

"At least it would be a more productive time than what we're having now," Frida shot back.

Before the king had a chance to react, Queen Isabel rose from her throne, her silk-slippered feet pounding on the stone steps as she marched toward Frida. Before she could blink, the queen's heavy ringed fingers connected with her cheek.

Frida stumbled back from the force of the blow, her head reeling as her hand flew up to cover her cheek. She could feel her face begin to swell as the queen's diamond left its mark on the corner of her eye.

Breathing heavily, Frida struggled to compose herself while the queen ascended the marble steps.

"You have no idea how long I have been waiting to do that," she declared.

The king looked between the pair, torn as to whom he should help. In the end, he called for a wide-eyed servant.

"You there, get the duchess some ice," he ordered.

The servant was quick to obey.

Frida let out a breath, regaining her composure. She squared her shoulders and straightened to her full height, determined not to be intimidated by her rival.

"If the queen has finished, am I free to leave?" Frida asked, her eyes never wavering from the king.

King Vicente glanced at his wife who was watching Frida, satisfaction written on her fair features. Frida ignored her.

"You will be placed under house arrest in your city apartments. There will be guards posted at your door. They will escort you in and out of your rooms until the court is satisfied with your questioning."

Was it her imagination, or did the king sound despondent?

She shook her head of the thought. She needed to find Cecilia as quickly as possible, which would be hindered by house arrest. Could she send word to King Anders? Would he help her escape?

"Please let me send her to the dungeons," Queen Isabel burst, launching herself at her husbands feet. Her knees hit the stone with a thud, but it did not seem to deter her plea, "even just for one night. She deserves to spend as much time as possible for the horrendous crime she committed against your niece."

"Hush Isabel," the king said tiredly, "nothing has yet been proven."

The queen scowled and crossed her arms over her chest, reminding Frida of a spoiled child.

"You may leave us." The king waved Frida away.

At his directive, Frida bowed low towards him, inclining her head briefly to the queen. She walked backwards to the entrance the servant had left her at minutes earlier. The same man met her now, an ice wrap in his hand.

Frida kept the ice on the side of her face, wincing at the cold. She followed him to a set of rooms on the at the very end of the palace, close to the servants' quarters.

Once they reached the serving hall, she was greeted by a familiar servant in plain clothes. He had trimmed his beard since the last time she saw him, but his pale features and slight frame were unmistakable. Pancho, the king's valet, greeted her with a wan smile.

"Pancho? What are you doing here?" she asked, pain shooting through her cheekbone as she spoke.

"The king has requested your presence," he explained.

"Already?" she raised a manicured eyebrow at him, "but what about Queen Isabel?"

A sly smile crept across Pancho's features. He had always been quiet and unassuming, the perfect servant to conceal her affair with the king. But the gleam in his eye stirred an unfamiliar panic within her.

"I am not referring to King Vicente, Your Grace," he nodded his head toward the long hallway to the servants' hall. Frida picked up her skirts as she hurried to keep pace beside him.

"Then, who?" Her skin crawled as she waited for the answer, her heart threatening to beat out of her chest.

Frida's legs trembled from more than just exhaustion by the time they reached the delivery area, behind the empty servants' hall. At the end of the alley was a dusty, black carriage. The same one she had arrived in earlier.

Pancho turned to her, his thin lips unfurling to reveal crooked white teeth.

"Pirate King Anders does not like to be kept waiting."

Frida had just enough time to register his words before panic rose in her throat.

"What do you want from me?" she demanded, whirling on the servant. She had thought him loyal all these years. Was he just waiting for the right moment to blackmail her to get what he wanted?

"The queen wants you to disappear, but King Vicente wants you alive," Pancho shrugged, "and you have something that interests the Pirate King."

"I was on my way there before I was summoned into this mess!" she burst.

Pancho frowned, "Makes no difference to me, Your Grace. I'm just following orders."

She narrowed her eyes, "Whose orders?"

He shrugged again, "Whoever's the highest bidder. And if you want to take my advice, I suggest you do the same. Your time in this king's court is numbered, Your Grace. Take back your life while you still can."

Scowling at the middle-aged man, she gathered her skirts and huffed into the carriage.

He shut the door after her, and knocked on the frame. In a moment, the carriage jolted forward. She drew the curtains shut to block out his piercing stare.

If Isabel wanted her gone, she would disappear. But she would make them rue the day they crossed her.

27

Not Part of the Plan

"Have you thought about what you will do when you arrive in Calgaria?" Alistar asked, tossing a ball of twine in the air.

Cecilia shook her head against her crumpled pillow. She'd languished in bed for three days, alternating between sleeping, and studying with Marcus. She'd avoided walking along the deck for fear Alistar would corner her, and only ventured out under the light of the stars, usually with Bella.

Yet, despite her best efforts to avoid him, Alistar had muscled his way into the medic's cabin and ignored her hints to leave her alone. Still, she endured his company with a smile.

"Are Duke Aurelius and his crew forcing you to sail with them? Or will they drop you off at the Fickle Islands?" he asked, nearly dropping the twine onto the floor.

"They're not forcing me to do anything," Cecilia sighed, "I decided to sail on the first ship out of Cova Rafael and," she gestured at her arm, "I'm not really in a position to run away."

The lie had come easily. She hadn't wanted Alistar to blame Marcus for helping her run away. There was enough tension between them without adding unnecessary stress.

"So, you *don't* want to sail to Calgaria?" he turned to face her.

She picked at her nails, leaning further into her pillow, "I don't know… where is this coming from?"

He shrugged, trying for a lightness that didn't match his eyes.

"Had you considered going anywhere else before you ran away from home?"

"What is this, an interrogation?" she snapped. She had no patience for him today, "I had no plans when I left except to get as far away from your mother as possible. Now I'm wondering if Calgaria will be far enough."

He flinched. His knee stopped bouncing.

She squeezed her eyes shut. "Don't tell me you're surprised. You know I never wanted to stay at the Villa."

"Yes but I always imagined you would go to the capital, not leave the country," he frowned. "This is so unlike you."

She opened her eyes to look at him. His white shirt was creased and ruffled, tucked into equally dishevelled brown trousers and shining black boots.

"I never wanted the life Frida laid out for me. You must know that."

"And I do," he took her good hand gently in his, pressing a gentle kiss onto her skin. The sudden movement made her flinch which sent a sharp pain along her injured arm. Alistar ignored the hiss that escaped her lips.

"I know you don't want to marry Mario. I don't want you to, either. That's why I'm proposing."

She looked at him blankly, "Proposing what?"

He smiled as though she had made a joke.

"Don't play coy with me. I proposed to you the night of your ball, and I'm proposing to you again now."

"Alistar-"

He held up a finger, cutting her off.

"I know you told me you didn't want to marry me then, but I am the ambassador to Calgaria. I have money, a title, status. I may not be recognised as a prince in my father's court but I will have influence in Calgaria. I can look after you with my own money. You will be far away from my mother, except when she comes to visit, and you will have the freedom to accompany me on my travels."

How could you grow up with someone and not really know them at all? she wondered.

"I don't think you understand. I do not want to get married." She tried to pry her hand from his strong grip. "Not right now. Not to you."

His face fell as though she'd slapped him. Still, she forged ahead.

"I'm an orphan. I have no dowry. I don't know who my parents are. My only semblance of a plan is to try to meet the Calgarian king."

He shook his head, his grip on her hand tightened. "If you want an audience with the king, I can grant it to you. Consider it one of my first priorities when we arrive."

She shook her head, "I don't want your help if it comes at a price."

"And what about these strangers you're sailing with? You trust them to help you?"

"They're not strangers-"

"What are they then? *Friends?* I've seen the way Duke Aurelius looks at you and there is no friendship there."

"They are helping me of their own accord," she argued, "with no strings attached."

"Are they really? What do you truly know about them? How do you know they didn't plan this entire scheme just to get you on board?"

"I'm an orphan with no memories of my past. They are the only people who have given me some hope of finding out who I am." Cecilia snapped.

The creases on Alistar's forehead deepened into a frown.

"So, you'll really trust these strangers you barely know, over someone who's known you your whole life?"

"Yes."

"Why?"

"Because they're not asking anything from me."

His pouted at the window. If it weren't for the blonde scruff lining his jaw, she might've thought him a petulant adolescent.

"You know I care about you," he frowned at the floor. "I do not think I'm asking much."

Only my whole life! She wanted to scream. Instead, she took a breath, measuring her words.

"You're asking me for something I'm not ready to give," her voice was steady. "Not to you or anyone else."

He rubbed his face in frustration.

"Will you think about it at least?"

No, she thought.

They were interrupted by a knock at the door

"Cecilia, are you awake?" Jeremy called from the other side.

"Yes. Come in," she said, ignoring Alistar's annoyed expression.

Jeremy stepped into the room, Bella trailing him with a covered tray. The smell of freshly fried bananas permeated the room. She hoped no one heard her stomach rumble.

"We brought fresh bandages," Jeremy greeted.

"And breakfast," Bella added organising a tray table over Cecilia's lap.

"Thank you," Cecilia flashed them a relieved smile. She turned to Alistar.

"If you'll excuse me, my bandage needs to be fixed up again and I know how you get around blood."

Alistar nodded, a grim set to his jaw as he rose. He flashed a wan smile at Bella and Jeremy, not bothering to utter a word of greeting. Cecilia watched him leave, if only to make sure he disappeared.

"What did he want?" Bella asked.

Cecilia shrugged, stabbing a banana slice.

"Nothing important."

***

Marcus was in trouble.

He knew it before Catalina called him into her office after catching him creeping out of the medic's cabin late at night. Again. He had only meant to check on Cecilia's recovery, but the five-minute check-ins had turned into hours long Calgarian study sessions.

Unfortunately for Marcus, his creeping about the deck did not go unnoticed by the captain. Or the young ambassador.

"Sit down." Catalina ordered as he entered her cabin. She stood behind her mahogany desk pouring herself a drink.

Marcus raised a brow at the amber liquid as he sank into a wooden dining chair on the opposite side of her desk. Catalina rarely drank while on duty, and never before noon.

"Bit early for that isn't it?"

The captain narrowed her eyes at him, her mouth pursed into a thin line.

"Are you in any position to judge me just now? Do you know how hard I had to fight to keep Duke Alarcon from tossing you overboard?"

Marcus leaned back into the chair, folding his arms over his chest.

"I know he doesn't like me, but that's a bit dramatic, isn't it?"

He flinched as her hand hit the table, a collection of papers scattering onto the hard timber floor.

"You're flirting with his fiancée." Her voice rose to a shout.

Marcus scoffed, fighting an amused smile.

"You can't be serious. He's not claiming Señorita Cecilia is his fiancé is he?"

Catalina stared him down, clearly not in a joking mood. Marcus raked a hand through his hair, waves bouncing as he shook his head.

"I heard her reject his marriage proposal the night I helped her escape. If they somehow became engaged since then, I think she would've told me."

"Yes, because you've been so honest with her," Catalina retorted.

Silence hung in the air as she took a long, slow sip of her drink her gaze never wavering from her brother-in-law. Marcus' jaw clenched, all semblance of joviality disappearing.

"What are you implying, *captain?*"

She lifted a shoulder in a shrug.

"Have you found time in all of your gallivanting to tell her what you were really doing the night you helped her run away? Does she know you're only helping her to reclaim your father's inheritance?"

The chair banged on the ground as Marcus rose to his feet.

"My inheritance has nothing to do with this," he shot back. "I am simply upholding the oath I made to my king – to serve and protect the royal family."

"Yes, you seem to be doing a *fine* job of that," she said into the glass.

"What is *that* supposed to mean?"

She watched him for a moment, glass poised at her lips.

"Don't get distracted. Or did you forget the oath you made Marcus? The one you made me swear to never let you break."

His jaw tightened as he walked to the window. It was a wet dawn. The sea swelled unpleasantly beneath them, carrying them through grey water and gloomier skies. Sheets of rain barred their view from anything but the closest islands and even they were dark and foreboding.

Marcus clenched his fists by his side, leaning forward onto the cool reinforced glass panelling.

"I am not getting distracted," he grumbled, "I know my place."

"Do you?"

"*Yes,*" he hissed. "My duty is to serve and protect the crown. That is exactly what I'm doing."

"If I didn't know any better, I'd say your feelings are getting in the way."

"I've known her less than a month!" he scoffed. "You're acting as if I've fallen in love with her."

"Have you?

He paused, incredulous, "No!"

"Good," She crossed her arms, "then perhaps you can stop flirting with her and riling the young ambassador."

He shook his head slightly, rolling his eyes. Catching her hard stare, he huffed.

"I wasn't flirting, but I'll do as you say. Captain." He grumbled.

She bristled at the title. If it had come from anyone else, it wouldn't sound like an insult. His eyes glazed over, settling on the painting behind her.

"Am I free to go?" he asked.

Sighing, she nodded.

Marcus raised his hand in salute. Ever the soldier, he turned on his heel and marched out of the room. She watched him leave, fixing her eyes on the door he slammed behind him. She barely flinched as it shuddered against the frame.

Her glass squeaked against the timber as she twisted it on the table, the amber liquid as dull as the dawn before them. In the silence of the room, she almost believed him.

28

Friendly Advice

"Thought I might find you here."

Jeremy sidled up beside Marcus who turned from his viewpoint at the starboard railing, the cool breeze mussing the surgeon's dirty blonde hair.

"Mind if I join you?" Jeremy asked, not waiting for an answer as he leaned forward on the railing.

"I would be glad of your company," Marcus smiled.

In the days since gifting Cecilia the book, his nights were usually spent helping her with the language. Not surprisingly, she was a natural. A fact that only further cemented Marcus' assumption about her.

"How goes our patient?" Jeremy asked. "You seem to see more of her than I do these days."

"Good," Marcus nodded, "resting."

A soft tune floated from somewhere along the bow, Orren and Soren kept their nightly vigil on the flute and fiddle. Most of the crew had gone below, with only those on night watch keeping track of the ship.

Sebastian stood like a sentinel at the helm, his eyes set on the dark horizon glinting silver in the moonlight.

"You've been unusually attentive with her, haven't you?" Jeremy noted, a sly smile creeping onto his lips.

"Not you too," Marcus shook his head, "Like I told Catalina, I'm just doing my duty in keeping her safe. Well… as safe as I can."

"No one was expecting the arrow, Marcus. You shouldn't beat yourself up about that." Jeremy patted him on the shoulder.

Marcus shrugged. It had been all he could think about for days. Who would want to hurt Cecilia and why?

If Duchess Alarcon had known Cecilia was aboard the *Sorrento*, would she have tried to harm her? Or did the threat lie elsewhere? He frowned at the moon. He had discussed the incident with Catalina dozens of times and they were still no closer to an answer.

There was one possibility that kept gnawing at him. He shut it out of his mind. It would be treason to even think it.

"Do you have any theories on who could have wanted to hurt her?" he asked instead.

Jeremy shook his head. A blanket of stars twinkled above them, a welcome sight after many moonless nights.

"No one was really looking in all the chaos. Although, my theory is that if anyone was a target, it would have been Alistar."

"Can't argue with that," Marcus mumbled. "Being an ass can most definitely get you killed."

Jeremy's mouth quirked into a smile, "You don't get on well, do you?"

Marcus chuckled, "That is an understatement."

"I can understand why. He's not exactly a likeable character – but I've never heard you call someone an ass before."

Marcus lifted his shoulder in a half shrug.

"This wouldn't have anything to do with Cecilia, would it?" Jeremy nudged his shoulder.

"Why would it?" Marcus frowned at the shadowed horizon.

"I've seen the way you look at her. Oh, don't give me that look." Jeremy crossed his arms at Marcus' scowl. "In all our years sailing together, I have never seen you take such an interest in a young woman."

"I am only doing my duty," Marcus reiterated, "I am a soldier.

She is my charge. That is all."

"You've been praying for her since she got shot. I haven't seen you in prayer since Claudio died. Admit it, Marcus. You care for her."

Marcus' scowl deepened, "I like her enough to not want her to die."

"No man is an island Marcus," Jeremy ignored his friend's frosty glare, "It is not good for a man to be alone."

"Better to be alone than to cause someone pain," Marcus mumbled.

Jeremy's face fell as Marcus' words fell into place.

"Just because your father and brother left behind widows doesn't mean you should close yourself off. Love is a risk we must all take."

"And you're going to take that risk with Arabella? Despite your father's thoughts on the matter?" Marcus challenged.

Jeremy reeled as though Marcus had hit him. His concerned hazel eyes turned dark under the moonlight.

"Love is something you fight for. But why would I expect you to understand? You've closed yourself off to it for so many years I shouldn't be surprised you don't recognise when it's staring you in the face." Jeremy pushed off the railing.

Marcus didn't bother watching his friend leave. Instead, he turned back to the ocean, listening as Jeremy's footsteps faded into the night, the flutist's serenade following suit.

Silence stretched out before him and before he realised the late hour, he was alone. Just like he wanted.

29

An Unwelcome Surprise

The soft click clack of knitting needles filled the medic's cabin as Bella attempted to teach Cecilia how to knit.

"You loop the thread around the needle like so, then you pull it back, loop the needle again and pull," she said demonstrating.

Cecilia attempted to copy her with little success, her thoughts wandering to a glittering palace. Jeremy had given her a sleeping draught to help with the pain, but with it came nightmares, or memories, she wasn't sure which. Her uneven rows fell into a heap on her lap.

"Have you ever tried sewing?" Bella set down her needles.

"Frida made me take up embroidery one summer," Cecilia leaned back against her pillows, "with about as much success as we're having now."

Bella frowned, "Nothing is enjoyable when you're being forced to do it."

Cecilia nodded, picking up the needles again. She wasn't sure what to do with them, but it felt nice having something in her hands.

"If you don't mind my asking, what was it like living with Doña Alarcon?" Bella asked, continuing with her knitting. "My sisters live near Cova Rafael. They tell me she is a tyrant in her household, but hardly anyone from the village knows anything about her aside from the fact she is the king's rumoured mistress."

Cecilia shrugged.

"She is certainly temperamental. I never knew what mood she would be in when I walked into a room. Sometimes she would blatantly ignore me, other times she would chastise me for simply existing." She fiddled with the woollen threads in her lap. "When the king came to visit, she would be the most reasonable person in the world, but when he left, she would be unpredictable."

"That seems like a nightmare," Bella glanced up from her needlework.

"I don't remember any different."

Cecilia had been so used to Frida's iciness; she couldn't remember a time the duchess was genuinely happy to see her. Even when Frida had adopted her from the orphanage, she didn't seem overly warm.

"And what about your parents? Do you remember much of them before you went to live with her?"

Cecilia picked up the knitwork again, if for nothing else than to avoid seeing the concern in Bella's big brown eyes. She looped the needle through the yarn again, brows furrowed in concentration.

"Not much," she shrugged. "Frida figured I must've hit my head or something in the orphanage that gave me some sort of childhood amnesia."

"Did she ever bring you to a physician about it?"

"Not that I can remember."

"Do you miss your parents?"

Cecilia frowned at the uneven row, "Can't miss what you can't remember."

Bella opened her mouth to speak again when a cheer erupted outside the door.

"What's going on?" Cecilia asked, setting the knitting in her lap.

Bella frowned, "I'm not sure. Only one way to find out."

Cecilia sat cautiously on the cot as Bella opened the door. She could only make out a wall of bodies gathered around something on the deck. Another cheer erupted as Bella spoke with one of the deckhands. She turned back to Cecilia, eyes shining with excitement.

"It's a duel!" she squealed.

"A what?"

She rushed over and tugged Cecilia off the bed by her good arm.

"Come and see!"

Cecilia followed her friend through the crowd to the front of the spectacle.

The sun blazed above them as the crew formed a tight knit semi-circle on the starboard deck, the railing making up the other border. Two men circled each other, their swords angled to the sky.

Under the golden sun, she could see the sweat glistening on Sebastian's dark skin. His opponent kept his back to her, one arm poised behind him. She cringed at the sound of metal grating on metal as the swords slid against each other.

In a flash, Sebastian lunged forward, his opponent stepping back just in time to miss the tip of the sword. Cecilia's heart fluttered as she recognised Marcus, his mouth curving into a smirk before making a quick thrust at Sebastian.

Despite the swarthy man's height and obvious strength, he was not quite quick enough to parry the attack. His shirt sleeve caught the brunt of the blow, followed by another quick attack from Marcus' sword.

It was a friendly match, Cecilia realised, as the pair exchanged wits as well as blows.

"You fight like my sister," Sebastian teased.

"Then maybe you should measure up!" Marcus quipped back.

The crowd laughed in assent. Marcus' lips twitched into a satisfied smile, though his gaze never wavered from his opponent. Marcus stepped away from Sebastian, both men waiting for an opening.

Sebastian swung first, his aim strong and true, but Marcus leaned back, bringing his arm up to parry the blow. He swung again, the clash of metal ringing in her ears while Marcus moved like lightning, his steps quick and sure. Before she could understand what was happening, Marcus spun, his sword raised against Sebastian's, as he stepped into the taller man's space, and in a blur, the edge of his sword was pressed against Sebastian's neck.

Sebastian's face broke into a grin as he patted Marcus on the shoulder. The crowd erupted in applause as Marcus lowered his sword, stepping away from his opponent. They bowed to the crowd the way she had seen actors do on the rare occasions she was allowed to accompany Frida to the theatre.

"Any more takers?" Marcus asked the crowd.

A murmur rippled through the audience before a voice piped up.

"I'll have a go."

Jeremy stepped into the circle, a hand resting on the scabbard at his waist. While he unsheathed the weapon like a soldier, the sight of the medic with a sword in hand was strange to Cecilia.

Marcus threw Jeremy a friendly smile, but even she could see the mischievous glint in his eye as they took their positions.

The duel wore on for longer than she thought. Jeremy was a surprisingly able swordsman, parrying Marcus' attacks and reading his penchant for short, sharp blows. She found herself unable to take her eyes off Marcus, his movements flowing gracefully into each other like a dancer. The swords flashed silver under the sun, their blows ringing in her ears.

Sweat glistened on Marcus' tan brow as he measured his opponent, both steady on their feet as they kept a respectable distance between them. Eventually, Marcus struck first, finding an opening. Jeremy tried to put distance between them but it was too late. With a flick of his wrist, Jeremy's sword flew out of his hand, clattering to the floor, as Marcus brought his sword up to Jeremy's neck.

A strange rush of pride swelled in her chest as Marcus handed Jeremy his sword, clapping him on the shoulder. Jeremy said something too low for her to hear, but the laughter on his lips showed there was no ill will from being bested in the fight.

"Is anyone else brave enough to try and best this man?" Jeremy challenged the crowd.

"I am."

Cecilia's heart dropped.

Alistar moved through the gathering, his gait measured as he reached the front. The smile died on Marcus' lips as he surveyed Alistar.

"Do you have a sword?" Sebastian asked, stepping out from the edge of the crowd.

Alistar shook his head. Cecilia thought he should be at least a little sheepish about it, but he seemed as confident as ever.

Sebastian unsheathed his sword from its scabbard, handing it to Alistar.

"Just promise you won't break it," he forced a smile.

Alistar nodded.

"If you need to back out, you can do so at any time," Marcus said as he took up his position.

"You would do well to remember that." Alistar countered.

They angled their swords to the sky, their blades grating against each other.

"Care to make this interesting?" Alistar asked.

"That was the initial plan," Marcus countered, "but I have a feeling you'll try to bargain anyway."

Alistar's glare was almost as hard as the steel in his hand. "If you win, I'll stop complaining about you to Captain Catalina."

"Seems fair," Marcus tested Alistar's blade, "And if you win?"

Alistar angled his face away from the crowd, but she could hear the satisfactory smile in his voice.

"You will stop hanging around my fiancée."

Cecilia felt the weight of every pair of eyes on her, scrutinising her every move.

"We're not engaged!" she protested.

Bella shot her a pained glance.

"I never agreed to marry you," She called again.

Despite the quiet murmur of the crowd, Alistar didn't seem to hear her. Marcus however, did. He glanced at her, his mouth set in a firm line. It was the opening Alistar needed. He swung his sword at Marcus, who momentarily distracted, was a touch too late to block the blow.

Alistar's sword cut through Marcus' shirtsleeve, but no blood rose to colour it. Marcus recovered quickly, striking Alistar's blade. He wasn't quite quick enough to parry another attack.

This time the duke's blade nicked the side of Marcus' shirt harmlessly to reveal a lean, tan bicep.

Cecilia's heart leapt when Marcus finally managed a blow of his own, slicing Alistar's shirtsleeve. Alistar hissed through his teeth, blood blooming on his free arm.

"You'll pay for that," Alistar spat.

"You'll have to catch me first," Marcus smirked.

He sidestepped Alistar, whose next thrust caught only the ocean breeze. He stumbled forward, past Marcus who tapped him on the bum with the flat side of his sword. A guttural growl followed as Alistar straightened himself up, slashing his sword in Marcus' general direction.

Marcus rolled on his feet, making sure to keep a careful distance from Alistar, like a lion waiting to strike. When he was close enough, Marcus flicked his wrist, the force of his sword catching Alistar by surprise.

The crowd bayed at the spectacle as both men fought for the upper hand. Marcus was by far the better swordsman, his steps sure and graceful but Alistar was able to hold his own.

Everything happened too quickly for Cecilia to comprehend. One minute, Marcus had the upper hand as Alistar stumbled backward. He fell flat on his back, his sword clattering to the ground. Then, before she could blink, Alistar swept Marcus' feet out from under him. Marcus lost grip of his sword. Before he could reach it, Alistar pushed it away. Marcus scrambled for control, bunching Alistar's shirt collar at his throat, his fist poised to strike.

"*No!*" Cecilia surged forward.

Marcus paused, his fist frozen in the air. It took him a moment to focus on her before he began to lower his hand. A sword appeared at his throat. Alistar had managed to reach one of the blades, pressing the sharp edge against Marcus' neck.

"I believe this makes me the winner," Alistar declared.

A quiet rage threatened to bubble over Cecilia as she met his smug grin. She almost regretted not letting Marcus punch him, except for the overwhelming desire to punch him herself.

Marcus leaned back slightly, pushing the sword away from him with a finger. He glared at Alistar through stony eyes. The duke did not seem to care.

A polite applause rippled through the crowd as some of the crew exchanged coins.

"Now, according to our little exchange, this means you must stop hanging around my fiancée." Alistar smirked.

"I never agreed to any such thing." Marcus hissed, picking his sword up off the floor.

"I am not your fiancée." Cecilia argued.

Alistar shrugged, meeting her gaze. "You will be."

It was all she could do not to slap some sense into him.

"What part of the word no, don't you understand?"

"What part of 'you don't have a choice' don't you understand?" he countered.

White hot rage boiled in her veins as he sauntered off, the crowd quickly dissolving behind them. Cecilia followed him to the mouth of the galley, Marcus hot on her heels.

"What do you mean I don't have a choice? I never agreed to marry you. What part of that is incomprehensible to you?"

Alistar whirled on her, pointing his sword in her direction. She took a wary step back, into Marcus.

"You were right about what you said before. You have no dowry, no connections and no prospects. If you want to find your parents, your best chance is finding someone who knew them, through my connections. If we marry, I can grant you unlimited access to the people and resources that you need."

"And who are you to make that choice for her?" Marcus demanded.

Her heart quickened as he laid a protective hand on her injured arm, his sword poised under Alistar's chin. The air rippled with tension so thick, it could break with a quick flick of his blade.

"Like I said," Alistar straightened, "Cecilia has little in the way of means to find her parents. I am her best chance. There is no other choice."

"You're wrong," Marcus countered, "there is always a choice."

She could tell be the set of Alistar's jaw he was about to say something stupid.

"Fine," she said before she could think better of it, "if I agree to your terms, will you stop behaving like a child?"

A grin spread across Alistar's face as he dropped his sword. The clatter of metal on timber rang in her ears like a funeral bell.

Marcus' fingers pressed into her arm, just below her wound. For once, she didn't mind the pain.

"You don't have to do this," he said in a voice so low only she could hear.

She turned to face him, his brows furrowed as his soft brown eyes searched hers.

"We can help you," he squeezed her arm again gently, "no strings attached."

The breeze picked stray strands of her hair as she shook her head.

"He's relentless. He won't stop until he gets what he wants. Better to give in to him now than drag the fight on."

Marcus shook his head.

"You deserve better than this."

'*You deserve better than him*,' the words hung in the air between them.

It took a few heartbeats for her to break his gaze.

"I will help you get out of this. I can connect you to King Lars without Alistar's help."

She shook her head, a sad smile playing on her lips. "I'm sorry," she whispered, releasing herself from his grip.

"Come now, Cecilia," Alistar called from the bottom of the galley ladder, "let us celebrate my victory with a nice bottle of bubbles."

Turning away from Marcus, she forced her face into a mask of neutrality. It took all her resolve not to look back at him until she reached the bottom rung. When she glanced back, he stood in the same spot she had left him.

Watching.

Waiting.

30

Storm's Brewing

"Why did you do that?" she demanded, following Alistar to his quarters on the first level of the galley.

"Isn't obvious?" he opened the door to his cabin.

"No, it isn't." Cecilia stomped inside.

He gestured for her to sit on the bed pushed against the far wall, sunlight streaming in from the small porthole window above. Instead, she stood to the side, disturbing a pile of papers stacked atop a heavy wooden desk.

Alistar fished for something in a sturdy timber trunk by the door. He emerged triumphant with a bottle of wine and two silver tumblers.

"What else was I supposed to do to make him stay away from you?" He popped the cork, making a mess of the sticky bubbles.

"Maybe I didn't mind his company. Did you ever think about that?" she scowled.

Alistar poured the drinks, his pale brows knitting together.

"You should stay away from him," he offered her a tumbler "he's not who you think he is."

She took it, setting it down on the desk beside her.

"Oh, and you know so much about him now, do you?"

The bottle wobbled on the desk as he set it down, all semblance of celebration forgotten. A flash of something dark crossed his face. In that moment, he reminded her of Frida before she flew into a temper. The steely calm before the storm.

His brown eyes narrowed as he moved deliberately to stand in front of her. She froze under his hard gaze. His breath was hot on her face, sending an uncomfortable tingle down her spine.

"I know more about him than you do. Trust me when I tell you to stay away."

"I am not your plaything," she willed her voice not to tremble. "Why should I listen to you?"

"Because he's dangerous."

So are you, she thought.

"I'm going to need more reason than that," she said instead. "I already know he's good with a sword."

She nodded at the bright red stain on his shirtsleeve. Jeremy would see to it later. She was in no mood for compassion.

"He is not the man he claims to be," Alistar argued. "The man who held the Dukedom of Reddan died twenty odd years ago. This man-"

"Marcus," she filled in.

"-is an imposter."

Cecilia lifted her eyes to the dark stained timber ceiling.

"I know he's not a real duke. I found out the night I met him."

"Then you should know better than to take him at his word."

"He's delivered me safely thus far."

Alistar glanced pointedly at her injured arm.

"I beg to differ."

She held his gaze.

"He told me he could arrange for me to meet King Lars, without needing to marry him. Unfortunately, I cannot say the same for you."

Alistar stopped pacing for a moment. He rested a fist on the desk, bumping the bottle.

Glancing down, she noticed a path worn into the tapestried rug underfoot.

"I gave you time and you have not given me an answer. What else was I supposed to do?"

"Wait for me instead of making assumptions. It's been less than a week."

He slammed a clenched fist on the wall beside her, "You said you would think about it."

"I did," her voice was barely more than a whisper.

"Well?"

She fought to keep her balance as the ship dipped on a rough wave. Alistar was temperamental at the best of times, but she had never been the subject of his wrath. Would he strike her if he didn't like her answer?

"If you say nothing, I'll take your silence as a yes." He continued.

Marcus' words flashed in her mind.

You deserve better than this.

She shook her head at Alistar, her heart thundering in her chest.

"I will not marry," her voice came out stronger than she felt. "Not you, not anyone. Not until I find out the truth of my parentage."

"But why?" he whined.

"Because," she straightened herself against the wall, "I have a right to know myself and share who I am with others. This is something I must do alone. Who would I be if I tied my identity to a husband?"

"But you'll tie your identity to your parents?" he stepped away from her.

"Right now, I do not know if I'm a princess or a pauper," she wished he could understand. "If I am a princess, I will have duties and responsibilities outside of myself. My identity will lie with my country and be crafted for me. I must find a place within that. If I am a pauper, I will be free of such things. But I will still try to find out who I am."

"You don't have to live as a peasant," he burst. "You can marry me and be a woman of luxury!"

"What if I don't want that life?"

He frowned, hurt. His outstretched hands fell to his sides, "What do you mean you don't want it?"

Cecilia sighed, "What I mean to say is that I would like to take some time to find out who I am. To reevaluate my life as it is, without having to keep someone else's expectations in mind."

"So… does this mean you will never marry?"

She shook her head. Her injured arm throbbed after banging it against the wall.

"If I marry, I want it to be by my choice, not because I was forced into it."

"I didn't say I was forcing you," he mumbled, picking up his tumbler.

"You didn't give me much of a choice," she leaned against the wall with her good arm.

He was silent while he downed his drink. The ship pitched dangerously beneath them, knocking her into the edge of the bed. Alistar caught her, drawing her up with him.

His fingers dug into her forearms to steady her. Bile rose in her throat. Would her head ever stop spinning?

"I'm trying to keep you safe, Cecilia," he murmured above the wind whistling outside, "Because I love you."

Her throat constricted at the earnestness in his voice. She took a useless step backwards into the wall. The room closed in on her as Alistar planted his arms on either side of her, the opened bottle spilling onto the tapestried rug beneath them.

"I don't wish to be parted from you."

His piercing gaze flicked between her eyes and her mouth. His lips skimmed her ear as she ducked under his arms.

"I'm sorry Alistar, but I do not care for you the way you want."

He looked as though she had slapped him.

"Don't tell me you've fallen in love with that rogue." He spat.

"I'm not-"

"He's a good for nothing scoundrel who will break your heart. And don't think of running to me when the time comes - because it will - and I'll treat you with the same carelessness you're treating me with now."

"Alistar I'm not in-"

He twisted to face her, his lips peeled back in a sneer. In the grey light of the cabin, he reminded her of Frida. She stumbled back, groping for the door.

"Have you considered why he appeared in Villa Alarcon the night you disappeared? Do you have any idea why he might have helped you run away?" he demanded.

She shook her head.

"I haven't had much time to."

Alistar's mouth twisted at the side.

"Don't you think it's strange that this random man from across the ocean just so happens to be at your birthday ball, with a ready escape out of the country?"

"What are you getting at, Alistar?"

"Don't be naïve, Cecilia. You are the lost princess of Calgaria. You can stop pretending you don't know."

She stared at him, open mouthed.

"What are you talking about?"

He shrugged casually, "Why else do you think a Calgarian nobleman – or whatever he is - has such a vested interest in you? Why do you think he put you on a boat to Calgaria and offered you no way of escape?"

"I'm going to Calgaria because it's as far away from your mother as I can get!"

"No. It's because he knows you are the real Princess Lilia. And I'll bet good money he's getting paid to deliver you to someone across the sea."

"Now you're talking crazy," she shook her head, "What proof do you have?"

"My mother was the one who stole you from the palace."

She balked at him. Was Alistar really admitting to her that his mother committed treason?

"How do you know?"

He picked up his drink, evidently enjoying her reaction as he drew the story out.

"She told me. I admit, I was sceptical at first. What reason would my mother have to kidnap a foreign princess? But when she told me her motive, well, it wasn't hard to believe."

Cecilia hesitated. She didn't want to ask, to give into Alistar's gloating, but she wanted – needed - to know what happened.

"Explain."

Her voice was barely audible over the rush of waves crashing against the hull. From the window behind Alistar, white foam splashed against the splotched glass. Silver light streamed through the grey clouds, briefly hiding the sun.

"When my mother was a young woman, she fell in love with a prince – my father. Her best friend's brother. Unfortunately, my father was promised to a foreign princess and Mother was left heartbroken. Until one day, two foreign princes came to Avinada to find a bride. The Crown Prince of Calgaria and his brother came to make an alliance. Prince Oslo did not seem to care much for Avinadan girls, but Prince Lars did.

"Mother was touted as a potential match for the younger prince. All seemed to be going well until her father became ill. Mother left the city to be with him when he died. When she came back, Prince Lars and Princess Minerva were engaged."

Cecilia's heart thundered in her chest. Alistar was obviously enjoying telling the story, and she could easily believe Frida's quest for revenge.

"The news was a blow to my mother who had now been left heartbroken twice," he continued. "She fought with Minerva, begging her to break the engagement, but the princess refused and cast her from the echelons of Avinadan society.

"She had to settle with Duke Alarcon, a widower twenty years her senior. She never got over the pain Lars and Minerva caused her, so when word reached her that they had had a daughter, Mother decided she would get her revenge."

"So... I was just a pawn in a game to her?"

"What do you think I am?" Alistar sipped at his drink.

The floor swayed beneath them, her trembling legs buckled at the unexpected tilt of the ship.

Cecilia's lungs burned in the stifling heat of the room. She needed to leave. Taking a deep breath, she fumbled at the door handle to steady herself.

"If this is all true," she managed, not quite meeting his eye, "why did she want me to marry Mario? He's a nobody in King Vicente's court."

"Because if my mother married you off to a lowly nobleman and presented you to the Calgarian court, she effectively cuts off your chance at marrying for political alliances."

The room pressed in around her as the ship groaned beneath them. The sun hid behind grey clouds, angry sea foam splashing against the window. Her heart beat so hard against her ribcage she was afraid it would jump out of her chest. Her fingers ached where they dug into the brass handle.

"I need to go. I need to... think," she gasped.

She half-expected Alistar to stop her. Instead, he watched with passive interest as she fumbled the door open, stumbling into the empty passageway. She pushed down the bile rising in her throat.

The smell of salt air and rain mingled on her tongue as she fumbled up the stairs, onto the deck. A cacophony of shouts, bangs and groans filled her ears as the crew fought to secure themselves.

A crack of lightning lit the sky above them, thunder rumbling through to her very bones. Without warning, the ship pitched to one side. Losing her footing, she stumbled into someone. She yelped as strong hands righted her.

"Where are you going?" Marcus yelled above the noise of the storm.

She drew back from him, her eyes darting frantically about the deck. Water spilled over the sides of the ship, gripping her heart with a new terror. Ahead of them, large waves swelled, the ship dipping dangerously into the unforgiving ocean. Surely, she hadn't come all this way to die?

"I'll take you back to your cabin. Stay there till the storm passes." Marcus yelled to be heard above the noise.

"Marcus!" Catalina shouted above him.

The captain stood at the helm of the ship, her mouth set in a thin line as she glanced between Marcus and the storm.

"In a minute!" he called back.

"We don't have a minute!"

He turned back to Cecilia, his hands gripping her shoulders.

"I'm taking you to the captain's cabin. Stay there," he ordered, his voice nearly drowned out by the crashing waves.

Cecilia's heart stilled as water rose over the side of the railing, splashing onto the deck. Trembling, she nodded, following him to Catalina's cabin.

"Stay inside until someone comes and gets you," he gave her hand a reassuring squeeze. "The last thing I want is to lose you."

Without another word, he turned back to the storm, leaving her alone in the captain's cabin. Thunder cracked overhead, demanding her attention as she retreated inside. Her scream was lost in the roar of the waves as the world crashed around her.

31

Hoist the Colours

Limbs aching from prolonged tension, Cecilia uncurled herself from the plush green sofa. The storm had spent itself, only the unsteady rocking of the ship serving as a reminder of the fray. The *Sorrento* broke through the tumultuous waves and into the shining sunlight.

Cecilia sighed in relief, her battered heart resuming a normal pace inside her chest. Her mind, no longer screaming from the terror of the storm, calmed enough to think.

She cast her eyes about the room. Papers which had been stacked neatly on Catalina's desk, were strewn messily across the floor. The roar of the wind had settled and soft rays of sunshine peaked out from behind fluffy white clouds.

Finding her footing, she gathered the papers from the floor, sifting them into neat piles on top of Catalina's desk. She hadn't meant to pry, but she skimmed the loose sheets of paper anyway, mentally marking Calgarian words she recognised, when a loose sheet fell to the floor.

She hadn't planned to read the paper as she picked it up, but it was hard not to notice the king's name, written in cursive black ink. To her surprise, the letter was in Avinadan.

Captain Catalina,

As discussed with Captain Cervantes, I am entrusting you to deliver my daughter Princess Lilia to Calgaria as soon as possible.

I understand she has been living in North Avinada for well over a decade, supposedly in the care of a duchess. I have not been able to substantiate this claim, but I trust you and Captain Cervantes will be able to find the truth.

As promised, once she is delivered home and you have obtained substantial evidence to prove her claim, you will be rewarded handsomely for your service.

Signed,

His Majesty King Lars V of Calgaria.

Cecilia covered her mouth with a hand as she read the words over again. If Alistar was right about her identity, Marcus and Catalina were not only ordered to bring her to Calgaria, they were also getting paid to do so.

The thin parchment slipped from her fingers, her heart racing as the words began to dawn on her. Alistar was right. She was the lost princess, the subject of legends and bedtime stories. So why had Marcus not told her outright?

A shout on the deck snapped her out of her thoughts, bringing her back to the task at hand. She rifled through Catalina's otherwise orderly desk, the storm making a mess of the contents in her drawers. An ink pot spilled onto a leatherbound journal, wetting Cecilia's fingers. She cursed under her breath, grabbing a white handkerchief to wipe her fingers. The ink clung to her skin.

She was beginning to give up hope when the ship rocked beneath her and a black box tumbled from the back of the drawer. The worn velvet was rough under her ink-stained hands. The silver lining peeled as she rubbed it gently with her thumb.

With trembling fingers, she flicked it open, laying its contents carefully on the desk.

The first scraps of paper didn't give her much information, the letters were foreign and the handwriting had faded with time.

She thumbed through the remaining slips of paper, leaving soft black smudges on the edges when she found something. It was a portrait of a woman and a young girl. They shared the same dark hair and serious features. The young woman looked no older than Cecilia did now. Though she wore a pale blue gown, her shoulders draped in a deep blue coat bearing the Calgarian royal symbol, she wore her hair in the classic Avinadan fashion, two long braids tumbling down her shoulders.

For a moment, Cecilia wondered who had painted her. Then she realised, the young woman in the portrait was not her – the little girl on her lap was. She had so few pictures of herself when she was a child, Cecilia almost forgot what she looked like. But the eyes gave her away. One hazel, one brown.

With trembling fingers, she flipped the portrait over. A woman's cursive handwriting greeted her on the other side.

Queen Minerva and Crown Princess Lilia of Calgaria.

Beside it, lay the chain Catalina had shown her when she'd first arrived, the golden lion's head glinted in the burgeoning sunlight.

The door banged open, revealing Catalina, Marcus and Sebastian drenched by rain and saltwater. Catalina's hand rested on the hilt of her sword; eyes narrowed in suspicion at the intruder.

"Señorita? What are you doing?" Marcus asked before Catalina could accuse her.

"Nothing," she lied, letting the portrait fall back into the box in front of her, stashing the necklace in her pocket with her other hand.

"What's that on my desk?" Catalina asked, removing her hand from her sword. Cecilia's throat tightened. She hadn't meant to snoop.

"It fell out of a drawer during the storm. I was just trying to put it back," she lied, fidgeting with the worn velvet.

"I'd appreciate it if next time you left the tidying up to me," Catalina frowned.

Cecilia nodded, stepping away from the desk. "Sorry," she mumbled.

Catalina opened her mouth to speak when a commotion erupted outside.

Sebastian and Catalina shared a glance before hurrying to the door.

Catalina paused, looking back at the captain.

"I expect you to be gone by the time I get back," she said.

She shot a pointed look at Marcus, who stood by the door, before rushing off.

"Care to tell me what all this is about?" he asked, raking a hand through his dark curls, flicking water onto his already soaked shirt.

"Why didn't you tell me I'm the princess?" she mumbled.

His brown eyes widened, "How could you possibly know that?"

"Because of this!" Cecilia held up the velvet box. "You knew I was the princess and you didn't tell me. Why?"

"It's not what you think."

She opened her mouth, anger rising in her throat when an urgent bell clanged outside.

"Pirates!" someone yelled, "Pirates ahoy!"

A new terror gripped her. Marcus swore, apologising quickly. He crossed the room in three quick strides, snatching her wrist and pulled her towards the door.

"Where are you taking me?" she demanded.

"We'll hide you in the infirmary. The pirate envoy must've seen us as we edged past the storm – Catalina sent word to them days ago that we needed to pass through. This should only be the greeting envoy to guide us past Puerto de Oro, but we don't want to take any chances," he explained as he led her out of the captain's cabin and onto the deck, still littered with debris from the storm. She tried to make sense of his answer.

Her stomach tied itself in knots as they drew closer to the medic's cabin. Despite the sun's reappearance, goosebumps ran down her arms.

"Ever since Pirate King Anders began his rule over The Fickle Islands, he laid claim to large swathes of sea to make up for the lack of land borders," Marcus explained. "He can't stand royal ships either, so he sends his own crews to examine any ship that sails past."

"What do they look for?"

"Anything of value. Precious metals, jewels and fresh food mostly, but we have nothing to worry about. Catalina has an amount set aside to pay them for admission to Puerto de Oro."

"He doesn't take anything else from the ships?"

Marcus shook his head, "Everything valuable on the *Sorrento* is secured and stored away. Sometimes his crews seek women to bring him."

"Oh."

"But I will not let any harm come to you," he promised. Despite her accusation moments earlier, his coffee-coloured eyes held no malice.

"Everyone on the deck!" An unfamiliar voice rang out across the ship.

"Do as he says," Catalina ordered.

"Stay close." Marcus squeezed her hand reassuringly as he led her onto the deck. A group of pirates swung from a galleon that had sidled next to the *Sorrento*.

Catalina stood in front of the pirate who had given the order, a young man who looked no older than twenty. His faded red tunic hung loose on his lean frame. A white shirt was tucked into dark pants, equally tucked into worn leather boots. An armoury hung on his belt, various daggers, swords and pistols sheathed on thick crocodile skin.

Sebastian stood like a sentinel at Catalina's shoulder, hand on the hilt of his sword as he watched the pirate take a turn about the deck.

Despite standing half a head shorter than Catalina, he regarded her casually. Cecilia stared in awe at his hair, the colour of ground paprika. She had never seen anything like it before.

Catalina's hand stayed planted on the sword at her belt as half a dozen pirates began spreading out on the deck.

"If anyone of your crew put up a fight, they'll be put to the sword." the young pirate said, his lips peeled back to reveal yellow teeth. He had addressed Catalina, but his words carried across the ship.

"Stand down," Catalina ordered her crew, most of whom stood in tense anticipation.

The young pirate, presumably the captain, snapped his fingers. In a flash, his men had surrounded the deck, knocking over barrels, ripping into sacks and overturning anything that had not been battened down. A trio of burly pirates made their way below decks, knocking down everything in their path.

"Before I forget," the young man turned back to Catalina, "Our fare?"

Cecilia watched as Catalina handed over a large pouch of coin. She glanced nervously at Marcus whose shoulders tensed as he watched the scene unfold, yet he stayed glued to the spot in the shadows of the cabin. The pirates had not spotted them yet.

Alistar's yelling tore her attention away from the young pirate who had seemed to notice her over Catalina's shoulder. A burly pirate dragged Alistar from the galley, a second leading Jeremy out, blood pooling from his lip.

"What's all this then?" the pirate asked, coming forward to survey the two young men.

Jeremy glanced nervously at Catalina as Alistar continued to struggle against the pirate.

"Do you know who I am? Do you know who my father is? I'll have you hanged for this," he yelled. The burly guard twisted Alistar's arm behind his back, causing him to grunt from the pain. The young pirate ambled over to the duke; his dirty blonde hair caught uselessly in his eyes.

"You must be Alistar Alarcon. I've heard much about you." The young pirate circled him.

Cecilia tensed, taking a small step back. Marcus attempted to shield her as best he could.

It was too late. The young pirate had seen them. His lips parted showing a mouth full of yellow teeth, a terrible gleam in his eyes.

Marcus stepped forward, one arm out to keep Cecilia behind

him.

"Ah, some undeclared passengers," the pirate greeted, ambling over to them, "and a pretty one at that."

"She is under the protection of King Lars of Calgaria," Marcus declared as the pirate approached them, his boots thumping on the timber floor. He hardly spared Marcus a glance as he pushed past his shoulder.

Cecilia's breath quickened as she stumbled back, her hand slipping out of Marcus' grip.

"You must be Cecilia Alarcon," the pirate said, "I have orders to bring you directly to my king."

"That was never part of the deal Skiv," Catalina called out, stalking over to him. Sebastian trailed her silently, his eyes firmly trained on Skiv.

Not looking back, Skiv snapped his fingers. Before Catalina could draw her sword, another pirate grabbed her arms, twisting them behind her back. She struggled against him, stomping her foot on the pirate's boot. He cried out, his grip loosening just in time for a second pirate to hold a dagger to her throat.

Skiv turned back to the captain, raising his voice to be heard above the racquet of his crew rifling through the ship's contents.

"Anyone who resists Pirate King Anders will be put to the sword. But... the king is not without mercy. If you let us take these palace dwellers to Puerto de Oro in peace, you will be given safe passage and a personal escort to Calgaria."

"No." Marcus shook his head, knuckles white on the hilt of his sword. "If you want her, you'll have to go through me."

Skiv turned slowly around to face Marcus before lunging at him with his dagger.

Marcus, who had been expecting the move, jumped out of the way, pushing Cecilia to the ground. She scrambled out of the way as metal screeched on metal.

Marcus swung to face Skiv, walking backward to the centre of the deck.

The pirates stopped what they were doing, both crews waiting with bated breath to see what the young men would do next.

Skiv snarled as the two men circled each other. It was the pirate who moved first. He lunged at Marcus who slipped past him, landing a blow on Skiv's shoulder. Blood gushed from his arm but Skiv did not cry out. Instead, he gritted his teeth and launched another attack.

From the corner of her eye, Cecilia saw Jeremy struggle against his guard. Sebastian raced forward only to be thwarted by another pirate who had appeared from seemingly nowhere.

As the fight between Marcus and Skiv carried on, she watched as more pirates swung from the galleon. Alistar protested against his guards, one of whom stuffed a rag in his mouth, the other pushing him to the portside guard rail where a gangplank had been erected between the ships.

Cecilia looked back at Marcus who had landed a few blows against Skiv, his dagger clattering loudly until it landed by her feet. Without thinking, she picked it up and tossed it overboard. Her joy was short-lived when unfamiliar hands clamped on her shoulders.

"Let me go!" she screamed as a burly man lifted her up over his shoulder.

"Cecilia!" Marcus yelled. She turned just in time to see his panic-stricken face as Skiv took advantage and landed a blow across Marcus' cheek.

A scream tore itself from her lips as she struggled against the arms that held her. The pirate only grunted and tightened his grip.

"Any more of that and you'll find yourself falling to yer death." grumbled a voice as thick as gravel.

Panicked, she stopped fighting as blue sea flashed beneath her.

"We have our bounty," a jubilant voice declared.

"Turn around now and we won't sink ya ship!" shouted another man, close to Cecilia.

The man who was carrying her set her roughly down onto

a timber deck. She turned around to see the *Real Sorrento*, one sail slashed in three diagonal splits.

Skiv had untangled himself from the fight, swinging back with a host of pirates onto the galleon's deck as the ship lurched forward.

Cecilia scanned the deck for any sign of Marcus and the others. She found him standing on the Sorrento's rail, his sword dangling from one hand, the other poised on the rope beside him.

Behind him, Jeremy tugged at his shirtsleeve. Even from this distance, she could see the fire in his dark eyes.

"Pitiful sight innit?" Skiv asked, sidling up to her, a small roll of rope in his hands.

Upon closer inspection, Skiv seemed younger than her, barely twenty, but the scarred cheeks and sun-weathered skin aged him.

"Who are you and where are you taking me?" she demanded, heart pounding in her chest.

"I'm Skivver, second in charge to Pirate King Anders. That's all you need to know," he said. "Now, if I leave your hands untied, how likely are you to hit someone?"

She jerked her chin up and looked him in the eye, trying to steady her trembling legs.

"I will fight you and your men until I am returned to my ship."

"Guess the ropes are staying on then," He snatching her hands, tying them in front of her. She struggled, wrists chaffing against the thick rope, but Skiv was an expert sailor and his knots would not come undone easily. Still, she felt better for trying.

"Raul, take the princess somewhere more comfortable. We reach land at nightfall." He shoved her into the arms of a wiry young man, with seedy eyes, his shirt hanging loosely from his thin frame. He flashed her a predatory grin exposing missing, yellowed teeth.

"If it weren't for King Anders' orders, we'd all be having a taste o'ya," he said.

Cecilia fought back tears as he pushed her across the deck and into the cramped captain's cabin.

'Please Ilio, if you're there, please, please get me out of here.'

32

For Whom the Bells Toll

The smell of burnt sugarcane, tobacco and alcohol pressed down on the pirate king and his company, as thick as the humidity that engulfed them.

Pirate King Anders reclined in his seat, his heavy leather boots propped up on the mahogany table in the centre of the room. His piercing blue eyes surveyed Duchess Alarcon, his face unreadable, as they waited for their final guest.

Count Sanchez sat beside the duchess topping up his glass with the pirate's house-made rum. She kicked her companion's leg under the table, only to earn a patronizing glare.

"So, you want to rule a kingdom?" Pirate King Anders broke the silence, a ring of smoke floating into the air as he huffed his cigar.

He didn't look like a king, Frida thought. He was barely thirty, with scruffy red hair and a blazing beard.

"Is that not everyone's dream?" she nodded, fidgeting with her skirt under the table. It took a lot to make her nervous, and despite her previous correspondence with the pirate king, he was more intense in person.

"Don Sanchez has told me about your goddaughter. Is it true what they say? That she is Princess Lilia?" He tapped the butt of his cigar into an old ashtray, resting on a bar stool beside him. Coloured bottles sat atop the shelf, each filled at various levels.

Frida inclined her head, but said nothing.

"He also said you wanted to use her status to rule by proxy." He continued. "Is that true?"

"It is true I wish to rule a kingdom," she said, choosing her words carefully.

He nodded.

"I cannot promise to give you Calgaria as it is not mine to barter, but if what your advisor told me is true and she is the lost princess, I can give you a stake in my kingdom... if you give her to me in marriage."

Frida unfurled her fan, batting the heat away. She raised it just enough to cover her satisfied smirk. One did not simply accept an offer of marriage, even from the pirate king.

"It is something I would consider." She inclined her head politely.

The Fickle Islands weren't Calgaria, but they had been enemies for time immemorial. Frida wanted to inflict as much pain on Lars and Minerva as possible.

Anders opened his mouth to speak when a young man swaggered into the room. He was not much younger than the pirate king, handsome in a foreign sense, and he carried himself with the ease and grace of someone used to power. An array of weapons hung from his belt, his long legs clad in finely stitched trousers. Frida decided it would be wise to hold her tongue.

"Ah," the pirate king grinned as he swept his feet from the table, standing to greet his guest, "if it isn't the future Crown Prince of Calgaria. How nice of you to join us."

Prince Derek smiled, clapping the pirate king on the back. He looked older than Frida imagined him, his ebony hair swept fashionably on his head. His blue eyes glinted with a hint of mischief in the grey afternoon light. He took a seat opposite Frida, his tall frame blocking her view of a stormy seascape in a golden frame.

"You've come just in time. I was about to offer the duchess a stake in my kingdom if she promised to hand over her goddaughter."

Derek cast his gaze lazily over her before turning to the pirate king, "Now, why would you do that?"

"Because," his eyes lit up gleefully, "I'm looking for a wife, and you're looking for a way to secure your birthright."

The Calgarian prince glanced back at Frida who met his cool gaze with a polite stare of her own.

"Explain," he ordered, like a man who was used to giving commands.

Frida bristled. She never liked being told what to do, especially when someone ordered her to do it. Still, she schooled her features into a friendly smile, keeping her tone light.

"My goddaughter Cecilia is your cousin, Princess Lilia. According to your law, she is the true heir to the Calgarian throne, at least until your investiture. She... ran away on the eve of her twenty-first birthday. I believe the man who helped her escape knows her true identity and may be trying to take her back to Calgaria."

Prince Derek ran a finger over his lip thoughtfully.

"How do you know she is the Calgarian princess? Many families have gone to my aunt and uncle to try and convince them that their daughters are the true princess. Why should I believe you?"

"Because we stole her from the palace, Your Highness," Mario blurted from beside her. Frida fought the urge to kick him under the table again.

The prince only raised an eyebrow at him.

In the heat, Mario's face turned an unsightly shade of red. Sweat clung to his thick brows, despite the breeze filtering in from the open window beside him. Grey roots began to show as the breeze tugged at his thinning hair.

Mario explained in great detail all that had transpired the night of Princess Lilia's disappearance. The young prince occasionally looked at Frida who continued to meet his gaze with a cool stare. She would not confirm or deny anything until the prince had dealt with Mario.

If Mario were to die for admitting to treason, she could blame her involvement on the ramblings of a madman. If the prince were to reward her however, that would be an entirely different matter.

She waited patiently as Mario finished, watching Prince Derek for any sign of hostility. Instead, she was met with passive interest.

"If I understand this correctly," Prince Derek said eventually, "you wished to present Princess Lilia to my uncle's court to claim her birthright, after marrying her off to this – count – so that you could rule by proxy?"

"That does seem to be the gist of the plan." Frida agreed.

"So how do you fit into this Anders?" Prince Derek turned to the Pirate King.

He shrugged, "I figured I could take Mario's place and marry Princess Lilia. That way I get a claim on her inheritance and your path to the throne is clear. She can't be the queen of two kingdoms."

Prince Derek leaned back in his chair, eyeing them thoughtfully.

"Now, hang on a minute," Mario burst, knocking over his chair as he flew to his feet, "What about me? Do I get a say in all this?"

"No," the pirate king declared. He leaned back in his chair, his long legs stretched out under the table. His hand fell to his waist. Frida recalled seeing a pistol hanging at his hip when he stood to greet the prince.

"What am I supposed to do then? Stand aside while you marry her? That's hardly fair. Come on Frida, tell them you won't do it."

Frida sighed. She had weighed the risks. Giving Mario Cecilia's hand was not the hill she would die on. Especially when a throne of her own, or part of one, was at stake.

"I think this new plan works better," she shrugged.

"Only because it works in your favour! You promised me a kingdom! Now you're going to leave me in the lurch? You conniving cow! You lying bi-"

A loud bang cut Mario's sentence short. He lurched to one side, his eyes bulging out of his red face. Like a stone, he fell to the floor, a crimson bubble spilling from his thin lips.

Frida turned back to the pirate king as he holstered his gun. The smell of gunpower filled the room.

"Well, that gets rid of that problem," he said, his tone matter-of-fact.

It took all Frida's strength to keep from looking down at Mario, sprawled on the ground. Pirate King Anders gestured to two men hidden in the corner of the room, who quickly wrapped Mario's body in a sheet.

She caught Prince Derek watching her and straightened herself. She would not appear ruffled. Instead, she focused on the painting behind Prince Derek as he and the pirate king entered another conversation, as though killing a man in polite company was a regular occurrence. Perhaps for the pirate king, it was.

Her thoughts were interrupted by a young man in ragged sailor's clothes bursting through the door.

The pirate king glanced at him and nodded. Unsure if the conversation was meant for her ears, Frida busied herself in admiring the room around her. A number of maps, faded weather reports and battle plans lay strewn about the room, both on tables and hanging on the walls. A crude tapestry of young women hung behind the pirate king at the head of the table, partially hidden by cabinets containing more liquor than a tavern.

The young man strode to the king's chair, conveying his message in a low voice. The pirate king nodded, waving his hand in dismissal before turning back to Frida.

"It seems you were right, Your Grace. The *Real Sorrento* has been intercepted and the young lady is now on her way here," he grinned.

Frida matched his smile.

"I suppose we ought to settle the terms of our deal then."

33

Rescue Plans

"Do you really need that may knives?" Catalina asked, from Marcus' shoulder.

"It doesn't hurt to be prepared," Marcus set three blades back onto the counter he'd picked them from.

At Catalina's raised brow, he unhooked one of the extra pistols from his waist.

"It's a suicide mission to do this alone." She leaned against the wall beside him, her arms and feet crossed in front of her.

"If I don't go now, who knows what he'll do with her?"

Catalina didn't need him to clarify who he was talking about. Hours had passed since the pirates had kidnapped Cecilia and the ship's sails had not been replaced. They had drifted along as far as the current could carry them, before the traitorous waves changed their course. Catalina was forced to drop the anchor while they readied the sails and waited for better conditions.

"Well, if there's one thing, I'm certain of," she said, eyeing him as he weighed a sword in his hand, "he won't kill her."

"There are some fates worse than death," Marcus said evenly, setting the weapon down.

Catalina lifted a shoulder in a shrug.

"Jeremy and Sebastian are at your disposal."

Marcus frowned.

"You didn't think I was going to let you do this alone, did you?" she asked.

"I don't remember telling you I had a plan."

"You didn't," her lips twitched into a slight smile, "but it's what Claudio would have done."

Marcus ran a hand through his hair, unsure what to say. He wished Claudio were here to help, to dive into this mission together. To watch his back.

"You know, I've been thinking about the oath you swore to me," Catalina continued. Marcus' hand hovered over a pouch of bullets. He forced himself to breathe, his heart booming in his ears as he waited for her next words.

"I've decided to renounce it and let you go."

"What?"

"I cannot promise to never let you fall in love. It's not fair to either of you."

He shook his head.

"You're mistaken *Captain*. I'm going after her because it is my sworn duty to protect the crown at all costs."

"You're about to sacrifice yourself for someone you care about. There's no greater love than that."

"Love or not, this is what I signed up for. What you signed up for as a naval officer. Don't start trying to lecture me about feelings at a time like this." He huffed, sheathing the bullets and tying them to a pouch on his belt

"Just because your father and brother died, doesn't mean their love wasn't worth having," she said gently.

Marcus checked his weapons again, shaking his head.

"What part of *this is my sworn duty* don't you – or anyone else on this heaven-forsaken boat – understand?"

Catalina frowned, pushing off from the wall. "She'll grieve you, you know, if you don't come back."

His mouth set in a firm line, "Better for her to mourn a soldier than a companion."

Catalina's eyes softened, despite the constant frown.

"Before I forget," she retrieved something from her trouser pocket, "take this."

She held out a long, carefully wrapped item. The cloth had faded to yellow over time, the hem frayed. Marcus reached for it carefully. It was a dagger, he realised. The silk slipped easily through his calloused fingers.

The white hilt was intricately carved with twin gold vines. The flash of polished silver glinted under the dim sunshine falling through the armoury's single window. A flame blade. He examined it carefully, the shape of it somehow familiar. Two C's entwined on the butt of the hilt.

Claudio and Catalina.

The dagger, though light, turned to lead in his hand. His brother's memory weighed heavily on his mind. Could he live up to Claudio's expectations? Could he live up to his own?

"This is Claudio's dagger," he said, his anger dissipating. "Why are you giving me this?"

"I'm trusting you to bring it back to me." Catalina curled his fingers around the hilt.

Her eyes shone under the pale sunlight. He couldn't remember the last time he had seen her cry.

"I will. I promise," he vowed.

The captain cleared her throat and straightened her jacket.

"You should get going. Sebastian and Jeremy are waiting for you."

Marcus cleared his throat and attached the dagger to his belt.

"Thank you, captain."

She waved him off, "Don't thank me yet. We still have a mission to complete."

"Of course. Someone has to keep you and Sebastian on your toes." His lips curved into a smile. She rolled her eyes, but matched his smile. With a casual salute, he turned on his heel and strode out of the armoury, taking the steps two at a time until he was met by the early afternoon air.

Grey sunshine bathed the deck as the sun peeked out from behind lazy clouds. He found Jeremy and Sebastian standing in front of a lifeboat on the portside of the ship. Bella stood with Jeremy, her soft brown eyes filled with concern when Marcus approached. Sebastian meanwhile stood stoic, nodding once at Catalina when she appeared behind Marcus.

"There you are," Jeremy greeted. "We thought we'd have to start rowing without you."

"By all means, feel free," Marcus gestured at the boat.

"Orren and Sorren will go in as back up if you need," Catalina assured them, before Jeremy could formulate a reply.

The twin sailors stood close by, waiting for their next instructions.

"How long until the sails are repaired?" Marcus asked instead, nodding at the mainmast. The sails had been torn in multiple places as the pirates swung back to their ship, leaving the *Sorrento* stranded.

"At least a few hours," Bella supplied. "My uncle and the sailmakers have already started work on repairing the mainsails, but the pirates seem to have stolen our spare sail as well."

"Not that you need to concern yourself with that just now," Catalina gestured at the boat Sebastian was already standing in. "Right now, you need to focus on bringing Cecilia back to the ship as quickly and safely as possible. Sebastian will brief you on anything I missed."

"If we're not at the docks by sunset, Catalina will meet us in Cova Zafiro at sunrise," Sebastian added as Marcus and Jeremy climbed into the boat which rocked unsteadily beneath them.

"Try not to get in any more trouble," Catalina ordered as Sebastian and Jeremy worked the ropes to lower the boat.

"I think it's a bit late for that now," Marcus frowned.

They hit the water with a jolt, the dark waves rising up to meet them. Taking up positions, the three men rowed together towards the twinkling horizon of the Fickle Islands, leaving the *Real Sorrento* fading into the distance.

34

The Fickle Islands

The sun glared from behind filthy clouds as Skiv shoved Cecilia into the captain's cabin. Men's shouts filled the air as the ship surged forward. The door slammed behind them.

"Sit," he gestured at a cramped dining table to one side of the room. A single, unmade bed stood on the other side; an equally untidy desk butted beneath it. A tiny sofa sat opposite.

Gathering her dignity, she straightened her skirt and sat at the table. Skiv took a seat beside her, producing a dagger from his belt.

The pirate's silver blade glinted under the sunlight streaming from the floor to ceiling windows at the back of the room.

"We're going to play a little game," he motioned to the dagger, laying it flat on the table. "You're going to tell me who you really are and I'll try not to scar your pretty little hands."

Cecilia curled her fingers into fists on the table, determined not to let him see her trembling. But Skiv was quick and snatched a hand, forcing it flat on the table. With a yelp, she struggled against him as he picked up the dagger.

"Please, don't. Stop. Please," she begged, hot tears welling in her eyes.

"Stop squirming. You'll only increase your chances of losin' a finger if you try to move."

Chest heaving, she stopped struggling, but her hand still trembled on the hardwood.

"Good," Skiv nodded, satisfied by her stillness. Her fingers shook as she pressed them into the sticky hardwood. Skiv picked up the dagger, holding the hilt in a fist. Cecilia didn't know much about daggers, but she knew you weren't supposed to hold them like that unless you were prepared to stab something. Her stomach dropped to her boots.

"Rules are simple. You tell me the truth, I won't hurt you. If you lie, or if you move, you're liable to taste metal. Got it?"

Cecilia gritted her teeth. She had tasted more than enough metal for one journey. Gripping the fabric of her skirt with her free hand, she nodded.

"Good," he flashed her a grim smile, "we'll do this slowly at first. Then quicker as the questions progress."

"Why are you doing this?" she mumbled, desperation overriding her fear.

He cocked his head to one side, his breath warm on her face as he poised the dagger for action.

"King's orders. Anything else?"

She thought for a moment, "How did you know who I was? Or where to find me."

"Your godmother's lucky guess," he looked at her hand, "or rather, not so lucky."

Cecilia swallowed the tears rising in her throat as Skiv took up the weapon and began stabbing it between the gaps of her fingers. The gentle *thud, thud, thud*, echoed in her ears, picking up the pace with each question.

"Who are you?"

"I am Cecilia Alarcon, ward of Duchess Frida Alarcon."

"Are you sure?"

"Yes."

"I think you're lying," Skiv sang as metal sliced the side of her finger. She yelped, pulling her hand back, but Skiv was stronger. He held her hand firmly on the table, the breath of the knife sent shivers down her spine. Steeling herself, she gripped her skirt harder, gritting her teeth against the pain as blood pooled between her fingers.

"My name is Cecilia Alarcon-"

"Is it? *Your Highness*," he sneered.

"My name is Princess Lilia," she tried, "Daughter of King Lars and Queen Minerva of Calgaria."

"Much better."

The knife thudded into the wooden table, missing her finger by a hairsbreadth.

"Why did you escape from Villa Alarcon?"

That was easy.

"I did not wish to marry Duchess Alarcon's advisor, Mario Sanchez."

"And who are your travelling companions?"

She hesitated. On the one hand, she did not want to give up Marcus' identity. On the other hand, she didn't want to lose a finger.

"Duke Aurelius and the Calgarian ambassadorial crew."

She braced herself as much as she could against the cold kiss of metal on her skin. Still, the pain surprised her.

"Wrong answer."

She hissed as blood bloomed from a second finger.

The *thud, thud, thud* of the blade beat in time with her heart.

"He said his name was Marcus," she choked out. "He helped me escape."

"What does he want with you?"

She swallowed, teetering on the edge of her seat as she steadied herself against the table.

"I don't know..." she stammered, lungs burning.

"You're running out of fingers," Skiv lifted the dagger higher.

"To bring me to King Lars and Queen Minerva," Cecilia burst, heart hammering in her throat. Any more of this and she might bring up her breakfast.

"Why?"

"To present me as the lost princess."

"And..?"

Skiv's hand was a blur over her own. She wondered how long he could keep this up without nicking her by accident. Warm blood stuck to her fingers, staining them scarlet. Briefly she wondered if it were possible to bleed to death from one's hand.

"To claim a reward? Money, land, I don't know. But the king said he would reward them with something."

"How do you know this?"

"I saw a letter from him on the captain's desk. I was looking for something else and saw he had signed it."

The dagger clattered on the table, the blade nicking the edge of her wrist. She flinched, drawing back her hand. This time, Skiv released her, handing her small grey rags.

"Very well. Two out of five ain't bad," he nodded as she fumbled with the cloth. "I'll get the medic's kit and clean ya up. The king didn't want ya marked too much."

She sank into her chair, clutching her hand close to her chest. The silence of the room filled the air as she focused on the galloping beat of her heart.

Sea foam sprayed against the window outside. If she squinted hard enough, she could imagine the silhouette of the *Real Sorrento* sitting stationary against the dull silver waves, shrinking further into the horizon.

She was sure the ship would have caught up to them by now. What else did Skiv's men do? She doubted Marcus would let her get away so easily. They couldn't claim their reward without her.

She slammed her good fist onto the table. Maybe Alistar had been right about the lot of them, Marcus especially. She had thought differently of him. He had been so accommodating to her on the ship — was that because he knew who she was the whole time?

And what of Bella and Jeremy? Had they befriended her under

false pretences too? Bella was so sweet it didn't seem likely, but how well did she really know any of them after a few weeks?

By the time Skiv came back with the medical supplies, a second pirate in tow with a tray of food, she was ready to hurt someone.

"Where are you taking me?" She flinched as the taller pirate took her hand in his big brown paws.

He was surprisingly gentle for a man who looked so intimidating. He was about Sebastian's height, but broader, his grey shirt stretched to its limit around beefy arms. Where Sebastian was tall and muscular, this man was thick and stout, his shoulders hunched like a bear. His shaggy dark locks fell into his eyes as he reached for a bandage.

Skiv grinned, hands on his hips as he watched the burly pirate work on her hands.

"The Fickle Islands, princess. Home."

"Your home, perhaps. Not mine."

Skiv shrugged, "It will be soon enough."

Pain exploded in her free fist as she slammed it into the table. Neither man flinched at the sound. Skiv raised an expectant brow at her while the brawny pirate pasted a poultice to her cuts. She hissed at the sting.

"Tayen will attend your physical wounds. Perhaps food will balm your emotional ones," Skiv nodded at a small, round tray on the table.

Seething silently, she watched Skiv saunter out of the room, leaving her alone with this strange pirate. Her traitorous stomach rumbled, echoing in the silence of the room.

"You should eat, Miss," Tayen mumbled, his attention never wavering from the bandage he tied around her fingers, "I'll be done in a tick."

She eyed him warily. Tayen barely glanced from his work.

"It's not poisoned if that's what you're thinking. You'd be no use to the king dead," he paused, "D'you want me to see to ya shoulder?"

She raised a brow at him puzzled.

"How did you know about that?"

"Your bandage has come undone." He motioned at the stray piece of bandage peeking from her elbow. She'd rolled her sleeves up, a slight reprieve from the afternoon heat.

Cecilia hesitated. Jeremy had only tied her bandage when she was unconscious. Since then, for the sake of decency, she had Bella help her. Despite Tayen's gentle manner, he was still a pirate. Pirates weren't decent men.

She shook her head.

"You've got short shirtsleeves. If you pull it up, I can manage. I wouldn't press, but ya bleedin'."

Cecilia looked at her arm. He was right. A trail of red blood bloomed above her elbow. She didn't have a choice.

"Thank you," she mumbled, pulling her sleeve up as far as it would go.

Tayen nodded gently unwinding the bandage, "Your welcome, Highness."

***

It was almost sunset by the time *The Happy Dagger* was within sight of the Fickle Islands.

"You 'right miss?" Tayen had asked after he finished bandaging her shoulder again. She moved her arm and flexed her hands, muscles taut against the firm fabric.

"Yes," she nodded, "thank you."

She caught the beginnings of a shy smile as he turned away. Against her will, she was beginning to like him. She appreciated that he didn't stare at her like the others, nor did he make any wayward comments. In fact, he barely spoke at all.

A slight chill hung in the air, despite the clear skies and afternoon heat. Stars twinkled in the heavens even before the sun bled into the horizon. Tayen shielded her from the prying eyes of the crew as they walked to the bow of the ship. He didn't say much, which she was grateful for. She wasn't in the mood for conversation.

The warm glow of the city greeted them as the ship turned into port. Puerto de Oro was a hive of activity. Sailors called to one another, shouting various orders as ships passed through the harbour. Some yelled greetings, others farewells. Cecilia caught a few whistles and curses in her direction and wrapped her arms about her, trying to shrink further into herself.

"Don't mind them, miss. Most sailors think it's bad luck for a woman to be on a ship," Tayen mumbled beside her.

"Why is that?" she asked.

He shrugged, "Old superstition. Though we've had some women take to the seas since Pirate King Anders took over the isle 'few years ago. But most sailors don't want much do to w'em. They forget their mothers came by boat."

"As sailors?"

"As slaves."

"Maybe that's why they believe it's bad luck," she guessed.

"Think it has more to do with them sailing away for good," Skiv answered, his voice bitter. She flinched, wary of his presence.

He leaned against the railing, showing her his empty palms.

"I won't hurt ya… this time," he flashed her a wan smile.

She took a small step away from him. Despite his tender age, she guessed he was barely older than nineteen, his hazel eyes held the seriousness of a seasoned sailor.

She turned her attention to the view below them. The port opened in a semi-circle. Sitting on the grassy hillside, square houses stacked on top of each other, their flat roofs blending into the house behind.

They sailed parallel to the port on the left side of the village. Great ships were cast into shadow, their outlines dark against the setting sun.

As the pirate ship glided into the marina, she marvelled at the sight of so many ships, boats and dinghies in one place. Vessels of every size crammed together in what she could only describe as organised chaos. Men's shouting grew louder as the harbour master shouted directions. Skiv yelled a greeting as the old, heavily moustached man tipped his weather-beaten hat at them.

Ahead of them, Cecilia could make out poles rising from one side, out of the way of passing ships. Iron cages were mounted on top of them, hunched, gangly limbs reaching through the rusted bars. Shadowed figures leered at them, their voices garbled by the elements. The sun plunged into the horizon, cloaking the nightmarish creatures.

Fear rooted her to the spot as she recalled stories of sea monsters washed ashore and held captive by pirates to spook trespassers. Skiv and Tayen flanked her on either side, providing a semblance of relief.

A garbled cry called out close by. She jumped at the gravel like voice.

"Don't mind the prisoners," Skiv offered. "They're calling for food."

"What did they do?" she whispered. Now, she could make out the desperate shadows, their faceless forms pleading with her.

He shrugged, "S'what happens to those who defy the king."

Bile rose to her throat, her stomach churning the contents of her meagre dinner. Guilt and fear mingled together as she fought to keep her food down.

"Can't we give them something?" She asked through gritted teeth.

Tayen averted his gaze as Skiv's face hardened.

"They don't deserve our mercy."

"No one deserves this!" she pleaded.

He cocked his head, pushing off from the railing. His face was a mask of steel, all semblance of the young boy, replaced with the hardness of a man.

"You don't know what they've done," he hissed.

"They're still human! They should be treated with dignity."

"They committed treason-"

"Against an unjust ruler!"

"You don't know what you're talking about, woman," he snapped.

She flinched as he raised his hand toward her. He pulled himself back, his fingers mere inches from her cheek. Cecilia flinched as something like guilt flashed across his face before he turned away.

"Tayen, take her away," Skiv ordered in a low voice.

Tayen motioned for her to step away from the rail. She watched Skiv stomp to the galley, fists clenched at his side. Biting back relief, she let Tayen guide her across the deck. Guilt pressed in on her as the cacophony of cries rang out around them, their voices pleading, desperate. Would she find herself in one of these cages if she dared defy the king too? She forced herself to keep walking.

A cry stopped her in her tracks. A young voice. A child, calling for its mother. Cecilia turned just in time to see a small figure slumped against the iron bars, lit briefly by the spilled remnants of the sun. Other figures appeared to be sprawled around the cage, silent and unmoving. Hollow eyes peered out from a small, dirty face, as the child leaned out against the cage. A hand stretched out, beseeching her.

"Mamá? I'm hungry." The young voice rasped.

Cecilia choked on a sob as she stumbled blindly behind Tayen who dragged her into the relative safety of the captain's cabin. The door shuddered in the frame behind them, but even its crash could not stop the child's voice ringing in her ears.

Knees trembling, she dropped to the floor, Tayen producing a bucket just in time for her to start retching into it. With tears burning her eyes, she heaved until there was nothing left in her stomach but an aching guilt.

35

Puerto de Oro

The child's plea haunted her as Skiv and his men escorted her through the village square. Apparently, he thought he could distract her with tales of the bloodthirsty king's history as the crew huddled around them in a protective circle.

With the image of the child fresh in her mind, the last thing she wanted was to hear about the pirate king's apparent goodness. What good could there be in a man who left a child in a cage to face the elements, surrounded by death on all sides?

Tayen, at least, was sympathetic in his silence while Skiv continued to drone on. The crew remained stoically silent against the cries of gulls overhead and children playing on the streets. Not that Cecilia could see much of the village, so tightly knit were the crew around her. She barely had space to walk on her own with Skiv and Tayen flanking her on either side.

"Pirate King Anders usurped our previous leader Captain Hogan five years ago. He restored peace to the islands during a time of civil unrest and promised to give womenfolk the right to sail," Skiv explained, uncaring that his words fell on deaf ears.

"Though not many menfolk are willing trade or sail with women yet. Reckon they should stay home and attend to better things."

Catching the last comment, Cecilia rolled her eyes. She didn't care if the pirates saw her disdain for their king. She would not let them see her cowed.

"At the moment, King Anders is endeavouring to make peace with former enemies across the seas." Skiv's pointed glance at Cecilia went unnoticed as she followed him through the village port. Tayen walked beside her, slowing his strides so she would not have to run to keep up. Her wrists chaffed against the rope that bound her to them. Despite all Skiv's theatrics about calling her a princess, she felt more like a prisoner than a guest.

"The city looks its best at night," Tayen murmured as they walked past curious onlookers. Ragged mothers called for dirty children playing under the light of iron streetlamps. Fishermen called to each other, some even greeting the crew who marched along behind them.

The smell of frying fish hung in the air, mingling with laughter from labourers entering the array of pubs and taverns that lined the main street. Couples loitered around the plaza square. Travellers lined the streets, looking for a place to revel or rest. Cecilia's skin crawled as drunk sailors or sweat soaked labourers leered at her or let out low whistles as they passed by.

"Ay señorita, how much for a bite?" a sailor called to her.

Tayen bristled beside her, murmuring something unsavoury to himself.

Cecilia burned at the comment. She was already self-conscious as the only woman in a crowd of men, must she be humiliated also? Her fists balled at her sides, only the fabric of her skirts keeping her from digging nails into her skin. She was beginning to regret not donning the travelling cloak Tayen had brought her on the ship.

He had been charged to bring her a set of clothes to change into after she was sick in the cabin, but Cecilia had felt too numb to get changed. She stared at the fine clothes, a rich green dress and dainty slippers, but her thoughts remained fixed on the child in the cage. How could she dress in such fine clothes when children were dying?

"Ignore them. The saltwater numbs their brains," Skiv said, his voice loud enough for the offender to hear.

"They spend so much time at sea, they forget how to talk to a woman," Tayen mumbled, glancing at her for the briefest of moments.

His comment reassured her as they made their way down a narrow gravel path at the edge of the village.

Her wrists itched as she rubbed them against the rope, her skin red and chafing. Skiv had said it was a safety precaution as he looped the end of the rope onto his own wrist, but she couldn't help feeling like a dog tied to its master.

Skiv navigated the trail expertly, his steps firm and assured. Tayen stayed beside her, slowing his gait to match hers. He caught her when she stumbled on loose rock, his arm reaching out to break her fall. She ignored the twist in her heart as she thought of Marcus steadying her when they reached the port in Avizon. Had she imagined the concern in his eyes? Or had that been a trick too?

Briefly, she wondered how he fared. No, she didn't want to know. He had betrayed her by keeping her identity a secret. She shouldn't care about what happened to him, to any of them. And yet...

She could picture Bella fretting away at her needlework, Jeremy somewhere close by. It was impossible to imagine one without the other, sharing teasing smiles and stolen glances. Both reassuring her in their own ways that everything would work out in the end.

They could not have known about her identity, she decided. If they had, they would have found some way to tell her.

"Almost there," Skiv announced as they rounded a hill.

They had traversed the length of the port on the western side attached to an inlet. They came to a juncture at the edge of the city; most of the foot traffic had petered out, with only young revellers acknowledging the motley crew. Once they rounded the sand hill, she could make out a stationary ship, its deck bathed in torchlight in front of what looked like a two-storey tavern.

"That's La Morada del Rey," Tayen murmured beside her.

The King's Abode.

Cecilia frowned. It looked more like a bawdy tavern than a palace for royalty. The dark walls were painted in shadow as they drew closer. The crew, which had remained largely quiet during their trek through the village, perked up. Conversations sprang up as they came closer, an excited buzz rippling through them.

Cecilia's heart hammered in her chest when they passed the main entrance, a dark blue door with huge bronze compasses emblazoned on the heavy timber. The smell of free-flowing liquor mingled with the bitter stench of vomit as musicians played a fast tune inside. Boots stamped in time to the beat, bottles clanging on timber as the ground shook beneath them. Women's laughter poured through the windows, cheap and gaudy. Cecilia hoped she would not be forced to join their ranks.

Someone grunted behind her.

"Come on princeling. Don't tell me you've found your sea legs *now*," a gruff voice said from somewhere behind her. She turned to see Alistar pick himself up off the ground, brushing the dust from his trousers, dried blood smearing the collar of his shirt. His blonde locks were a tangled mop on his head, and his eyes were dark either from bruises or lack of sleep.

He threw a dirty look at the pirate that had taunted him. For the first time, she noticed the rope in his mouth and wrists. Obviously, he was not afforded the same luxuries as she was. As much as she wanted to hurt him for disregarding her proposal rejection, she couldn't help but pity the sight of him. Straggly blonde locks plastered against his olive skin, his eyes blazing at the man who taunted him moments before. She turned back to Tayen before he could catch her staring.

The burly pirate looked straight ahead, barely sparing her a glance.

"Don't show weakness," he mumbled in a voice so low she wondered if he meant for her to hear him.

Skiv held up a hand to halt the procession as they rounded the corner. Before she knew it, they had come to a stop at the side of The King's Abode. Up close, she could appreciate the brocade decorations that lined the building, painted to be the same colour as the stone. Skiv turned to Cecilia, gathering the rope that tied them together.

Barely sparing his crew a glance, he raised two fingers in the air, pointing them back in the direction which they came. Wordlessly, they shrunk into the shadows, taking a despondent Alistar with them.

"This is where we leave you," Skiv slipped the rope from her wrists, "You'll be given sleeping quarters and something to eat. Make yourself at home. You will be given a day or two to settle in before the wedding. She'll see to all your needs."

Before Cecilia could ask who *she* was, a familiar figure in a scarlet dress appeared at the side entrance. Her ebony curls were piled high on top of her head, a predatory grin plastered across her face.

"Cecilia, my dear." Frida greeted, reaching out to take her hands. Cecilia stepped away from her, stumbling into Tayen.

"No," she turned to Skiv, "take me back to the ship. Take me to King Anders, I don't care. Just take me away from *her*."

Frida gave her a tight smile, her tone light as though cajoling a child.

"Come now Cecilia, you don't really mean that. You know I won't hurt you."

Cecilia shook her head as Frida drew closer, hands outstretched.

"Don't touch me," Cecilia cried, her words rising with every syllable.

Frida froze in place. She inclined her head in a nod.

"As you wish."

Cecilia threw herself at the ground between Skiv and Tayen. Skiv pulled at her arm, drawing her up. Frida stepped into the doorway.

"Will you allow me to show you your room at least?" Frida asked, her voice even.

Skiv glanced between the two women. He nodded once at Cecilia.

"Tayen and I will be back for you in the morning. The king does not like to leave his brides unaccompanied if he can help it."

"I can look after her-" Frida interjected.

Skiv shook his head, folding his arms over his chest.

"I'm sure you can, Your Grace, but the king does not take chances. We will be back tomorrow."

Cecilia's stomach churned at the thought of being left alone with her godmother. But a small seed of relief bloomed at the thought of Skiv and Tayen coming back for her. She may not trust the pirates, but she would prefer their company over her godmother's.

"Very well," Frida conceded, "Come Cecilia, there is much we must do."

With a final, pained glance at the pirates, Cecilia followed her godmother through the arched doorway and into the house, praying they would keep their word.

36
Disarray

Marcus slumped into the tavern chair as Sebastian and Jeremy sank in at the table beside him.

"Thank Ilio we made it," Sebastian sighed as a waitress set a jug and tall tumblers of ale in front of them. Sebastian snagged three clean looking cups from the empty table beside them and poured cold water from the jug.

"I think I've had enough water for the day," Jeremy said, taking a long swig of ale. A thin white moustache lined his top lip.

"We must keep moving," Marcus picked up a cup of water. "Who knows where Cecilia is by now."

"First, we must eat and rest our tired bodies. We've been rowing all evening – we need a break." Sebastian leaned back in his chair.

"Yes, but Cecilia-"

"You won't be much good to her dead on your feet," Sebastian interrupted.

Jeremy nodded his assent.

"Marcus, as your friend I'm telling you to rest. As your doctor, I'm ordering you to."

Marcus huffed, leaning back in the chair. Like a petulant child, he crossed his arms over his chest. He knew his friends were right, but he didn't have to be happy about it.

"Besides, while we're here, we can find out if anyone knows anything. Perhaps we can discern when she arrived and what the pirate king hopes to do with her?" Sebastian suggested.

"I suppose you're right," Marcus grumbled, his stomach protesting over the din.

The trio had docked at the inlet on the eastern side of the port, close to the edge of town. Sebastian said it was close to The King's Abode – the official residence of Pirate King Anders.

"There's a ship attached to the side of the tavern via the jetty. On the other side, it backs onto a series of cane fields. Once we rescue Cecilia, we can travel north-east through the farms and backroads, until we reach the land bridge that takes us to Isla Esmeralda, then make our way to Cova Zafiro," he said.

They were silent as a waitress set their food on the table, the smell of roasted herbs and meat wafting from the plate. Marcus could barely contain the rumble of his stomach as he and his mates helped themselves to roasted pheasant and vegetables with a side of greens and a platter of bread and cheese.

"So how do we go about finding Cecilia?" Marcus asked, ripping a slice of bread.

Sebastian shrugged, "News travels fast here. I don't doubt we'll find out soon enough."

Before he had finished chewing a mouthful of bread, a scraggly pair of sailors took up residence at the table beside them.

"D'you think this one will last? The king's other two wives died pretty early into their marriages." The younger, lanky pirate asked his companion, pouring them generous tumblers of ale. The spark in his bright brown eyes betrayed his youth under the faded clothes hanging from his thin frame.

His companion was older with a weathered face and greying hair. He stroked the meagre scruff of his grey chin before answering.

"There's something different about this one. Rumour has it she's a lost princess."

"She'd have to be lost if she's marryin' the Pirate King. Royalty never marries into this place."

The older man knocked the boy's head so hard Marcus was surprised the lad didn't keel over.

"Don't let me catch you sayin' that again," he hissed, glancing at the trio who were suddenly engrossed in their roast potatoes. "The king's doin' what he needs to do to secure the future o' the isles."

"What does that mean?" The boy rubbed the back of his head.

"Didn't ya hear, the Calgarian prince is in town? 'Parently he's lookin' to secure an alliance with our king."

"What for?"

The old man shrugged. Marcus' grip tightened on his knife.

What kind of an alliance would Derek want with the Pirate King? Calgaria and the Fickle Islands had been enemies for most of their country's long histories.

"So, this princess King Anders is supposed to wed," the younger man poised his drink to his lips, "is she Calgarian? I thought their princess was dead?"

The old man sighed; a look of weary resignation settled across his wrinkled face.

"Fortuna, give me strength," he muttered under his breath. "The Calgarian princess is not dead. She was kidnapped, but rumour has it she was raised in Avinada."

The younger man stared blank-faced at his companion. The old man resumed as though speaking to a child, "An Avinadan noblewoman and a foreign prince have arrived on our shores. Doesn't that seem like an odd coincidence to you?"

The young man shrugged with feigned confidence, "I've seen stranger things."

Marcus and Sebastian shared a smile at the young man's audacity as Jeremy rolled his eyes.

"I'm sure," the old man said, as he sipped his drink. "Nevertheless, King Anders would do well to make sure this bride doesn't die on his watch, lest we have another war on our hands."

The young man nodded, taking a long swig of his ale. Marcus knew it was risky but he couldn't hide his curiosity any longer.

"Pardon me, I don't mean to interrupt," he addressed the older sailor, ignoring Jeremy and Sebastian's warning glances, "I couldn't help but overhear. You said the Calgarian prince is on the island? Do you know how long he's been here for?"

The old man eyed the group warily. They were all dressed in simple sailor's clothes. Brown trousers, black boots and white sailing shirts. They wore weapons on their belts, same as every other man and their travelling cloaks hung over the wooden chairs.

"Why d'ya wanna know?" the old man asked, eyeing them warily.

Jeremy shrugged, "We're just curious, that's all. It's not often we hear about our prince traversing these islands."

"You're Calgarian?" the old man asked, noting the accent. His eyes lingered questioningly on Sebastian. His dark skin and short curls stood out against Jeremy's pale skin and dark blonde hair. Marcus, though he shared his mother's Avinadan colouring, spoke with a strong Calgarian accent.

"Yes," Marcus cleared his throat before Sebastian could speak, "we have been travelling for some time and have heard little news from our home country."

This seemed to please the sailor who nodded, leaning back into his chair.

"What d'ya wanna know?"

"Anything you can tell us."

"M'name's Carrigan. This is Elmar," he introduced himself and his companion. "We can only tell you what we've seen or heard, mind."

Marcus nodded.

"That will help us greatly," He smiled, pressing his hands together in thanks.

Sebastian and Jeremy exchanged wan smiles with the sailors, refraining from giving their names.

The companions listened with keen interest as Carrigan told

them about watching Prince Derek disembark from a merchant ship a few days prior.

"Seems he's staying at The King's Abode which you'll find at the Trinity Inlet on the edge of town. An Avinadan noblewoman seems to be staying there too. Disembarked from the same ship he did. That sorta thing's not unusual around these parts, mind, but it's a bit strange for two foreign nobles to be on the island at once," he said.

"Usually having an Avinadan nobleman around wouldn't arouse suspicion but even stranger was she brought prisoners with her.

"Then yesterday evening, *The Happy Dagger*, that's the king's ship, rolls in and a young woman is given a full crew escort through the town," Carrigan said, pausing for a drink.

"And what makes you think this woman is a princess?" Marcus asked.

Carrigan shrugged, "Rumour mostly. But me son works at The King's Abode, and he said she bears a strong resemblance to the foreign prince. And she's got different coloured eyes."

Marcus' heart raced.

"You mentioned before that your king had plans to marry her for a political alliance. How can he be sure she's the right woman?"

Carrigan set his drink down, the glass almost half empty.

"You're not asking the right question," Carrigan shook his head. "Why does he want an alliance with our age-old enemies? Who or what is he looking to conquer?"

Sebastian cleared his throat, glancing at the door of the tavern. Marcus recognised a pair of pirates who had taken Cecilia the days before.

He tightened his grip on the meat knife, no longer resting on the succulent roast pheasant.

Anger bubbled to the surface as he watched the sailors, a lanky fellow with blazing hair and a dark haired, burly young man, wave over a waitress.

Jeremy placed a warning hand on Marcus' shoulder as they

watched the pirates order drinks. Marcus recognised the young man as Skiv, the pirate he fought on the *Sorrento*.

"Don't." Jeremy planted a hand on Marcus' shoulder before he could rise. "Not now."

Marcus brushed off his friend's hand, already on the edge of his seat. Carrigan caught his gaze.

"Listen to your friend, boy. Skiv's young but he's a good fighter and favoured by the Pirate King. You cross blades with him here, you'll regret it."

Marcus set his jaw, staring daggers at Skiv, who remained oblivious to his ire.

"How do we get to The King's Abode?" Marcus asked, turning back to Carrigan and Elmar.

Elmar laughed, "The King's Abode isn't just somewhere you go. You have to be invited."

"Or taken as prisoner," Carrigan mumbled.

"Marcus, you better not be planning what I think-" Jeremy started

"How much would it take to get in?"

"As a guest or prisoner?" Carrigan glanced at Jeremy who groaned, slumping into his seat. Sebastian remained tight-lipped as always.

"Either."

The old man's eyes gleamed with interest.

"You got coin?" he asked.

"Enough."

"I'll see what I can do," he held out a hand. Marcus shook it. Carrigan grinned to reveal yellowed teeth, "Pleasure doing business with ya."

37

Nowhere to Run

"So, they've let you out." Alistar greeted as he settled in the sand beside Cecilia. She turned to face him, her windswept hair tumbled over her shoulders. She offered him a wan smile, trying to hide her disappointment. Since her arrival the day before, she had hardly spent a moment alone.

"I threatened your mother I'd run away again if I couldn't have a moment alone." Cecilia smiled to herself.

She'd never stood up to her godmother before, especially not for anything so insignificant as a beach stroll. Still, she was grateful for the small win - even if she had guards watching her every move.

"Without your rogue?" she could hear the tightness in Alistar's voice, "Where would you go?"

She shrugged, "To find him I suppose."

She was surprised at the words as they tumbled out of her mouth.

"Do you think he'll come for you?" Alistar picked at the tuft of grass in front of him.

The roar of waves crashing against the shoreline filled the silence, a cool breeze tugging at their clothes and sending goosebumps down her arms.

She'd tried to put Marcus out of her mind. He was getting paid to bring her to Calgaria, the letter from the king had confirmed that. The betrayal stung, but he was her only chance of escape.

"He always has before," she shrugged, leaning back on her hands. Coarse sand bit into her skin, "I don't think he'll stop now."

The sky bled orange, casting a golden glow across the ceaseless ocean. From their secluded sandbank nestled close to The King's Abode, they were sheltered from the prying eyes of people walking along the beach, most of whom were waved on by guards.

"You know, my offer still stands," Alistar broke the silence between them. "If I marry you -"

"Can you stop with that already?" she snapped.

"Frida will sacrifice you as long as it means getting a piece of my kingdom. She told me Anders killed Mario. What if he kills you too?" Cecilia turned back to The King's Abode to keep her voice from cracking, "I can't have more blood on my hands."

Her throat burned with unshed tears. She had never liked Mario, and in truth, her future felt lighter now he was dead. Still, her stomach churned at her relief. Was she really so callous? Someone cleared their throat behind them, breaking her from her thoughts. She turned to see Skiv and Tayen, their ragged clothes whipping in the wind.

"Time to head back, Your Highness," Skiv held out a hand to help her up, "Pirate King Anders is awaiting your presence."

Cecilia ignored it, gathering her skirts as she stood and straightened. No matter how many times he addressed her as Your Highness, she couldn't get used to it.

"Cecilia is just fine," she grumbled, "I'm not royalty yet."

"King's orders" Skiv shrugged, "Duke Alarcon, the king has called for your presence at the tavern."

Alistar stood dusting sand from his clothes. "Duty calls," he shrugged at Cecilia, following Tayen up the sandy embankment.

"What will happen to him?" She asked when she was sure they were out of earshot. Skiv shoved her gently forward.

"S'up to the king, but if he behaves himself, I guarantee he won't end up in a cage."

Cecilia shuddered, the memory of the child flashing in her mind. She had spent the night haunted by what she could have done to help him. Regret seeped into every waking moment.

"Did the king follow on my request to free the child?" she asked.

Skiv's lips drew into a thin line. Her skin crawled under the ocean breeze. He had told her when she sent word to the king not to expect much. Yet still, she hoped.

"Got there too late. He was buried this afternoon, which is more than most get."

Cecilia's stomach dropped to her boots. Skiv caught her before she could tumble onto the coarse sand path which meandered back to The King's Abode. Her throat closed, tears spilling onto the sand as her choked sobs filled the air.

Skiv didn't speak again until he had returned her to her room. He lingered in the doorway, shuffling on the faded rug outside her door. Framed by the dark timber, the last rays of sunlight spilling through her open window, he looked older than his nineteen years.

"I know you don't want this life, but...Pirate King Anders is a dangerous man. If you try to run away or cross blades with him, it won't end well. Just a thought..."

"Why are you telling me this?" she asked, wary.

"Because," he shoved his hands into his pockets, "if you run away – it's not just you who'll end up hurt. Me and Tayen, we're s'posed to look after you. If you run..."

Realisation dawned on her.

If she ran away, their lives would be forfeited.

"Then come with me," the words tumbled out before she could think.

He shook his head glancing over his shoulder, as he stepped into the room. He stopped, just in front of her before continuing in a low voice, "I can't do that. If either of us gets caught helping ya, we'll both die. I'm not scared of death, but I won't lose my brother."

Fire burned in his dark eyes, his ruddy hair shining in the final rays of sunshine. Cecilia gripped the vanity behind her.

"You have two choices," Frida announced as she swept into the room, stopping short at the sight of Skiv and Cecilia. Skiv cleared his throat, straightening himself to bow at the duchess.

"Am I interrupting something?" Frida frowned at them.

Skiv shook his head.

"I was just leaving," he said, turning away from them. Without glancing at her, Skiv turned on his heel and left.

Cecilia turned her attention to her godmother. Duchess Alarcon busied herself in arranging the two frocks in her arms against Cecilia's thin bedframe under the window.

"You can either wear this lovely blue number the king picked out, or this gorgeous red one I brought from home."

The duchess ignored Cecilia's tired stare and fussed over belts and accessories to accompany each dress from a small trunk by the side of the bed.

"And if I don't want to wear either of them?" Cecilia sighed, leaning heavily against the vanity. Frida's usually genial smile faltered.

"You are going to meet the Pirate King. You should wear something more presentable than... that," Frida huffed, her hand encompassing Cecilia's general direction.

"What if I do not wish to meet him?"

"I'm afraid you have no choice, my dear," Frida's frown deepened, "This marriage is happening whether you like it or not."

"Marriage?" Cecilia's resolve faltered, "Who said anything about marriage?"

Frida's lips parted in a satisfied grin. Her beady eyes lit up and a familiar sense of dread washed over Cecilia

"I did," a rich baritone voice greeted from the door.

Frida turned first, dropping into a low curtsy. Cecilia eyed the stranger, his strong countenance sparking a flicker of familiarity.

"It seems marrying you off might be the only way for me to secure my throne."

38

A Marriage of His Convenience

"Greetings, Your Highness," Frida straightened to her full height, offering the prince a dazzling smile.

The prince dipped his chin in greeting, his piercing blue eyes never wavering from Cecilia's. She dropped into a polite curtsy. He frowned, crossing his arms as he leaned into the doorframe.

"So, you're the usurper who wants my throne." He pushed off the frame, huffing into the room. Despite his casual appearance in dark trousers and a dark blue sailor's shirt, his ramrod back and air of authority exuded an arrogant confidence.

"You're Prince Derek." It was more a statement than a question.

A memory flashed in her mind of a young blue-eyed boy, as she took in the sight of the man before her.

"I am." He gestured for them to sit at the circular table in the centre of the small room.

"So tell me, *Cecilia*," he elongated every syllable of her name, "why should I believe you are my long-lost cousin?"

She took her place opposite him at the table, "I was hoping you could tell me."

His eyes settled on the golden emblem at her throat. She had worn the chain after being taken captive by Skiv, who had searched her pockets on the ship.

"Were did you get that?" his voice hardened.

"I found it," Cecilia's hand rose to the pendant.

"Give it to me."

"What? Why?"

"Do as you're told!" Frida scolded, reaching for Cecilia. Cecilia held onto the pendant, but Frida was quick. She yanked the chain from her neck, delivering it the prince's waiting hand.

"If you're a paid actress, you're doing a terrible job at convincing me to take your claim seriously," he pocketed the pendant.

An unfamiliar grief began to bubble in her throat. The pendant was the only claim she had to petition the Calgarian king and queen. Now it was gone.

"Please," she hated the tremble in her voice, "I just want to find my family. That necklace...I thought it might help."

"Is that why you're pretending to be Princess Lilia?" The prince scoffed, "Do you think the king and queen would fall for your lie so easily?"

"I'm not lying," she clenched her fist in her skirt, "I just want to know who I am. I can't remember anything about my life before I was taken by the duchess."

"And you think it will be easy to claim the life of Princess Lilia?" He poured himself a cup of wine. Someone had set a fresh bottle on the table. "Do you think it will be easy to assume the identity of a dead girl? To steal my throne? Become queen?"

Cecilia shook her head.

"No, that's not my intention at all."

The prince narrowed his eyes, "Then why did you leave Avinada?"

"I wanted to run away from *her*," Cecilia pointed at her godmother. Frida sat unbothered; her hands clasped in front of her. Cecilia turned her attention back to the prince his mere presence invading the tiny space.

"Who brought you thus far? Surely you didn't set sail on your own?" He sipped his drink.

Cecilia pursed her lips. Marcus might have betrayed her by keeping her identity secret, but the *Real Sorrento* was still her best chance of getting home. If only she could find a way to escape.

"I believe there was a rogue agent, Your Highness. He introduced himself as Duke Aurelius Reddan," Frida supplied.

Prince Derek narrowed his eyes at Cecilia, his long fingers forming a fist on the table.

"I think you and I both know that's not his real name," he ground out.

Cecilia held her nerves and his stare. Marcus had mentioned something about protecting the royal family. Had he been the prince's protector?

"Tell me his name and I won't harm you," he promised.

The taste of copper filled her mouth as she bit down the corner of her cheek.

"For goodness' sake Cecilia. You're not a mute!" Frida hissed.

Cecilia shook her head. "I don't know."

She flinched as the prince banged his fist on the table. In a heartbeat, he picked up her injured hand, fingers still bandaged from the ordeal on the ship.

"I spoke with Skiv. I know you're lying."

"Then why do you need me to tell you?" The words were out of her mouth before she could stop them.

"Don't ask stupid questions, Cecilia. That's none of your concern," Frida scolded.

The prince's eyes flicked to the duchess who tried to placate him with a smile.

"You should listen to your godmother. She's a smart woman."

Cecilia gritted her teeth as his fingers dug into the soft skin at her wrist.

"Promise me you won't hurt him."

The prince's grip relaxed enough for her to wriggle out of. He nodded once.

She hesitated.

"You have my word."

She watched him for a moment. His countenance relaxed, though his fist remained firm on the tabletop. Something about the way he dipped his chin at her tugged at the edge of a memory.

Her heart twisted in her chest. Could she betray Marcus to this stranger? Unable to hold the prince's gaze, she turned away.

"He said his name was Marcus," she murmured.

The prince sucked in a breath.

"Did he act alone, or did he have accomplices?"

She shrugged.

"There were two farmgirls in Avinada, Your Highness," Frida cut in. "I believe I have dealt with them appropriately."

Cecilia's stomach knotted into itself as the prince nodded.

"Very well," Prince Derek drained his cup, "I trust you will see to Señorita Cecilia while she prepares for the wedding festivities. I would stay for tomorrow's ceremony, but I do not have the luxury of time."

Frida nodded, schooling her face into a polite grin.

"Why are you doing this to me?" Cecilia asked as he stood from the table.

"Because you are in the way of my birthright." The prince straightened himself, resting a hand on the back of his chair.

"But I don't want the crown," Cecilia fought to keep her voice from breaking, "I just want to find my family."

The prince hesitated, his blue eyes hardening.

"Well," he cleared his throat, "that's too bad."

Cecilia didn't bother to curtsy as he left.

A flash of blue fabric filled her vision, hitting her square on the head. Frida had thrown a dress at her.

"Get dressed," she ordered," you meet your fiancé in an hour."

39

Rules of Engagement

Frida adjusted the leather belt on Cecilia's waist. Where it would usually be filled with an assortment of weapons, hers remained empty, save for the dagger Marcus had given her in Avizon, and a red scarf.

She tried not to wince as Frida pulled her hair into a thick braid, leaving two strands of hair to frame her face. The older woman pushed her onto the corner of the bed, quickly applying kohl to her eyes and rouge to her lips. Skiv appeared in the doorway, their escort for the night.

"The Pirate King is waiting," he said by way of greeting. He didn't quite meet Cecilia's eyes as she followed him out of the room.

Music pounded from somewhere beneath them as Skiv and Tayen accompanied Frida and Cecilia down a thin timber passageway.

They had been stationed near the king's chambers, attached to the tavern in a quiet inlet. Cecilia fought to keep her footing. After spending weeks on the ocean, she'd become accustomed to the familiar rock and sway of the boat. Now she was on dry land, her mind struggled to keep up.

Tayen caught her as she stumbled over her skirt.

"Careful, Highness," he mumbled, letting her go as soon as she was steady. Cecilia flashed him a grateful smile, careful not to let him see the tears in her eyes.

She had hoped someone from the *Real Sorrento* would have come for her by now, but no sign of help had appeared. They wouldn't abandon her to the pirates, would they?

Her fists clenched at her sides. Everyone had seemed so genuine, Jeremy, Bella, Marcus. He had given his word to protect her… was it all a lie?

Had she imagined the anguish in Marcus' face as he watched the pirates take her away? Would he keep his promise to protect her? Had she been right to trust him at all?

Alistar was right, there was much she didn't know about him. Least of all why Prince Derek was so upset he had helped her.

"You could at least pretend to be happy you're about to become a queen," Frida hissed as the sound of men's revelry drew closer.

"I never wanted this," Cecilia's argued.

"Don't be ridiculous, Cecilia, everyone wants this," Frida snapped.

Cecilia shook her head. She didn't want to marry a criminal; someone who let children die cruel deaths.

What if you could stop them? What if you could save the children? She thought.

Her heart thundered in her chest. Could she stop King Anders? If she assumed her role as queen, would he give her authority over the isles? And if he did, could she bring justice to the community?

Her thoughts were interrupted by a loud bang followed by a series of whoops and cheers.

They had reached the end of a long hallway which opened into what appeared to be a dark storeroom. Burly men in stained clothes pushed barrels of ale along the length of the room, others poured fresh cups of amber liquid, stacking them on trays carried by young women in colourful dresses.

Cecilia scrunched her nose at the stench of sweat, ale and tobacco as Skiv led them to another door. Sweat beaded on her brow as they stepped through the cramped hallway.

The sound of revelry magnified, the sharp notes of the violin piercing her ears. Men's boots thundered on the ground beneath them, their shouts and jeers as oppressive as the evening heat.

Skiv motioned for her to follow him to what appeared to be the edge of a stage. Ahead of them, a large wooden dais stood bathed in golden light. Two thrones sat in the centre, a pair of dirty leather boots draped casually over an armrest.

Peering around Skiv, she caught sight of a long arm hanging from the other side, an unlit cigar poised between two long fingers.

"Time to meet your future husband," Frida murmured from beside her.

Cecilia rolled back her shoulders, straightening to her full height. She would do her duty, not to Frida, but to the people.

Frida's lips curved into a dreadful smile as she pushed Cecilia on stage. She regained her balance as she approached the throne. Strong arms steadied her.

"Princess Lilia."

It was less a question than a statement. Cecilia looked up to find a handsome young man standing above her, soft green eyes peering out from underneath a mop of red curls.

"I don't believe we've been properly introduced. I am Pirate King Anders." He clasped her hand. She nodded, steadying herself.

He was younger than she had expected. His suntanned cheeks were hidden beneath a neatly trimmed beard.

In his dark trousers, billowing ebony jacket and impossibly stain-free white shirt, he looked like a swashbuckling rogue. He was certainly a far cry from the scraggly pirate she had imagined.

His sharp green eyes glinted as dangerously as his weapons at the belt as they raked over her.

"She's a mute!" a man yelled from the crowd when Cecilia did not speak. Heat rushed to her cheeks. She averted her gaze.

The pirate king flicked her a charming grin.

"So, this is to be my new wife?" he raised his voice. The crowd cheered in answer. Keeping a firm grip on her hand, he gestured toward the two thrones. His blue-green eyes never wavered from her own, "You like what you see?"

Her skin crawled as the crowd cheered and brayed at their master. Cecilia wiped her free palm, slick with sweat, on the side of her dress. She didn't care if it was unladylike. The last thing she wanted was to impress these men.

The pirate king held his arms out as if to embrace as her. She stepped backwards, garnering a laugh from the crowd. King Anders' smile never changed but his eyes darkened. He pulled her into an embrace as whoops erupted from the audience below.

"You're on my island now, you play by my rules, understood?" he whispered, his breath hot against her ear.

She nodded, stomach churning in dreadful anticipation.

"Good girl," he pulled back from her, keeping one hand in a vice-like grip. "Now, let's have a look at you."

He spun her in a graceful circle about the stage, as if showing off a partner he was about to dance with. Cecilia's stomach knotted itself again.

"Look at those eyes," King Anders winked at her, "those are the eyes of Princess Aramyth. *Royalty.*"

Anxiety bubbled in in her chest, constricting her throat. Her lungs burned for air and she wondered if her stomach could digest itself from nerves.

"Maids, and scallywags," the pirate king addressed the crowd again, "before you tonight stands Princess Lilia, the lost princess of Calgaria. My future wife."

The crowd hollered in response. She burned with humiliation at the lewd remarks thrown her way.

She scanned the room quickly, searching for an escape, an open window, an unmanned door. Eagle eyes peered at her from scarred pirate faces, their weathered hands not far from well-used weapons. Anders wrapped an arm around her waist, his fingers digging into the fabric of her dress.

Her heart leapt as she recognised Sebastian and Jeremy sitting in a quiet corner of the room, their eyes never wavering from her. It was all she could do not to untangle herself from the pirate king and run over to them.

The Calgarians had not abandoned her after all. Hope rose in her chest. If Jeremy and Sebastian were around, surely, Marcus would be with them? She flinched as Anders leaned his head close to hers. Her skin prickled against his warm breath.

"Don't get any bright ideas my sweet, my men have been trained not to let any woman escape. Especially someone as valuable as you."

40

Friend Turned Foe

Moonlight spilled into the dark cell as Marcus peeled himself off of the cool dirt floor. He coughed dust, dirt and human misery assaulting his nose.

"So, you leave for a month and get kidnapped by pirates," a familiar voice greeted from the shadows, "and you say I'm the troublemaker."

Marcus turned to face Prince Derek, flanked by two blazing torches and an armed guard. He shook his head, as much to clear the hair from his face as to shake the dream before him.

"Derek? What in Ilio's name are you doing here?"

"First of all," the prince folded his arms in front of his chest, "it's *Prince* Derek to you. "Secondly, I'm here on official business."

Marcus' brow quirked as he straightened himself. In two quick strides, he stood at the cell door, Derek's face split in two by the iron bars. "What kind of business can Calgaria have with the Fickle Islands?"

"That is none of your concern."

Marcus frowned. The finer details of royal business may not be his concern, but the whereabouts of the Crown Prince were. Or at least, they had been. Until Cecilia.

"Why are you here?" Marcus knew he risked Derek's ire, but curiosity got the better of him.

"I followed the bitter stench of betrayal and it led me here."

A wave of shame washed over Marcus.

"Derek - I…"

"Save your apologies," the prince's mouth hardened. "I know all about your little mission to return my supposed cousin to Calgaria and replace me as heir to the throne. You may not think I am petty, but I will not give up my birthright so easily. Especially to a foreigner."

Marcus bristled.

"She is no foreigner. She is Calgarian and the king's daughter."

"And an Avinadan," the prince took a step toward the cell, his eyes narrowed at Marcus. "She is a half-caste. She would not be fit to rule."

"Take care with what you say, brother," Marcus tempered his voice, careful not to betray the sting in the prince's words.

Derek tutted.

"I am not, nor have I ever been your *brother*."

The words cut deeper than any physical wound the prince might have bestowed. Marcus' fist tightened around the solid bars in front of him. Flecks of rusted paint peppered his skin.

"Besides," Prince Derek continued, "I couldn't take the throne with Lilia in the way. Pirate King Anders and I came to an understanding."

"Cecilia is not yours to trade," Marcus hissed, taking a step forward.

Derek tutted at his friend; his dark blue eyes as cold as Calgaria's winter glaciers.

"You didn't think I was going to sit back and let you deliver her to my uncle on a silver platter, did you? The Calgarian throne is mine and I won't let some foreign usurper take my birthright."

"She's not a usurper, she is the king's daughter," Marcus burst, "whether you like it or not, she's the rightful heir to the throne. I was fulfilling my duty!"

The prince's face darkened.

"And what duty is that, Marcus?" Derek's low voice carried in the stony darkness. "Your duty to me or your desire to claim your inheritance?"

"My duty is to the crown!"

"Your duty is to *me*!"

"My duty is to *my king*!"

Something akin to sadness flickered behind the prince's hard eyes.

"What's done is done," His voice turned to stone. The prince jerked his head at the guard to open the door. Marcus didn't protest when he was shoved onto his knees.

He barely had time to register Derek's fist when pain shot through his jaw. Strong hands clamped on his shoulders.

Derek straightened.

Despite the pain blooming across his face, Marcus raised a questioning brow at the prince. Twenty years of friendship was a hard habit to break.

"Are you trying to stop me?" Marcus spat blood to the side, despite the pain.

"I'm not trying," the prince promised, his voice as sharp as a blade, "I will stop you."

He barely had time to duck as the prince lunged forward. Marcus threw himself to the side, rolling onto his feet. He lunged at the guard who had been holding him, knocking him to the ground and swiping his sword from its scabbard.

For a prince so stringent on security, Marcus thought, he should've chained his fists.

A blade flashed before his eyes. Marcus swung his weapon just in time to parry the blow, the force of it sending a shock through his arm.

Metal clanged against metal as his blade met the prince's.

"You are no longer under my protection, Marcus," the prince ground out, "I care not whether you live or die."

Marcus pushed the prince from him. Derek's back thudded into the iron bars, yet he barely flinched. He lunged at Marcus who stepped out of his way. Derek stumbled further into the empty cell. Taking advantage of the prince's momentary distraction, Marcus ran into the dimly lit hall, slamming the iron doors behind him.

He turned to face his oldest friend.

"I will not fight you, Derek."

The prince's face turned red, his lips twisting in anger. He slammed a fist against the iron bars.

"I'll kill you!" he yelled.

"So be it."

A flash of gold glinted under the spilled moonlight by his boot. Without hesitation, Marcus pocketed it, a thin golden chain slipping through his fingers.

Stepping over the unconscious guard, Marcus hurried through the stone hallway, Derek's screams following close behind.

The pendant burned a hole in his pocket, every passing step bringing him closer to his goal.

Retrieve the princess. Bring her home.

He would worry about everything else later.

Muffled voices came from a door at the end of a long hallway. He turned to the right where golden light streamed from the edges of a stone passageway. Glancing behind to make sure no one was following; he took a tentative step forward.

The air smelled different here. Tobacco mixed with rum and revelry. A fiddler picked up a fast tune as women laughed at a sailor's bawdy joke.

From his vantage point, on the second storey of a tavern, he could see casks of ale lined several walls, along with muskets, pistols and several rounds of ammunition. He tightened his grip on his sword hilt, his free hand patting a dagger on his belt.

Claudio's dagger.

Checking there was no one else on the level, Marcus stepped into the light. The crowd beneath him was so caught up in music and ale, they paid him no attention.

He could see Jeremy and Sebastian in the centre of the room, their faces grim as they watched a couple on stage.

Pirate King Anders towered over a petite woman, his fingers raking through her hair, like claws.

A young woman, her dark hair woven into a solitary braid tumbling down her back, stood facing him. Though he could not see her face, he could feel the anger radiating from her small frame.

Cecilia.

His stomach dropped as the king threaded himself around her, bunching the blue fabric of her dress in his fist.

A clang of stone on iron threw him into action. Derek would find him soon and exact his vengeance.

Without looking back, Marcus leapt over the railing. He could deal with the prince later. Now, he had to save the princess.

41

The Intruder

Pirate King Anders led Cecilia to the carved wooden thrones in the centre of the stage. She took her seat beside him, schooling her features into a mask of neutrality. She could not let the pirate king read her thoughts so easily.

A man servant stepped up to offer her a cup of ale. She shook her head. Anders however, picked up the proffered drink, replacing it with a second, half empty glass. The pirate king raised the cup to his lips, but did not swallow.

Cecilia glanced away before he could catch her watching him. A thought came to her, unbidden.

A sober pirate is a man keeping watch for trouble.

The crowd grew raucous and reckless as the night wore on. Maids in low cut dresses and painted faces worked the room expertly, weaving their way through men wanting ale, attention and affection.

On more than one occasion, Cecilia's skin crawled under the gaze of hungry men, their beady eyes devouring her as if she were nothing more than a piece of meat. She swallowed, keeping her eyes above their heads, trying her best not to stare at Jeremy and Sebastian. She did not want to risk drawing attention to them if they had come to rescue her.

Still, neither of them had tried to approach her. The only flicker of recognition between them was a faint nod from Jeremy when she took her seat beside the king.

A bell chimed and King Anders stood to his feet.

"Garçon, another drink," the pirate shouted over the chaos, raising his glass high in the air. A cheer erupted from the crowd. Taking the encouragement, the pirate king grinned, winking at Cecilia.

"I like my rum the way I like my enemy's ships. On the rocks!"

The room erupted again. Men hollered and whistled, thumping their boots on the creaking timber floor. Cecilia watched as the crowd raised their glasses knocking back their fill and requesting more. King Anders, downed his drink, setting it down on a wooden stool beside him as he sank heavily into the throne.

Maids wove around the room again, though their numbers were fewer than at the beginning of the evening. Cecilia watched the final contingent filling cups and batting away unwanted advances. The men seemed oblivious to their dull eyes and shallow smiles.

Cecilia's heart beat loud in her ears. Were these women pillaged from other crews? Would she share their fate once the pirate king tired of her? To wear a harlot's dress, and smile at filthy men who saw her as nothing more than an object to be used and discarded? No. She would put an end to such things.

The fiddler, a short, stocky man, rose his voice to dedicate the next tune to the fast women in the tavern. Cecilia bunched her fists into the fabric of her skirt.

"Not a fan of large gatherings, love?" King Anders asked drawing her from her thoughts. He hooked a calloused finger under her chin, tilting her head at him.

She steeled herself to meet his cold blue-green eyes, hoping he could not read her discomfort.

How could a man call himself a king if he did not look after the least of his subjects? How could he sleep knowing children died from his torture? That even the maids who tended him were used and discarded by the men he entertained?

"I am not used to so much liveliness in one place, my lord." She forced her tone to be light.

He chuckled, letting go of her chin to brush a stray strand of hair behind her ear. She looked away, hoping he would mistake her aversion for shyness instead of disgust.

"Ah yes, your godmother kept you on quite a tight leash, didn't she?" Anders kept his hand on her cheek, forcing her to look at him. Her cheeks flushed her discomfort. He merely smiled.

"I can see why. One look at your beauty and all men who laid eyes on you would be fighting for your hand."

His tender voice grated on her nerves. She shuddered as he leaned in close, rum and tobacco mingling on his breath, and did her best not to pull away.

"If this party bores you, say the word and we can go somewhere more...secluded. This party is beginning to wane on me."

Cecilia's skin crawled as he angled her head towards him. His eyes were fixed solely on her lips.

The crowd whooped and hollered again. The sound of metal clinking on glass sent shivers down her spine. She jerked away, shaking her head of the noise.

The pirate king chuckled again and pulled her close.

"They're signalling for us to kiss, my love." He stood, drawing her up with him, "We cannot disappoint them."

Before she could think, he swept her into his arms, dipping her low to the ground. His lips pressed firmly against her own. She squirmed, trying to scream against him, but the sound garbled. He only gripped her tighter, holding her head in place with a strong hand.

Anders finally broke the kiss, raising an eyebrow at her before turning to the crowd. Cecilia closed her eyes, wishing she were far away. Using the armrest of the nearest throne to steady herself, she willed her legs to stop trembling.

Without thinking, she wiped her mouth, rouge staining the back of her hand.

The crowd saw and booed her.

Let them jeer. Those abhorrent dirty animals, she thought miserably.

"It seems my new bride is shy when it comes to public displays of affection," the pirate king announced to the crowd. Someone called out for more beer. The rest of the men laughed.

"Yes, one more round for the night and then the rest of you pay your way. I must attend to my lovely new bride," he said, his eyes roaming over her greedily.

Cecilia's breathing quickened as he stepped towards her again. She knew what was coming next, yet she stood frozen as Anders towered over her, gently raking his fingers up and down her arms.

"What do you say, love? Shall we make our way to the bridal chambers?"

Frantic, she searched for an excuse that would satisfy him. Surely, he could not take her to the bridal suite without first performing the wedding ceremony?

Steeling herself, she put a hand on his chest. She had seen Frida flirt with the king a thousand times before. Could she emulate the wretched woman, now?

Forcing a smile, she looked at him through her eyelashes. His heartbeat quickened beneath her palm.

"Would it not be proper to wait until after the wedding, my lord? After all waiting makes the heart grow fonder, does it not?" She kept her voice just loud enough for those in the front rows to hear.

He closed the gap between them, taking her head in both his hands. It was all she could do not to pull away.

"But I want you now, my sweet." His voice betrayed his desire.

Girding her resolve, she wet her lips, "If you want me, you must wait." She took a small step back. As an afterthought, she flashed him a quick smile. "At least until tomorrow. Then I'll be all yours."

He brushed her lips with his thumb.

"Nobody tells the king what to do," he frowned, "but because it is you who is asking, I will give in. Just this once."

Her smile widened at the edges. Her knees almost buckled at the weight of her relief. Instead, she glanced at where Jeremy and Sebastian had been sitting. They were nowhere to be seen.

"But let me at least have one more kiss." Anders pleaded, drawing her attention back to him.

Before he could move, a steel blade glinted between them, the tip of a sword pointed under the king's chin. If Anders was surprised, he didn't look it. Instead, he levelled a cool gaze at the intruder.

"You must be Captain Cervantes," the pirate king greeted, his voice even, "I was wondering when you'd show up."

Cecilia's heart leapt in her chest as Marcus stepped toward the king, a steely determination in his blazing brown eyes.

His clothes were a little worse for wear, his dark shirt was stained with dust and blood. His hair was a dark halo against his grim face, a thin trail of blood trickled from his cheek.

"Touch her again and I'll strike you where you stand," Marcus challenged.

Anders let out a brief chuckle, releasing his grip on Cecilia. It was the opening she needed to pull away from him. Marcus stepped into the space between them, putting an arm out to shield her.

"I'd admire your courage little soldier, if you weren't so stupid as to think I am unarmed. Or that you wouldn't be outnumbered."

In a flash, Anders drew his own sword, pointing it at Marcus' throat. It's blood red tassel swung under the golden candlelight. Behind him, Cecilia could make out several pirates reaching for their weapons.

"Cecilia, get behind me," Marcus barely spared her a glance. She moved to obey.

"Oh of course," Anders chuckled as Marcus took a careful step backward, "the soldier is in love with the princess. How predictable. How... pathetic."

"Why does everyone keep saying that?" Marcus mumbled.

Murmurs ran through the crowd, an excited buzz rippling through the room. Cecilia's breath caught. If she stepped in between them, they would be forced to put their swords down. Fear rooted her to the spot as Marcus' rapier tested the pirate's sword.

Anders spared her a glance over Marcus' shoulder.

"I hope you remember this night, my sweet," he addressed her. "My love will not be rivalled."

Before Cecilia could think, Anders swung his sword at Marcus. Strong hands yanked her to the floor. Prince Derek loomed over her, his sword glinting in the golden light.

"Perhaps your death would suit me better," he sneered.

Cecilia froze as Derek raised his sword above her. Two blades blocked the prince's blow, holding his fury at bay.

"Over my dead body," Marcus vowed.

The prince frowned at him.

"That can be arranged."

42

Smoke & Mirrors

When your back's against the wall, dazzle them with smoke and mirrors.

The advice his father had given him as a boy rang in Marcus' ears as he and the pirate king blocked Cecilia from Derek's blade.

"Get her out of here!" King Anders roared at his men as he and Marcus pushed Prince Derek away. The same brigand who had taken Cecilia from the *Sorrento* dragged her from the stage behind him.

Marcus whirled to fight the brute, only to be met by Derek's blade. He lunged at Marcus who narrowly missed the sword's razor edge. The prince's face darkened.

"You hurt her, young prince, then our deal is nullified," the pirate king's voice came from beside Marcus.

Derek frowned at the pirate, his shoulders drooping. It was the opening Marcus needed. He slashed at the prince's arm. Derek hissed, gripping the wound.

Meanwhile, Marcus spun to face the king.

"Where are you taking her?" he demanded. The pirate flashed him a cruel grin.

"Somewhere you'll never find her."

Marcus circled the pirate king, both watching the other for an opening. A grunt from behind him forced Marcus to turn. Pain sliced his arm as Derek's blade shone red in the firelight.

"You're outnumbered Marcus," Derek warned, a sinister edge to his voice.

"Has that ever stopped me before?" Marcus raised an eyebrow at his old friend. Switching his attention, he managed to block the prince's attack.

Rage contorted Derek's features as an ugly growl tore itself from his lips. Blinded by emotion, Derek would be quick to contain. Still, Marcus danced around his friend, keeping his back to the stage. The king watched them for a moment before joining the fray.

Three blades met, the sharp clang of metal ringing in the air. The crowd hollered in uproar. Glass bottles crashed nearby as tables and chairs were sent flying. Someone had started a brawl and bloodlust ran rife through the tavern.

Good, Marcus thought, he needed a distraction. The prince and the pirate joined forces against him, pushing him back against a wall.

Marcus tensed, unsheathing his dagger.

A familiar scream above them threatened his composure. Derek took the opening, slashing Marcus' wound again. Gripping his sword tighter, Marcus fought to keep focused.

"That was a cheap shot," he ground out.

Derek's mouth hardened into a thin line.

"I'm just getting started."

Marcus reached for his dagger, blocking the prince's blow before it could pierce his heart.

Metal rang in ears, blades a blur as his opponents pressed against him.

Bracing himself on one leg, Marcus kicked a wooden barrel beside him. The king stumbled out of the way, his blade narrowly missing Prince Derek. Marcus leapt over the barrel, landing in time to parry the prince's attack.

The smell of alcohol threatened to overpower them as ale spilled onto the floor.

"What the hell did you do that for?" the pirate king growled, regaining his balance and slashing at Marcus, "Do you know how expensive this is to make?"

Marcus snorted in answer.

"Marcus!" A familiar voice rose above the din. He glanced behind his opponents to see Sebastian, his shirt torn at the collar, pointing toward the staircase.

Cecilia.

Before Marcus could take a step, Derek lunged at him, blue eyes blazing with unbridled hatred. Marcus sidestepped the prince, causing him to slip on the ale. Marcus dropped to a crouch beside him.

"Forgive me brother," he murmured. Derek's eyes widened as Marcus brought his fist down on the prince's head. He prayed Derek would wake up with nothing more than a headache.

"You shouldn't have done that to my ally," the pirate king levelled his blade under Marcus' chin.

"He was my friend first," Marcus challenged.

"Some friend you turned out to be."

Marcus batted the sword away with his own before lunging forward. The pirate king, expecting the attack, blocked him easily.

"Let the princess go," Marcus demanded, as they circled each other, ale licking at their boots.

"Never."

Their blades rang out against the din, Marcus pushing them closer to the edge of the stage, toward the rowdy crowd. If he could make it to the stairs, he could find Cecilia and get her out of there.

The pirate king lunged again. Marcus blocked him expertly, forcing the pirate to retreat against a stage wall.

"You'll never have her, you know," Anders taunted, flinching as Marcus' blade tasted skin.

"Shall I describe to you how she tastes?" Growling, Marcus lunged forward, his dagger missing the king's head by centimetres.

King Anders laughed.

"Is that the best you've got?"

"I wasn't aiming for you," Marcus smirked. A torch clanged to the ground by their feet.

The pirate lunged forward. Marcus sidestepped him racing to the edge of the stage. Anders lost balance, tumbling into Prince Derek who was beginning to peel himself up off the floor. Marcus' dagger glinted in the firelight, as he leapt into the throng of thugs. Small flames licked at his ankles, the stage floor crackling beneath him.

"I'll make you pay for this!" Anders yelled, scrambling to his feet.

But Marcus was already gone.

43

A Fiery Escape

Cecilia didn't need to turn to know it was Tayen who had bundled her into his big, burly arms. Skiv's red hair bobbed along in front of them as they hurried down a maze of narrow passageways. She screamed as they plunged into darkness.

"Where are you taking me?" she demanded, lungs constricting in the oppressive heat.

"Somewhere safe," Skiv called from somewhere ahead of them.

Cecilia strained her ears for any sign of a fight behind them. Apart from Tayen's heavy footsteps and her own heartbeat, she could barely make out a sound, save the distant crash of furniture.

After Marcus and the prince started duelling, a fight had broken out in the tavern. In the ensuing chaos, Skiv pulled her to safety, bundling her into Tayen's waiting arms.

Despite his previous kindness, she wasn't sure she welcomed the sight of him.

"Please, Tayen. You're hurting me," she cried.

He mumbled an apology and loosened his grip but didn't let her go until they turned into a short hallway, illuminated by a small torch.

Skiv fumbled for a key at a large wooden door. Cecilia closed her eyes, imagining a dungeon at the end of the road.

Instead, a cool breeze hit her skin as they tumbled out. Two horses stood saddled and ready in the dirty yard. Cecilia balked to see Sebastian holding them steady. Tayen set her gently on the ground. She looked between the men, confused.

"What on earth is going on here?" she held onto Tayen's arm for support. Her legs trembled as she struggled to comprehend the scene before her.

"It seems the pirates grew a conscience and decided to help you escape," Sebastian answered, holding out a hand.

She stood slack-jawed, staring at her companions.

"No. I have to go back."

Sebastian's dark brows furrowed in confusion.

"Señorita," he handed her the reins to a bay mare, "we are here to rescue you. To take you home."

"But Calgaria is not my home!" she stomped her foot.

Skiv and Sebastian exchanged looks. To her surprise, Tayen spoke up.

"You deserve better'n what King Anders was offerin' you," he said. "No one should use people the way he does. The way he did our sister." He nodded glumly at Skiv.

"If you're really the lost princess he says you are, you need to be with your family. And if you're not… well, you deserve a life better'n the one you'd have here."

"But I can help!" she protested.

"Help who? Your Highness? We're beyond helpin'." Skiv jerked his chin at Tayen.

"The children! The ones dying in terrible contraptions. The ones on the street with no choice but to become pirates or-"

"And what d'you think you can do?" Skiv snapped. "Tell the king to turn our way of life around to suit your superior sense of morality?"

Cecilia's back stiffened.

"I want every person on this island to have a fair chance at a good life."

"And who's sayin' we don't have a good life?"

"Are you happy with how your life turned out?" Cecilia challenged.

Skiv's features darkened, as he closed the small distance between them. Sebastian stepped in front of her before Skiv could raise his hand.

"Get out of here before I change my mind for helpin' ya." He stabbed Sebastian's chest with his finger. Sebastian didn't flinch.

Behind them, the tavern creaked and shuddered. The mare skittered as the smell of smoke filtered across the yard. Cecilia mounted quickly.

"There's an abandoned cottage on Isla Esmeralda where you can spend the night," Tayen said, patting the horse. "Tonight's our lowest tide of the year so take the sandbar across. The tide'll wash away ya tracks by mornin'."

A large bang sounded behind them. Women screamed. Glass boomed and shattered. Men called for buckets as orange flames licked at the edges of the tavern.

"You should go," Skiv jerked his chin toward the cane fields, "King Anders'll have your heads if he catches you here."

The mare whickered and shuffled beneath her. She turned to Sebastian.

"What are we waiting for?"

Before he could answer, Marcus sprinted around the corner, soot falling around his shoulders.

Her heart leapt at the sight of him. Before she knew quite what she was doing, she urged the horse into a canter towards him, her arm outstretched. Glancing up, he swung himself into the saddle behind her. Sebastian motioned for them to head into the cane fields, the dark stalks spreading out before them.

She looked for Skiv and Tayen, but they were nowhere to be found.

Probably for the best, she thought.

The tavern groaned behind them, flames lashing the roof. A crash spooked the horses into action, the trio leaping into the field as the fire crackled.

Bells rang in the distance, the clanging soon drowned by the thunder of horses' hooves.

In the years ever after, it was the screams of the damned that haunted her the most.

44

The Truth of It

Fire roared in their ears, heat prickling over her shoulders as sweat beaded on her brow. Despite Marcus shielding her from the brunt of the heat, the fire was inescapable. Flames crackled dangerously around them, fields alight as far as the eye could see.

"Anders has figured out we're in the cane fields," Marcus shouted above the crackle of flames. "He'll be lighting his cane on fire to smoke us out."

Cecilia coughed, her lungs struggling to cope. Charred pieces of cane rained down on them, burning her nose, her hair, her hands. She shook her head, cane trash raining on her clothes.

Beside them, Sebastian urged them faster; the horses, recognising the threat, obeyed, speeding down the narrow tracks.

Although the fires lasted no more than a few minutes and smoked themselves out quickly, the threat, and sweet smell of burnt sugar, lingered menacingly in the air.

"What's the bet Anders' men are waiting to catch us on the road?" Sebastian called over his shoulder. Cecilia could barely make out his words, over the rush of wind.

"It's a high probability," Marcus called back.

"What do we do?" she shouted.

She didn't want to continue through the cane fields with the threat of fire so close and constant, yet she worried about Anders' men on the road. She shuddered to think what they would do to her.

"There's a mountain village not far from here," Marcus rose his voice, careful not to yell in her ear, "From there we'll make our way to

Cova Zafiro. Catalina will pick us up."

"She didn't wait for us at Puerto de Oro?"

She felt Marcus shake his head, his chin brushing the back of her head gently.

"We told her to leave the harbour as soon as Alistar and Jeremy boarded the ship. If they left while the tavern burned, they may've set sail before Anders thought of closing the harbour."

"You rescued Alistar?" she asked, perplexed.

She could hear the smile in his voice.

"I came to rescue you. Alistar was just collateral."

They continued in silence, the wind making conversation impossible. They wove in and out of narrow tracks left by cane cutters until the fires were well and truly behind them. The moon hung high in the sky, a blanket of passing clouds briefly blocking them from sight.

Sebastian motioned for them to slow when they reached the edge of the vast cane fields. Cecilia chanced a glance over Marcus' shoulder. An orange glow shone in the distance. She brushed cane trash from her sleeves.

"Do you need to stretch your legs?" Marcus asked, nodding at the stretch of road before them.

Cecilia shook her head, "No. Let's keep moving."

Sebastian watched them curiously before clucking his horse forward.

The road opened out to flat plains lined with tall grass, stretching out to the base of a small mountain. Mud squelched beneath the horses' hooves as they followed the well-worn path.

Grey clouds glinted silver under the moonlight, the smell of freshly fallen rain mingling with the scent of smoke on their clothes. The crackle of fire gave way to the sound of night birds hooting and crickets chirping in the distance.

They passed by a few sleepy fishing villages, slowing only to pass through. As they passed, Cecilia could hear the gentle rush of waves crashing against the shore somewhere to her left. For a moment, she let herself lean back into Marcus' chest, closing her eyes to let the cool ocean air wash over her skin.

"Comfortable?" Marcus' voice interrupted her reverie.

She startled forward, mumbling an apology.

Sebastian rode beside them, the sound of hooves crunching on gravel melding into the natural nightlife around them. Yet, despite the flat roads and moonlight, they were careful to keep conversation to a minimum.

In the brief peace of the scene around them, Cecilia fought to keep her eyes open. Yet somewhere in the journey, she nodded off to the gentle sway of the horse and Marcus' steady heartbeat.

She had no memory of entering the small clearing they found themselves in a short time later.

They reached a narrow creek, hidden by a small grove of trees. They were near enough to see any incoming traffic on the road, but far enough to hide from anyone who happened to pass by.

Dismounting, she stretched her weary limbs, legs aching with exhaustion. Marcus caught her arm to steady her.

"Careful, Señorita," he offered her a weary smile.

She shrugged him off, walking to the nearby creek. The still water glittered under the spilled moonlight, a forest full of trees illuminated by stream and heavens alike.

Hot tears burned her throat, anger, relief and disappointment mingling together.

"Señorita," Marcus' voice came from behind her, "what's wrong?"

"I have to go back," she choked.

He leant against a young tree, its juvenile leaves skimming Marcus' dark locks. His brows furrowed in concern.

"Did you lose something?"

She shook her head.

"Then why do you wish to return?"

"Because I have to be his queen."

Marcus shifted uncomfortably, crossing his arms over his chest.

"You barely knew the pirate king two days, and you want to marry him?" He couldn't hide the disgust in his voice, "I didn't think you were the power-hungry type. But I guess you're just like your godmother."

He pushed off the tree, walking along the creek line.

"Hey!" Cecilia followed him, "That's not true!"

"Oh really?" he whirled on her, "Then why else would you want to marry a monster like him? Certainly not for his charm or looks!"

"There's nothing wrong with his looks," Cecilia argued. Not that she had cared what the pirate king looked like. Much.

Marcus shook his head, raking a hand through his hair.

"I can't believe you. A powerful man demands to marry you and you accept because he's handsome."

"It's not like that." Cecilia snapped, "Maybe if you would listen to me instead of assuming the worst, you would understand that I don't want to marry him."

"You just said you wanted to!"

"Hush! You're frightening the horses." Sebastian reprimanded patting their horses down.

"Sorry," Marcus apologised to the sky. After a moment's pause, he faced her again. "Help me understand."

Cecilia took a deep breath.

"I don't want to marry the pirate king, but if becoming his queen is the only way I can help people, then it is a responsibility I am willing to bear."

Marcus' dark eyes softened as understanding dawned on him.

"As Calgaria's princess, you will have power and influence. You will make decisions that will affect people's lives for the better-"

She shook her head.

"It doesn't matter what influence I have over people *there*," she stepped towards him, pleading with him to understand, "if I can't change the lives of people *here*. I saw a child die, Marcus."

She shut her eyes at the memory. Tears spilled down her cheeks. She wouldn't wipe them away.

"What does it matter what I can do in Calgaria when innocents are dying here every day?"

When she opened her eyes again, Marcus' gaze was soft but firm.

"You have the makings of a great queen," he murmured.

Despite herself, Cecilia warmed at the compliment.

"You know," he leaned forward conspiratorially, "Calgaria and the Fickle Islands will need someone to help smooth diplomatic relations after this. If we get you back in time, I think you can make some stipulations as part of a peace treaty."

Cecilia's heart leapt in her chest. All was not lost!

Thank you Ilio! She prayed silently. Outwardly, she grinned at Marcus.

He cleared his throat, raking a hand through his perfectly messy hair. She noticed a dark stain pooled on his sleeve.

"You're bleeding," she pointed at his arm.

Marcus glanced at his sleeve.

"Oh," he frowned, "I'd forgotten about that."

Cecilia reached for her waist, untying the scarf Frida had added to her ensemble at the last minute.

"Take this," she thrust it at him.

With a grateful smile, he peeled off his shirt, revealing a lean, tanned torso. She forced herself to look at the wound on his arm. It was deep, but not fatal.

"So, you think I'm really the lost princess?" she asked, watching as he knelt by the creek.

Wiping the grime away from his wound, he nodded.

"I was going to tell you before we got to Calgaria." Even under the moonlight she could make out the goosebumps covering his arm as he winced under the cool water, "but with everything that happened after Alistar boarded the ship- I guess I just couldn't find the right time."

Cecilia nodded at her boots.

"I would've appreciated you finding a way to tell me. Especially since you were getting paid to bring me back."

"Would it have made you think differently of me?" he reached for the scarf, "of this whole… misadventure?"

She shrugged, kneeling beside him. Gently, she began to wrap the scarf over his arm, covering the wound. His fingers brushed hers as he held the top of the makeshift bandage on his shoulder.

"Maybe…" she tightened the bandage around his bicep.

"If I'd told you from the start who you were, would you have believed me?" he pressed. "If you knew I was paid to bring you home, would you still have come?"

She bit her bottom lip, thinking for a moment.

"I… don't know," she said finally, tying the bandage tight at his shoulder, "but I would've appreciated the honesty."

The softness in his voice when he next spoke, surprised her.

"I'm sorry. For not telling you. And for calling you shallow. You did not deserve that."

She shrugged, avoiding his gaze, "It's alright."

"It's not."

Something about the quiet authority in his voice forced her to look at him.

"I should not have lied or called you names according to my misjudgement. For that, I apologise."

His eyes shone in earnest.

"I forgive you," Cecilia whispered.

Marcus smiled in relief. Under the spilled moonlight, he looked like a prince, his dark hair crowned by the moon, setting shadows dancing across his handsome face. Something about the softness in his gaze set her heart racing.

"I hate to interrupt, but we need to get going," Sebastian's voice startled them apart. She hadn't realised how close they had drifted together.

Marcus shook his head, stepping away from her. He pulled his shirt on, walking toward their horse. With a sigh, Cecilia dusted herself off.

"Would you like to take the reins, or shall I?" Marcus asked, stroking the steed's nose. She shook her head.

"You take them."

Marcus mounted first, holding out his good arm to help her on behind him.

They continued at pace, alternating between a walk and a canter, the twinkling stars guiding their path.

"I'm sorry too," she murmured as they passed the edge of a sleepy fishing village. She rested her chin on Marcus' shoulder, speaking so softly she could barely hear her own voice.

"What do you have to be sorry for?"

"For putting you in more danger than you needed to be, and..." she hesitated, "for not giving you an opportunity to tell me the truth earlier."

A long moment passed before he spoke again.

"You have nothing to be sorry for."

She shook her head, glad she didn't have to face him.

"I don't expect you to trust me after this," he continued, "but I hope you can believe me when I say that I will do everything in my power to get you home safely."

"I know."

Marcus turned his head just enough to flash her a warm smile, his brown eyes glinting under the mischievous moon.

Not for the first time, she wondered what it would be like to kiss him.

45

Villa Fortuna

"You let them escape?" Pirate King Anders roared over the crackle of the tavern. The wooden structure leaned dangerously to one side as black ash rained from the cane fields behind them.

Skiv struggled against the men who held him as Pirate King Anders kicked Tayen, lying beaten and bloodied on the ground.

Tayen's head lolled on the dirt, his battered arms wrapped protectively around his middle. Strong hands clamped on Skiv's shoulders. His crewmen. Their betrayal cut deep, but King Anders' cut deeper.

"What in the seven hells possessed you to let them go?" Anders demanded as his boot met Tayen's back. A sickening crack sent shockwaves down Skiv's spine.

A semi-circle of Anders' men gathered to watch the scene, a fair distance from the burning structure. Firefighters had arrived and were pouring buckets of sand into the ever-growing flames, but Skiv knew it wouldn't be enough to temper the mighty fire.

Tayen groaned, the mournful sound the only reassurance he was alive.

"Answer me!" Anders yelled, his face now inches from Tayen's battered form. The burly pirate shook his head, his jaw clenched in defiance.

The pirate king raised his fist to strike again.

"It was me!" Skiv burst, lurching forward, "I did it. I let them go."

The pirate king whirled on him, straightening himself to his full height. His green eyes blazed with barely contained fury, his tattered shirt tugging on the warm evening wind.

"We both know you're only taking the fall to spare him," he took a swaggering step toward Skiv, his fist still clenched by his side. Skiv braced himself for the punch that would inevitably come. He would welcome it, he longed for the pain

Instead, King Anders turned swiftly and landed another blow on Tayen. Skiv's knees buckled at the gurgle of blood spilling from his brother's mouth.

"Don't' make me ask you again!" Anders demanded.

A woeful moan escaped Tayen's lips as he sunk deeper into the dirt, his skin covered in burning ash.

"Please–" Skiv fell to his knees beside him, "Tayen–"

"Shut up Skiv! Get the brute on his knees," Anders ordered his men.

Two solid guards stepped forward, manhandling Tayen's battered form until he was forced to kneel. They held one arm each to stop him from toppling over. Skiv's heart lurched in his chest to see his brother look so young, so vulnerable.

Tayen, while two years older, had always been the softer of the two. He looked like the scared little boy he had been when their father died. Skiv squeezed his eyes, shutting out the image.

"I will not ask you again, boy. Why did you let them escape?

The roar of fire rushed behind them, men shouting orders filled Tayen's silence. Skiv recognised the Calgarian prince distantly calling for his horse. Still, Tayen said nothing.

A gunshot rang out.

Despite the heat from the fire, a cold sweat broke across Skiv's skin. Dark blood poured from a wound in Tayen's abdomen, but he remained glaring defiantly at the pirate king.

"You killed my sister," Tayen murmured, his voice barely audible above the flames. Blood dripped into the dusty ground as he spoke, "I promised to avenge her if it was the last thing I did."

The pirate king's voice hardened.

"Well then," he cocked the gun at him a second time, "give her my regards."

Skiv flinched at the gunshot. Tayen slumped to the ground. Skiv's anguish was lost to the night as the hands that held him shoved him back into the relative safety of the charred cane fields.

"Throw him into the fire," Anders ordered.

Skiv screamed as two crewmen dragged Tayen to the edge of the nearest cane fire, his body lost to the flames.

He fought to overthrow his captors. Someone landed a blow on his jaw and he welcomed the pain. With a roar, he struck his attacker, raining down blow upon blow until the face beneath him was as battered and bloody as his brothers.

He felt the shackles at his wrists too late as he was hauled to his feet, dragged to stand before the pirate king. Shaking with anger, grief pouring down his face, Skiv fell to his knees.

King Anders rolled his eyes.

"Get up. Pirates don't mourn traitors," he ordered.

Skiv shook his head.

"He's my brother!"

King Anders ignored him, instead nodding at the guards who held him. Skiv didn't fight as they hauled him off the ground.

"Gather the prisoners and Lady Alarcon. We have a ship to catch." he ordered his men. They dispersed quickly, each moving with haste to get to their posts. All except the two who had thrown Tayen to the fire, their hands clamped like a vice on Skiv's shoulders.

The pirate king stood before him, his face cast in shadow as the tavern continued to burn. Flames bloomed from his shoulders; his cruel mouth twisted into a sneer. He was half pirate, half demon.

"I will give you one chance to prove yourself to me. If you fail, you'll meet a fate worse than death," Anders promised.

"Kill me. At least then I'll be with my family," Skiv bit back.

The king clocked his shoulder as he moved past, his voice so low only Skiv could hear.

"I will not grant you mercy in death. Not like I did the rest of them."

***

"We're not far from Villa Fortuna. If the village lives up to its name, we might be able to find some fresh horses to continue our journey," Sebastian said as they made their way towards a fresh set of untouched cane fields, "And take care what you say from now on, the cane hears everything."

The smell of salt air carried slightly on the evening breeze, mingling unpleasantly with the taste of ash and smoke on Cecilia's tongue.

They passed through the town in a walk to avoid suspicion, despite the empty roads and late hour.

Fields of tall cane spread out around them, separating each house at irregular intervals.

On the other side of town, she spied a steaming cloud rising high into the night air from tall spires. The mill was lit at regular intervals, still partly hidden in shadow, but nonetheless intimidating even from a distance.

Most homes they passed were asleep for the evening. Drawn curtains hid them from prying eyes. Every now and then, a front door was lit dimly by an outside lamp, a beacon for those who had spent too long at the tavern. Winding their way through the centre of town, they reached a fountain in what looked to be the town square.

Even under the moonlight, she could make out the dirty water spilling from the lips of a marble mermaid, her stony face distorted by shadow. The gruesome sight made Cecilia's stomach twist with a nervous flutter.

"This way," Sebastian guided them on towards another stretch of road, this one cobblestoned. Not far ahead, a tavern glowed golden at the end of the street. As they drew closer, an off-tempo fiddle and raucous music wafted over them, drunk patrons singing loudly and off-key.

The trio dismounted once again stretching their aching limbs. Marcus and Sebastian immediately set about tying the horses to a communal lean-to outside the ramshackle building.

Cecilia stood by the dark mare, making note of the old building. From her vantage point among the horses, she could see couples as they loitered in shadows on the tavern's veranda, too lost in their own world to take notice of the strangers in their midst.

A wooden sign swung gently above the tavern entrance, three overlapping horseshoes branded onto the well-worn wood, The Lucky Mare painted in red lettering beneath it. A light tune filtered through the laughter and revelry.

"Fancy a dance?" Marcus asked, sidling up beside her.

Cecilia shook her head, thankful the dark cloud passing over the moon hid the blush on her cheeks.

"You're bleeding, again," she said instead. From the dim streetlights, she could make out the dark stain spreading across the red scarf, trickles of blood running down his arm again.

Sighing, Marcus tore a strip of fabric from the hem of his shirt, his brows furrowed in concentration.

"What are you doing?" She frowned.

He paused to glance at her quickly.

"Making a bandage."

"Out of your shirt? Are you sure that's sanitary?"

His mouth quirked into a teasing smile.

"You don't think Jeremy would approve?"

"I don't think I would approve," she surprised them both with a laugh, "but I suppose we can make an exception."

"If you need a fresh bandage, I've found one," Sebastian said, throwing a white ball at them. Marcus caught it with one hand, winking at her. She raised what she hoped was an unimpressed eyebrow.

The ghost of a smile lingered on Marcus' handsome features as he rolled up his sleeve. She untied the scarf, securing the bandage firmly over the wound again, this time under his careful instruction, as he slung the strip of his shirt over his other shoulder.

"Hold the base of it here," he instructed, covering his hand with hers as she wrapped the fabric around his arm.

"Tell me if it's too tight." She murmured.

Cecilia tried not to think about the flutter in her stomach as her fingers softly grazed his skin as she worked. She tried not to let her gaze wander to his forearms or think about pushing away stray strands of hair framing his high cheekbones.

Had she thought him handsome an eternity ago when she first saw him at Villa Alarcon? Days without a razor saw dark stubble pepper his jawline which gave him an air of maturity she hadn't noticed before.

With a final tug, she tied the linen bandage, her fingers hovered uncertainly over his bare skin.

"How's that?" she admired her handiwork.

"Good," he grinned, "thank you."

She couldn't help the smile that bloomed under his gaze.

"Alright, the coast is clear. Let's get going." Sebastian's voice brought them back to the situation at hand, "Untie as many horses as you can, quickly."

They set to work, Marcus swiftly untying rope from the wood. Most of the horses stood where they were, taking the liberty to graze a little further than they had been able to.

"That's enough, let's go," Sebastian ordered, holding two fresh horses by the reins.

"How do you feel about sharing again?" he asked.

A loud bang startled the horses as the untied steeds took flight and the ones Sebastian held jittered nervously.

"Hey you! What are you doing with my horse?" a shadowy figure slurred from a tavern door.

"I guess we have no choice," Marcus answered as he helped Cecilia mount a bay horse, scrambling quickly behind her as Sebastian called something out over his shoulder.

A gunshot rang out into the night. Horses' hooves thundered against the worn earth as more shots rang out after them. So much for going unnoticed.

The world was a blur as Marcus urged the horse faster. They followed the road out of the square to the deserted main thoroughfare. The group of horses they released galloped beside them, some overtaking them, others breaking off to follow their own paths. A commotion rang out behind them. They were being pursued.

Hooves pounded against stone as they passed an old brick church, a clock tower chiming beside it. The numbers were hard to make out in the rush under the moonlight. Cecilia counted ten chimes, the sound echoing behind them, long after leaving the town. Had they really been riding for half the night?

Once on the open road, Sebastian took the lead while they brought up the rear. A small mountain range surrounded them, its face covered by forest. She ignored the twinge of sadness at the thought of Mount Aramyth, the constant sentinel shadowing Villa Alarcon. Avinada may not be her native country, but for better or for worse, it was the only home she'd ever known.

"Lean into me if you feel unsteady." Marcus murmured against her ear.

After a moment's hesitation, she leant back carefully against his chest. He edged closer in the saddle, his thighs squeezing hers a little tighter as he brought his arms in closer, cocooning her against him.

The horses didn't break stride.

Fields of grass opened out before them, the dark horizon inching closer. The moon hid behind silver clouds when Sebastian slowed to a halt. A bridge appeared ahead of them; the steady rhythm of the ocean crashed nearby. Cecilia shivered under the night air, her flimsy blue dress barely a barrier to the wind's cool teeth.

They sidled up beside Sebastian, easing from a canter to a walk as they stopped at the edge of a sandbank.

The moon moved from behind a dense cloud, uncovering a pale path snaking from the bottom of the sandbank to the next island.

"That must be the sandbank Tayen told us about," Sebastian nodded at the path, directing his words to Cecilia.

"We're going to trust the word of a pirate? After everything he did?" Marcus asked, voice wary.

"He and his brother sacrificed themselves to help me escape tonight," Cecilia argued, "I trust them."

"We could take the bridge," Sebastian suggested with a shrug, "but I don't want to take our chances with highwaymen."

"Would there not be highwaymen on the sandbank?" Cecilia asked, trepidation creeping into her voice.

Sebastian shook his head.

"The only people who would cross a sandbank at low tide at night are criminals, fugitives or fools."

"And which one are we?"

She could hear the smile in Marcus' voice as he urged their steed down the sandy embankment.

The ocean breeze was chillier on the shore than it had been on the bank. The trio dismounted, taking off their boots and tying them together, tossing them onto their shoulders.

"It'll be easier to cross the water when your boots aren't dragging you down," Marcus explained.

The path was wide enough for them to walk two abreast, Marcus and Cecilia in front with Sebastian bringing up the rear.

Cecilia relished the feeling of wet sand between her toes. How long had it been since she had last strolled along the beach? Or a garden? Or anywhere for that matter? She had eventually grown accustomed to the rock of the boat beneath her, but nothing was better than the feel of her feet on solid ground.

Cold water lapped at her ankles as they passed through the first stretch of water. She shivered in the cool breeze, her hair whipping out from the orderly braid Frida had styled her in so many hours ago.

Her stomach rumbled angrily, the sound lost against the lap of the waves and the occasional horses' sigh. They trudged along in silence, all conversation drowned out by the indominable wind. Shivering, she rubbed her arms to try and mitigate the cold, pushing herself faster to try and generate some warmth.

The sandy path snaked its way through to the next island, darker in patches covered by water, brighter where the tide stayed at bay. Inky black ocean surrounded them on both sides in an endless horizon. Stars dotted the sky above them, shining briefly from behind inconstant clouds.

A gunshot pierced the otherwise quiet night. The horses startled, whinnying in fear. Marcus tugged their horses head down, attempting to stop it from bolting.

"Pirates! On the bank!" Sebastian yelled from behind them.

A second gunshot rang out, this time followed by a soft plink beside them. Marcus steadied their steed as Cecilia scrambled for the horse. Water splashed at her calves until it came up to her knees. Either they'd hit a deep patch of water, or the tide was rising. Knees trembling, Cecilia fought down the rising panic bubbling up her throat.

With Marcus' help, she pushed herself into the saddle, scooting forward to give him enough room to sit behind her. Sebastian, already mounted, hurried beside them.

A third shot rang out, this one closer than the rest. Sebastian swore as his horse startled. Marcus plunged them into the water. The horses' hooves pounded unsteadily on the shifting sand beneath.

"We need to keep moving," he said through gritted teeth as he fought for control over the fast-panicking horse.

"The tide–"

"I know," his voice was steady, "we don't have far to go."
"But the pirates- what if there are more on the other side?"
Marcus shook his head.
"One problem at a time, señorita,"

46
Family Ties

The ocean chill cut through to his very bones as they emerged soaking from the water and onto a stretch of solid sand. Chancing a glance behind his shoulder, Marcus could just make out shadowed figures stranded on the sandbank behind them.

They had ridden through the rising tide, almost swimming at some points, until they reached the zenith of the sandbank. The sound of gunshots had died down as they raced ahead, bullets missing them far and wide. Now, all that broke the night's serenity were the frightened shouts of the stranded.

Ahead of them, past the grassy sandbank on Isla Esmeralda lay more fields. Tall grass cast strange shadows along the dirt path as they cantered through the quiet island corner. The island, at least to the north, was sparsely inhabited by farmers, their lands stretching as far as the eye could see.

Marcus had no doubt the pirate king had stationed sentries along its coastline. They had no time to dally.

The moon moved westward, followed by persistent clouds in a game of cat and mouse. Briefly Marcus wondered where the *Real Sorrento* would be stationed and if she would see them at all.

Cecilia sighed against him. She had begun to doze off after they passed the first distant cluster of houses, her head lolling off to the side. Gently, he pulled her back in the saddle to lean against him. She hadn't protested, likely too tired to notice.

"We'll be coming up to Skiv's safehouse soon," Sebastian announced. Though his voice was low, it sounded loud in the silence of the night.

Marcus nodded.

He was hesitant to stay at a place once inhabited by pirates, even if they had helped them escape the pirate king. Skiv was the one who had taken Cecilia in the first place. He had proudly proclaimed himself second to the king. Had he really had a change of heart to help them, or was he leading them into a trap with false repentance?

Marcus scanned the road ahead of them. They had not seen anyone since leaving the men stranded on the sandbar. Even if they had managed to extricate themselves from the rising tide, they were too far from Isla Esmeralda to reach her shores.

Sebastian clicked his tongue and Marcus followed him down a narrow side road. Had he not followed Sebastian, he might have missed it, hidden by a grove of trees. Beyond them, into the clearing stood an old, weatherbeaten cottage, surrounded by more silver grass. Even under the moonlight, the old home looked nostalgic, as though it was missing the people who inhabited it, yet welcomed anyone who could breathe new life.

"Señorita," Marcus shook her gently awake as they rode to the far side of the house, "we're here."

She yawned, stretching her arms in front of her before slipping to the ground. He followed suit, tying his horse to a sturdy panel on the back veranda. They joined Sebastian at the front door after a quick walkaround.

"Doesn't look like anyone's been here for a while," Sebastian said as he searched for a key, finding one under a tattered rug lining the entryway.

With a groan, the door creaked open and the trio made their way into the house. Marcus hadn't noticed how chilly the wind was until they were inside, the door shut firmly behind them. It wasn't exactly warm, but it was better than standing in the frigid air all night. He motioned for Cecilia to stay by the door while he and Sebastian inspected the house. Creeping through the cottage, they examined each room.

It was sparsely furnished, but homely. There were only two bedrooms, with two small beds in each. Drawers held a meagre supply of tattered clothes. Portraits of a young family popped up in each room, one of the occupants obviously an artist.

Satisfied there were no threats, he joined Cecilia and Sebastian in the living room.

"Find anything?" Sebastian asked.

Marcus shook his head.

"Good. It's another few hours' ride until we reach Cova Zafiro. I think it's safe to say we won't get there without at least a short rest."

Cecilia tried to hide a yawn behind her hand. Marcus, fatigue setting in, yawned as well.

Sebastian offered to take the first watch, protesting slightly when Marcus offered to take it.

"Will you sleep if I don't take it?" Marcus asked, knowing his friend far too well.

After a moment's pause, Sebastian shook his head.

"Will you need some company?" Cecilia asked, rubbing her eyes. Marcus shook his head.

"I'll feel better knowing you've had some sleep. Besides," he stifled another yawn, "I'm not tired."

She nodded, unconvinced.

Before settling in for the night, they made sure every window, curtain and door was closed. Cecilia gathered pillows and blankets from the bedrooms while Marcus and Sebastian set up their sleeping quarters in the small living room.

"I found this in the kitchen," Sebastian said proffering a selection of dried meats and crackers, "It's not much, but it should keep us going until we reach Cova Zafiro."

Giving into his hunger pangs, Marcus sat on the floor, eating in companionable silence. Once they had satisfied their stomachs, Sebastian rolled the rest of the bounty into a linen cloth, packing it in a satchel procured from a saddlebag.

They decided to give Cecilia the sofa, which she accepted gratefully. Marcus set up camp on an armchair opposite the front door, while Sebastian set up a thin layer of blankets by the empty hearth, opposite the sofa.

Together, they provided a sandwich of protection against any potential intruders, which save for the rats crawling in the ceiling, would not be many.

"Are we leaving at first light tomorrow?" Cecilia asked from beneath her blankets.

"No," Sebastian's voice was tired but firm, "we must be at the docks before then. We rest for an hour or so, then we leave."

Cecilia groaned from under her covers.

Fighting drooping eyelids, Marcus stretched his limbs, knocking a slip of parchment from a cabinet beside him. Gingerly, he picked it up. It was a family portrait.

A thin young woman with kindly brown eyes, and a slightly older man with grey peppering his brown hair. Together, they were flanked by three children – a bright, ruddy haired lad with bright blue eyes, a tall dark-haired boy who despite his large size, seemed to shrink into his parents, and a pretty young girl with strawberry-blonde hair.

Something about the two boys seemed familiar. Marcus' suspicion was confirmed when he read the scrawled note on the back of the portrait.

In loving memory of our beloved Papa. The Skivver family, Seraph and Albert Skivver with their children, Albert Jnr, 8, Tayen, 10 and Cecilia, 12.

Skiv.

Marcus yawned. Perhaps the pirate's change of heart was genuine after all?

47

First Light

It was still dark when Cecilia woke to someone shaking her shoulder. Groaning, she shivered pulling the blanket tighter around her, defending herself from the chilly night air.

"It's time to get going," Marcus' gentle voice sounded thick with sleep. She pried an eye open.

"Five more minutes?" she pleaded.

He met her entreaty with a tired smile and weary shake of his head.

"We've already slept longer than we ought. We should've been on the road at least an hour ago."

Sighing, Cecilia pushed herself from the sofa tugging the blanket around her shoulders as if keeping the last dregs of sleep.

"Where's Sebastian?" she peered around the room in the dim light. The outside world was as dark and quiet as when they had arrived. Surely it couldn't be close to dawn yet?

"He's outside. Everything's packed and ready to go," Marcus answered.

Folding her blanket haphazardly, she placed it gently on the sofa before following him outside. She regretted leaving the blanket as he locked the door behind them, placing the key back under the rug.

Her skin prickled in the cool air as she waited by the stairs. Moonlight streamed from behind a solitary grey cloud, blankets of stars peering at them through the black-blue sky.

A rustling by the veranda caught her attention as she spied a dark, solitary figure round the corner. She froze, her throat constricting in a silent scream until Sebastian came into view leading a horse.

"Where did you find that?" Marcus asked, skipping down the stairs.

"She was grazing nearby. I found some extra tack in the barn while you were inside and saddled her up," Sebastian shrugged.

"Did you see anyone else around?" Marcus scanned the dark fields behind Sebastian who shook his head.

"I watched her for a time. I couldn't see anyone," he patted the beast's neck. "Besides, she's friendly."

Sighing, Marcus rubbed a hand down his face.

"Very well. Cecilia, do you think you can handle riding on your own?"

Cecilia straightened, indignant.

"You've seen me ride before." She crossed her arms over her chest. Had she had more time to sleep, she might have been more agreeable.

Marcus rubbed his eyes with both hands, pushing hair out of his face. She caught him murmur something about coffee.

"Never mind. You take the mare and we'll ride to Cova Zafiro. We have only a few hours until dawn and we need to be on the *Real Sorrento* before then."

With a final check to make sure they weren't being followed, the trio made their way out of the field and out onto the open road.

***

A faint silver streak in the eastern sky alerted them to the presence of dawn. A blanket of grey clouds hung low across the mountain, despite the slow- settling humidity. Sweat clung to Cecilia's back, as the trio made their way to the outskirts of Cova Zafiro.

They had alternated between a walk and a canter for most of the journey, until the first rays of dawn peaked over the horizon. The men expected trouble on the road. Their rest, while short, had given Pirate King Anders ample time to gather his resources and send out messengers and search parties ahead of them.

Cecilia had no doubt the island's ports had closed by now.

"Do you think Catalina will wait for us if we're late?" She asked no one in particular.

"She doesn't have much choice." Sebastian answered.

They barely spoke as they passed a sleepy village, its inhabitants not yet risen. Had they the privilege of time, they would have bypassed it altogether. As it was, the quickest way out was through. So, they walked through the town, Sebastian and Cecilia riding ahead with Marcus bringing up the rear.

The clip clop of horses' hooves was the only break in the silence as they plodded towards the small town. Beyond the sparsely inhabited streets, the grey mass of sea swept into the mouth of the fishing village below, revealing a wide bay. A bright twinkle on the water caught Cecilia's eye. She hoped with all her heart it was the *Sorrento*.

Sebastian came to a halt beside her, Marcus following suit as they stood at the top of a hill, overlooking the town.

"We can't stay here," Sebastian murmured.

"I agree," Marcus sidled up beside him, scanning the horizon. "Did you pocket the spyglass you found?"

Sebastian nodded, rifling in his saddle pack until he found what he was looking for.

He produced a small, golden object, expanding it to its full length, before putting it to his eye.

Cecilia looked between him and the twilight scene with bated breath.

Finally, his lips curved into a smile.

"I think I see her."

Grinning, Sebastian handed the spyglass to Marcus who nodded.

Cecilia watched with keen interest as the men fashioned a torch from a fallen tree branch, Marcus' torn strip of shirt, and a box of matches they had swiped from the cottage.

In the distance, a light twinkled off the water. At first, Cecilia thought it must be sun over the water, but a glance at the clouds suggested the sun would not make its appearance yet. Besides, the twinkling was intermittent, stopping at times as her companions blinked out a response.

It was a code.

"What are they saying?" she asked, glancing between the two parties.

"They'll meet us on the shore," Sebastian answered, his face awash with relief.

Marcus offered her a bright smile.

"Not long now and you'll be on your way home."

Home, she thought, *I don't think I know what that is anymore.*

***

Cecilia's stomach rumbled. She had hoped to hide the sound as they waited on the beach, the horses untethered and unsaddled.

"I think one uninvited horse on a ship is more than enough," Sebastian said as they mulled over what to do with the beasts.

The trio had made their way onto the sand, Sebastian leading them to a secluded spot hidden by rocks and small, hardy trees. The horses, not seeming to mind human company, grazed nearby. It was in the silence Cecilia's stomach rumbled. She tried to mask the sound, wrapping her arms about her middle, but it was no use.

"We should probably eat something," Marcus suggested, proffering last night's rations from a bag slung over his shoulder.

She didn't have to be asked twice. Setting up a meagre picnic on a faded blanket procured from a saddlebag, the trio ate quickly, polishing off the small stash of crackers.

The smell of freshly baked bread and salt air mingled on the wind. Another stomach rumbled and Cecilia was grateful she wasn't the only one who had been left wanting.

"Should we go into to town and buy some more food?" Marcus suggested, smothering a yawn.

Sebastian's lips pursed as he thought about it.

"It's dangerous. Cata's sailors are on their way. I can see them on the horizon now. Besides, what if we get caught?"

"One, I'll be quick," Marcus counted his excuses on his hand, "two, I'll go on my own to avoid suspicion and three, I'm going to endeavour not to get into trouble."

Sebastian frowned, crossing his arms at the younger man. "And when has point number three ever worked out for you?"

Marcus grinned at his friend, throwing a wink at Cecilia.

"Fine," Sebastian sighed, "Cecilia and I will remain here. You go into town and get only what you can carry, but be quick. If Orren and Sorren get here before you're back, we'll leave you behind."

"Understood," Marcus threw him a mock salute.

Cecilia watched him walk the short distance into town. Her stomach lurched from more than just hunger pangs as he disappeared into a small building on the edge of town. Anxious, she picked at her fingernails.

"How are you feeling?" Sebastian asked drawing her attention to him.

"I think I should be asking you," she fought to stifle another yawn, "did you get any sleep at all?"

He gave her a tired smile and a barely perceptible shake of his head.

"It's been quite an eventful night for you. Your third marriage proposal in about as many weeks?"

"Something like that," she shrugged, "and not to anyone I want to marry either."

Sebastian glanced in the direction of the sleepy town.

"Do you think King Anders will pursue me all the way to Calgaria?" Cecilia picked at her thumb, "If I am who he says I am, I doubt he would give me up so easily."

Sebastian shrugged.

"We won't let him take you again."

"Did you know?" she asked, "that I was the lost princess?"

He shifted on the sand, casting his eyes over the water. Cecilia huffed, leaning back into the coarse sand.

"It seems everyone knows who I am, except me." She lamented to the ocean.

Sebastian shook his head vehemently.

"You may not have the identity you thought you had, but no one can decide who you are for you," the earnestness in his voice surprised her. "You might be a princess with titles and responsibilities, but it's up to you to determine what you will do with that power."

Cecilia stared at him, stunned, until the words began to sink in.

"Thank you," she said, unsure what else to say.

He picked at a stray strand of leather from his arm guard. He was still dressed in his usual sailor's uniform, but until now Cecilia hadn't noticed the leather armour he wore, wrapped around his arms and waist.

"They were going to tell you." Sebastian filled the silence once more.

"When?"

He shrugged, "Marcus and Catalina had it all planned out."

The breeze picked up strands of loose hair from their faces.

"All I know is Marcus had orders to bring you from Villa Alarcon to King Lars and Queen Minerva. That being said, we should have all been more honest with you from the start. Marcus was sworn to secrecy, but ever since you've boarded our ship, he has been looking for a way to tell you the truth. In all my years sailing with him, I have never seen him so protective of anyone, besides Catalina and Adela. You mean a great deal to him."

Cecilia swallowed the guilt she felt at accusing Marcus. He had been nothing but kind to her since the moment he set eyes on her, and yet his secrecy cut deep, despite his noble intentions.

They sat in silence for a few minutes, until Sebastian stood abruptly. Cecilia followed his line of sight to a boat close by, two figures sat inside. He let out a low whistle and began making wild gestures with his arms. Cecilia looked between him and the figures on the boat, one of whom had dropped his oars to gesticulate back.

What on earth are they trying to communicate? She thought.

She heard Marcus before she saw him, his boots crunching softly on the coarse sand.

The sun had risen slightly, casting a light glow against the grey clouds which were still keeping the rain at bay. Her stomach rumbled loudly as the smell of freshly baked bread filled the air. Marcus handed her a brown parcel, the steam of the fresh bread roll leaving its mark against the paper.

"Thank you." She took it gratefully.

"A pleasure, señorita."

She ignored the flutter in her stomach as his face spread into a charming smile. Instead, she unwrapped the sweet treat, delighting in the warmth of the bread and sweetness of the sugar.

Marcus interrupted Sebastian's wild gesticulations to hand him his morsel. Sebastian shook his head.

"I won't eat until we board the ship."

Marcus conceded and sat beside Cecilia as they waited for the boat, Orren and Sorren now recognisable, to make their way to the alcove.

Marcus had already picked away at half of his loaf, tucking the rest in the bag. Cecilia tried not to pick too eagerly at hers, but the soft bready goodness melted easily on her tongue. She had finished her treat by the time the twins made their way ashore.

They met the lifeboat on the water's edge. The sun had risen higher now, the village illuminated by the pink and orange rays.

With hurried greetings, the trio clambered onto the boat, Orren and Sorren pushing them back out to sea.

In a few minutes, they were back on open water, Marcus and Sebastian taking up oars with the young men. The boat cruised quickly in the water, despite Sebastian's shoulders drooping from the fatigue.

"The captain didn't want to take her chances docking in the harbour in case it was closed. We'd have met you further north but we were delayed by Alistar and Jeremy." Sorren said, barely missing a beat as he worked the oars.

"What happened? Did they make it back to the ship?" Marcus' brows furrowed with concern.

Sorren nodded.

"The duke was hysterical. He wanted to get back to the tavern to rescue the lady here," he nodded politely at Cecilia. "When we saw the tavern go up in flames, he tried to fight his way off the ship. He barely let anyone work the deck without putting up a fight. Jeremy's been keeping him sedated. He was very worried about the welfare of Señorita Alarcon."

All eyes turned to her.

"I'm fine." She cleared her throat.

Sorren nodded seriously.

Wind battered the small boat as they rowed through a smattering of rain. Cecilia rubbed her arms with her hands, hoping the movement would retain some warmth in her weary bones.

They reached the *Sorrento* as the rain began to fall in earnest, splattering the water beneath them.

Cecilia clung onto the rope ladder on the side of the ship for dear life, not daring to look at the ocean below. She clambered behind Marcus, weaving his way expertly up the ropes, Sebastian and the twins behind her.

Catalina stood waiting on the deck to greet them, Bella and Jeremy by her side. Bella engulfed Cecilia in a tight embrace, as Marcus and Sebastian stepped on deck. The captain met them with a bright smile.

"Good to see you back in one piece," she greeted.

"It's good to be back." Marcus yawned.

"The three of you had better have a rest. I'm sure you've had a very long night. When you're ready, we will have a debrief in my cabin. The rest of you," she turned to her crew, "make haste. We must leave these waters immediately. I want us in Calgaria yesterday."

"Aye, Captain," the crew chorused.

Catalina came over to Cecilia and put a hand on her shoulder, offering her a friendly smile.

"I can't tell you how glad I am to see you."

Cecilia returned the gesture.

"Me too," she admitted and realised she meant it. Despite their previous animosity, she was genuinely glad to see the captain.

Bella grinned beside them as Catalina dashed to the helm, the ship lurching beneath them as the anchor lifted and wind filled the sails. As Marcus and Sebastian walked toward the galley, Bella looped her arm through Cecilia's.

"She actually means it too," she leaned conspiratorially into Cecilia. "She was very worried when the three of you didn't come back with Jeremy and Alistar."

"Really?"

"Truly," Jeremy echoed, "She asked Bella and I how we thought you would fare, especially with your arm. I'll need to have a look at that, actually."

"It's fine," Cecilia shrugged. "It aches, but so does the rest of me. It's Marcus who needs tending. Someone sliced his arm when he fought off the pirates at La Morada del Rey. We patched it up with a bandage, but it was only temporary."

"Always in some sort of trouble," Jeremy murmured untangling his arm from Bella's, "I'll catch him before he sleeps. I'd patch him up in the medic's cabin but Alistar's holed in there until further notice."

"Señorita Cecilia," Catalina called from the helm, "I'd like to see you in my cabin later. After you've had a rest."

"Aye, captain." Cecilia nodded.

Bella beamed at her.

"Two days on the Fickle Islands and you've turned into a full-blooded pirate," she winked.

Cecilia grinned, as her friend regaled her with the latest titbits of life aboard the ship while they walked to their shared cabin.

"Sleep as long as you need," Bella stood by the door. "Catalina will be busy on deck for the rest of the day and likely into the night. We'll catch up with you after, and you must tell me about the pirates. Are they really as nasty as people say?"

Cecilia lifted a shoulder in a half shrug, remembering Skiv and Tayen, "Not all of them."

Bella's smile widened but she dropped the matter. After a moment, Cecilia shut the door behind her, grateful for the comfort of her bed. By the time her head hit the pillow, she was fast asleep.

48

Memories

The bright afternoon sunlight filtered through the small porthole window, the light hitting Cecilia's eyes painfully as she stirred awake. Slowly, she stretched her stiff limbs, careful not to bump her injured arm. The pain had stayed at bay for the better part of the night, easier to ignore with adrenaline coursing through her veins. Now she was alone, the pain gripped her once again.

Shuddering in the sudden cold of the cabin, she reached around for the cotton blanket by her feet. Her mind was still foggy from dreams she couldn't remember. She rubbed her eyes again, taking stock of the room around her.

Her heart slowed as the familiar cabin settled around her, Bella's sewing projects momentarily abandoned on the trunk at the foot of her bed.

Groaning, Cecilia peeled herself from the mattress, borrowing Bella's wooden comb to untangle the mess of waves out from her disorderly braid.

Her clothes were significantly dishevelled, her once crisp dress now bleak and rumpled. Cecilia sighed. She was too tired to choose another outfit.

Ruffling her hair, she let it hang in loose waves over her shoulders. The sun shone between a haze of fluffy white clouds, as she made her way out of the galley the spring humidity giving way to a cool ocean breeze. She scanned the deck, finding no sign of Catalina, and made her way to the captain's cabin.

Cecilia knocked on the green door. After waiting a few moments with no response, she gently pushed it open.

Catalina's cabin was quaint, orderly and empty. Only the bed near the window spoke of human presence. An array of sheets lay tossed and tangled on the straw mattress, speaking of a night with little sleep. Cecilia made her way further in, examining the small array of trinkets and tokens on Catalina's desk and vanity.

The majority were small; golden painted beads, scattered seashells, a beaten leather cased compass and a gold pocket watch, its face paused at ten minutes to two. Beside it sat two golden framed portraits, one of Adela who seemed to have been no older than three.

Dark ringlets framed her face, a halo of wildflowers sitting crookedly on her head. She was not looking at the artist, instead engrossed in picking the petals of a yellow flower. Did Adela feel the same loneliness Cecilia felt at her age? She knew the little girl's ache for her mother would never truly go away. At twenty-one, the desire to find her family only intensified.

She moved onto the next picture, this one a wedding portrait. Cecilia was immediately struck by how young Catalina looked in the painting, her eyes clear and bright, dark waves tumbled over white-sleeved shoulders. Cecilia realised she had only once seen the captain in anything other than her uniform.

The groom on the other hand, wore a military uniform, distinctly different to the one Catalina wore now. A dark, navy jacket cut at an angle just above the waist, a white button-down shirt beneath it and black trousers. He stood beside her chair, one hand resting on her shoulder, the other firm at his side.

He had a boyish roguishness in his hazel eyes that made it difficult to look away from. She wondered if it was the same thing that drew her to Marcus. The resemblance between them was obvious now, they had the same high cheekbones and strong jawlines. Claudio's hair seemed a few shades lighter, erring on the side of brown rather than black, and he was slightly broader in the shoulders.

The ship fell heavily on a rough wave, the unexpected force of it knocking her into the vanity, causing the frame to fall into a semi open drawer.

She opened the drawer to fish it out, her knuckles brushing rough velvet. Gingerly, she brushed the surface of it until she recognised it as a velvet box. It was the same one Catalina had asked her about when she first arrived on the ship.

She looked cautiously over her shoulder, her breath bated as she listened to the sounds outside. The crew called out directives while gulls cried overhead. The ship swayed to the rhythm of the waves, creaking in response to the sudden burst of wind in the sails.

Taking her chance, she opened the box, small scraps of paper falling onto the floor. She gathered them quickly, shuffling through the small portraits of a young girl.

Cecilia turned one of the small portraits over in her hand. The inscription, scribbled in pencil, was in Calgarian. Despite her limited lessons in the language, the words were easy to guess.

Crown Princess Lilia of Calgaria, 4 years old.

Behind the portrait, her fingers skimmed a crisply folded, rectangular piece of white parchment. She unfolded it carefully, a slight tremble in her hands as she read the words.

Her heart stirred at the handwriting, her father's handwriting she realised with a start. As she read the words trying desperately to glean as much as she could from them, a glint from the box caught the corner of her eye. She followed it, lighting upon a small jewel bracelet.

The small gold pendant matched the one Prince Derek had taken from her. A memory flashed in her mind.

'Lilia', her mother's voice crooned as the young woman sat opposite her. The floor was covered in stuffed animals, some hers, some her cousin's. They had been playing pirates and princesses until Derek hit himself in the head with a sword. The nanny had taken him out of the room as tears poured down his face.

Her mother appeared in the doorway, watching with furrowed brows as her nephew was led out of the room. The princess brightened at her mother's presence, holding out her teddy bear.

'Play with me Mamá?' she asked, her voice tiny in her own ears. Her mother nodded, holding one hand behind her as she sat down, her blue skirts spreading around her like waves on the shore.

The girl loved it when her mother smiled, her brown eyes crinkling at the corners. She stood and plonked herself in her mother's lap, the scent of jasmine enveloping her like a warm embrace.

'Lilia, I have a gift for you,' her mother said, holding the velvet box in front of them. 'Do you remember how you said you liked Mamá's jewellery?'

She nodded, as she watched her mother toy with the box.

'This is an early birthday gift.'.

Her eyes widened as her mother opened the box to reveal the prettiest, daintiest necklace she had ever seen. It matched the necklaces her parents wore. A lion's face indented on a soft gold circlet.

'Shall I put it on you?' her mother asked. The girl nodded her enthusiasm, watching with bated breath as her mother draped it over her head and fastened the matching bracelet.

'Now your father and I shall be with you wherever you go,' she promised.

Grinning, the girl threw her arms about her mother's neck.

The door swung open as tears poured down Cecilia's cheeks. She remembered. She remembered her mother. The bittersweet memory lingered in her mind's eye as Marcus, Catalina and Sebastian spilled into the cabin.

A grin slipped from Marcus' face, immediately replaced with concern as he crossed the small room, Catalina close behind. Sebastian hung back, watching patiently.

"Are you alright?"

"What's wrong?"

Marcus and Catalina's voices blended together as he led her back to the sofa.

"I remember," she sobbed.

"You remember?"

"Remember what?"

Catalina gently handed her a tumbler of water. Grateful, Cecilia took it.

"The bracelet," Cecilia held the tiny piece of jewellery out to them, "I remember when my mother gave it to me. Before my birthday. I was in the nursery and Derek had gone with the nanny and she came in and..." her voice broke.

Marcus took a seat beside her.

Inadvertently, she leaned against him. Hesitating, he wrapped an arm around her shoulder, stroking her free hand with his thumb.

"Do you remember anything else?" he asked, his voice gentle.

She shook her head, "No. Not yet."

Catalina pursed her lips.

"Perhaps as we get closer to Calgaria, your memories may begin to come back. In the meantime, maybe we can try and jog your mind? Marcus said you still understand Calgarian?"

Cecilia shrugged.

"We can settle that later," Catalina continued awkwardly, "in the meantime, we must discuss what happened on the Fickle Islands."

Then gently, "You do not have to stay if you don't wish to. You've been through enough already."

Cecilia shook her head.

"I want to stay," she sniffled. "Besides, I didn't spend all that time on Isla Fortuna without picking up some bits of information which could be useful to you."

Marcus' lips quirked into a grin.

"I knew we could count on you."

49

Patched Up

Cecilia paced outside the medic's cabin as she waited for Jeremy to finish up with Alistar.

The sun was beginning to set, casting a warm golden glow about them. The rain had passed long ago and there was nothing, save the incoming night that would shadow them from any would-be pursuers.

But not even the threat of pirates was as nerve-wracking as facing Alistar again. Catalina had warned her the young ambassador had been locked up for his own safety and that of her crew.

"Are you sure you want to do this on your own? He might be agitated when you go in," Catalina warned as she walked with Cecilia to the medic's cabin. The younger woman shook her head.

"Hopefully once he sees I'm alright, he'll calm down."

Catalina pursed her lips into a thin line, unsure about the ordeal. Beside her, Marcus stiffened, his hand reaching for the hilt of the sword strapped to his waist. He was never without a weapon now, Cecilia noted. The hilt of a new white dagger had gleamed at her since they left The King's Abode.

"I'll go with you. Just to make sure he doesn't lay a hand on you."

Cecilia shook her head.

"I'll be fine. He won't hurt me."

Marcus frowned.

"I'll be outside. Just in case." He posted himself at the door. Cecilia gave him a small smile, relieved to have him close by.

She hadn't been alone with Alistar since their conversation on the beach the day before, yet it felt as though an eternity had passed since then.

Gathering her courage, she raised her hand to knock on the door. To her surprise Jeremy appeared in the doorway.

"Sorry," their apologies overlapped.

Jeremy offered her a friendly smile.

"Can he have visitors?" she asked, keeping her voice low.

"He's still a bit sleepy. The last sedative hasn't completely worn off yet, but he'll be glad to see you."

"Thank you."

He grinned, *"De nada."*

Cecilia took a tentative step into the cabin. It was much like she remembered it, bottles and vials organised haphazardly on benches and shelves. The cot stood against the far corner of the room. Alistar brightened up as he recognised her.

"You came," he sat up, nearly bumping his head against the wall.

"Hello," she waved, creeping in.

"Jeremy said you were here, but I didn't want to believe it until I saw you." He held out a hand to her.

"I'm here." She accepted his hand awkwardly, taking a seat on the chair beside his bed. The one Marcus had occupied during her recovery.

"Did Anders...?" Alistar swallowed, trying to find the words to finish his sentence.

She shook her head, "He didn't hurt me."

"Good. Good."

The silence stretched before them as they sat side by side on the cot.

"How did you get out of the tavern?" she asked at last.

"Jeremy and Sebastian bundled me out. Said they were there to rescue you," he shrugged. "I was just collateral."

- 303 -

"Your mother...?" Cecilia picked at her nails, "Was she in the tavern too?"

Alistar turned his face away.

"If she was, I didn't see her."

"So you don't know if she got away in the fire?"

Alistar shook his head, "Would you care if she did?"

Cecilia looked at her hands, knotted in her lap. Jeremy had poulticed and tied fresh bandages around her fingers, but the pain had faded. However Frida treated her, she treated Alistar worse. Still, she was the only mother they'd ever known.

"I suppose it would be better for us both if she didn't," she mumbled.

Alistar sighed, "So, you started the fire, huh?"

"I don't know who it was," she shook her head. "I'm just glad we got out."

Alistar frowned into the silence, "She underestimated you, you know."

"I think we all did."

He bumped her shoulder gently, "I always knew you had some fight in you."

She met his gaze, there was a hardness in his eyes that hadn't been there before, but it gave way to a small smile.

"So... what's next?" he rubbed his hands together.

She blew out a breath, leaning back in the chair, "I haven't had time to think."

"You know you're running out of time. We'll be docking in Alcary soon."

"Don't remind me."

She settled in this familiarity with Alistar. Despite the turmoil he had caused, he was the closest thing she had to family.

"I know you may never look at me the way you look at Marcus, but I can give you a good life." Alistar said gently.

Her brows furrowed.

"What do you mean, the way I look at Marcus?" she asked.

"Your eyes go soft when you look at him."

She scoffed, shaking her head, but excuses would not come.

"You can deny it all you want Cecilia, but I've seen the way you look at each other. It's like nobody else exists."

"He was lying about knowing who I was this whole time!" she finally exclaimed.

"So, you're upset he didn't tell you who you were in the first five minutes of meeting you?" Alistar crossed his arms.

"He had a whole voyage to do so," she mumbled. Even as she said the words, the fight had gone out of her. What good was holding a grudge when he'd already apologised? She picked at her fingernails, already chipped and uneven from worrying at them throughout the journey.

"Cecilia," Alistar paused, forcing her to look at him, "I am by no means Marcus' biggest fan, but even I can see he has done nothing but protect you since he first met you. Your well-being is his highest priority."

She sighed.

"Ever since you danced together on your birthday… the way he was looking at you… you can't deny that."

Cecilia wanted to shrug him off, to dismiss him as some jealous lover. But there was no malice in Alistar's voice. Only a sad resignation.

"So, what are you saying?"

"I don't know," he threw his hands up. His blonde locks tumbled into his eyes as he rested his head on the wall.

"You're free to make your own decisions. Just, stop being blind to the men in love with you."

"Men? Plural?"

He rolled his eyes at the ceiling.

"My offer still stands. If you want it to."

Cecilia scrunched her face, realisation dawning.

"Geez - you don't have to look so put off!" he exclaimed.

Cecilia snorted.

"I'm sorry – just, you're like a brother to me. Or a really annoying cousin. Well, a less ruthless cousin."

He barked a laugh.

"You're the closest thing I have to family," she explained. "I can't see you as anything else."

"Alright," he held his hands up in surrender, "I will not ask again."

A flood of relief surged through her, despite his sober demeanour. Outside, the dinner bell clanged.

"I should get going," Cecilia stood, dusting herself off. "Can I get you anything?"

Alistar shook his head.

Cecilia waited awkwardly, before slipping out the door and into the early evening sun.

50

Siren's Way

The sun cast the last rays of colour across the open ocean, the silver waves glinting under the golden display. The faint trace of Calgarian coastline peaked over the edge of the gunwale, barely more than a shadow on the horizon.

Cecilia's heart leapt at the sight of it. The first sight of land since leaving the Fickle Islands three days ago. Her first sight of Calgaria. Would it ever truly feel like home?

"Do you have room for one more?" Marcus gestured to the makeshift wooden bench Cecilia perched on. She scootched along the small seat, giving him ample space to sit. Aside from the debriefing in Catalina's cabin, they had barely spoken about the journey. Something had passed between them on the Fickle Islands, Cecilia was sure of that. She just couldn't understand what.

"Getting in some study before we make landfall?" Marcus nodded at her book. After her reunion with Alistar, she had poured over the study book Marcus had gifted her.

Its once pristine pages were marked with notes and scribbles from both their hands.

"I want to make a good impression with the king and queen. I know my mother will speak Avinadan," Cecilia couldn't help a small smile, "but I want them to see that I'm willing to learn what it takes to be a royal."

Marcus flashed her an approving grin.

"I'm sure they will approve of you regardless," he slipped into Calgarian.

Cecilia matched his grin.

"Dinner?" he offered a plate of fresh, crispy tortillas. The familiar fried doughy smell, filled Cecilia's stomach with more than just hunger.

The closer they sailed to Calgaria, the more foreign Cook's dishes became. It was strange to see such a mundane Avinadan dish after a week of fish broth and bread.

"Thank you," Cecilia took a tortilla from the pile, dipping the warm, pan-fried dough into a small container of fresh tomato salsa.

She relished taste of maize against the hint of chilli. Would it be her last taste of home?

"Are you ready for tomorrow?" He set the plate between them.

Cecilia sighed. All she could think about was meeting her parents. Would they like her? Would they accept her into the family? Would the kingdom accept her at all?

"I've imagined every scenario I could possibly think of. I've played out every possibility of how the meeting will go, in my mind, but my nerves do not fade." She picked idly at the tortilla.

"You have nothing to worry about," he nudged her shoulder gently, "they will love you."

"How can you be so sure?"

'Because," Marcus hesitated. Her stomach flipped at his stare. She stopped picking the tortilla. "They would be fools not to."

A commotion at the gunwale startled them both. Marcus pulled away, leaning toward the sound.

"We're passing through Siren's Way!" Someone exclaimed from the poop deck, only to be shushed by a fellow crewman.

"What's going on?" Cecilia tried to peer over the top of the gunwale from their small alcove.

"I'll show you," Marcus offered her a hand. Grateful for the small contact, she took it.

The ocean which had moments before glinted silver under the

moonlight, turned a glorious, luminescent blue in the water. Following the light, she appeared at Marcus' shoulder at the bow of the ship.

"What is this?" she gasped, gaze fixed on the ocean before them. In the near distance, bright streaks of blue crashed on reefs alongside the ship, as though illuminated from the depths itself.

"We are passing through Siren's Way. It's a series of reefs that mark the halfway point between the Fickle Islands and Calgaria," Marcus explained. "Legends say that on clear nights, if you listen close enough, you can hear distant, ethereal music. Ships used to wreck here frequently as sailors would stop for a night to find the source of the sound, only to get caught in a storm the next morning."

Behind them, a soft melody floated across the deck. They turned to find Orren sitting on an upturned barrel on the far side, swaying to the soft rhythm of his flute. Sorren stood beside him, a fiddle resting between his chin and shoulder as he plucked gently at the strings.

Cecilia glanced from the twins to Marcus, his hip leaning against the rail as he watched the brothers, now facing the ocean on the starboard side.

"They always play as we cross Siren's Way. It is a form of worship for them, a prayer that Ilio will protect us and deliver us safely to the other side."

"And does He answer their prayers?"

Marcus thought for a moment, his mouth twisting to the side in a lopsided frown.

"I suppose so."

"Does he answer yours?"

"Once."

Something about the intensity in his gaze made her heart flutter.

"What did you ask for?" Her words were barely more than a whisper.

His fingers stretched to fill the distance between them. She loosened her grip on the gunwale. Before he could brush her skin, his fingers curled away. He rested his hand on his sword hilt.

"It doesn't matter." He turned away, his dark eyes scanning the inky horizon. Swallowing her disappointment, she followed his gaze, watching as the bright blue waves pushed and pulled against an invisible shore.

A soft melody filled the air as Orren and Soren picked up another tune. It sounded vaguely familiar, the melody reminiscent of another time, another life. A grand white hall with a white domed roof, stained glass windows lighting the marble walls in a kaleidoscope of colour.

As the song faded into another, unfamiliar tune, he shot her a soft smile. Embarrassed to be caught staring, she looked at her hands, now resting on the rail in front of them. They were small compared to Marcus'; his long fingers, rough and callused from years of training with the sword.

Was she supposed to leave him at the docks after everything he had done for her?

"Marcus, can I ask you something?"

He turned his full attention to her, his face bathed in moonlight.

"Of course."

"What happens when we dock in Calgaria? Will I be able to say goodbye to my friends or will you take me straight to the palace?"

He paused before answering.

"The king's guards will alert His Majesty to the *Sorrento's* arrival. Once we dock, you will be taken to The Marble Palace where you will meet the king. If it makes you more comfortable, I can arrange for Arabella to attend you."

"You won't be coming?" surprise coloured her voice.

He shook his head.

"Once the king's men meet us at the docks, I am released of my charge." He straightened his posture, like a soldier fulfilling his orders.

"Oh." She tried to hide the disappointment in her voice. She hadn't thought about what he would do after returning to Calgaria.

He was a soldier. Of course he would attend to his duties. Still, her heart sank at the thought. Would they ever share this familiarity again? Or would they be separated by rules and decorum?

"And if I wanted you to accompany me? As my…" she searched for the right word… protector, bodyguard, *friend?* "Personal escort," she said finally.

He flashed her an amused smile.

"It would be an honour, Your Highness."

He gave her a polite bow. A strange sadness swept over her at the gesture. Whether or not he knew it, a wall had come between them. If she were the princess, it should be natural for him to address her so formally. Still, she hated it.

"Just Cecilia," she held his gaze, "please."

He pursed his lips, unsure.

"I cannot," he shook his head. "You are the future queen. I am a soldier. I shouldn't be so familiar."

This time Cecilia stepped closer, laying a trembling hand on top of his on the rail.

"You saved my life. More times than I can count. You have been my guardian and my friend. Please, Marcus," her voice cracked, "call me by my name."

He swallowed, his dark eyes searching hers.

"As you wish," he nodded, "Cecilia."

They barely noticed as the bright ocean glow faded into the inky abyss, or the final notes of Sorren's fiddle lingering sweetly in the air. Or the double masted ship flying towards them, its bright white sails twinkling a warning behind them.

51

The Uninvited

Marcus remained on deck, watching the stars twinkle in the heavens. Cecilia had gone to bed and the twins had packed away their instruments.

He watched them bow their heads in prayer, offering thanks to Ilio. For the first time in a long time, he did the same.

Ilio, give me the strength to deliver her, he prayed. *Give me the strength to let her go.*

By tomorrow afternoon, she would resume her rightful place as heir to the throne and he would resume his role as the royal family's protector. They would still see each other, but the wall of protocol and etiquette would hinder any kind of attachment they might have.

So why did it feel so strange?

He knew their roles from the start. She was a princess; he was a soldier. This was their destiny. They had become friends, a dangerous decision given his recent history with the crown prince.

He turned away from the horizon, the moon illuminated the inky sea below. He could not afford to be distracted from his duty. Especially not by her.

And yet...

She consumed his every thought, his every waking moment. His days were not the same if he did not see her smile. She was the first and last person he thought about, morning, noon and night. Some of it was duty, but the rest...?

Sighing, Marcus turned back to the deck. Most of the crew had retired for the night in preparation for the morning's duties. Tomorrow they would dock in Alcary and Marcus would let this journey fade into nothing more than a pleasant memory.

With a final glance at the ocean, he made his way below decks, so consumed in his thoughts he missed the shadow of a menacing galleon as she raced to catch up with the *Sorrento*.

***

Moonlight danced off the blade between Anders' fingers as he stood at the helm of *The Happy Dagger*. He watched his helmsman navigate the bioluminescent waters of Sirens Way, chasing the *Real Sorrento* already on the other side of the crossing.

Doña Alarcon stood beside him, wrapped in a thick brown shawl, unused to the night chill of the ocean.

"How far are we?" she asked the helmsman, a stoic man with ash blonde hair and a crooked nose.

"We're almost at halfway through the crossing. We're making good time and won't lose her yet," he answered.

Anders smiled to himself, twirling the dagger across his knuckles before sheathing it abruptly. He turned to Doña Alarcon.

"Prepare the hostages and bring them on deck. We shall be in need of them soon."

"Yes, my lord." She nodded, turning back to hurry down the steps to the galley.

A sly grin crept across his face as he murmured to himself.

"Five lives for the price of one."

***

Frida made her way through the cramped galley to an unmarked door at the top of the stairs. She found Brutus, her manservant, guarding the door. She had recruited him once she found him fleeing the tavern fire on Isla Fortuna.

Brutus had shown initiative, luring in Cecilia's kidnapper's relatives in addition to the prisoners she had taken. In all, there were three women, a man and a child.

"The king wants the hostages to be brought on deck. We are fast approaching the *Real Sorrento*." she said by way of greeting.

Brutus nodded, unlocking the door behind him, taking a small oil lamp from beside his heavily booted foot.

Frida squinted into the dark cabin, the dim lamplight casting shadows across the room. As her eyes adjusted, she could make out the figures of the women and the child huddled together; the man, who was stripped of weapons, positioned himself between the group and the intruders.

The stench of human misery assaulted Frida's nose. She failed to stifle a cough, instead turning to Brutus who continued to stand stoically at the door.

"Lead them to the deck, she ordered, turning on her heel and escaping into the fresh night air. When she returned upstairs, Anders greeted her with a wide grin, a predatory gleam in his eyes.

"Not long now, my dear." He held his hands out to her.

Frida gave him a winning smile, ignoring the warning twist in her chest.

In the few days they had spent together, Frida was becoming increasingly uncertain about the mental stability of the infamous pirate. She had trusted her dealings with him in the past, but she was beginning to think the man behind the letters and the man in front of her were two entirely different people.

In the hours before they set sail with the hostages, Frida had seen Anders shoot one of his own crew for letting Cecilia escape.

The cool ocean chill brought her back to the scene at hand. She stood beside the captain at the bow of the deck, his back to the ocean, as the five hostages were brought out, their clothes dirty and tattered.

Among them were the rogue's mother and niece, the two girls Frida had imprisoned for helping Cecilia escape and Antonio Salvador, an apparent business associate of Duke Aurelius.

The girl, no older than eight, clutched her grandmother's dirty skirt, silent tears running down her cheeks as Anders knelt in front of her. Moonlight bathed his pale face in an unearthly shade of silver, resembling him to a ghost. Frida admired the young girl's pluck to continue looking him in the eye.

"The fate of your lives belongs to a young woman on the ship we are about to embark," he told her, before addressing the rest of the motley group.

"Pleading with me is useless, so save your breath. You will need it if negotiations fail." He glanced pointedly at the gangplank leading to the dark ocean below.

The girl began to whimper.

Anders frowned sympathetically, taking her hand from her grandmother's skirt.

"It would be a shame for such a young life to be lost."

"You will not take her," the grandmother stepped between them, squaring her shoulders. "I will not let you."

Anders stood, straightening himself to his full height to tower over the older woman.

"Is that so?" he challenged, glancing at the girl. "Well little one, I guess you will have to stay with me since your grandma has kindly volunteered to lead you all to a watery grave."

***

A scream pierced the air. A child's cry.

Marcus glanced at Catalina, her face pale under the moonlight. She matched his worried expression. They knew that cry.

It was impossible, of course. They had left Adela and Rosalina in the safe house in the city.

He glanced at Sebastian, concern echoed on his dark features. Without a word, the trio dashed out of the captain's cabin, leaving behind a flurry of maps and charts.

A shout from the crows' nest confirmed what he recognised too late; a galleon flying pirate colours was gliding up behind them.

"All hands ahoy!" Catalina yelled, her voice ringing clear across the deck. "Pirates incoming!"

Sebastian clanged the ships bell, its urgent warning bellowing across the deck. Sailors piled out of the galley, immediately manning their posts ready for an attack. The buzz of an incoming fight rippled through the air as soldiers drew their weapons. A rumbling beneath them let them know the cannons were manned.

"Arm yourselves!" Catalina shouted, her voice clear above the racket as the pirate vessel sidled up beside them. Moonlight spilled across the water revealing Pirate King Anders leaning out on the rigging of his ship, his lips curved in a deadly smile.

Beside him were five prisoners, a tall, filthy man, two tattered young ladies, an older lady and... his breath caught...

No.

Beside the younger woman stood Rosalina, her dark curls pushed from her face, her mouth stifled by a rope. Her hands, tied in front of her, clutched a child's pink shoulder for dear life.

Adela.

Marcus' heart fell into his boots at the sight. Adela's pink dress was torn at the collar, and tears stained her dusty cheeks.

"*No*," Catalina turned pale against the ship's wheel. Her knees buckled beneath her, the ship almost crashing into *The Happy Dagger*.

Sebastian was beside her in a moment, laying a steady hand atop her own as he gently corrected the ship.

"Evening captain," Pirate King Anders called across the water, "Fine night for a trade, don't you think?"

52

Hunter's Moon

The deck was a cacophony of chaos as Bella and Cecilia stumbled out from their cabin. A child's scream pierced the air, sending a chill up Cecilia's spine.

Somewhere above the din, Pirate King Anders' voice rang out. He had come for her after all.

"What's going on?" Bella asked a passing officer scurrying to his post.

"Pirates. You both best be getting below decks."

The officer extended an arm to herd them below when the pirate king's voice rang out again.

Stepping away from the officer, Cecilia hurried past him to the base of the helm. Sebastian stood like a statue behind Catalina, fury burning through his stoic features as he held the captain upright. Cecilia followed his gaze. Beside Pirate King Anders stood five prisoners, their wrists bound in rope in front of them.

Bright moonlight illuminated the deck ahead of them. Her heart thundered in her chest as she recognised them all.

Liz. Jeleni. Antonio. Rosalina. Adela.

They're here for you. Your life for theirs.

Cecilia trembled at the thought.

"Ah, my sweet, I'm so glad you could join us," King Anders' voice jolted Cecilia back to attention.

"What do you want, Anders?" The fury in Catalina's voice was palpable.

The pirate turned his attention from Cecilia to the captain.

"Oh, nothing much. Just your family in exchange for my wife."

"Tell me it's not true." Bella gasped softly beside Cecilia. She shook her head as the pirate continued.

"You have something of mine aboard this ship and I do not intend to leave without it."

"My passengers are all freemen and women. I did not steal anyone from anywhere, if that is what you're implying." Catalina snapped.

"Nevertheless," the pirate continued, "my terms are simple. You exchange the princess and I will release your family."

"And if I refuse?"

In a flash, Anders motioned one of his pirates who ripped Adela out of Rosalina's grip. The older woman surged forward but was forced back into line by Skiv. Undeterred, Rosalina continued to squirm against his grip. Cecilia watched him whisper something in her ear. Rosalina's eyes widened, but she nodded, ceasing her struggle.

The pirate king shoved Adela toward the edge of the deck closest to the *Sorrento*, holding her tightly in front of him like a shield. In his free hand, a dagger shone, the metal glinting in the moonlight.

"*No!*" Catalina stumbled forward as though drawn by an invisible string.

"I will not harm the child if you give me what I want." Anders held the dagger in front of Adela's throat.

Cecilia held her breath. She did not doubt the extent of Anders' cruelty. Had she not seen him sentence a child to death already? Catalina tore her gaze from Adela, glancing briefly at Cecilia, an apology all too evident in her dark eyes.

Cecilia stepped forward. The choice was easy.

"I will go with you, just let them go," she pleaded.

"No," Catalina shook her head.

"*Yes*," Cecilia held the captain's gaze. She would not force the captain to choose between her duty and her family, "I will go with you," Cecilia addressed the pirate king, her voice ringing clearly across the deck, "but you will release the hostages first."

King Anders flashed her a menacing grin.

"Fine." He jerked his head at the crew manning the prisoners. "Release them and bring me my bride."

"No!" Another voice broke through the shadows. "You will not take her."

Cecilia turned to see Marcus weaving through the assembled officers, Jeremy at his shoulder.

"I was wondering when you would show up again," King Anders greeted, his smile souring. "I can't say I'm pleased to see you."

"You will not harm the hostages," Marcus drew closer to the ship's edge, "nor will you take Señorita Cecilia."

"You are not in any position to be making bargains." Anders gripped the dagger at Adela's throat tighter. The girl trembled under the pirate's threat.

"Then I will fight you for them," Marcus challenged, "their lives for mine."

"No," Cecilia gasped.

Marcus' chin turned slightly in her direction, his hard gaze never wavering from the pirate king. He considered the offer, the rough lap of waves the only sound cutting through the silence.

"Alright," the pirate king shoved Adela away from him, "I'll take that challenge. Your life for theirs and whoever wins gets to keep the princess."

Marcus swung his cloak from his shoulders to reveal dark leather soldier's armour, the Calgarian Lion emblazoned on his chest. Cecilia's heart pounded in her ears.

Would he kill Anders for her freedom? Would he die for her? She couldn't bear to find out.

"Marcus," she called out. Could she persuade him to let her go? To live and fight another day?

Instead, he walked to the nearest edge of the deck as the pirate king swung down from *The Happy Dagger.*

A triumphant grin creased the pirate's face as he landed, blowing Cecilia a kiss. She glared at him, crossing her arms defiantly over her chest.

The pirate king shrugged, turning to face Marcus who stood ready to fight, his sword catching the moonlight.

"Like I told you, my sweet," Anders threw a glance at Cecilia, "my love will not be rivalled." With that, Anders lunged in one swift motion, bringing his sword down toward Marcus.

Marcus stepped out of the way, blocking him.

"Cecilia, come with me," Jeremy rushed her, herding her away from the fight and into a sheltered alcove where Bella waited.

"No, I can't leave," Cecilia protested, "I have to do something!"

"You can't stay there either! If Anders kills Marcus-" Bella shook her head, "We swore an oath to protect you."

"But we have to do something!" Cecilia stomped her foot.

The sharp ring of metal on metal drew their attention back to the fight. Marcus blocked the pirate's parry expertly before landing a blow across the pirate's cheek. Blood trickled down Anders' freckled face, dripping into his fiery beard. With a ghostly grin, the pirate wiped his face with the back of his hand, smearing blood like war paint on his face.

With a cry, he swung his sword down upon Marcus.

"Now!" Marcus cried barely managing to block the deadly blow.

As silent as a passing ship, dark figures swung from the *Real Sorrento* onto the top deck of *The Happy Dagger*, aiming straight for the prisoners.

A scream pierced the air again.

It took a moment for Cecilia to recognise it as her own.

53

Chaos

"That's the signal. You two, stay with Alistar. He'll protect you if things get gnarly," Jeremy ushered them into the medic's cabin.

"But-"

"No buts Cecilia. I'm your doctor and I'm ordering you to stay safe!"

"Let's go." Bella tugged her by the sleeve. Cecilia pushed down the protests that threatened to spill over as she followed them to the medic's quarters. Alistar stood by the door, dagger in hand as the girls piled in.

"Make sure they stay put," Jeremy ordered.

"You have my word," Alistar nodded.

"Good," Jeremy breathed a sigh of relief, leaning a hand against the doorframe. "Now, you two take care of each other."

Cecilia fought the urge to roll her eyes.

"What will you do?" Bella hung by the doorway.

"Join the fight of course," Jeremy grinned.

Moonlight caught the hilt of a dagger on his belt, and Cecilia realised with a start he was also dressed for a fight. Despite the medic's armband, he wore similar leather armour to Marcus. Had they been expecting this all along?

Before she could question him, Bella surged forward to plant a quick kiss on his lips.

"Come back to me," she ordered.

Jeremy's eyes widened as Bella recomposed herself.

"That's the plan," he fumbled, raking a nervous hand through his hair.

With a final nod to Alistar and a lingering glance at Bella, he returned to the fray.

"Well," Cecilia stared at her friend, "that was unexpected."

***

Beads of sweat broke out on Marcus' brow. His arm stung where Anders had lashed out, reopening the wound from their previous fight. Marcus hissed, earning a menacing grin from the pirate king.

"You should give up while you still can, boy." The pirate growled as they circled each other.

"Never," Marcus spat, eyeing his opponent for an opening. The pirate lunged again, his jabs short and sharp.

"I should kill you for what you did to my tavern." Anders jabbed his sword.

Marcus gritted his teeth, returning the blow with one of his own.

"You're a traitor to the crown!" Anders continued.

Marcus blocked another blow.

"Tell me something I don't know," he ground out.

The ship's bell rang out against the clang of metal, officers and pirates alike descending into chaos around them. Men shouted orders at each other. But Marcus would not be distracted.

His blade found the pirate king's wrist. Swearing, the pirate dropped his sword. Marcus took advantage, stepping into the pirate's space, jabbing an elbow into his chin.

The pirate king doubled over, blood trickling from his lip.

"Bastard." He swore.

Marcus snatched the pirate's sword, holding both weapons in front of him.

"I've been called worse."

***

As soon as Jeremy's footsteps dissolved into the chaos, Cecilia rummaged around the cabin for anything sharp she could find.

"Cecilia, what are you doing? You can't go out there. I won't let you." Alistar demanded from where he stood at the cabin door.

She ignored him, pulling out his military-issued dagger from underneath the cot pillow.

"Hey! That's my spare!" he protested.

"You're not using it."

"Still," he crossed his arms, "That's mine."

"You're not seriously thinking of going out there are you?" Bella asked around a fingernail.

"I cannot sit idly by as others bargain for my life. I am not an object to be exchanged." Cecilia strapped Alistar's dagger to her belt, "I cannot have any more blood spilled for me."

"Wait for Marcus to win the duel with Pirate King Anders," Bella held a hand out.

Cecilia shook her head.

"I read somewhere once, there is no greater love than to lay down one's life for one's friends. You have all become the closest thing I have to family. I will not let harm come to you if I can help it."

She tightened her fists at her side, unclenching them slightly as she met Bella's gaze. Her friend's dark eyes shone with tears, her bottom lip trembling.

"You shouldn't have to do this," she whispered, her voice barely audible from the commotion outside.

"I must."

"Then I'll go with you." Alistar nodded to himself, "I'll protect you."

Cecilia shook her head again.

"You're still drowsy from the sedatives."

"But you can't fight!" he argued, "What if you get killed?"

Cecilia hesitated. The pirate king would not kill her, but a stray bullet or dagger might. She took a deep breath.

"I'm going. You can come with me or not, but I have to do something."

Bella nodded, pulling her in for a tight hug.

"If this is what you think is right, you have my support. But I will stay here. Someone has to tend the wounded."

Cecilia nodded.

"Thank you. For everything."

Bella flashed her a thumbs up, holding Alistar back by his shirtsleeve. Rolling her shoulders back, Cecilia flashed her friends a brave smile and stalked out the door.

54

Leap of Faith

Cecilia ducked and weaved her way through the throng of fighters swarming the area, stepping her way around wayward fists, arms and elbows. She scanned the deck, narrowly avoiding a flying crate. A man cried out as the wooden box hit him square in the chest with a sickening thud. Cecilia hurried forward until she was at the bottom of the helm.

Marcus and Anders were locked in a battle of blows on the starboard deck, their swords clanging as each fought for the upper hand.

Kneeling behind a water barrel, something flashed at the corner of her eye. A blade glinted in the moonlight mere inches from her hand. Without a second thought, she snatched the knife, the bloody handle immediately staining her skin. Like a hot coal, she dropped the cursed object.

A movement caught the corner of her eye. The captain's cerulean coat was unmistakable under the bright moonlight. Stepping out from her hiding place, Cecilia hurried to catch up to her.

She had barely reached the starboard side before the captain was met by two young pirates, their daggers glinting under the pale moonlight.

Catalina's sword was an extension of her arm. She whirled on them with the grace of a skilled warrior, pushing one pirate into the blade of his companion. Bracing herself against the gunwale, Catalina pushed them both, screaming, into the dark depths below.

Bile rising to her throat, Cecilia fought the urge to vomit. She stepped close to the billowing blue coat tails as Catalina felled another sailor, the burly man falling into the swell below.

Cecilia's feet were moving before she could understand what was happening. She had barely reached the gunwale when Catalina spun on her, sword at Cecilia's throat.

"It's me," she pleaded, hardly daring to breathe.

"For goodness' sake, why didn't you say anything? I almost killed you." Catalina pulled her sword away.

"I'm here to help." Cecilia offered weakly.

Catalina side stepped her, the sickening sound of a body hitting the deck following half a second later. Cecilia fought the instinct to check the ground.

"If you want to help, get back to the medic's cabin. You're no use to us if you can't fight."

"Marcus taught me–"

"He taught you self-defence," Catalina snapped, pausing to shove a stumbling pirate out of the way. "You're a liability if you stay out here and you're no use to us dead."

Cecilia flinched at the captain's words. She was right of course, but the words still stung.

"I want to help." Cecilia said weakly.

"Then get back to the medic's cabin," Catalina pushed past her.

The captain leapt onto the gunwale, a gangplank secured between the two ships. A silver blade flickered in the air.

"Catalina! Duck!" Cecilia yelled.

Without hesitation, the captain hit the deck. A burly pirate ran straight into the ledge, his torso hanging over the side of the ship. With a scream, Cecilia knocked his head with the butt of her dagger, sending him toppling into the water below.

The captain stood to her feet, straightening her jacket.

"You're confident with that thing?" she nodded at the dagger in Cecilia's hand.

"Yes." She lied.

"Alright," Catalina pursed her lips, "let me know if anyone makes a swing from the gangplank," she ordered as she leapt onto the narrow timber frame.

"Aye captain." Cecilia nodded, hands immediately gripping the edge of the narrow board for support.

Catalina sheathed her sword, swapping it for a cutlass.

Cecilia kept watch as pirates rallied around the ship, circling the *Sorrento's* crew like magpies. She kept her eyes above the action, avoiding the bodies that lay injured or dying, littering the decks.

"Captain, watch out!" Cecilia yelled as a mean looking pirate, dagger in hand, swung his own cutlass towards Catalina.

Without looking, Catalina ran forward on the gangplank, pushing the pirate into the watery depths below.

The Captain straightened herself, waving Cecilia forward. Taking a deep breath, she hurried across the narrow strip, careful to keep her eyes locked on the ship in front of her.

She leapt onto the ship's deck beside Catalina.

"What now?" she asked as a group of blue coats formed a protective line in front of them.

"We take back our people," Catalina grinned, straightening her coat.

Catalina whistled to her officers, a handful forming a protective guard around them as they fought their way to the upper deck. Cecilia held her dagger in front of her. She couldn't do much, but it was better than nothing.

Skiv stood with the prisoners, holding Rosalina by the shoulder. His eyes were dark and sunken and a thin red line marred his face.

"Skiv," Cecilia greeted, stepping forward before Catalina could draw her sword against him.

"Step aside," Catalina ordered, her sword at the ready.

"We won't be doing that," a velvet voice said from behind them. Frida stepped out of the shadows, gripping Adela's shoulder.

Cecilia's fingers tightened on her dagger, "Frida? What are you doing here?"

The duchess' lips curled into a familiar snarl.

"All this time I spent shaping you into the perfect little pawn and this is how you repay me? By throwing in your lot with them?" The duchess nodded at the *Real Sorrento*. Cecilia followed her gaze. Anders and Marcus were still locked in a battle of blades.

A shadow at the port side caught the corner of her eye.

"Let the child go." Catalina ordered. Cecilia turned back to her godmother, a detached look in her beady eyes.

"I should never have let you live if I'd known you would be this much trouble," the duchess continued.

"Why did you do it?" Cecilia asked, glancing between the captain and the duchess. Catalina frowned.

"I wanted revenge," Frida shrugged. "Your mother talked King Vicente out of marrying me. She said her brother was too good for me. Then she stole the prince I was supposed to marry. She took away my happiness, so I took away hers."

Frida stepped forward, her grip on the child loosening as she walked towards Cecilia.

"I want to bring you to Calgaria myself," the duchess' voice dropped, sending an uncomfortable shiver down Cecilia's spine. "I want to drag you before the throne and have Lars and Minerva beg me to spare your life."

Cecilia's heart hammered in her chest. She licked at cracked lips, her throat dry.

With a thud, the duchess hit the deck like a sack of bricks. Cecilia turned to find Catalina massaging her knuckles.

"If there's one thing I can't stand, it's monologuing."

"Mamá!" Adela cried, launching herself into Catalina's arms.

Cecilia turned to Skiv who stood awkwardly by the prisoners.

"You're not going to arrest us?" she asked, keeping her dagger close.

Skiv shook his head, "I promised I'd help ya. 'Sides, Anders killed my brother. I owe him nothing."

Catalina looked up from embracing Adela and Rosalina.

"Are you sure you want to do this Skiv? Anders might be occupied now but he'll find out if you help us." Catalina warned the young pirate as he helped herd the prisoners to the forecastle, the *Sorrento's* sailors forging the path ahead.

"I know the risks I'm taking," Skiv answered, "I swore on Tayen's grave that I would avenge him."

The clang of metal on metal filled the air as they reached the forecastle, taking the stairs two at a time. They were further from the *Sorrento* than she would've liked, but at least it wasn't as crowded as the rest of the deck, swarming with sailors from both ships. At this distance, it was hard to tell friend from foe.

Catalina whistled at her crew. Orren and Sorren who had been engaged in fisticuffs moments before, disposed of their opponents like rag dolls before joining their captain at attention.

Catalina glanced at Adela, Rosalina already covering the girls' eyes.

"Help this man release the hostages and swing them across to the *Sorrento*," she ordered, "Keep them in my cabin until we can make a clean breakaway."

Nodding, they rushed to obey, testing ropes before beckoning the hostages forward.

"Do not betray me, Skiv. Or I'll have your head," Catalina muttered, moving to help Adela, clinging desperately to her grandmother's hand.

He gave her a lopsided grin, the gesture transforming his face.

"Better you than him." He nodded in Anders' direction. The pirate king clutched his arm, circling Marcus. Even from this distance, Cecilia could feel the tension radiating from them.

Ilio, help us, she prayed silently.

"I want to go home," Adela choked out a sob.

Catalina drew her daughter into a hug, pressing a kiss to the girls' head.

"We're going home now, I promise. We just need to get to the *Sorrento.*"

"How?"

"Remember in the stories I read to you about the man who lived in the jungle? How he would swing from one vine to another?"

Adela nodded.

"Well, we're going to do something similar. Only with ropes instead of vines."

Cecilia's heart leapt to her throat as Skiv secured a rope around her waist.

"What are you doing?"

"This is the quickest and safest way back to the ship."

"By jumping?" she exclaimed.

"It'll be over before you know it. Trust me."

Cecilia glanced up to find Rosalina hanging back as the twins readied themselves with the two women hostages. Antonio threw her an unconvincing wink as he gripped his rope for dear life.

Skiv stood on the gunwale, rope wrapped around his arm and feet. Catalina held onto Adela and Rosalina, who for the first time looked terrified.

"There is no other way?" she asked, turning to Catalina, her eyes wide with fear.

Catalina shook her head.

"I'm sorry."

"On the count of three," Skiv yelled, struggling to be heard above the din.

Cecilia joined them on the gunwale, searching for Rosalina's hand. The older woman clutched her tightly.

"One. Two. Three!' Skiv yelled, leaping into the night.

Taking a deep breath, Cecilia launched into the air, Rosalina's hand tight in hers.

They flew through the night, the wind at their back, the *Sorrento* surfacing beneath them. For a moment, she thought, all would be well.

Until she heard it.

The unmistakable sound of a gunshot.

Cecilia screamed.

Then she fell.

55

A Beautiful Place to Die

A shadowed figure slipped onto the ship, his dark cloak secured around his broad shoulders. He marched with authority across the deck, blue coated officers and pirates alike fighting out of his way.

He had come for one purpose and one purpose only.

Revenge.

He scanned the deck for any sign of his target. Of course, as a woman, she wouldn't be in the thick of battle.

And yet.

A movement on the pirate ship caught his eye. Even from this distance he could see her wild dark locks whipping in the wind. She had changed into unassuming travellers' clothes. Even swinging from a rope, she was the picture of royalty.

Close by, the soldier circled the pirate king, narrowly missing a fatal blow.

The intruder picked his target, raised his pistol in the air and fired.

***

Marcus swung his sword, but the pirate king was prepared. King Anders knocked the weapon out of his grip, sending it clattering to the floor. His lips parted in a cruel grin as Marcus dived for the weapon, the pirate's sword cutting through the air.

A shot pierced the night.

Marcus scrambled out of the way, but it was too late.

A searing pain cut his side. He dropped his dagger, the white hilt glinting in the moonlight. Pushing himself onto his knees, Marcus pressed his hand to the wound.

Warm, sticky blood covered his skin, staining his new brown shirt.

"Well, well, well," Pirate King Anders grinned down at him, "it seems your old friend meant what he said. He doesn't care if you die after all."

***

Cecilia hit the deck hard. Her knees buckled beneath her as she stumbled from the landing. She had barely managed to keep her grip on the rope when the shot sounded.

"Soldiers ho!" someone yelled in the near distance. The ship's bell clanged for the second time that night as strong hands herded her forward.

Rosalina squeezed her hand. Cecilia turned to face the older woman flanked by Jeleni and Catalina, who held Adela protectively at her chest.

"What on earth are you doing here?" Cecilia blurted as they hurried forward.

"We'll explain later," Jeleni shook her head.

Another shot sent them sprawling to the ground.

Turning to find the source, Cecilia found Marcus, blood seeping from a wound at his side. Above him, Pirate King Anders grinned, his taunts lost in the chaos of the din.

"Where is she?" Prince Derek's voice sent a shiver down her spine. She knew who he was looking for.

Cecilia untangled herself from Rosalina's grip, ignoring her companion's protests as she stalked towards Marcus and the pirate king.

"I'm here!" she yelled, turning in a slow circle until she found the prince.

Prince Derek was dressed finer than she had seen him last. In dark trousers and a fitted ebony shirt, a sword at his hip and gun in his hand, he looked more mercenary than prince.

He was close enough for her to see the fury of oceans behind his sharp blue eyes.

He levelled his pistol at her, and she knew deep in her bones, he would not miss his mark.

She took a deep breath, the world slowing as she rose to meet her fate. She glanced at Marcus, but his gaze was locked firmly onto the prince. Perhaps it was for the best.

She closed her eyes and waited for the inevitable.

***

A shot pierced the darkness. Followed by a man's dreadful scream.

***

Marcus holstered the pistol at his hip. Derek swore, clutching his hand to his bleeding cheek.

The prince was a good shot, but Marcus was better.

King Anders lay in a pool of blood beside him, a knife protruding from his back. One of his own men stabbed him in the confusion.

In the moments after the gunshot, the world slowed down. Cecilia stood frozen, accepting a fate that wasn't hers to claim.

Yes. She would be safe.

He reached for his sword as he stumbled forward.

"Marcus!" someone called his name.

A familiar pair of hands rolled him onto his back.

- 334 -

The stars shone brighter, as though welcoming him home.

Hello Marcus, they twinkled in greeting, *we've been expecting you.*

"Marcus, you idiot, you better live." Jeremy's voice was far away.

"Marcus," her voice was close now. Sweet. Sad. Beautiful.

"Please… please don't leave me."

Soft fingers threaded through his own, squeezing his hand as though transferring life to his broken body through sheer willpower. The languid waves lapped against the ship's hull as the ocean breeze tugged at his hair.

So, death had come for him at last and Marcus had broken his vow.

Under a blanket of stars and the watchful eyes of his love, it really was a beautiful place to die.

56

Where the Shadow Ends

The first rays of dawn played at the edge of his vision as his senses returned slowly. The ship rocked constant and steady beneath him, the familiar splash of waves against the hull filling his ears. Sailors yelled orders across the deck. A cool chill sent shivers down his spine, despite the warm blankets layered on top of him.

Carefully, Marcus tested his left hand to find it curled on top of his chest, his arm in a sling. His right hand was otherwise claimed.

Turning, he saw Cecilia, fast asleep in the chair beside him. Her hair tumbled in waves down her shoulders. Even in sleep, her fingers held tightly to him as though keeping his soul in his body by her mere touch.

If this was death, he could get used to it.

While his mind settled back into the present, he looked about the medic's cabin. The table behind Cecilia remained a mess of vials, potions and bandages. He imagined Jeremy and Bella working over him, Bella comforting Cecilia, waiting to see if he would wake or not.

A mountain of bloodstained rags sat in a bucket in the corner of the room, matching Cecilia's stained clothes. Her lips were turned down as if not even sleep could ease her anxiety.

Smiling, he ran his thumb gently along her knuckles, his heart near bursting at the sight of her. Deep down, he knew it could never be. He was a soldier, sworn to protect her. He could only ever love her from afar.

And yet it was enough to know in this moment that he loved her.

After a few minutes she stirred, bolting up in her chair.

"You're alive?" she burst, "thank Ilio!"

His reply was cut short as she threw herself into his arms. Her shoulders shook as she sobbed, her tears spilling onto his shirt. He returned the hug, holding her as close to him as possible, inhaling the salty scent of her.

Tears continued to stream down her cheeks as she pulled away from him, her hands finding his face. Her palms were soft under his stubble as she rubbed her thumb along his cheek.

"I thought I lost you," she whispered.

He cupped one hand in his, giving her the briefest shake of his head.

"Not even death could keep me from you."

At last, a smile broke across her face.

It was as though he had seen the sun for the first time after an eternity of grey skies. Her eyes- one honey-brown and one hazel-sparkled, filling him with a strange warmth. Had his skin ever known the summer sun? Not so until now.

He tasted the salt of her tears, her lips strong and full against his own. For a moment, he froze, dreaming. Then the sun broke through and he melted against her, pulling her into him like a ship to shore.

At last, they broke apart, his lungs burning. Not that he would mind if these were his last moments. But death held no allure for him now.

A knock at the door severed their attention.

Not waiting for an answer, Jeremy appeared in the doorway, an amused grin lighting his face as he crossed the cabin. Bella trailed behind him holding a tray with a small vase of flowers. The familiar scent of beef stew sent Marcus' already fluttering stomach into uproar. How long had it been since he'd eaten?

"Are we interrupting something?" Jeremy grinned at them, a knowing glint in his eye.

Cecilia's cheeks flushed red, as she avoided everyone's gaze. Marcus on the other hand, couldn't wipe the grin from his face, leaning on his good elbow.

"Is that for me?" he nodded at the tray in Bella's hands.

"It's the least we can do after you cheated death last night," Jeremy smiled. "But for Ilio's sake Marcus, don't do that to me again."

Marcus grinned as Bella set the tray across his lap, throwing him a conspiratorial wink.

"I'll try not to," he promised, picking up a spoonful of stew.

Jeremy made a sound between a laugh and a sob, holding his face in his hands before facing them again. For the first time, Marcus noticed the dark circles under his friend's eyes.

"I'm so glad you're alright," Bella smiled.

"So am I," he flashed her a winning grin.

"Alright," Jeremy clapped his hands together. He regained his regular jovial composure, though his eyes were still clouded, "once you've had something to eat, we'll head to the captain's cabin. You have some visitors who are eager to see you."

A child's bright laughter wafted through the thin cabin walls. Adela, he realised. With a pang, he recognised his mother's voice a few moments later.

Swallowing the sudden rise of emotion, he asked, "How are they?"

Jeremy's lips pursed into a thin line, "They're well. Considering the circumstances."

"Eat," Cecilia encouraged him gently, "we'll see them soon.

Under the watchful eyes of his friends, Marcus wolfed down as much stew as he was able. Jeremy frowned when he was finished.

"Surely, Rosalina taught you better table manners than that?" he asked as he cleared the tray.

Marcus shrugged, "I was hungry."

***

Cecilia tried not to beam with pride as she walked arm in arm with Marcus toward the captain's cabin. She suspected he didn't really need the support to walk the short distance from the medic's cabin, but she wasn't about to refuse him.

Not after she'd almost lost him.

After Marcus shot Prince Derek, she wasn't sure he was going to live. Soldiers descended on him, swatted away by Jeremy and Sebastian, brandishing their own weapons.

Only after the pirates retreated and Catalina exchanged stern words with the prince's sailing commander did the soldiers eventually retreat.

Cecilia had expected the prince's ship to shadow them to Calgaria, but when she woke that morning, the *Real Sorrento* was alone.

"Do we know what happened to Prince Derek last night?" Marcus asked as they approached the captain's quarters.

Cecilia shook her head.

"Catalina will have all the details."

Before they could reach the door, it flew open, nearly smacking them in the face as a small, squealing figure launched herself at Marcus. This time, he didn't have to pretend to lean on Cecilia as she helped steady him on his feet. Adela glued herself to his legs.

"Adela, come back here. Give your uncle a chance to come in before you launch yourself at him." Catalina ordered from the doorway. She flashed them a relieved smile as Adela tottered back to her side.

"I'm glad to see you up and about," the captain greeted.

"So am I," Marcus winced.

Inside the cabin, the gathered audience shifted to make room for them at the small sofa nearest the door. Bella sat at the cramped table in the centre of the room, flanked on either side by Liz and Jeleni who were interrogating Jeremy. Even from this distance, Marcus could see the beads of sweat on his forehead as he answered the sister's latest question. Bella grinned between them, as she watched Jeremy squirm.

Antonio stood beside his brother, bemused by the line of

questioning. In another corner of the room, Skiv and Sebastian stood deep in conversation while Adela floated between Catalina, who was perched at the front of her desk, and Rosalina who stood to greet Marcus.

"Mijo," she breathed, holding her arms out.

"Mamá."

Cecilia stood back as Marcus relaxed in his mother's embrace. The previous night had taken its toll on them both. Rosalina's red eyes betrayed an anxious night.

"I'm alright, Mamá," he assured her, "I'm alright."

It was another minute before she finally released him, checking his free arm.

"The sling?" she pointed at the injury.

"A precaution," Jeremy assured her. "He suffered some rather nasty cuts, in addition to the bullet scrape."

"I can't believe you're here," Marcus interrupted them. "How?"

Rosalina's face fell.

"We were kidnapped. The day you left, a man came to the house asking for help. I tried to send him on his way but he grabbed me and held me against the kitchen wall. I screamed for Adela to run and get help, but he caught her," she bit her lip. "He said he would hurt her if I didn't come with him."

Adela shifted uncomfortably on Catalina's lap.

"He brought us to an abandoned night house, and stored us like old wine in a damp cellar," she wiped tears from her eyes. "That's where we met Antonio, Liz and Jeleni. It seems this man was working for Duchess Alarcon."

"I think it was the same man who followed you from our safehouse," Jeleni supplied.

"Brutus," Antonio added, "I enlisted him to help me break the young ladies out of prison and he betrayed me instead."

Rosalina nodded, "The next thing we knew, we were being taken to the cargo hold of a ship to the Fickle Islands." She continued, "He presented us to Pirate Anders and the next thing we knew, we were on another ship, bound for Calgaria."

Marcus squeezed his mother's hand.

"You're safe now," he reassured her. Rosalina nodded, gripping his hand. Cecilia wished she could take away their pain, or avenge it somehow. Perhaps, if Anders died, she wouldn't have to.

"We will dock in Alcary and figure out the next steps from there," Catalina assured the group. "For now, I think we all need to rest."

The group disbanded immediately. Bella led her sisters out of the cabin. Jeremy sighed, motioning for Antonio to follow them out.

Morning sunlight streamed through the captain's window to reveal the Calgarian coastline inching closer. Grey mountains towered into a bright blue sky.

Cecilia caught Marcus watching her.

In a few hours she would be home.

She would meet her parents, become a princess and inherit a whole new world.

57

The Prodigal Daughter Returns

The blare of trumpets echoed throughout The Marble Palace. Birds startled from their posts lining the king's outer balcony, their small figures cutting through the morning haze as the lazy sun rose into the clear blue skies above.

King Lars leaned against the marble guardrail on the balcony overlooking the shimmering city of Alcary.

The sprawling white buildings blinded him to the silver horizon. He had received word the *Real Sorrento* was days away from docking. Now, she was expected to return, carrying the most precious cargo.

White sails twinkled in the distance. The king's heart thundered in his chest, his palms sticky with sweat. After sixteen long years, his daughter would finally be home.

"There you are, my love." His wife's familiar voice floated from the doorway behind him. He turned to find Queen Minerva, her face as bright as when they had wed twenty-three years ago. Her soulful brown, hazel eyes mirrored the hope he felt in his soul.

"Can we truly be sure this is her? I'm not sure my heart could bear another false hope after so many years." She held her hands out to him.

He pulled her close, planting a reassuring kiss on top of her dark tresses.

"She is the one. Ilio has had His hand in this, I am sure of it."

The queen nodded against his chest, a trembling sigh escaping from her lips. They stood for a moment, the cool mountain air settling around them.

A palace guard cleared his throat from the palace doorway, his ice blue coat garnering him the rank of colonel. He wore a grin that shone through his eyes as he addressed the king, forgetting formality for a moment.

"Your Majesties, the *Real Sorrento* has arrived," he announced.

The king stepped out of his wife's grip, taking her hand.

"Take us to her at once," he ordered.

The guard did not have to be told twice, his grin never fading as he led the royal couple hurriedly through the familiar marble passages of the great palace and into the glistening city below.

***

Cecilia could scarcely recognise herself.

To keep their anxiety at bay, Rosalina, Liz and Jeleni had spent their nights holed up below decks working on a dress Bella had begun to fashion for Cecilia's presentation to the king. The result was the most beautiful dress she had ever laid eyes on.

Bella grinned, brushing away invisible pieces of lint from Cecilia's shoulders.

"Well?" her smile betrayed her eagerness.

"It's beautiful," Cecilia breathed.

Delicate gold vines trailed from the navy bodice, down the elegant navy skirt. Her shoulders were covered by delicate capped sleeves, lilies embroidered on each.

Liz had pulled her hair up in a fashionable updo, revealing the delicate, embroidered collar at her throat.

The hem picked up to show the polished leather of Catalina's new boots, which she had lent Cecilia for the occasion.

"Give us a spin!" Liz encouraged. Cecilia turned and was met by a series of oohs and ahhs.

"You look like a princess!" Adela sighed from Rosalina's lap.

- 343 -

"I feel like one," Cecilia laughed.

The nerves which she had so valiantly kept at bay all evening were back in full force. Her stomach churned as the ship rocked around in Calgaria's fussy waters.

A knock on the door startled her back to the present.

"Who is it?" Bella called out.

"It's me," Marcus answered.

"Come in."

Cecilia almost didn't recognise Marcus when he walked in. He had changed into what must be his guard uniform, dark leather armour and boots, his sling long forgotten. His face was clean shaven, and handsome, though she missed the shadow of stubble on his jawline.

In his hands, he held a long, thin velvet box, the colour had faded from a navy hue to a dusty blue. Bella and the girls exchanged glances.

"We'll leave you alone." Rosalina stood, placing her hands on Adela's shoulders.

"But I want to see what's in the box!" the youngster whined.

"Hush, Adela. We will find out after."

The girl pouted, crossing her arms over her chest.

"Let's see if we can't find something pretty for you to wear in your mother's cabin?" Liz suggested, tearing the girls attention away from her uncle.

"We'll see you on deck." Bella winked, closing the door behind them.

Butterflies took flight in Cecilia's stomach as Marcus cleared his throat.

"I hoped you might wear this when meeting your parents today."

He popped the box open to reveal a gorgeous sapphire pendant, embedded in gold and hung on a matching golden chain, woven to resemble woodland vines.

She had never seen anything so elegant.

"I... I don't know what to say. Thank you. Where did you find something so beautiful?" she asked, gingerly picking it up from the velvet casing.

"It was a gift from Queen Minerva to my mother many years ago. It was meant to be passed from mother to daughter. She wanted you to have it."

"Oh," she set it back in the case, "it is very lovely. I'm sure Catalina or Adela would love it."

"Cecilia," he took her hand, "it's *yours*. It was always meant to be."

It took her a moment to understand.

"*Oh*. Thank you."

His eyes softened as he smiled. He seemed to be doing that a lot recently.

"Would you like me to help you put it on?"

"Yes, please." She fought to keep her voice steady.

Her stomach flipped as he stood behind her, his gentle fingers brushing stray strands of hair from her neck. Her breath caught as his fingers brushed against her skin as he fought with the clasp.

"Thank you," she breathed, catching their reflection in the mirror. "I don't know how I would've coped these last few weeks without you."

He turned to face her, taking one hand in his.

"And I, you. Perhaps," his smile turned sad, "if you were a simple woman, and I were a simple man, we could carve out a simple life together."

Their eyes met in the mirror, as his words settled between them.

"I-" She turned to face him, his steady brown eyes already locked on hers. When had they become as familiar as her own?

Her fingers found the fabric of his shirt. His breath quickened as she tucked a stray strand of hair from his face.

"May I?" She asked, her voice so soft she wasn't sure he heard her.

He nodded.

Tenderly, he drew her face up to meet his, covering her lips gently with his own. He drew her closer to him, his free arm wrapping around her waist to steady her from falling. She wanted to continue kissing him, to take in the scent of mint and leather, to lay her hand against his strong heartbeat.

A knock at the door broke them apart.

"Two minutes," Catalina called from the other side of the door.

"No," Cecilia shook her head, "I'm not ready."

Marcus stroked her cheek with his thumb. "You'll be alright. I will be with you every step of the way. So will Bella and the rest of our friends. We're all here for you."

Cecilia shook her head again, panic rising in her chest.

"What if they don't like me? Or… or what if I'm not the kind of daughter they expected? What if I look nothing like them? Or if Derek comes back and forces them to get rid of me?" her anxious thoughts bubbled over.

"Cecilia, look at me," Marcus ordered gently. Hesitating, she met his gaze.

"King Lars would not have sent me halfway across the world if he did not think you were his daughter. Make no mistake, he doesn't expect you to be the same girl you were when you were taken." He tucked a strand of hair from her face. "They're your family, they love you. Together, you'll find a way to make it work."

His confidence assured her, but doubts still lingered.

"What about Prince Derek? What if he comes back to finish the job?"

Marcus caught her hand, giving it a reassuring squeeze.

"I'll deal with that if the time comes. Today, is between you and your parents. We can figure the rest out later."

She swallowed her anxiety. *Her parents*. What a strange thought.

"Do not give voice to those anxious thoughts. You've seen for yourself the evidence we collected. You remembered Queen Minerva giving you the bracelet. You recognised Derek despite not seeing him for sixteen years," he assured her. "And if that is still not enough, you bear a striking resemblance to the queen."

"You're sure?"

"Absolutely. Don't you trust me?"

A wry smile played at his lips, a teasing twinkle in his eye.

"Cast the anchor!!!" Sebastian's voice rang out over the din of the ship.

Cecilia turned to him, eyes wide.

"I can't do this." She shook her head.

Marcus pressed a quick kiss to her hand.

"You can and you will. I will be right beside you every step of the way."

Catalina knocked on the cabin door, poking her head inside. Cecilia startled at her appearance.

"We'll be disembarking in ten minutes, Your Highness," Catalina winked.

Cecilia nodded. The captain disappeared as quickly as she had appeared, leaving the two of them alone again.

"Come on," Marcus led her to the door, "you don't want to miss your first sight of Calgaria."

58

Homecoming

The sun shone high in the sky as Cecilia stepped out of the cabin, her hand resting comfortably in Marcus' elbow as he escorted her onto the deck.

Great, grey mountains flanked them on either side. Despite the early hour, the docks thrummed with activity, stevedores and fishermen shouting greetings and orders alike.

Butterflies fluttered in a dizzying pattern from her heart to her stomach as the ship steadied in its berth, her fingers numb with anticipation. She tried not to look too far ahead of her, for fear she would burst into a puddle of tears.

The ship moored before she was ready.

Her fingers tightened around Marcus' bicep.

"You're going to be fine." He whispered in her ear.

Nervous, she nodded.

They ambled past Alistar, who bowed as she passed.

"You will make a wonderful princess, Your Highness," he said, addressing her by her title for the first time.

She inclined her head at him. Would she ever get used to such formality? She stopped to embrace Bella and Jeremy, flanked by Liz and Jeleni.

"How can I ever repay you for helping me?" she asked.

"Be a good queen and rule your kingdom well. We can talk about payment after," Jeleni smiled wanly. Liz nudged her sister who broke out into a grin.

"Don't mind her, she's just teasing. I'm sure you will be the perfect princess," she assured Cecilia, who let out a deep breath.

Catalina and Sebastian stood at attention as she and Marcus drew near the foot of the ramp. Cecilia's heart pounded against her ribs as the royal carriage rolled onto the docks in front of them. She willed her trembling knees to stop shaking, forcing herself to meet Catalina's soft smile.

"If you need a ship to escape on, Marcus knows where to find us," the captain flashed her a teasing grin.

"I might take you up on that," Cecilia chuckled, tension easing from her shoulders.

Adela flashed her a double thumbs up beside Catalina.

"Go on," Sebastian nodded in the direction of the royal carriage, "they're waiting for you."

Cecilia turned to see the king leap from the regal vehicle, his royal cape dancing in the wind as he raced ungracefully down the grey stone path, the queen trailing close behind.

Gripping Marcus' arm for strength, she allowed him to lead her quickly down the ramp, their feet settling on solid ground for less than a second before the king, eyes shining with tears reached them.

"Lilia." He breathed as he took her into his arms.

Cecilia breathed in the strong scent of her father as he held her close, rose and sandalwood and something familiar she couldn't quite place. His chest shook against her as tears streamed down his pale face.

Through her own tears, she saw the queen, a thin woman, almost identical to her, standing at the king's shoulder. She was regal, in her pastel blue gown and silver cloak, but her face spoke a mixture of relief and longing.

"Oh my daughter, how I've missed you," she exclaimed in perfect Avinadan.

"Mamá," Cecilia gasped, throwing herself from her father's arms, into her mother's.

She inhaled the scent of jasmine on her mother's skin as she buried her face into her neck. While her father's embrace was strong and welcoming, her mother's arms felt like home.

59

A Final Promise

The familiar scent of oak and parchment filled the king's study. It was much tidier than the last time Marcus had stood in the room waiting to receive orders.

The maps and papers that had been scattered about when Marcus received his commission had been tidied in the weeks since he had returned with Cecilia. Leather-bound books and journals were stacked in neat rows along the wall of shelves at the far end of the room.

"Ah, Captain Cervantes," the king looked up from a pile of papers at his desk, "how are you faring?"

"Well, thank you, Your Majesty." Marcus stood at attention before the king.

After he escorted Cecilia to the palace, Jeremy had put him under immediate medical respite. It had been weeks since Marcus was able to rejoin his fellow soldiers in training. Prince Derek, whom he had expected to beat them to Calgaria, had not yet returned.

"I have been meaning to thank you for returning my daughter to me," the king grinned. "Nothing I can say or do can ever amount to the immense gratitude I have for you and what you have done for my family."

Marcus bowed his head as the king continued.

"As promised when I commissioned you, I am restoring your birthright, all of your father's wealth, land and titles which were stripped from him by his father. Your father was a good friend, and a pioneer for peace between Calgaria and Avinada. I am sorry he could not see how far our countries have come."

Marcus' eyes shone.

"Thank you, Your Majesty,."

"And I hope you will accept my apology. He and I both married Avinadan women, where he was ridiculed, I was celebrated. I should have done more..." the king trailed off.

Marcus shook his head.

"I will accept your apology, Your Majesty but I am not sure I can accept the reparations." he said carefully, lowering his gaze.

The king raised a brow at him.

"Why not? Is it not what we agreed to? Or is there something else that troubles you?"

Marcus hesitated, "May I speak freely, my lord?"

The king nodded.

"I am unsure if I can accept the dukedom and all that comes with it, should I accept the position of Chief Sentinel."

"You will take the promotion?" The king frowned, mirroring Cecilia.

Marcus took a deep breath.

"My role as your guard is to protect and preserve the royal family. I will do anything I can to ensure Cec- the princess' safety. Also," he hesitated, "when she found out I was helping her for a reward, I betrayed her trust and a part of myself. Now... I don't know if I can accept the reparations."

The king frowned thoughtfully.

"She has forgiven you?" he asked.

Marcus nodded once, "Yes, my lord, but I still feel... tainted."

The king stroked his grey-stubbled chin.

"And if I offer it to you as a gift? Would you accept a gift from your king?"

Marcus shifted uncomfortably under the king's gaze.

"I would not want to offend you."

"You would offend me more by not taking it. Besides, I have spoken the matter over with my daughter," he beamed. "She concedes it is a fair price to pay for your efforts to return her safely. You may talk it over with her if you'd like."

Marcus stared numbly at the king, a keen excitement beginning to uncurl in his chest like the first blooms of spring.

"She truly does not mind?"

The king shook his head, "If you don't believe me, ask her yourself."

Marcus looked at the king curiously, but the older man simply winked, a mischievous glint in his hazel eyes.

"Now that's settled, I must be off. I have some things to attend to before Cecilia's investiture next month. I have no doubt you two have some catching up to do."

"Thank you, my lord."

"No, Marcus," the king flashed him a genuine smile, "thank you."

The door to the king's study opened and a doorman appeared.

"Felix, please escort Captain Cervantes to the Rose Gardens." He turned to Marcus, "A final gift before you return to your ancestral home."

Marcus bowed low to the king before following the teal-caped guard down the marble hall. The last time he walked through these corridors, he had felt certain it was his destiny. Perhaps that was more true now than ever.

***

Cecilia set her book down on the marble bench beneath her. Words swam in her mind, Avinadan and Calgarian blurring together in an unintelligible mess until she couldn't remember what was up and what was down. Sunlight streamed in overhead, the crystal blue sky peeking in from a glass dome in the centre of the roof.

Clear water trickled from the large fountain in the middle of the courtyard, shimmering with an array of rich colour from its mosaic bottom. White and pink water lilies floated along, battered by a lazy breeze.

An array of exotic green plants and bushes hemmed in around her. Despite the bustling glow of the city, Calgaria was a cold kingdom set in a permanent state of white, blue and grey, despite the arrival of spring.

She missed the colour and warmth of Avinada, the lush green mountains, the golden sandy beaches. So, she found herself studying in the Rose Gardens, the closest she had come to feeling at home.

"Have I caught you at a bad time?" Marcus greeted, leaning against the marble entrance closest to her. She pretended not to notice the bouquet of flowers in his hand.

"I'm just taking a break," she sighed, picking up the dictionary. "My investiture is in a matter of weeks and I can't seem to wrap my head around any of the everyday phrases, let alone the formal language."

"It's alright," he assured her, "Calgarian is not an easy language to learn."

Cecilia leaned forward, "Are those for me?"

"Oh," he crossed the courtyard, holding them out to her, "yes. I hope you don't mind; I picked them on the way over here."

"They're beautiful," she sniffed, motioning him to sit beside her.

"Your father said there was something you wished to speak to me about?" He sat on the bench, trying to keep his voice light.

"Yes. I - we wanted to know if you intended on staying in Calgaria. I know my father gave back your inheritance, but I - we weren't sure if you intended on staying in the city. Jeremy said he would, although Antonio and the Cifuentes sisters would be heading back to Avinada."

"Except for Bella."

"Right," she continued, "I know Sebastian and Catalina are setting sail too. I just… I would hate to see you leave again so soon."

She looked at the flowers in her lap.

"Cecilia," he murmured, taking her hand, all formality lost between them, "I promise, I am not going anywhere. I will be right here whenever you need me."

She met his gaze, her eyes turning to honey in the morning sunlight.

"You promise?"

"Of course." He flashed her a playful grin, "someone has to keep you from running away."

"What?" she laughed, "don't you trust me?"

He winked.

"Just this once."

***

ACKNOWLEDGEMENTS

This book would not be possible without the support of my parents. Thank you for instilling a love of reading in me, and for letting me tell you about this story for so many years. It's finally finished! Hopefully, one day I can get you that house in the Bahamas.

To Faith Briggs—though you'll never get to hold this book in your hands—thank you for letting me tell you this story when I should have been doing my homework. And thank you for the book of folk tales that kickstarted my love of writing. May we meet again in heaven.

To my friends who have let me share my writing journey with you— Sarah, Lai, Jo, Mikayla, Makeleigh, Brooke, and Alice—thank you for your enthusiasm, encouragement, and support through the years.

And a special thanks, of course, to my publisher, Crystal Leonardi, and editor, Georgie Montague. This journey wouldn't be possible without your help, and I can't thank you enough for helping me polish and refine this story.

Finally, as a Christian, I believe God is the ultimate source of creativity and storytelling—without whom, this story would not be possible.

About the Author

Catherine Duffy is an Australian author and journalist based in Far North Queensland. With a background in creative writing, English literature, and journalism, Catherine brings a thoughtful and imaginative voice to her work.

A lifelong lover of stories, she enjoys reading across genres—particularly fantasy, science fiction, and contemporary fiction. Her love of travel was sparked early, adventuring across the country with her English father and Salvadorian mother, an experience that continues to inspire her storytelling.

When she's not writing, Catherine can be found at the beach, curled up with a good book, or affectionately annoying her dog.

Her debut novel, Runaway Cecilia, marks the beginning of an exciting new voice in Australian fiction.

Socials

Instagram: @something.cat.pens

FROM THE PUBLISHER

Catherine Duffy's debut novel, Runaway Cecilia, is a sweeping romantic fantasy that deftly weaves classic fairy tale elements into an original, richly imagined world. Set across the fictional lands of Avinada, the Fickle Islands, and Calgaria, this enchanting retelling of Rapunzel offers readers a coming-of-age journey brimming with intrigue, danger, heartache, and hope.

From the opening pages, Catherine displays a confident narrative voice and a strong command of prose. The story opens with a gripping prologue that establishes high emotional stakes and hints at the deception and betrayal to come.

At the heart of the story is Cecilia. Raised under the tight control of the calculating Duchess Frida Alarcon, Cecilia begins the novel as a sheltered and dutiful young woman. But as truths begin to unravel and suspicions take root, her courage, resilience, and inner strength are tested. Her decision to run away and reclaim her identity is both empowering and emotional, marking the beginning of a beautifully rendered journey of self-discovery.

Pirate battles, secret identities, courtly drama, and a daring rescue all contribute to a cinematic reading experience.

Runaway Cecilia is a luminous debut from a fresh Australian voice. With imaginative world-building, heartfelt relationships, and a timeless message about freedom and the courage to claim one's destiny, this is a novel that will appeal to fans of romantic fantasy and classic retellings alike.

Catherine Duffy has arrived—and Runaway Cecilia is only the beginning. Congratulations Catherine, it has been a joy to work with you to bring Runaway Cecilia to life.

Crystal Leonardi
Bowerbird Publishing
www.crystalleonardi.com

www.ingramcontent.com/pod-product-compliance
Lightning Source LLC
Chambersburg PA
CBHW050613170726
48283CB00001B/232